TORIES AND TURNCOATS

GEOFF BAGGETT

Cocked Hat
Publishing

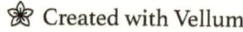 Created with Vellum

Patriots of the American Revolution Series

BOOK SIX

ALSO BY GEOFF BAGGETT

Dedicated to my fellow re-enactors and living historians. These amazing friends and dedicated educators lost an entire season of events, camping, fellowship, and fun to the scourge of the Covid-19 pandemic. Still, they persevere and eagerly await new adventures in 2021. Huzzah!

Cover Photography - Kim Baggett
Cover Subject - Bob Roberts

Cover Design - Natasha Snow
natashasnow.com

PART I

THE BONDS OF FRIENDSHIP

1

A NEW FRIEND

Sunday, June 7, 1750
William Newman Farm
Near Williamsburg Township, South Carolina
On the Banks of the Black River

Will Newman could barely contain his excitement. Finally, his father had given him permission to trek west toward the High Hills of Santee. Though he was seventeen years of age, Will had never traveled such a great distance unaccompanied. Indeed, as the only child in a motherless family, he had always lived the life of a sheltered, overprotected youth. His doting father had monitored and controlled his every waking moment since birth. But, at long last, the day that he longed for had arrived. He was striking out into the world on his own, if only for a short while.

It promised to be the journey of his dreams ... seven days of just him, his flintlock, and the lush South Carolina landscape. He would wander the rolling hills east of the Wateree River and live off of the bounty of the land. It would be a rite of passage for the strikingly handsome young lad. Surely, after such an impressive excursion as this, his father could no longer deny him the rights and privileges of independence and manhood.

Will focused intently on his preparations for the journey. The family's huge oak dining table was covered with clothing, supplies, and hunting accouterments. He was attempting to consolidate as much of his gear as possible inside his large oilcloth knapsack. He had precious little room for belongings and supplies in his cypress-log dugout canoe. The sleek, narrow vessel was designed for speed and ease of navigation, not for hauling cargo. And besides, once he beached his canoe near the headwaters of the river and headed into the hills, he would have to carry all of his belongings on his back. Therefore, packing light was an absolute necessity.

The distinctive click of the latch on the rear door of the house interrupted Will's planning and thoughts. His ruddy-faced, portly father, the elder William Newman, stepped swiftly into the dining room and then slammed the door closed behind him. He swatted frantically at his neck and face.

"These damnable bugs!" Mr. Newman exclaimed in a thick Irish brogue. "I swear I just spied a mosquito the size of a hummingbird down at the hog lot. And the gnats! Son, those little bastards are suckin' me dry of every ounce of me blood. God help us! These damnable, damnable bugs! Why on earth did I ever leave County Cork?"

Will rolled his eyes and then shook his head slightly. His father's fond, reminiscent references to Ireland, a place he had never even visited, always elicited the same sarcastic response from his son.

"I know full-well that you have never set foot in Ireland, Father. You were born in Craven County barely a mile from here. Charlestown is the farthest you have ever traveled from this river-bank." He paused, looked at his father, and then raised his eyebrows mockingly. "But, you do sound like you learned to speak in County Cork."

Will's father stepped closer and gave his son a playful slap across the backside. "None of that, now. Boy, I will suffer no sass from the likes of you." He shook his head in mock disgust. "I swear, for the life of me I can nay understand how you came to speak the King's English like a British schoolmaster. Your Irish-born grandfather must be rolling in his grave."

Will chuckled softly and gave his father an affectionate nudge with his elbow. He then refocused his attention back upon the task of packing. His father stood silently and gazed upon his only son with eyes of love and concern. Will was the only family that he had left in the entire world. For seventeen years, the two of them had relied upon one another, for there was no one else. It was hard for William Newman to relinquish control and allow his son go out into the world on his own. But, deep down, he knew that it was time. As hard as it was for him, he simply had to release the tethers that bound young Will to hearth and home.

Mr. Newman stepped forward to examine the items on the table. He uttered a sarcastic grunt. "I see your tent shelter, plenty of fishing line, hooks, and nets." He pointed at Will's shooting supplies. "You appear to have ample powder and lead. But, I do not see any food. Are you plannin' to maybe eat anythin' on your journey, lad?"

Will suggested with a straight face, "The blackberries, scupper-nongs, and paw-paws will be plentiful in the hills. I will have plenty to eat."

His father gasped. "Good God, Boy! Have you lost your ever-lovin' mind? You can nay survive for a week on wild berries! If you can do no better than tha', I must take back my word and insist that you stay at home. I can nay be responsible for you wanderin' off into yon hills and then starvin' to death."

"I am only going to be gone for one week, Father," Will retorted.

"I'll have you know ... a true Irishman can starve in half that time!"

His father held his breath for a moment and then both of them erupted in hearty laughter.

"I am only teasing you, Father." Will pointed at his cargo-swollen shoulder bag. It was a lovely woven tapestry haversack with a wide leather strap. "I have packed two pounds of rice, a sack of roasted, dried corn, and at least a pound of venison jerk meat. That will be plenty to feed me for a week, especially if I can shoot some small game along the way."

"I heard you speaking to Mr. Jenkins at the butchery last week. Do ya truly think there are buffalo in those hills?"

Will nodded enthusiastically. "I heard reports from two different men in Williamsburg. Mr. Jenkins even had some fresh buffalo tongue on display in his shop."

Mr. Newman nodded and licked his lips. "It's been many a year since I tasted one of those delicious beasties. You know, there was a time when we could see them in the woods across the river. It was rare, but I saw them with my very own eyes. Bears once wandered these woods, as well. Son, there is nothing quite so delicious as a slab of bear meat roasted over an open flame." He stared, wide eyed, for a moment as his mind recalled a fond memory from his childhood. "Your grandfather killed a huge black bear not a quarter-mile from this very spot." He shook his head in disappointment. "But, those days are long gone. Too many people are here now."

"But, not in the High Hills of Santee," Will declared. "Most likely, bears and elk still roam those highlands. Fewer people have settled up there."

Mr. Newman frowned. "I am quite certain that the buffaloes and bears are scarce there, as well. Souls are floodin' into our beloved South Carolina, I'm afraid."

"What about mosquitoes? Are they migrating here, too?" Will teased.

"Those little buggers have always been here, and in large numbers." He scratched a large welt on the side of his neck. "People say the white man drove the Indians from this place. But, I will go to my dyin' grave believin' it was the bitin' critters that made them all flee." He patted Will on the back. "You know, Son ... I almost envy you goin' to those hills. Perhaps, away from all these damnable bugs, you'll be able to get a good night's sleep."

Will nodded knowingly. "I certainly hope so."

Mr. Newman stared at his beloved son with eyes of concern. "You must keep an eye out for Indians, Will. There has been trouble in the backcountry in recent months."

"No one has seen a Cherokee on this side of the Wateree for more than five years," Will assured his father.

"Still, you must remain vigilant at all times. You will be straying dangerously close to the lands where they roam. 'Twould be nothing a'tall for a band of the savages to venture across the river, especially in such a deserted country as the High Hills. And there are always bandits and ruffians on the loose in the backcountry, just looking for a victim to rob or something to steal. You must be especially watchful at night."

"I promise to be careful, Father."

Mr. Newman nodded. He seemed satisfied that his son understood the gravity of the dangers associated with upland travel.

"What if you shoot a buffalo or a bear? How do you plan to get the meat home? Surely, you'll not attempt to straddle a carcass across the bow of your tiny canoe." He chuckled at the notion.

"I have no intentions of shooting either one, Father. Without a horse, I could never get the meat to my canoe. And I would never want to kill such a majestic animal and allow it to simply go to waste. No, I would just like to see some with my own eyes, before they are all gone from the Carolinas. For eating, I will stick to small game ... rabbits, turkeys, and such."

Mr. Newman nodded. "I think that is wise, indeed. Of course, even if you did not shoot any game, at all, you could still have a splendid excursion."

Will smiled warmly at his father. "Indeed. It is the journey and experience that I seek more than anything. Just getting away by myself is what is truly exciting for me."

"So, you're that anxious to escape your troublesome old papa, are you?"

Will stood silently for a moment. He turned and faced his father. "You know what I mean, don't you, Father? Do you understand why I need to go?"

His father inhaled deeply and nodded. "Yes, I do. Oh, to be young again!" He glanced back at the items on the table, anxious to avoid an emotional display. "So, am I to assume that you will depart early in the mornin'?"

"Yes, sir. Dawn tomorrow. I want to get as far upstream as I can tomorrow and then make camp. I doubt that I can reach the headwaters in one day, even on this lazy, slow river."

"'Twould be a feat, indeed, even in a canoe. I would plan on two full days for travel upstream, four days in the hills, and then a leisurely float downriver on your final day."

Will nodded. "That is my plan."

Mr. Newman patted his son fondly on the shoulder. "Well, then ... it appears that you have everything well in hand. I shall allow you to continue your preparations. We can talk more over supper tonight. Mrs. Harmon is preparin' us a roast goose, buttered corn, and some of her delicious onion-fried potatoes." He nudged his son. "I hate to say it, but she is a much better cook than your mother ever was, God rest her soul."

"Well, you do pay the Widow Harmon for her labor. So, I suppose that makes her a professional cook." He smiled playfully.

"As well I know it." Mr. Newman nodded thoughtfully. "Perhaps I should propose marriage to the widow and save all of this money that I pay her for cooking and keeping our house."

Will chuckled sarcastically. "I am not so certain that she would entertain such an arrangement. 'Twould mean less money and much more work for her in the end."

His father's head bobbed up and down. "'Tis true, 'tis true. And, if you think about it, a wife would, no doubt, cost me even more money in the long run. All the rosewater, petticoats, ribbons, and bonnets." He scowled and then shook his head. "No. I shall leave our arrangements as they are."

"A wise decision, Father," Will affirmed.

Mr. Newman shrugged. "Oh well, 'twas worth considerin', I s'pose." He simultaneously stretched and yawned. "Son, if you will pardon me, I think I shall enjoy a quick nap whilst the sun is still up. Oh, how I do love a Sunday nap!" He shuffled toward the stairs and then called over his shoulder. "But, be sure to wake me if I have not roused by suppertime. 'Twould be heartbreakin', indeed, if tomorrow's breakfast turned out to be my next meal."

~

Noon - Two Days Later
On the Black River - South Carolina

WILL PADDLED STEADILY against a slight current. The air was heavy and wet. By mid-morning, he had already shucked off his hunting frock and shirt. It would be scandalous, indeed, to be seen naked above the waist publicly. But, he was nowhere near civilization. There was likely not another soul within ten miles in any direction. So, Will was not at all worried.

The Black River certainly lived up to its name. The murky water was stained black by tannins from the thousands of cypress trees that lined its banks and filled the surrounding swamplands. Some of the cypresses in the remote swamps and backwaters adjacent to the river were enormous. Their trunks were so huge that five men could not hold hands and reach around them. Throughout the stagnant, shallow waters, bony cypress knobs protruded upward around the bases of their parent trees. There were occasional sprigs of Spanish moss dangling from limbs overhead, though the moss grew rarer with each mile traveled inland away from the coast.

The smell of the river and the surrounding swamps was rich, dank, and earthy. The warm waters of lowland South Carolina literally teemed with life of almost every imaginable form. From the tiniest worms and bugs to the biggest and most fearful predators, everything that existed in the wetlands lived either to eat or be eaten. As a result, there were also the many signs and odors of death and decay.

The animal life along the more remote portions of the river fascinated Will. He had seen water birds of every imaginable variety. Countless blue herons populated the area. They stood as still as statues atop cypress knobs while they scanned the turbid, black waters for their next meal. He spied hundreds of long-legged white egrets, as well as gigantic pileated woodpeckers, and majestic white-headed eagles. Screeching, high-flying hawks hunted throughout the swamplands. Occasionally, flocks of vultures circled menacingly overhead as they smelled the death of some unseen, unfortunate creature below.

The water teemed with life, as well. Frogs and fishes leapt from the dark waters with great regularity. There were plentiful beaver, otters, muskrats, and minks. Turtles of all shapes and sizes sunned on logs with their legs and necks outstretched. Snakes of every sort dangled from the trees and slithered on top of the water. Will had even been surprised to see a particularly large alligator lurking near the eastern riverbank almost ten miles upstream from his home. His father had long ago assured him that the gators did not travel that far upstream. He made a mental note to set the man straight when he returned.

William Newman, Jr., reveled in the peace of the remote wilderness and the glory of his solitude and independence. This was the farthest that he had ever ventured from home without the company and supervision of his father. He began to imagine all of the sights that he would see in the hills and the strange beasts and people he might encounter. He looked forward with great anticipation to witnessing an elk or buffalo grazing in a remote meadow. He prayed that he might witness things that he had never seen before.

Soon, Will spotted a small creek about a hundred yards ahead and to his left. His father had described the tiny waterway over supper two nights prior. It held deep water for almost a mile toward the west. He planned to paddle along that creek until the water shallowed out and then make his landing. Soon, he would leave the dark, humid river behind and make his way on foot into the sunny, glorious hills.

～

Three Days Later

WILL SQUATTED QUICKLY behind a patch of thick underbrush. He carefully placed his trusty .54-caliber flintlock smooth bore on the ground beside him as he scanned the grassy meadow. His weapon was primed and ready to fire and carried a load of buckshot. Just moments before, he had heard the distinctive gobble of a tom turkey. It sounded like it was a couple hundred yards away. Will licked his lips hungrily. Fire-roasted turkey would make for a delicious supper, as well as a fine breakfast for tomorrow. He was growing weary of fish, squirrels, and rabbits.

He decided to try and call the turkey in close enough for a shot. He retrieved his polished wing bone turkey call from his haversack and popped the narrow tip into his mouth, holding it with his right hand. He then cupped his left hand beneath the other end, covering the hole in the bone. Immediately, he began a choppy kissing motion with his lips, sucking the air across his palm and through the length of the hollow wing bone. The device emitted a sharp, pulsating call that sounded exactly like an amorous hen. He paused after calling for a few seconds and listened. The turkey gobbled once more. It sounded closer than before.

Once again, Will placed the tip of the call in his mouth and repeated the process. Suddenly, he saw the huge bird emerge from the trees at the far end of the meadow. He crouched lower and repeated the call. The gobbler strutted forward quickly, his tail fully fanned. Will tucked the turkey call back into his haversack and then reached for his gun. Lifting it to the firing position, he pulled the hammer back slowly until it was fully cocked. He trained his sights on the bird and waited breathlessly for the opportunity to fire.

The turkey was about thirty yards away from him when it suddenly stopped. The cagey bird had, no doubt, caught Will's scent. It knew that something was not right. The turkey turned to make his retreat and, just for a moment, gave Will a perfect broadside shot. He pulled the trigger. The weapon unleashed a shower of sparks and billowing smoke beside Will's right cheek, followed immediately by a powerful boom. The recoil of the gun slammed against his shoulder. Once the smoke cleared, he spied the stricken bird sprawled in the grass. It was down on its right side, shaking in spasms and kicking helplessly at the air beneath its feet.

Will waited for a couple of minutes as the blood and remnants of life drained from the doomed bird. Finally, when it was thrashing no more, Will stood upright. He quickly reloaded his gun. Afterwards, he walked across the meadow and retrieved his prize. Holding it upside-down by its legs, he gave the turkey a quick examination. It was an impressive bird, indeed. Its spurs were almost three inches long and its beard was a full twelve inches in length. It would make a fine meal. Will felt like celebrating. His harvesting of such a magnificent animal made what had already been a good expedition even better.

It had been an amazing three days of hiking and exploration. Will had covered a leisurely twenty miles during his trek through the High Hills. He traversed the high country westward and walked all the way to an overlook where he caught a glimpse of the Wateree River. He camped on an open hilltop that evening to watch the lovely sunset and monitor the boat traffic on the river. He saw several small vessels. All were making their way north from the Santee, obviously headed toward the bustling Fredericksburg Township.

The views in the hills had been breathtaking and unforgettable. Red cedars, giant oaks, and tall pine trees covered the rolling ridges. The trees and thick grasses were lush and green. There were ample springs that provided clean, refreshing water. The atmosphere was pleasantly cool and dry and not at all like the humid, heavy air in the river lowlands. The weather throughout the week had been ideal, with only a single rain shower on his first afternoon of hiking. Most days, a stiff, refreshing breeze blew from the west, providing coolness and comfort. It was, in a word, perfect.

Will imagined that he might settle down and build a cabin in a place such as this. But, alas, the time to return home was drawing nigh. He was almost heartbroken that had to depart the following morning. He was tempted to turn toward the west, take off walking, and never look back. But, for the moment, he had little time for daydreaming. He definitely had more pressing matters at hand. There was camp to make and supper to cook. He would have to save his dreams of running away to the backcountry for the coming night's slumber.

It was two hours before nightfall. Will selected an ideal campsite near a small, bubbling spring. The water flowed from between two slabs of sandstone at the base of a large rock outcropping. It trickled downhill, filling a small, pebble-lined pool. The water was cold and very clear. It would serve him well for both his overnight stay as well as the return trip to his canoe on the following day. He pitched his wedge tent about fifteen yards west of the spring, beneath a stand of tall pines. The westward vista would provide a perfect view of the evening's sunset. The ample pine needles would ensure a soft mattress for his bedroll.

After clearing a large area for his campfire, he retrieved his flint and steel and quickly ignited a crackling blaze. He then took his turkey to the spring to clean it and prepare it for cooking. It took over a half-hour to pluck and butcher the turkey. When finished, he filled his cooking pot with fresh water and then carried the water and meat back to his campsite.

The fire had died down and formed a sizable bed of coals, which was perfect for roasting his meal. Will impaled the breast meat and leg quarters on an iron spit and then suspended them over the fire for roasting. He cut up the bones and other remnants of the bird and placed them in his cooking pot to boil. He carefully placed the pot on a flat stone beside the glowing coals of the campfire. The bones and fat would cook up a fine broth. Later, he would add rice, salt, and spices to the mixture to form a hearty soup.

Once the meat and soup were cooking, there was nothing to do but wait. Will retrieved his clay pipe and tobacco pouch from his haversack and then sat down inside the open door of his tent to enjoy a smoke. After smoking a tasty bowl of Virginia burley, he felt inclined to partake of some whiskey, as well.

"Why not?" he declared out loud. "Now is as good a time as any to give it a try."

Will lay his pipe aside, dug into his knapsack, and nervously retrieved a small corked bottle of the contraband drink. He had actually pilfered the bottle from his father's private supply on the evening before his departure from home. He had never tasted whiskey, but fully intended to give it a try at some point during his trek. Since he was stepping so boldly across the threshold of adulthood, he reasoned that a nip of liquor should be an element of the overall experience. Such a luxurious evening as this was the perfect opportunity to perform a whiskey experiment.

He crawled forward and gave the spit a turn, exposing the uncooked side of his meat to the heat of the flames. Then, he sat back, popped open the cork, and took a hearty drink of the amber liquid.

It was not as he had expected. His lungs closed momentarily from the bitter, searing sensation. He became frantic, fearful that he may never breathe again. But soon, his airway opened up and the burning in his throat gradually subsided. The whiskey scorched a path all the way down to his belly. Will coughed and gagged. It had been a bit too much to swallow, especially for one's first drink.

"Christ, Almighty!" he exclaimed. "Why would anyone desire to drink this stuff? It's Satan's piss, straight from the gates of Hades!"

He paused for a moment, shrugged, and then took another tentative swig. This time, he was more judicious in his volume of intake. He rolled the whiskey around in his mouth and then allowed it to trickle down the back of his throat. It was a much more controlled swallow, and only slightly more enjoyable. He took a couple more similar swigs before popping the cork back into the bottle. He turned and tossed it inside the tent, then he lay back and rested his head on his knapsack. The experiment was done. He could safely check liquor off of his manhood list.

Will felt completely relaxed. A warm, fuzzy numbness began to work its way through his members. His fingers and toes began to tingle. It was a brand-new sensation for him, and he liked it. He felt his eyes growing heavy. Soon, they were closed.

WILL FELT something strike his foot. Still sleepy, he willed his eyes to open. He glanced down at his feet. He saw nothing but his tan stockings and his black shoes with their shiny brass buckles. Then, an unexpected voice ripped him away from his comfortable world of lazy slumber.

"Your meat was getting a bit overdone. I gave it a turn. I hope you do not mind."

Will, his vision still somewhat fuzzy, was seized with terror. He had not heard a human voice in almost a week. He bolted upright and immediately reached for his gun so that he might fend off this unwanted invader. As he did so, he slammed his forehead into the sturdy oak sapling that was serving as his tent pole. The force of the blow was vicious and elicited a loud thud. He immediately lifted his left hand to his wounded, throbbing skull. Despite the pain, he continued to search for the gun with his right hand.

"Whoa! Whoa! Calm down there, friend!" the mysterious voice begged. "There is no need for alarm. I mean you no harm. I was just passing through a hollow down below when I smelled your fire."

Finally retrieving his rifle, Will swung it in the direction of the voice and pulled the flintlock into the cocked position.

"I said I mean you no harm!" the fellow declared in a distinctly harsher voice. "Please, put that gun down before you hurt someone."

Will squinted at the fellow who was kneeling on the far side of his campfire. He was a handsome, friendly-looking young man with dark hair and dark brown eyes. He was clad in an impressive pair of tanned buckskin breeches, a checkered red homespun shirt, a dark blue wool weskit, and a sage-colored linen coat. A black floppy hat adorned his head. He held his hands out to his sides in an ovbious non-threatening a gesture. He reached downward and slowly opened the lapels of his coat.

"See? No pistols." He pointed to his right. "And my rifle is over yonder with my horses."

Will cut his eyes in that direction. Two horses grazed happily about ten yards away. One was wearing a saddle. The other was a pack horse loaded with several burlap bags. The huge animal carried a medium-sized iron pot tied atop its load. A rifle leaned harmlessly against a nearby pine tree. Will glanced back at the young man. The fellow removed his hat and placed it on the ground beside him. His long, untied hair flopped down loosely into his face. He raked it back from his eyes with his right hand and tucked it inside the back of his coat collar. His movement was relaxed and comfortable, as if he had brushed his hair back in such a manner thousands of times before.

"What are you doing here in my camp?" Will demanded. "Why did you sneak up on me? Did you strike me in the leg?"

The fellow chuckled. "There was no sneaking involved, friend. And, yes, I did give you a little nudge. You were not easy to rouse. Words did not get the job done, so I had to take other measures. As I said before, I was just passing by when I smelled your fire. I rode up that narrow draw to the north. When I came into the clearing, I saw your legs sticking out of the tent. I called out, but you did not answer. I feared for a moment that you might be dead. So, I tied off my horses and ran over here to check on you. That is when I heard you snoring." He smiled. "So, I figured you were not dead after all. I gave your meat a quick turn and then gave you a little tap with my boot."

Will grinned sheepishly as he lowered his gun. He carefully released the hammer to the half-cocked position. He confessed, "I think my father's whiskey may have had something to do with my condition."

The fellow's eyebrows raised in surprise. "You have whiskey? Would you, perhaps, have a nip to share with a fellow pilgrim?"

"Perhaps." Will stood and then stepped around the campfire to approach the young man. "My name is Will Newman. I live southeast of here, near Williamsburg on the Black River."

The young man smiled, stood, and then extended his hand to Will. They shook. "I am Bat Austin, from Jackson's Creek."

"Bat?" Will echoed, confused.

"That is what people have always called me." He sighed. "Will, I suffer from an ancient name that has been in my clan for generations. It is such a mouthful that my family shortened it for me, and mercifully so."

"So?" Will asked impatiently. "What, then, is your given name?"

He cleared his throat slightly. "Bartholomew."

Will nodded slowly and then grimaced teasingly. "I can see why you prefer Bat."

The fellow chuckled. "Without doubt!" He nodded toward the roasting spit. "Do you have some meat to spare? It has been a while since I enjoyed a hot meal."

Will nodded. "I have plenty." He knelt down and checked his broth pot. "Please, sit down. Allow me to fish out these bones and then we shall have some soup, as well. I have some rice to add to the pot."

Bat licked his lips hungrily. "I have not tasted rice in a long time. We do not get much of it over in the west."

"You live west of here?" Will inquired, intrigued. "The place you named did not sound familiar to me. I was wondering where it was located."

Bat nodded. "Jackson's Creek is north of the Congaree, not far from the forks of the Broad and Saluda."

Will's eyes widened. "I did not know that any white folk lived that far west! That is very close to Cherokee country, is it not?"

"It is, indeed. And, no, not many of us live out that way. Although, more settlers seem to be trickling in each spring season."

Will sighed deeply. "I would love to see it all, someday. The western lands, I mean. I have never been out that far west before. I have never even laid eyes on an actual Indian."

Bat grinned. "Well, then, Will Newman ... how about you get that rice cooking? I will go and relieve my horses of their saddles and cargo. Then, I will tell you all about the western lands and the

Cherokee whilst we enjoy our supper. I have stories that will make your ears burn with horror and with joy."

Will smiled back and nodded. He thought happily, *"I believe I like this fellow ... Bartholomew Austin."*

AFTER A HEARTY AND CONVERSATION-FILLED SUPPER, the two young men continued to talk into the late hours of the night. Their lips were well-loosened by the remainder of Mr. Newman's pilfered whiskey. The two young men became instant friends. They were thrilled when they realized that both of them were exactly the same age of seventeen years. Other than that, however, the two of them shared very little in common.

Will explained that his father was a planter, but also made money in transporting goods on the various rivers throughout the lowlands. He grew large crops of rice and indigo, but his real wealth was earned through his small fleet of flat boats and the store that he operated in Williamsburg Township. His boats enabled him to not only move his own crops down to Charlestown, but also the crops and wares of his neighbors. He was also able to bring back imported goods from the port of Charlestown to sell at his store. The endeavor had been quite lucrative over the years.

Bat's father, on the other hand, was a humble farmer and prospective millwright. Indeed, he had only recently constructed and begun operation of a grist mill on Jackson's Creek. The tiny mill was much-needed for the small but growing number of farmers in the region. With the help of his sons, Mr. Austin milled the corn for his neighbors for a nominal ten percent fee. The business was small but growing.

Their families were vastly different in size, as well. Will was the only child of his parents' marriage. His mother died during his birth and his father never remarried. He was quite accustomed to being the center of attention in his father's life. Will explained to Bat that his father was quite restrictive when it came to extending freedoms to his son. He had traveled to Charlestown with his father many times. However, this trek in the High Hills of Santee was his first exercise in true freedom, and quite a milestone in his life.

Bat, interestingly, came from a very large family. He already had three brothers and one sister, and swore that his mother seemed to be "hatching" another one about every third year. As the oldest son in a large family, Bat had been free to roam the wilderness of South Carolina since he was a young boy. He was quite accustomed to being out on his own. Indeed, for the past three years, he had been making trips alone to the various townships throughout the region. He hauled cargo and conducted business for his father. For a lad of seventeen, he bore many responsibilities, had traveled to many places, and had experienced numerous adventures. Will could not help but feel envious.

"So, then, you here in the hills for a pleasure trip?" Bat asked, fascinated at the notion.

"I suppose you can call it that. I simply had to get out from under my father's foot and do something on my own. I pestered him for weeks to let me go on an expedition to the west. He finally relented and granted me permission for a one-week journey."

"Well, the High Hills are not exactly what I would call 'the west.' But, they certainly are beautiful, are they not?"

"Oh, yes! I have never seen such beauty or felt such comfort during the warm months. I cannot believe that, in the month of June, I have actually needed a fire to keep warm at night."

"The nights in these hills do bring a chill." Bat tossed a small log onto the campfire. "Did you not bring a horse?"

Will shook his head. "I had no need for one. I was able to paddle my canoe for a good part of the journey. I came by water most of the way and then struck out on foot. I have been up here hiking in these hills ever since. Truth be told, I was hoping to catch a glimpse of a buffalo or a bear." He frowned, disappointed. "But, I have not seen a single sign of either."

Bat looked slightly amused. "You'll not see any buffalo this far east. Bears, maybe. But no buffalo. They are much further west, deep in the mountains of the Cherokee."

"I do not understand. A man in Williamsburg told me that there were buffalo here," Will protested. "He had fresh buffalo tongue for sale in his butchery last week."

"He was a charlatan and full of shite." Bat insisted. "The fraudster must have been selling beef tongue and calling it buffalo. I have walked the trails throughout this region for five years and I can promise you that there are no buffalo here." He paused thoughtfully. "And, as best I can recall, I have only seen two or three rather scrawny bears."

"Well, that is disappointing, indeed," Will remarked. "I must have words with the butcher the next time that I go into town."

Bat chuckled. "I would enjoy hearing that particular conversation."

"What about you? Why are you up here in the hills?" inquired Will.

"Oh, I was just heading home from a salt lick near here. I've been cooking and rendering salt from mineral water at the lick for the past week. I harvested about all that my poor old horse can carry, so now I am taking the products of my labor back home to Papa."

"Is your salt lick far from here?"

"It is three or four miles to the northeast, right at the foot of the High Hills. It is a very small mineral spring, but it puts out strong, salty water. I rendered about fifty pounds over the last week."

"Is that good?" Will asked. He knew nothing about rendering salt.

"Pretty good for just one fellow with a small pot. Four or five men with a couple of big pots could make a hundred pounds in a couple of days."

"How long will it take you to get home?"

Bat stretched and then leaned back on his elbows. "Two days. I have to travel north a bit so I can cross the Wateree at Pine Tree Hill. They have a small rope ferry there that can handle my two horses. What about you? When are you returning home?"

"I leave in the morning. My father expects me home in two days. I will camp near my canoe landing tomorrow night and then float downstream the following day. The current should carry me home with ease. I'll be having supper at my own table the day after tomorrow."

Bat sat up straight and then stretched again. "Well, I suppose we had best get some sleep. We both have a long day of travel ahead of us." He nodded at the stew pot. "But, at least we will have plenty of meat and rice for a hot breakfast."

Will nodded and stood. "Indeed, we shall. But, before I bed down, I must first make use of the privy."

"Good luck finding one of those out here in the hills," Bat teased.

Will grunted. "You know what I mean!" He pointed to his right. "That middle pine tree over there is my own personal privy. Tread at your own risk."

"Ah!" Bat responded. "I am happy you informed me. I shall endeavor to avoid it at all costs."

Will chuckled as he ambled toward the pine tree. He soon disappeared behind the wide trunk in order to seek a measure of privacy. Bat walked over to his gear to retrieve his blankets and then quickly began constructing a pallet beside the fire.

Suddenly, Will leapt from behind the tree. His breeches fell down to his ankles as he ran. He was frantically kicking his right leg and screaming hysterically. The breeches quickly entangled his feet and he tumbled clumsily to the ground. There was something long and shiny attached to his right leg.

Will screeched, "My God! My God! My leg is on fire!"

Bat threw down his blankets and ran to Will's aid. He quickly identified the object hanging from Will's leg. It was a viper ... a venomous copperhead snake ... and its fangs were firmly embedded in the flesh of Will's calf.

"Be still! It is a snake! The bastard is still on you!"

Bat whipped out his razor-sharp hunting knife and then leapt onto Will's back. He slashed at the snake just below its head, severing it from the three-foot long body. He tossed the reptile's long body to his right. The decapitated snake twisted and writhed haphazardly on the ground. Bat then grabbed the snake's head and then used his knife to pry its inch-long fangs from Will's leg. Watery blood flowed out of the holes in Will's flesh. Bat held the head up in the firelight and squeezed the sides of the snake's triangular head. No poison dripped from its fangs.

Bat growled in frustration. "Damn it! The beast emptied all of its poison into you."

Will's breath was short and labored. He could feel his heart racing. "Oh, God, Bat! What am I going to do?"

Bat placed a reassuring hand on his shoulder. "You are going to calm down and be still. You will not die. I will not allow it."

2

GETTING HOME

Bat quickly removed Will's shoes, stockings, and breeches so that he might inspect and determine the severity of the wound. He groaned in frustration.

"Damn it, Will. I need you closer to the fire. I cannot see the bite."

Without asking permission or giving warning, Bat jumped up, grasped Will beneath his arms, and then dragged him on his belly nearer to the campfire. He immediately grabbed a huge handful of pine needles and tossed them on the barely-glowing bed of coals. He tossed some small sticks of pine onto the freshly-ignited tinder, followed by several dry, fallen limbs from an oak tree. The fire blazed quickly and brightly.

Will seemed frantic. He lay on his belly, groaning, writhing and kicking at the ground. Bat knelt beside him, placing Will's body between himself and the campfire. He grabbed his friend's injured leg to immobilize and inspect it. There were two small holes about an inch and a half apart in the meaty muscle of his right calf. Both holes oozed watery-looking blood.

"Well, the good news is that it was not a rattlesnake that bit you. It was a highland moccasin, one of those coppery-colored devils. They hide all over these hills. They are not normally aggressive and do not bite unless disturbed. You must have squatted and dropped your shite right on top of his head. He must not have appreciated it very much."

Will groaned, growing frustrated. "How is any of that good news?"

"Because I have never seen anyone die from a highland moccasin bite. I have seen fevers, and sometimes the flesh around the bite will turn black and rot and look really bad. But, I have never heard of death from the bite of this particular kind of snake. I suppose that if you had to pick a poisonous viper to nip you in the arse, this would be the best one."

Will kicked at the ground. "I am not laughing! This is not humorous! How can you poke fun at me as I lay here wounded and suffering?"

Bat placed his hand on the back of Will's knee and pressed it firmly toward the ground. "Be still! Calm down! If you do not, the poison will spread throughout your body and overtake you."

Will instantly complied. He inhaled and exhaled slowly as he tried to calm himself. But the pain was increasing and becoming almost unbearable. The burning sensation from his calf had already worked its way up his leg. He felt a dull ache in his crotch. He was so very afraid.

"I fear it is already spreading, Bat. I can feel it burning between my legs. I have an ache in my bollocks. It almost feels as if I have been kicked down there." He paused and then buried his face into his hands. "Oh, God! I am going to die, aren't I?"

"I already told you ... I shall not allow you to die."

Will inhaled deeply and then inquired hopefully, "So then, you must have treated the bite of a snake before?"

"No, but I have seen it done. One time my father treated a neighbor's snakebite. I watched everything he did. The other time, I saw an old slave heal a small boy bitten by a rattler. I believe the old negro knew what he was doing."

Will felt Bat moving. He glanced over his shoulder. Bat was kneeling beside his leg, hunting knife in hand.

"What are you about to do to me?" Will shrieked, panicked.

"I have to open up the wound and suck out the poison."

"Suck out the poison? How?" Will demanded.

"With my mouth."

"Christ, Almighty!"

Bat grinned. "I would say that right now is, indeed, a pretty good time to call upon the name of the Lord. Are you a Papist?"

Will gagged. "Hell, no. I am a baptized and confirmed member of His Majesty's Church."

Bat chuckled as he held his knife over the wound. "You should be mindful of your callous combination of profanity and theology, William Newman. I believe that James, the brother of our Lord, once declared, '*Out of the same mouth proceedeth blessing and cursing. My brethren, these things ought not so to be.*'" He paused and then took a deep breath. "Here it comes. Get ready and start praying. I am going to count to three. One ..."

He counted no further. Immediately, he slashed laterally across the snakebite, intersecting both holes and gouging the blade into the thick, rock-hard muscle. Will howled from a combination of surprise and agony. Bat had cut deeply into his flesh. Thick, black blood gushed from the open wound. Immediately, Bat leaned forward and placed his lips over the bloody cut. He sucked hard, drawing out a mouthful of metallic-tasting blood. He turned his head immediately and then expelled the contents of his mouth into the campfire.

Will beat his fists on the earth and grass. "Oh, my God, that hurt!" His head whipped around. He glared angrily at Bat. "You said you were going to count to three!"

Bat lifted his canteen, poured a generous amount of water into his mouth, sloshed it around, and then spit it onto the ground. He wiped his mouth on his sleeve. "I figured it best not to wait any longer. You were beginning to whine like a spoiled little girl." Bat grinned. A trickle of bloody water stained the corner of his mouth.

"Is that all, then? Are you quite done?" Will asked, somewhat more calmly.

"No. I have to burn the wound and then pack it with a poultice."

"Burn it? Why?"

"I do not know. But, that is what the old slave did to the little boy's rattlesnake bite, and the lad survived. So, I am going to imitate his every action."

"How will you burn it?" Will begged with fearful trepidation.

Bat pulled a tiny set of coal tongs from his leather pouch. "I shall use my pipe tongs and fetch a coal from the campfire."

Will groaned and then once again buried his face in his hands. Bat wasted no time. He turned and fished a small, glowing coal from the campfire. Then, he gently spread open the flesh of Will's two-inch-long cut.

"This is going to burn like hell," Bat warned.

"As well I know it. Just get on with it!"

Bat thrust the searing-hot coal into the open cut. Will's flesh popped and hissed. Smoke and steam erupted from the wound. The campsite was flooded with the obnoxious odor of scorched hair and burned meat. Bat kept the hot coal in contact with Will's exposed flesh despite the boy's uncontrollable writhing and kicking. He moved the searing coal back and forth inside the cut. Will howled, uninhibited, from the pain. He pushed himself up on his hands, arching his back and burying his pelvis into the ground.

"My God, my God, my God ... please help me!" he wailed.

Finally, when Bat withdrew the blood-cooled coal from the wound, Will's arms and back suddenly relaxed. He immediately stopped screaming and then collapsed, silent and unconscious, onto the dusty ground.

～

Twelve Hours Later

Will awakened slowly. He lay flat on his back on a soft bed of pine straw. Disoriented, he remained still for a moment and surveyed his surroundings. The cheerful, dancing light of a camp-fire illuminated the ceiling of pines overhead. In the sky to his left, there was the faint, purple glow of the coming dawn. For a moment, he could not recall the place where he lay. But soon the memories of the previous evening rekindled within his mind. He remembered the pleasant experience of getting to know his new friend, the unexpected shock of the painful snakebite, and the excruciating agony of Bat's medical treatments. His final recollection was of the young man thrusting a flaming coal into the exposed flesh of his leg.

Will's throat burned and ached from thirst. His head throbbed mercilessly. It even hurt to move his eyes. Despite the fact that his entire body was soaked in sweat, he felt quite cold. It felt like every inch of his body ached and throbbed. He wanted to sit up, but no matter how hard he tried, he could not budge his arms or his legs.

Resolving himself to his incapacitated state, Will glanced downward to examine himself. He was clad only in his sweat-soaked white linen shirt. His right leg was bent at the knee and elevated several inches in the air. He could feel the presence of a heavy lump on the back of his calf, held in place by a wide, tight bandage.

Will inhaled a deep, painful breath and then attempted to whisper a single syllable. He wanted to call out the name of his new friend. But, the word would not come. It could not seem to escape his parched, dry mouth. He licked his lips with his sandpaper tongue. Once again, he sucked in a labored, gasping breath and then repeated his desperate call. This time, the sound of his weak, gravelly voice penetrated the pre-dawn silence.

"Bat!"

The blanket on the far side of the fire rustled as Bartholomew Austin rose to a sitting position. He rubbed his eyes groggily and then looked toward his injured friend. He smiled. "Will! You are awake!" Bat tossed back the covers and then darted to Will's side. He knelt beside him. "My God, you are soaked in sweat. How do you feel?"

Will's body shuddered as a violent rigor descended upon his members. His teeth chattered. "I'm v...very cu...cu....old."

Bat gently felt of Will's forehead and chest. "Your body is much fevered, as I suspected it would be. I will fetch your blanket."

Bat disappeared from Will's field of view. He returned quickly, carrying Will's large, gray wool blanket. He spread it across his body and then tucked the loose edges beneath him.

"I found this in your tent. It should warm you right up. I will stoke the fire, as well."

Bat quickly added some pine needles to the campfire, followed by several large sticks of dry wood. It quickly crackled into a cheerful blaze. He then returned to Will's side, pewter cup in hand.

"You must be thirsty."

Will nodded. His mouth was so dry that he could not even attempt to form any more words.

"I have some tea for you. It is warm, but not hot, and it should satisfy your thirst. I added some honey earlier. The sweetness will help nourish your fever."

Will nodded and then smiled slightly. Bat knelt beside Will's head. He used his left hand to gently raise Will to a partially-sitting position. He lifted the mug to Will's lips with his right hand. Will gagged at first when the bitter tea landed upon the back of his tongue. But, once his parched mouth and throat were sufficiently moistened, the drink flowed easily. He drained the cup. The sweet tang of the honey lingered upon his lips. He licked the tasty sweet-ness with the tip of his tongue.

"Do you want some more?" Bat asked.

Will nodded. He groaned, "It is very satisfying."

Bat smiled approvingly. "You can have all you want. We need to get as much water into you as we can."

Bat returned soon with another cup of the refreshing beverage. Will was not quite so greedy with this one. He drank about half of the sweetened tea and then indicated that he had partaken enough. Bat placed the half-emptied mug on a wide, flat rock beside the fire.

"You have been sleeping for a long time, Will. But, that is good. Your body will require much rest in the coming days."

Will nodded slightly. "What else did you do to my leg? It feels very tight."

"I put a poultice on it and wrapped it snugly."

"What manner of poultice?"

"I mixed some of your pipe tobacco with about a half-pound of salt and some clay. I packed it onto the wound and then I wrapped everything with strips of linen for a bandage."

"That will heal the bite?" Will inquired hopefully.

"I do not know for certain. The salt should help draw some of the poison out of your flesh. Do you remember that slave man that I told you about, and the little boy with the snakebite?"

"Yes," Will responded weakly.

"Well, he made a poultice with salt and white clay and bound it on the boy's leg. I assumed that I should do likewise."

Will looked slightly confused. "What about the tobacco?"

"That was my own idea. When I was a child, my father placed wet tobacco on my bee stings and insect bites. He also rubbed it on me whenever I got into a patch of sumac. It always eased my itching. I figured that, if it helps with swelling and itching caused by bugs and plants, then it certainly could not hurt your snakebite."

Will closed his eyed and then took a deep breath. The warmth of the blanket and the toasty campfire had already managed to drive the cold from his bones. He could actually feel a tiny bead of sweat forming on his brow.

"I am grateful for all that you have done, Bat. I feel better already."

Bat smiled encouragingly. "I am glad that you do. But, do not be fooled, my friend. It will get much worse before you truly get better. The poison must work its way out of your body. You will have some rough days ahead, I am afraid."

"How many days?" Will asked fearfully.

"Three or four is my best guess. Hopefully, then, you will be well enough for travel."

Will closed his eyes and sighed. "How will I ever get myself home in such a condition?"

Bat patted his shoulder. "You need not worry about that. I have already made plans to take you home."

"But, Bat ... my home is in the opposite direction from yours."

"You need not concern yourself over it. An extra week or two of travel will do me no harm. Besides, it has been a couple of years since I have traveled that far to the east. I think I might enjoy a brief visit to the lowlands."

"Won't your family be worried about you?"

"I will send word to them. If you are doing better in a couple of days, I will ride to the Wateree and flag down a boat. I can send a letter addressed to the store in Fredericksburg Township. The owner will then forward it on to my father. That is how we deliver messages back home. Once Papa reads the letter, he will understand." Bat grinned. "For certain, I cannot leave you alone and unattended in these hills."

"If you could just get me to my canoe, I could float downstream and make it home by myself," Will declared bravely.

"Nonsense! I will deliver you overland. We will head northeast and cross through Megert's Swamp. I can have you home in a few days."

"I do not know how I could ever repay such sacrifice and generosity."

"There is nothing to repay. Civilized people help one another."

"But, we scarcely know one another, Bat."

His new friend grinned. "Well, that will change over the next few days, I reckon."

Noon - Four Days Later – Thursday, June 18, 1750

WILL SAT COMFORTABLY inside the open flap of his tent, smoking his pipe and sipping from a mug of steaming-hot turkey broth. The surrounding tall pines shielded the campsite in comfortable, cool shade. A brisk, refreshing breeze swept across the hilltop. Will was alone in camp. Bat had departed at dawn to post a letter to his father by way of a passing riverboat.

Will's fever was gone, and he was finally able to get dressed and move from his fireside bedroll to his more comfortable tent. His leg still ached below the knee, but the horrid burning and throbbing were finally gone. Bat's medicinal birch bark tea, a recipe that he claimed was gleaned from the Cherokee, had worked wonders, indeed.

It had been a torturous three days. The evening following the night of his snakebite, Will's fever went so high that it afflicted him with a confused delirium. He spouted strange words and curses and was not himself, at all. He sweated profusely, soaking his clothing and blankets. Bat feared that the boy might, indeed, die before sunrise. But, somehow, he managed to cling to life until the dawn.

Bat rested little throughout the first two days following Will's injury. Caring for his patient proved to be a round-the-clock task. He constantly doused his afflicted friend with cool spring water, forced fluids down his throat, and treated his festering wound. Besides the fever, the malodorous wound was the most troublesome aspect of Will's injury. The flesh around the snakebite turned a mottled black color, with tiny lines of green and blue reaching outward toward the pinker, healthier-looking tissues. Despite his constant changing of the poultice and bandages, the flesh around the wound continued to blacken in color and emit a putrid odor. Bat feared that if Will did not die, he might at least lose the leg.

Finally, Bat had little choice but to attempt to clean the wound of its poison-scorched tissue. He used his razor-sharp patch knife to cut out a four-inch circle of dead, blackened flesh from Will's leg. Once again, he burned the wound with hot coals and then packed it with tobacco and salt. He covered the makeshift poultice with soft clay from the bottom of the spring pool. Thankfully, Will had remained unconscious throughout the entire torturous procedure. He slept soundly throughout the night and then, quite miraculously, his fever broke the next morning.

Forty-eight hours later, Will was well on the mend. Now, at long last, it was time for him to go home. Since he was already several days late in returning, he knew that his father must be sick with worry. He prayed that the man was not overly tortured by his unexplained tardiness.

Will heard the sound of a horse's hooves approaching from the west. He perked up and maintained watch in that direction. Soon, Bat's smiling face appeared over the top of a large sandstone boulder. He rode confidently into the camp, jumped nimbly from his horse, and then sauntered over to the campfire. He poured himself a mug full of tea from a steaming brass pot.

"You look spry. Are you all packed for our journey?" Bat inquired jovially.

"Everything but my tent," Will responded. "I did not know how long you would be and had considered taking a nap before our departure." He paused as he knocked the ash from his clay pipe into the palm of his hand. "Did you manage to hail a boat?"

Bat took a swig of the steaming tea and then nodded. "I did, indeed. The first couple of passers-by ignored me, but when I waved a silver coin in the air, the next boat headed straight to the bank. It was a small flatboat loaded with tobacco and tea. The owner gladly received my letter and my coin."

"And you are certain that it will reach your father?"

"Of that I have no doubt. The boat will reach Fredericksburg before nightfall. My father should receive the correspondence before supper tomorrow night. There is no need to worry."

"What will you do with your salt and other belongings, since I am replacing those items on your pack horse?"

"I have picked out a good spot to hide both the salt and my father's iron pot. So few people venture up here, I am reasonably certain that they will remain undisturbed until I return."

Will nodded, satisfied with Bat's plan. He tossed the contents of his mug onto the ground beside the tent. "Well, then, I suppose it is time to go." He used the tent pole to pull himself to his feet. "If you will help me drop this tent, we can be on our way within the hour."

"Not so fast!" Bat objected. "I brought a small surprise with me. I made a trade with the boat crew." He grinned. "It is a wonder, indeed, how much one may obtain for five pounds of salt."

"What did you get? Tell me!" Will demanded eagerly.

Bat smiled teasingly. "What would you think about cooking up a pound of smoked middling meat and a dozen eggs before we go?"

"Oh, sure," Will retorted. "And I suppose we could sop up our drippings with a loaf of freshly-baked bread, as well."

Bat bit his lip and nodded. "I believe that can be arranged."

Will narrowed his eyes and glared disbelievingly at his friend. "Are you being sincere?"

Bat grinned proudly and nodded. "I have the makings of a fine meal in my saddle bag."

Will inhaled, excited. "Well, then! I think that, since you have obtained such a tasty treat, I could be persuaded to remain here on this pleasant hill for just a little while longer."

～

Early Afternoon
Near Megert's Swamp – East of the High Hills of Santee

BAT GLANCED over his shoulder to check on Will's condition. It became apparent to him that the still-recovering young man was in need of a rest. The duo had been traveling for almost three hours, and a brief break was warranted.

"Let us stop for a moment," Bat urged. "You do not look well. I fear that I have pushed you too hard."

Will did not respond. He merely nodded. His face was beet-red and sweaty. He appeared to be experiencing a significant amount of pain. Bat imagined that his friend's injured leg dangling from the side of the horse must have aggravated the wound and caused the leg to become swollen and irritated. Without doubt, the fact that he had no saddle and was riding the pack horse bareback made the journey very difficult for him. Bat made a mental note to stop more often and give Will the opportunity to elevate the afflicted leg. Truly, there was no need for them to rush.

They halted their horses in the shade of a small thicket. As soon as they stopped, Will carefully dismounted and then slowly sat down against a small maple tree. He popped the cork from his copper canteen and drank several eager, thirsty gulps. Bat removed his bedroll from the back of his saddle and carried it to Will.

"Here ... put this under your leg. Lie back and rest for a while. We are in no hurry. Hell, we can stop here and make camp if you do not feel like going any further."

Will took another quick drink of water and then shook his head. "I think I have a couple more hours left in me. We need to at least cross Megert's Swamp and get to the high ground on the other side before nightfall."

Bat nodded. "I reckon we can do that. But, we can enjoy a few moments of peace right here before we ride again. Your leg needs the respite." He sat down beside Will to share the shade of his little tree. "I may even take me a little nap."

"Go ahead. I will wake you when I am ready to move," Will promised.

Bat lay down on his back in the soft grass beneath the tree, perched his black felt floppy hat over his face, and was snoring within seconds. Will grinned and then shook his head. He was very tired, himself, but he could not imagine lying down and then falling into an immediate state of deep sleep. He envied Bat's apparent ability to simply turn off his mind and rest so soundly.

Will took another drink of water and then leaned his head back against the smooth bark of the maple tree. He closed his eyes and relaxed his body and mind. But, moments later, something disturbed his peaceful rest. He heard a strange noise. It sounded something like air being expelled from a large bellows. Immediately, he sat upright and scanned the area to search for potential danger. He saw something move in a small clearing about fifty yards to his left. Some manner of beast was emerging from the thick woods into the grassy clearing. Will's heart skipped a beat. For a moment, he wondered, "*Is it a bear?*"

Then, quite unexpected and unimaginably, five more of the huge, furry beasts emerged from the woods. Now there were six of them, all rooting and grazing in the thick grass of a small clearing. Will could scarcely believe his own eyes. The grazing animals were buffalo!

Will smacked Bat across the chest with the back of his hand. "Bat! Have a look at this!"

Bat growled, "Leave me alone, Will! I was dreaming about my neighbor, the lovely Miss Velma Pinson. And I was just getting to the good part."

"Bat, wake up! You must see this! There are buffalo here! I see six of them!"

"Horse shite," Bat grumbled from beneath his hat.

"Sincerely, Bat. Look!"

Bat groaned, disgusted, and then snatched his hat from his eyes. He sat up and peered in the direction where Will was pointing. Sure enough, just as Will claimed, six large-bodied American Bison were grazing in a meadow barely fifty yards away. Bat's jaw dropped in disbelief and amazement.

"Well, cock and pie! I would never have believed it had I not seen it with my own eyes." He glanced at Will and grinned. "You had best write this day down somewhere. I am reasonably certain that we have just witnessed something that we will likely never see again."

Will's face beamed with pleasure. "I am just glad that I finally got to see some buffalo." He sighed happily. "My experience on this journey has been made complete."

Two Days Later – Southwest of Lynches Creek

TRAVEL HAD BEEN PAINFULLY slow and difficult through the swamplands that surrounded the headwaters of the Black River. The horses slogged along with great difficulty through thick mud and, on occasion, belly-deep water. But, finally, Will and Bat emerged into the dry lands to the east. They began to make quicker progress through higher-elevation woodlands.

"Good God, I am glad to be clear of that nasty business," declared

Bat. "That last swamp was one putrid, unpleasant place. I fear that I may have a few leeches feasting upon my bollocks." He raised up in his saddle and pawed at his itchy privates.

Will laughed and then teased, "Do you reckon they might be starving to death?"

"Not likely," retorted Bat.

Will rolled his eyes sarcastically. After a while, he reflected upon Bat's analysis of the wetlands they had just crossed. "You are right about those bottomlands, for certain. The Scape Whore Swamp is not for the faint of heart. Many men have been lost to its mud and waters."

Bat cocked his head. "That is such a strange name for a place. Do you know how it came to be called thusly?"

Will chuckled. "According to my father, there was once a woman of dubious reputation who was being hunted by county officials. She was a lady who received recompense for her intimate services ... if you know what I mean."

Bat grinned and nodded.

"Well," Will continued, "The story goes that after being run out of her home by a gaggle of jealous Craven County wives, she disappeared into these wild, remote wetlands and then somehow managed to make her escape into North Carolina. Thus, the legend of a whore who fled through the critter-infested swamp gave birth to the strange moniker, Escaped Whore Swamp. Of course, the name been shortened over time by the local folk."

"I am almost sorry that I asked," Bat mumbled, chuckling.

"Thankfully, the swamps and bottoms are most definitely behind us now. There should be nothing but dry land between here and my home."

"Let us pray so," Bat affirmed.

The young men rode onward. Less than an hour after departing the backwaters, they discovered a narrow, rutted road. They halted at the roadside and observed for evidence of traffic.

"I believe this is the Williamsburg Highway," Will declared hopefully.

Bat grunted sarcastically. "It is not as I expected. It does not look like much of a highway. There is not a horse or wagon to be seen."

"It is the best road that we have around here. It goes from the river's headwaters all the way to Williamsburg."

Bat glanced in both directions. "Do you know exactly where we are, then? How far do you think we remain from your home?"

"I will know once I get a good look at some landmarks. Let us go." He guided his horse to the right and then led it onto the well-worn path. A few minutes later, he spotted a familiar home.

"That is Mr. Alonzo McCoy's plantation. I attended a ball at his house last fall. That fellow has some strikingly beautiful daughters." He winked playfully at Bat. "I know the way for certain from here. We are about a day's ride from my home."

Bat looked at the overcast sky. "We only have about four hours of daylight left. We can get in a couple more hours of travel and then stop to make camp."

"Agreed."

"Are you sure you are up to it?" Bat asked, concerned. "How is your leg holding out today?"

"Just knowing that I am so close to home and my own bed has made me feel much better. Come on, let us keep moving." Will did not wait for a reply. He pointed his horse toward home and snapped the reins.

∾

Late Evening
Encamped Along the Williamsburg Highway

WILL BELCHED LOUDLY. "That was delicious, I must say. I have never had the pleasure of feasting upon quail before. I do not think they live in abundance near my home."

"We were lucky to stumble upon a covey," Bat declared. He patted his belly. "I do enjoy roasted quail for supper."

Will and Bat both sat cross-legged under the open side of Will's wedge tent. They were encamped alongside the highway near a cluster of small oaks. The weather was uncharacteristically cool and pleasant for summer in the low country. As they had done each night during the return trip, they turned the tent sideways beside their campfire and lifted one side as a makeshift roof. Thus, they converted the small wedge tent into a larger lean-to. It provided more room for the both of them to sleep comfortably beneath the shelter.

They sat in silence for quite some time, alternately sipping hot tea and drawing smoke from their clay pipes. The mood of both men seemed somber and contemplative. After a while, Bat broke the silence.

"You seem downcast, Will. Are you not happy to be almost home?"

"Oh, yes! Very much so. But, strangely, I am also sad. I had such a wonderful adventure in the High Hills. I am a bit stymied, to be honest. I find it difficult to understand how I can feel both joy and sadness at the same time. It seems a bit odd."

"Not as odd as you think," Bat encouraged. He fetched a burning stick from the fire to re-light his pipe. "What will you do after you get home?"

"What do you mean?"

"I mean ... what are your plans? What are you going to do with your life? You seem, to me, to be a fellow in search of something. You are an intrepid young man who just wandered the frontier and survived an encounter with a deadly viper. Surely, after all that, you must have developed some man-sized plans for your future."

Will shrugged. "I suppose that I will continue in my father's business. I already work in his store several days a week and accompany him regularly on purchasing trips to Charlestown."

"So, then, you intend to follow along in your father's footsteps? Become a planter and an entrepreneur?"

"I do not see that I have much choice. Is that not what young English men do?"

Bat shrugged. "I believe that, here in the New World, a man can do anything that he sets his mind upon."

"So, then, what about you?" challenged Will. "Have you any big plans for your future?"

Bat poked out his lips and thoughtfully nibbled at the inside of his cheek. "I am still formulating them. I am in no rush." He glanced and Will and smiled.

The sound of horses approaching from the southeast invaded the silence and peace of their evening.

Will cut a concerned glance at Bat. "It is a bit late for anyone to be out on the roadways."

Bat shrugged. "It could be anything."

"Should we get our guns?" Will asked.

Bat shook his head. "It would not do us any good. That sounds like a dozen riders or more ... far too many for the two of us to confront with our two rifles."

Will craned his neck to peer down the highway. "They are coming from the direction of Williamsburg. Perhaps I will know some of them."

Minutes later, fifteen men on horseback appeared out of the trees that surrounded the roadway. Seeing the fire and tent near the road, they immediately altered course and approached. Will and Bat stood to meet them. The riders trotted to within twenty paces of the fire and then stopped.

The apparent leader of the group, a distinguished-looking middle-aged fellow, raised his hand in a friendly wave. He declared in a very proper and educated English accent, "Good evening, young gentlemen."

"Pleasant evening to you, sir," Bat declared.

"I am Levtenant Sidney Polkinghorne of His Majesty's Craven County Militia. I am in command of this patrol."

"'Tis mighty late into the night for the militia to be prowling about," Bat observed. "You must be careful you do not accidentally ride off into one of these rivers or sloughs."

The lieutenant chuckled. "Indeed. We had a close encounter with a large gully a few miles to the east. That experience compelled us to decrease our speed dramatically."

"What brings you out in the nighttime, sir?" Will inquired, curious. "Your presence on the roadway at this hour seems a bit odd."

"Oh, a great tragedy has befallen our area, I am afraid. One of our more influential planters along the Black River has reported a missing person in our region. Word has reached all the way to Charlestown. The South Carolina militia has been called out in force to scour the countryside from Lynches Creek to the Wateree River."

Bat and Will cut uncomfortable glances at one another. Will's face burned crimson red. He could feel his heartbeat pulsating in his temples. Surely, his father had not alerted the governor and activated the militia on his accord.

Will cleared his throat slightly. "What is the name of this missing person?"

"He is a young man by the name of William Newman. He is the son of the elder Mr. William Newman of Williamsburg. The lad should be about the same age as you fellows. Are you familiar with him?"

Bat laughed out loud. Will rubbed his forehead in disbelief and embarrassment. Finally, he inhaled deeply and then replied. "I, sir, am William Newman."

～

Thursday, June 25, 1750
The William Newman Estate on Black River

BARTHOLOMEW AUSTIN SPENT several restful days with the Newman men. But, the time for his departure had arrived. He was standing with his horses on the gravel driveway and securing his rifle and bags to the side of his English saddle. He heard footsteps behind him and turned. Will Newman was approaching, walking alongside his father.

The ever-red-faced Mr. Newman declared emotionally, "Mr. Austin, I cannot sufficiently express my gratitude in words. You saved my son's life and returned him to me. I shall never be able to repay you."

"There is nothing to repay, Mr. Newman. Besides, your restful guest room and bountiful table have been refreshing blessings to me. That widow woman of yours is quite the cook. I have gained at least five pounds since our arrival. You should consider marrying her and keeping her around here full-time."

Will chuckled out loud. William cut his eyes at his son and then elbowed him in his ribs.

Mr. Newman declared, "Well, Bartholomew, you must know that our home is always open to you. If you or anyone in your family are ever in this region and have need of a bed or a meal, you should come here to our home. Our eager hospitality awaits you."

Bat nodded respectfully. "Thank you, Mr. Newman. I do, indeed, look forward to returning someday."

"Please, make it sooner rather than later." Mr. Newman smiled and patted Bat on the shoulder. He inhaled deeply. "Well, I shall leave you boys to your goodbyes. I have much work to do." He tipped his hat to Bat. "Please write and let us know that you have returned home safely."

Bat tipped his hat in response. "Yes, sir. I will."

The elder William Newman turned and then shuffled along the pathway toward the barn. There was a moment of uncomfortable silence. Finally, Will extended his hand to Bat.

"Everything my father said goes double for me. I will always be grateful to you."

Bat grinned. "Do not get all sentimental on me. Contrary to what you and your father seem to believe, you were not going to die." He winked. "But, perhaps you can return the favor someday."

Will's eyes widened. "I would prefer not to suck any blood from your leg, if it can possibly be avoided."

Both young men chuckled happily. However, silence quickly descended upon them. Will's eyes began to water.

"Sincerely, Bat. I am grateful. I know that you truly did save me. I will never forget it."

Bat declared, grinning, "As well you shouldn't." He turned, placed his foot in the stirrup, and then swung his leg nimbly over the back of his horse. He stared at Will with a gaze of deep friendship. "Until we meet again."

"Until we meet again," Will echoed.

Without another word, Bat clucked to his horse. The animal trotted down the narrow lane toward the highway, followed closely by his empty pack horse. As Will watched him disappear beyond the trees, he wondered if he would ever actually see Bartholomew Austin again.

3

ROSEWATER AND RIBBONS

April 23, 1751

Wwilliam Newman called from the hallway, "Son, pour me a snifter of brandy, if you please. The latest edition of the Gazette awaits you in yon parlor. I will join you after I have relished in the joy of my evenin' constitutional."

Will grinned knowingly. His father's daily "constitutionals" were never walks for exercise or fitness or even to help settle his supper. They were always frantic races to the backyard privy. After eighteen years, Will could pretty much set his watch according to the precise regularity of his father's bowels.

After dispensing a hearty dose of brandy for his father, Will poured himself a generous glass of whiskey and then nestled into his favorite fireside padded wingback chair. His father had already stoked the fire, lighted the silver five-candle stand on Will's side table, and placed the newspaper on his footstool. He picked up his copy of the *South Carolina Gazette* and quickly scanned the date.

"Latest edition," he growled disgustedly. "This paper is from last week!" He shrugged. "Oh, well."

He sat back, sipped his whiskey, and then began reading the week-old news. Fifteen minutes later, his father appeared, red-faced and sweating, as was usual. He retrieved his brandy snifter from the serving bar and then clumsily plopped down into his sturdy, wide rocking chair. He swirled the amber liquid inside the bowl-shaped glass, gave it a discriminating sniff, and took a tiny sip. He closed his eyes and sighed with pleasure.

Will peeked over the top of his newspaper. "I do hope you washed your hands tonight."

His father opened one eye and, feigning anger, glared at his son. "I am weary. I'll not tolerate any impertinence from you tonight, boy."

Mr. Newman reached back and retrieved a small pillow from behind his buttocks. He tossed it playfully at his son. Will snagged the pillow from the air just before it hit him in the face and then nimbly dropped it onto the floor next to his chair.

"Nice try, old man," Will teased.

"Humph!" his father grunted. "If I had truly desired to hit you, I would have."

Mr. Newman took another swig of his brandy and then carefully placed the glass on his side table. He propped his feet on the brick hearth and then laced his fingers together and rested his hands atop his swollen, ample belly. After staring into the fire for a short while, he asked his son, "Well? What is happening in our world? Have you any interesting news to report?"

Will yawned. "Not much. But, it seems that Parliament has passed a *Paper Currency Act* forbidding the northern Colonies from issuing paper money."

"As well they should. Why should any of our British Colonies have need to print worthless paper when we have access to the King's coinage and currency? It is folly, I tell you. Loyal British subjects should be spendin' British money."

Will grinned teasingly. "That is interesting, Father. I do not believe that I have ever once seen you turn down Spanish or French coinage at our shop."

"Copper, silver, and gold coins are another matter altogether, young William. I care not which government issues them. Coins struck from precious metals have inherent value, no matter where they are minted. But, paper currency is spurious and prone to all manner of malice and fraud. I stand with His Majesty and Parliament on this new policy. I say, 'well done,' for passin' such a wise and patriotic act." He paused and sipped from his glass. "What else does that worthless Charlestown rag reveal?"

Will scanned the front page. "It says that the Creeks and the Cherokee are currently embattled in a bloody war against one another in the far west."

"Good! As long as the savages remain busy fightin' one another, they will leave His Majesty's citizens alone."

"But, the *Gazette* also reports that several English traders have been killed in the conflict down in the remote territories west of Georgia."

"Such men should know better than to conspire and do business with the savages," his father pronounced with an air of British judgmentalism. "All loyal subjects of the Crown should remain here within the boundaries and protection of the Colonies and His Majesty's soldiers."

"But, Father, one day I may be required to travel into those lands in the service of the King. I am an active member of the Craven County Militia. If I am ever called up, I will be required to go and serve, perhaps even in those faraway Indian territories."

Mr. Newman scowled and fumed. "Militia! Militia! Militia! That is all that ever seems to be on your mind these days. How I rue that horrid day when I sent them in search of you! Had you not been exposed to them thusly, you likely would have never joined their worthless ranks." He took a deep breath and endeavored to compose himself. "William, you are a gentleman and someday you will be the master of this estate and sole owner of our well-regarded and lucrative family business. You had best get all of this soldierin' folly out of your mind and concern yourself with things that truly matter."

Will rolled his eyes, an all-too-common response to his father's typically judgmental comments. However, he concealed his display of youthful mockery safely behind the folds of his newspaper. The elder William Newman was an opinionated man and apt to share his point of view with liberality and enthusiasm. Will need never wonder how his father stood on any particular issue.

Will turned the page to scan the stories on page two. As he surveyed the various headlines, he mused, "I wonder if Bat has seen any effects of this Indian war. He lives dangerously close to the Cherokee lands."

His father suddenly sat upright. "Good heavens, Will! I almost forgot!" He reached inside the lapel of his coat and produced a folded letter wrapped in a blue ribbon and sealed with a wide daub of yellow wax. "You received a correspondence from Bartholomew today. I received it at the shop shortly after noon."

Instantly losing interest in the newspaper, Will folded it and then tossed it aside onto the floor next to his chair. "What a wonderful surprise! I am most pleased. I have not heard from him since before the New Year. I was beginning to wonder if something untoward had happened to him during one of his travels or adventures."

"Perhaps he has good news to share." His father smiled as he handed the letter to his son. "I always enjoy your reading of his entertaining letters. He lives a very curious and interesting life out on the frontier," he paused. "Though, such a life would be foreign, indeed, to gentlemen such as ourselves."

Will ignored his father's last statement. He cracked open the stiff wax seal, peeled away the ribbon, and then quickly unfolded the letter. He scanned its message quickly. His face flushed red. He instantly flashed a huge smile.

"Well?" his father demanded. "Are you going to read it for me? What news does Bartholomew have to report?"

Will lowered the letter to his lap. He smiled so hard that his face began to ache. "It says that he is to be wed next month. He has invited us to travel to Jackson's Creek so that we might attend the celebration of his nuptials."

~

Saturday, May 29, 1751
Early Evening
The Home of Bartholomew Austin – Jackson's Creek, South Carolina

THE WEDDING CELEBRATION of Bartholomew Austin and the lovely Rachel Lott was in full-swing. The meadow beside the Austin home was illuminated with numerous lanterns, candles, and campfires. Music, singing, dancing, games, food, and drink were in abundance. Will was most intrigued by the tomahawk-throwing contest at the far end of the glade. He greatly desired to sneak away from his father and experiment with the fascinating weapon. No doubt, before the evening was done, he would have ample opportunities to do so. The merrymaking would likely continue into the wee hours of the morning, long after the groom stole his bride away to their honeymoon bedchamber.

The wedding had been a simple but elegant affair officiated by an Anglican vicar from Charlestown. Bat's father had insisted upon a state-recognized officiant, and had paid handsomely for his river passage from the coast. As a loyal subject of King George II, Bartholomew Austin, Sr., would settle for nothing short of a marriage recognized and ordained by the Crown.

Since there was not yet an established Anglican church in the area, Bat's father elected to host the ceremony on his lawn. Thankfully, the weather had cooperated. It had been a beautiful, sunny day. The setting was perfect. The wedding took place without a single hiccup. It was a day that neither of the newly enjoined families would ever forget.

Will was smitten with the hearty frontier folk and the vast, unspoiled, sparsely-populated countryside. Conversely, his father had barely ceased complaining since the moment their boat turned west onto the remote Congaree River. Clearly, he did not appreciate any aspect of the backcountry or the lifestyle it afforded. He described the territory west of the Wateree as "uncivilized," "barren," and "most undesirable." The only positive attribute that he had reluctantly assigned to the landscape was the "relative absence of blood-sucking insects."

Will could not disagree more. He felt the tug of the open country upon his young, adventurous heart. Ever since their boat landed at the mouth of Jackson's Creek, he had determined that he would live there someday. He considered speaking to Bat about the possibility of purchasing or receiving grant for land and settling nearby. Surely, his friend would have a working knowledge of the King's system of distributing land.

Throughout the early evening, Will and his father hovered quietly near the edge of the meadow and observed the boisterous festivities from a distance. They sat on a small bench and sipped whiskey and ale, chatted with the occasional curious guest, and patiently awaited their turn to congratulate the bridegroom and bride. They deduced that, with over two hundred neighbors and guests present, it would likely be a while before the newly-married couple would find the opportunity to visit with them.

Finally, about two hours after the ceremony concluded, Bat and his bride stole away from the greeting line and went in search of his friends from back east. They approached the Newmans at twilight. Bat was devilishly handsome in his perfectly-matched dark blue coat, weskit, and breeches. His dazzling white stockings, shirt, and cravat made his dark suit appear all the more stunning. He was hatless. His shiny, dark brown hair was pulled back into a perfect queue and secured with a long black silk ribbon.

Rachel wore a lovely off-white linen short gown and matching petticoat, accented by a white neck scarf that was block painted with a dark blue and yellow flower pattern. A thin lace bonnet covered her head, providing a glimpse of the blazing red hair underneath. Her hair was wrapped in a tight bun and decorated with a bright yellow silk ribbon that dangled from beneath the back of her bonnet. As she approached, Will was overwhelmed and mesmerized not only by her extraordinary beauty, but also by her delightful smell. She bore the intoxicating aroma of sweet, fragrant rosewater.

"Mr. Newman! Will! What do you fellows think of our little country celebration?" Bat inquired.

"There is nothing little about it," retorted Will as he and his father stood to greet the newlyweds. Each man removed his hat and bowed in honor of the bride. Rachel Austin offered her right hand, covered in a sheer white silk glove. Will received her hand and then kissed it in a most gentlemanly manner.

"Mrs. Austin, I am afraid that we have not been properly introduced. I am William Newman of Williamsburg Township on the Black River. This is my father, the elder William Newman."

She smiled warmly at them both. "Bat and I both welcome you gentlemen to our home." She giggled and then leaned forward to offer Will a most affectionate hug. "Will, I feel like I know you already. Bat has told me all about your adventures in the high country last year."

Will glanced teasingly at Bat. "Well, that makes only one of us, Mrs. Austin. I am a bit confused. You see, I must reluctantly inform you that your husband did not mention a single word of you whilst he tended to me throughout my many days of snakebite-induced illness. How, pray tell, could he have overlooked so important and beautiful a subject?"

Rachel feigned a stern look at Bat and then smiled and shook her head. "Mr. Newman, you must understand that his silence was evidence of neither artifice or malice. In truth, we did not know one another at that time. We only met this past January. That is when my mother and I joined my father at our new home here on Jackson's Creek."

"Ah!" Will exclaimed, nodding. He cut a teasing glance at Bat. "That explains the other troubling matter, then. It helps me comprehend the rather abrupt ceasing of correspondence from my good friend. The last letter that I received from him before your wedding announcement was way back in mid-December. Should I assume that your romance and engagement have consumed every moment of his time and attention since?"

Rachel's face flushed a bright crimson that was evident even in the dim glow of firelight and candles. She responded shyly, "I suspect so."

"Your courtship has been rather brief, has it not?" Will's father asked with a mild tone of suspicion and judgment. "Was yours an arranged union?"

"It was long enough to be respectable, Mr. Newman," Bat responded confidently. "And ... no, ours was not an arranged marriage. We have wed for love, not for dowry or business. We met in January at a social gathering. After that, we courted for three months before I asked Rachel's father for her hand. Neither of our families saw any need to tarry."

"So, then, it was love at first sight," Will observed admirably.

Bat and Rachel looked lovingly into one another's eyes and then each smiled and nodded slowly. Bat glanced at his friend and winked. "I think that I have chosen rather well, don't you?"

"Indeed," Will answered. "You married up, that much is certain. I feel sorry for Rachel, though. Once she hears the chorus of unpleasant noises that you make in your sleep, she may experience inescapable regret."

Bat's head spun toward Will in pained disbelief. Rachel stared at Will, wide-eyed. Her face burned bright from embarrassment. Then, suddenly and quite unexpectedly, she burst into uncontrollable giggling. Her laughter was contagious. Bat and Will could not help but laugh, as well. Mr. Newman was tempted to join them, but his gentle-manly airs would not allow him the freedom to do so. Instead, he covered his mouth with his handkerchief and intentionally looked the other way, even as the edges of his lips curled into an undeniable grin.

After their laughter subsided, Rachel leaned her cheek against her husband's chest and smiled at Will. "Husband, I like this witty, brash young man. I can see why you love him so."

Bat wrapped his arms around her and kissed her gently on the forehead. "I quite agree. I rather think that he was worth saving from the grip of that deadly viper, don't you?"

"Indeed," she agreed happily.

"Amen!" Mr. Newman concurred wholeheartedly.

Bat took his wife's hand and offered it to Mr. Newman. "My dear, will you escort Mr. Newman to the dancing area and introduce him to a backcountry jig? I would like to have a moment of privacy with Will." Bat glanced at Mr. Newman. "Sir, do you mind?"

Will's father smiled and bowed. "'Twould be a pleasure, indeed." He offered his right arm to Rachel. She immediately guided him toward the sound of the violins.

Bat and Will watched them disappear into the crowd. Once they were out of sight, the two young men sat down on the bench that Will had been sharing with his father.

"Well? What do you think?" asked Bat.

"My God, Bat. She is positively dazzling. And that red hair! I hope she does not turn out to be more woman than you can handle." He playfully punched his friend in the thigh.

"I think that I shall do just fine." He paused and inhaled a deep breath. "I trust that your travel here occurred without difficulty?"

"It was a lovely journey, and much easier travel than I had imagined. There is good, deep water all the way to the mouth of your creek. I imagined in my mind that this place would be much more remote and quite difficult to reach."

"Well, it is quite remote," Bat affirmed, "but, it is not at all difficult to get here by boat. What do you think of our beautiful country? Do you approve?"

"I love it!" Will blurted immediately. "There is room to expand and wander, and no swampland close by." He paused thoughtfully. "I think that I must settle here someday."

"Someday soon, I hope?"

Will sighed and appeared somewhat downcast. "No. I am bound to my father right now. The estate and his businesses have a claim upon me for the foreseeable future. But, that will not always be so. Could you assist me in filing for a grant from the Crown? Perhaps I could go ahead and secure land now, even if I do not settle it for a few years."

Bat patted Will affectionately on the shoulder. He grinned. "I think something can be arranged."

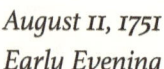

August 11, 1751
Early Evening

WILL WAS ALONE, as was usual on most nights during mid-week. More and more, his father seemed to always be away from home and traveling for business. Will's days of work in the family shop were long, to be sure, but his nights alone in the oversized Newman home seemed even longer.

Will, slightly intoxicated after a second glass full of whiskey, reclined lazily in his familiar chair and unfolded with great anticipation a newly-arrived letter from Bat. It was his first correspondence from his friend since returning home from the backcountry. The letter read:

Dearest William,

I trust that this letter finds you and your father in good health and spirits. It was truly a joy to welcome you both to our home here on Jackson's Creek. I pray that you may return for another visit at some time in the near future.

I am happy to report that married life is most agreeable to me. The bliss of our union and the joy found in the intimacy shared with a loving wife is more wondrous than I can describe. Mrs. Austin, in addition to being my loving bride, has become my dearest and most valuable friend. Ours is a home that is filled with love, wonder, and adventure. I can only hope and pray that you might someday find a similar abundance of joy in a marriage to the bride of your choosing.

I am also pleased to inform you that our new home will soon be inhabited by three souls. It seems that the Lord Almighty intends for me to have many arrows in my quiver, as my lovely bride is already expecting the birth of our first child. We will welcome this miracle of our love in the New Year. I invite you to pray earnestly for me as I step forward into the role of fatherhood.

Concerning our discussions on the evening of my wedding, I have secured information from my father regarding the process of patenting land on Jackson's Creek. He will be most helpful in assisting you in selecting suitable acreage in this region, as well as procuring, completing, and filing the appropriate documents with the Crown. Both of us stand ready to assist you should you decide to enter into such an endeavor. Your presence as a loyal friend and neighbor would be yet another source of unspeakable joy in my life, should you choose to remove to these environs and establish a homestead.

I look forward to hearing from you very soon. Please offer your father my kindest regards.

Ever Your Affectionate Friend,
Bartholomew Austin

Will carefully refolded the letter and then placed it on the table beside his empty whiskey glass. A small tear formed in the corner of his left eye. He felt honored to share in Bat's happiness. He prayed silently that he, himself, might find that kind of joy in marriage someday. He rose and poured himself another generous shot of whiskey. He walked over to the parlor window that faced toward the west, lifted his glass high as a toast to his friend, and then drained it dry.

September 1, 1751
Newman's Mercantile – Williamsburg Township

WILL SPUN around and angrily hurled a bolt of expensive cloth against the wall of the shop. He shouted, "I cannot believe it! Surely, this is some manner of sick joke! How could you do something like this to me ... your only son?"

His father remained perfectly composed. "I was merely acting in your best interests, William. Miss Kirby comes from a very wealthy and influential family. Her father is Spencer Kirby, the King's Chief of Surveying for this entire region. This marriage will be a most beneficial arrangement for us all."

"What you actually mean is that you acted in your own best interests, and that such a marriage will benefit your business and your bank accounts," Will accused, seething with rage.

"I rather think that our two interests are inherently intertwined, don't you?" He waved his hand to highlight the various portions of the impressive building in which they stood, as well as the goods stored there. "Think, boy. This property, my business, and my fortune will all be yours someday. You, too, will be a wealthy and influential man in South Carolina. A union with the Kirby clan makes much sense, both economically and politically."

"But, Father! I have not met this girl! I have never even cast my eyes upon her!"

"That is of no consequence. She is a maiden of fifteen years and chaste. You, as her husband, will be the recipient of a substantial dowry. I have been informed that it is upwards of four hundred pounds in gold and silver coin ... an almost unspeakable sum in the New World. You will be a wealthy man on the very day that you swear your vows."

Will stepped pleadingly toward his father. "But, do you not understand, Father? Do you truly know me so little? Fortune is not what I seek in a marriage. I want a wife whom I can adore. I want to experience life with a woman of my own choosing in an intimate and loving partnership." Tears formed in his eyes. "I want the kind of marriage that Bat and Rachel have discovered."

Mr. Newman sighed as he shook his head. "Bartholomew is a nice young man, William, but he is a backwoods fool. He will never have anything of longstanding consequence. You, on the other hand, have a much different future ahead of you."

Will was trembling in fear and rage. "People often measure the value of things by very different standards, Father. I am quite convinced, now, that you and I must."

His father smiled coldly. "Which is all the more reason that I should be the one making this particular choice for you. A wife is not something to be selected spuriously by an immature boy. Trust me, one day you will be grateful for my wisdom and for my provision in this matter."

Will took two steps toward his father. He stomped one foot and then almost growled at the man. "I refuse to be party to any arranged marriage. This is not Ireland. This is America."

His father did not relent. "Our geography matters not. William, you simply have no choice in the matter. I am your father. The contract has been signed. It is a legal, binding document." He exhaled in frustration. "Frankly, I do not understand why you find the notion so objectionable. My marriage to your mother was arranged, and you know full-well that we were happy together and that over the years we grew to love one another deeply."

Will glared incredulously at his father. "I know no such thing! How could I ever know that? My eyes have never even looked upon my mother. You know full-well that she was deceased before the midwife placed me on her lifeless breast! An African slave-woman nursed me until I was almost three years old. Now, that is a face I actually remember!" He slammed his fist onto the counter beside him. "That negro was more of a mother to me than the dead woman who birthed me."

Without thinking, William Newman lifted his right hand and slapped his son with rage and fury. The crack of flesh impacting flesh was wickedly sharp and loud. Will recoiled from the blow and stumbled to his right. He hesitated for a moment, temporarily frozen in disbelief. His father had never raised a hand to him before. After several uncomfortable seconds, he stood upright. He held his right hand against his still-stinging, red cheek. He scowled in hatred at his father.

"You will not disrespect your mother, God rest her soul! I will not tolerate it!" Mr. Newman stepped forward and wagged his plump finger in Will's face. "Now, you listen to me, boy. Your whinin' and complaints will cease, and cease immediately. 'Tis time for you to grow some bollocks and act like a responsible, adult man. You *will* obey me. You *will* honor me. You *will* wed Miss Mary Kirby. And you *will* do your duty for me and for our family."

Will inhaled deeply. He squared his shoulders, stood tall, and faced his father. "Yes, Father. I will obey you. I will do my duty, honor your contract, and wed this girl. But, I refuse to honor *you* any longer. You have broken my heart and my spirit. I am quite certain that I shall never forgive you."

He stormed past his father, threw open the shop door, and then made his exit. He angrily slammed the door closed behind him. His stunned father stood and stared after him in disbelieving silence.

～

June 4, 1752
Sunday Afternoon
Anglican Church – Williamsburg, South Carolina

WILL STOOD RIGIDLY in the reception line. He was awash in a fog of disbelief. One after another, the people in attendance filed by to shake his hand and offer well-wishes for a prosperous future. But, Will did not even have the presence to look any of them in the eye, much less speak to them. He still could not believe that his young life had come to this tragic moment of a forced joining. Any and all affairs of the heart had been cast aside in order to make room for a family business covenant. His father could not be any happier with the outcome. Will, on the other hand, wanted to climb up into the small bell tower of the church, wrap the ringing rope around his neck, and hang himself. The deed was done. He was wed to the Mrs. Mary Kirby Newman.

It was not as if she were an unattractive or unpleasant girl. On the contrary, Mary Kirby was quite beautiful, indeed. She was petite, with curly brown hair, sparkling blue eyes, a narrow waist, voluptuous hips, and an impressive bosom. She commanded the attention in every room that she entered. But, Will noticed from the outset that she seemed to enjoy that attention, particularly when offered by eligible men, entirely too much.

For the most part, Mary had been polite, courteous, and attentive throughout their nine-month courtship. However, she had her unpleasant moments. Though such moments were rare, she displayed on more than one occasion a short and vicious temper. She had much more frequently placed on full display her propensity toward wanton prideful presumption, seasoned with a healthy dose of overindulged ingratitude.

Their first encounter was but a harbinger of things to come. Shortly after their engagement had been announced publicly, Will visited Mary in her home and presented her with what he thought to be a most elegant and thoughtful gift. He offered her a light blue silk ribbon for her hair and a bottle of pleasantly fragrant rosewater. Her response to the gift was nothing short of rude, dismissive, and arrogant. She promptly informed Will that she only wore silk ribbons that her father imported from Egypt. Furthermore, she would never wear such cheap swill as rosewater, since she had no desire to "smell like a whore from a brothel down by the river." She required, instead, the expensive French perfume that her father purchased for her on his yearly trips to Paris.

Will considered fleeing at that very moment, if flight were at all possible. He even entertained the notion of enlisting in the King's Navy and escaping the continent altogether. But, as a man of honor, he remained determined to stand fast and fulfill his contractual commitments. He took her insults like a man and persevered in what he considered to be a doomed, lifeless premarital relationship.

So, for nine months the most talked-about young couple in Craven County attended all of the balls and other appropriate social gatherings throughout the region. They dined under the supervision of their chaperons at the finest restaurants. They went on scheduled courtship walks and lovely carriage rides. Still, despite all their outings and interaction, there was absolutely no passion or curiosity within their relationship. There was no spark. Will could discern absolutely no personal, intimate connection between them. To him, it felt as if he were purchasing a new mare for his stable, albeit a very beautiful, pampered, expensive, arrogant, and overly talkative mare.

Mary Kirby was a lovely girl. But, in Will's eyes, that was exactly her problem. She was a bit too cognizant of her own beauty. In addition, at a mere fifteen years of age, she seemed to him little more than a rotten, spoiled child.

Though they rarely talked about one another's lives or hopes or dreams, Mary was always willing to converse about the subject of marriage, itself. Indeed, it seemed to Will that Mary was much enamored with the notion of getting married, even if she appeared indifferent as to the identity of the bridegroom. She seemed relieved by the fact that her father had chosen a mate for her. Such an arrangement provided a more rapid path to the main event ... the wedding.

And what a wedding it had been! For the past three months, Mary and her sisters had been planning, shopping, and purchasing items for the grand occasion. Finally, after all those months of unbridled expense and feverish preparation, the day had arrived. Mary and her family relished in the pomp and ceremony of it all. Will's father seemed quite pleased with himself, as well. His plump, pink complexion appeared a bit more rosy than usual and he bore a smile that appeared as if it might never diminish.

The wedding itself was, to Will, a bitter disappointment at best. He suffered through the event rather than relishing it. He wandered aimlessly throughout the entire day, simply going where he was told and doing as he was instructed. He discerned that the Kirbys viewed him as nothing more than a necessary accessory. He felt disposable, unnoticed, and replaceable.

Thankfully, Mary and her family had managed to organize a wedding ceremony that required only his minimal involvement. He had three simple tasks to perform: hold the bride's hand, say the words, "I do," when prompted, and then kiss the bride when instructed. Of course, the Kirby family expected that first kiss to be gentlemanly and dignified. Will was to peck his bride gently on the cheek beside her lips and nothing more. A full-on lip-to-lip encounter would be considered far too vulgar and uncouth.

Will could scarcely believe the moment when, as his troubled mind wandered in an effort to escape the torment, the vicar was required to confront him twice with the question, "Mr. Newman, do you take this woman to be your lawfully wedded wife?"

He did not even hear those words the first time. He barely heard them the second time. Actually, Mary had given his hand a stern jerk to recapture and refocus his attention. Then, in that moment of distraction and lapsed attention, he had actually managed to forget the designated response. He would never forget the look of frantic confusion on the vicar's face when he answered, "I reckon … I mean … sorry Vicar … I can … I will … I do!"

The entire church erupted with thunderous laughter. Mary's face turned three shades of red before it landed on a deep purple hue. Will stole an embarrassed glance at the parents of the bride and groom. Mary's father was actually laughing. Her mother appeared on the verge of apoplexy. His own father covered his eyes in shame. Will wanted to die. He was barely out of the starting gate, and he was already in deep shite.

With that epic failure behind him, Will paid a bit more attention throughout the remainder of the wedding. Finally the vicar's proclamation came: "By the powers vested in me by His Majesty King George II and by our Lord Jesus Christ, I now pronounce you husband and wife." Will landed a perfect, dispassionate kiss on his new bride's cheek at exactly the right moment. And that was it. He was a married man, like it or not.

One hour later, he found himself languishing in the torturous, seemingly endless receiving line. He thought that he might melt from boredom and heartbreak until he saw two most welcome and familiar faces. Bat and Rachel Austin appeared in front of him. The lovely Rachel swaddled a tiny baby against her breast. Suddenly, Will's heart swelled with joy.

"Bat! Rachel, dear! I was not sure if you had come!" The two friends shook hands.

"We arrived a bit late, I am afraid, and had to sit in the very back. It was for the best, though. Rachel had to take the baby outside twice. The little scrapper made a little too much noise for our neighbors, if you know what I mean."

"William, who are these people?" his wife interrupted rudely.

"Forgive me, Mary. This is Mr. and Mrs. Bartholomew Austin of Jackson's Creek. They are two of my dearest friends."

"I have never heard of Jackson's Creek. Is it near Charlestown?"

"No, Mary. It is two days' travel west of here, in the backcountry."

"Oh," she responded haughtily. "Well ... thank you all the same for coming to our wedding."

She immediately turned to greet another guest. Will ignored her. He stepped back and removed himself from the line. He motioned for his friends to join him.

"So, this is baby Drury?"

Rachel beamed. "In the flesh! The pride and joy of my life. He is the exact image of his handsome father. Would you like to hold him?"

"May I?" Will asked, surprised. "I would be very honored."

"Of course," Rachel answered, smiling warmly.

Will reached out and took the tiny baby into his arms. He moaned with pleasure, "He is absolutely perfect." He could barely remove his eyes from the tiny, beautiful little boy.

"Where will you two celebrate your honeymoon?" inquired Bat.

Will sighed. "We will remain here in Williamsburg for two nights. Mary's father owns a rental house in town. We will rest there for two days and then depart for a two-week stay in Charlestown on Wednesday morn. I say 'rest,' but I believe Mary's family has almost every waking moment that we remain here filled with some manner of social event."

"Would you be free for dinner tomorrow noon?" Bat invited. "There is a tavern with excellent food near our inn. We would love to host you. We have much catching-up to do."

"I am not certain. One moment ..." He stepped forward and

nudged his wife. "Mary, might we have dinner mid-day tomorrow with the Austins? They have invited us out."

She scowled. "William, you know that my mother has a ladies' dinner planned for the morrow."

"Then, I am not expected to attend?"

She rolled her eyes. "Do not be daft, William. It is a ladies' dinner, after all. Your presence would neither be expected nor welcomed."

"Would you mind, then, if I dine with my friends?"

"I care not. You may do as you wish." She immediately turned her back to him and resumed her conversation with an older, wealthy-looking couple.

Bat turned and gave his wife a somewhat shocked, wide-eyed look. He turned and subtly leaned forward to whisper in Will's ear. "It looks like *you* may have *your* hands full." His wife, overhearing the observation, elbowed him sternly in the ribs.

Will did not say anything in response. He merely frowned and, for a moment, lowered his eyes in shame. Somehow rescuing his pride, he took a deep breath and then declared, "It looks like I will be alone in representing the Newman clan. But, the four of us can still have a jolly time together tomorrow." He playfully tickled baby Drury's nose.

"Actually," Rachel countered, "I think the two of you should spend a bit of time alone. I know that it has been a while since you were able to visit with one another. Whilst we are in town, I have some shops that I would like to visit. My days in civilization are so very rare."

"Are you certain that you would not mind us dining without you?" Bat clarified.

"Not a'tall. It will do you both some good to have a little bit of man-time. I have plenty to keep me occupied."

"Very well," Bat declared. "Then, let us dine tomorrow, Will. Just the two of us. Noon at the River Room Tavern."

"That sounds wonderful, indeed. I will be there."

Will offered the baby back to his mother and then shook Bat's hand.

Bat smiled warmly. "Until tomorrow."

"Until tomorrow," Will echoed softly.

Will's entire face filled with a smile. Finally, he had experienced a moment of warmth and joy on what had been, for him, a sad and disappointing day.

4

THE WICKED CAROUSEL OF LIFE

Noon the Next Day - The Dancing Fox Tavern

The mood was somber. Will and Bat huddled together in a quiet, solitary corner of the tavern. Each man nursed a tankard of ale. It was Will's third tankard, actually. He had arrived over an hour ahead of their scheduled dinner meeting in order to get a head start on his drinking. Besides being slightly inebriated, he seemed uncharacteristically quiet and reserved. His hands were shaking slightly. He was not himself, at all. It was obvious to Bat that something was troubling him deeply.

Bat leaned forward and rested his elbows on the table. "What is wrong, my friend? You are not behaving like the Will Newman that I remember."

Will drained the frothy remnants of ale from his stoneware mug and then held it high in the air in order to capture the attention of the bar wench.

"I think you have had enough ale, Will. The day has barely begun. You should not wish to finish the remainder of it in a state of wanton drunkenness."

"Oh, I am not so certain about that," Will countered, wagging his head sarcastically. "Alcohol is exactly what I need to help get me through this day ... perhaps through every remaining day of my cursed, miserable life."

"Damn it, Will! What is troubling you so?"

Will lowered his head. His shoulders began to shudder and his chest heaved slightly. He seemed on the verge of tears. He inhaled a deep, composing breath and then timidly looked his friend in the eye.

"Bat, I do not know how to express the words that I need to say. I have things that I want to ask you, but I cannot bring myself to do so. I am far too embarrassed."

Bat placed a reassuring hand on Will's forearm. "You can ask me anything, my friend, and without shame. You need never fear being ridiculed or judged by me."

"I simply cannot, Bat. It is entirely too ..."

His friend interrupted him somewhat harshly. "Ask me, Will. Just talk to me. I must know what manner of torment has afflicted you."

The bar wench appeared at their table, sloppily filled Will's mug, and then moved quickly to tend to her other customers. Will stared numbly into the pale, tepid drink.

"It is a very personal query, Bat. Indeed, it is far too sensitive a subject to mention in company."

"As I said before, you may ask me anything, my friend. You should know that you can trust me."

Will leaned back in his creaky ladder-back chair and inhaled deeply. He glanced all around him to make sure that no one else could hear and then leaned closer to his friend.

He whispered almost inaudibly, "It is a question concerning the marriage bed."

Bat smiled slightly. "Oh, I see. What about it? What do you need to know?"

Will grimaced, then asked hesitantly. "What should it be like?"

"What do you mean, exactly?"

"I mean ... between a man and his wife. What should it be like?" Will stared at his friend, consumed with anxiety. "Specifically, how should a wife comport herself?"

Bat rubbed his chin and hesitated for a moment. He chuckled uncomfortably. "Well, I cannot speak for all wives, of course. I have only had the one, and Rachel is the only woman I have ever bedded."

Will scooted forward in his chair. "And?" he inquired anxiously.

"And ... Rachel is a passionate woman. From what I can tell, and based upon the racket she makes inside the privacy of our bedchamber, she thoroughly enjoys our intimate moments. If she does not, she certainly has me fooled."

Will's chin dropped to his chest. He took several deep, thoughtful breaths as he pondered Bat's testimony.

Bat leaned in toward his friend. "Why these curious questions, Will? Were things not as you expected last night?"

Will shook his head. "No. Not at all. Our union was nothing short of aloof and dispassionate. Mary seemed almost completely removed from the encounter. Ultimately, I think she felt disgusted, perhaps even violated."

Bat sat up straight in surprise. "Sincerely?"

"Yes!" Will exhaled in exasperation. "Mary treated our wedding night as if it were an appointment with her physician. She disrobed under the cover of darkness and then slithered beneath the covers. Of course, I had no idea what to do. It was all brand-new to me. So, I undressed, as well, and then climbed in beside her." He paused and looked forward, almost staring through his friend to the wall beyond as he relived the traumatic moment in his mind. "Then, when I approached her in the bed, she uttered the most confounding thing."

"What?" Bat demanded. He leaned forward in his chair with curious anticipation.

Will answered quietly, "She whispered to me, '*You are my husband now, and I am fully prepared to perform my wifely duty. Now, do your business, and quickly so.*'"

Both of Bat's eyebrows lifted so high that they almost touched his hairline. "She said *that* to you?" He seemed genuinely dumbfounded.

"Indeed. Word for word. I shall never forget it for as long as I live. I felt as welcome in her bed as a dead, rotten catfish. Now, I am at a loss as to my next course of action."

Bat bit his lip. "Will ... umm ... I hate to ask you, but I must. You did consummate your vows, did you not?"

Will looked ashamed. He nodded slightly. "I suppose that is the most accurate way to describe it. She would not allow me to place my hands on her, at all. To be honest, the deed was difficult for me to accomplish. But I finished ... eventually."

"What did Mary say? How did she respond to your intimacy?"

Will took a huge gulp of the fresh ale. "She sobbed the entire time." Will continued, "Afterwards, as she put on her shift and left the room, she informed me, *'You should not expect to do that again any time soon. It was positively revolting.'* Then, she disappeared into the kitchen and spent the next hour soaking in the bathtub. I lay there alone, feeling as if I had gone to the privy on her. I finally managed to go to asleep. I assume that she slept in another bedchamber in the house. When I awakened this morning, she was gone. She left a note saying that she had taken a carriage to her parents' home."

Bat was aghast. "I am so very sorry, Will. It is not supposed to be like that. Not at all. The marriage bed is intended by God to be a glorious, warm, and loving experience. What you have described to me has no resemblance to that ideal." He paused thoughtfully. "Perhaps Mary's mother did not teach her or prepare her for the events of the bedchamber."

Will shrugged. "Perhaps. But, now I fear that I am doomed to a lifetime of sleeping beside a frigid, disinterested wife ... that is, *if* she will even sleep in the same room as me. I must assume that, though she desperately desired to be married, she has no practical or personal use for an actual husband."

"I pray that is not the case." Bat reached across the table and patted his friend's shoulder. "I must say, though, that I am not entirely surprised. I still cannot comprehend this entire notion of an arranged marriage. I know that many folks are still wed under such traditional circumstances and have been since the dawn of man. But, I just do not understand how it actually works. Rachel and I met ... we just stumbled across one another ... and then we fell in love. Marriage to her and intimacy with her are wonderful. It just makes sense. It is perfect."

Will smiled at his friend. "I envy you both."

Bat grinned happily. "I won a great prize in my sweet wife, that much is certain."

Will nodded and smiled in admiration. "That is very, very true."

Bat's face became more serious. "But, now we must pray that God will soften the heart of your wife and that the two of you will, over time, grow to love one another as deeply as we."

A tear leaked from Will's right eye. "Thank you, Bat. Your friendship and your prayers mean more to me than you will ever know."

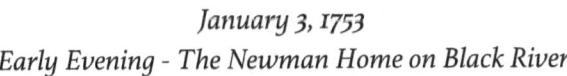

January 3, 1753
Early Evening - The Newman Home on Black River

IT WAS A FRIGID WINTER NIGHT. Will reclined lazily in his favorite chair in the parlor. He was drinking copious amounts of whiskey and reading, his two favorite nighttime activities. His father had joined him for a short while earlier in the evening, but then begged his leave to go outside and make his usual after-supper trip to the privy. Since it was so cold, Will was reasonably confident that his father would make quick work of emptying his bowels so that he might once again inhabit his rocking chair beside the toasty parlor fireplace. But, as of yet, he had not returned.

Mary Newman, seven months pregnant, waddled into the parlor in search of warmth. She tossed two small logs onto the ample bed of coals in the fireplace and then carefully lowered herself into her own rocking chair near the fire. She retrieved a woven wool blanket from the floor beside the chair and used it to cover her cold, aching, swollen legs. She rocked quietly and stared silently at her husband. Her gaze betrayed a deep-seeded attitude of bitterness and disgust.

To be sure, their marriage was off to a fragile, shaky start. Mary had originally assumed that she and her new husband would live within the borders of Williamsburg Township. She considered herself to be a civilized girl of the town and had absolutely no desire to live in what she deemed the *wilderness of the provincial country.* Will, on the other hand, had far different plans. He would not even consider living in town full-time. His desire was to remain at his father's home on the Black River and continue enjoying the lifestyle that he had always known and loved.

Their initial discussions of the matter were acrimonious, to say the least. On day three of the marriage, their first day of honeymooning in Charlestown, their disagreement over the matter boiled over into a full-blown confrontation. Mary screamed through tears of rage that she would never leave the immediate proximity of her mother. Will then informed her with absolute certainty that she was his wife and she would damned well go where he bid her to go.

Ultimately, obeying the admonition from her father, Mary packed her belongings and accompanied her husband to the river country. But, her surrender was not without emotion, rancor, and protest. After arriving on Black River, their initial pitched battle of harsh words devolved into a long, slow war of relational attrition. Mary avoided Will. Will avoided Mary. And throughout it all they continued to grow apart in their silence and bitterness. The discovery of Mary's pregnancy had, fortunately, brought about something resembling a "cease-fire." But, tensions remained high, and they were slowly but surely building to a point of explosion.

Mary cleared her throat in an effort to gain her husband's attention. Will remained silent and stolid, refusing to even acknowledge his wife's presence in the room. Instead, he continued to drink from his half-full glass of whiskey and read his latest book. Will's face was flushed red. It was also apparent from the unmistakable bulge in the front of his breeches that he was aroused by what he was reading.

Will was being held mentally captive by the words of a popular erotic novel, Edmund Curll's *The Potent Ally, or Succours from Merryland.* The illicit book was one of a series of erotic fiction stories that described the female body in the form of a topographical metaphor. It described in great detail the various anatomical portions of a fictional woman named Merry. It described her ample female features as a tasty landscape that required "exploring, tilling, and planting." Its content was quite lewd and was regarded as obscene within most British social circles.

Finally, Mary could remain silent no longer. She blurted loudly, "Have you no shame?"

Will glanced over the top of the book and glowered at his wife. "Whatever do you mean, dearest wife?" His words dripped with sarcasm and disdain.

"You know perfectly well what I mean! You sit there, right in front of me, and read that disgusting, pornographic drivel!"

"This book is fine literature. I will have you know that it is highly regarded in Europe. I paid a high price for it." His speech was slurred by his drunkenness. He could barely enunciate the word, "literature."

She grunted sarcastically. "Well, I say that you were cheated out of some well-earned silver. The only value of that particular waste of paper is found in hanging it on the wall of the privy. At least then we may make use of it for cleansing our bums. I am quite sure that such vulgarity is welcomed in France, where the men are libidinous louts and the women are all salacious whores. But, it is certainly not regarded as worthwhile reading in England or His Majesty's provinces."

Will lay the book face-up in his lap, still open to the page that he was reading. He drained his glass of whiskey and then reached for the bottle and poured himself another shot. He drained it, as well, and then clumsily filled the glass once more. He sat back in his chair and swirled the glass in his hand while admiring the motion of the pungent amber liquid. He patted the book and smiled a wicked, contemptuous grin.

"Did you know that the central character of this incredible book is a woman named Merry? She is a beautiful, bountiful, and sexually expressive woman. But, her name is not spelled the same as *your* Mary. Rather, it has an 'e,' as in 'Merry Christmas.'" He took another swig of whiskey and then smacked his lips. "I find that to be so filled with irony, don't you?"

She screamed angrily, "You positively disgust me."

Will shrugged. "Tit for tat. You see, a man must seek personal satisfaction somewhere. Why else do you think the upstairs of the taverns and brothels are so popular amongst gentlemen?" He lifted the book on one hand to display before her. "Since I would never demean myself with such immoral endeavors, I must seek my tiny measure of imaginary satisfaction within the pages of a book."

"What, exactly, is that supposed to mean?" she demanded.

He angrily slammed the book closed and then leaned forward in his chair. He pointed at her with the hand that was holding the whiskey glass, clumsily slinging the fluid all over rug that covered the parlor floor. Frustrated and angry at himself for making such a mess, he furiously slung the glass into the fireplace, shattering it against the brick. Shards of glass rained down into the fire. Mary jumped and lifted her hand in front of her face, fearful of his sudden and most uncharacteristic explosion of violence.

Will growled, "Woman, you know exactly what I mean! The only thing in this house that is colder than your icy, forbidding heart is our marriage bed."

A tear formed in her eye. "How can you be so cruel to the woman who bears your child?"

Will chuckled sarcastically. "Oh, that! Well, 'tis no small wonder ... a miracle, even ... seeing as how our wedding night was the one and only time that I have ever plowed your garden. If not for that one miserable night, I would almost have to believe that you were the recipient of an immaculate conception." He re-opened his book. "Seven months!" he hissed. "You were closed off to me from the very beginning and remain so to this day."

Mary's pride and heart were wounded. The object of her personal shame had been actually verbalized and laid bare. She burst into tears. It took a while for her to compose herself. Finally, she found the resolve to respond to her husband's vitriol and condemnation.

"Respectable, godly, and proper English women do not appreciate the lust of the bedchamber. That is the way of it. My mother taught me thusly, just as her mother taught her. The sexual act is sinful and repulsive at its very core. It is in no way natural. It serves no function other than to propagate our species."

Will stared at his wife through disbelieving, drunken, bloodshot eyes. He mumbled, "I feel sorry for you, and for your mother." He inhaled deeply. "It is not supposed to be that way. Not at all." He shook his head. "Your frigid ancestors have robbed you of a life of happiness and fulfillment in marriage. Now, I get to stare each day at the fruitless branches of their barren tree."

Mary gasped. "How can you say such a thing? Are you saying that I am an insufficient wife?"

He grunted. "You are no wife to me, at all, if you truly wish to know the truth."

She took several deep, enraged breaths. "I cannot be like one of the women in your tawdry books, Will."

"As well I know it."

Mary cast her blanket aside and rose to her feet. She was openly weeping and about to storm from the room, when the door suddenly swung open with great force and violence. It slammed against the wainscoting, denting the wood and knocking flakes of paint from the wall. Mrs. Harmon, the widow who cooked and kept house for the Newmans, stood trembling in the hallway. Her face was ashen and she was breathing rapidly.

Will shot to his feet. "Mrs. Harmon! What is wrong?"

She burst into tears. "Will, it is your father! I discovered him collapsed on the pathway to the privy! He will not get up!"

Will tossed his book aside, exploded from his chair, and then sprinted past the Widow Harmon. Mary followed him as rapidly as she could.

WILLIAM NEWMAN, Sr., was dead. It was an untimely death, to be sure. He was only forty-five years of age when he died on the gravel pathway to the privy. Shortly before breathing his last, he begged his son for forgiveness for forcing him to enter into a contract marriage.

Will granted that forgiveness through a fountain of uncontrolled tears. Then, Mr. Newman passed quietly, clutched tightly in the arms of his one and only son. The last words that he heard spoken were Will's. The last face that he had seen was Will's. It was a peaceful, albeit heartbreaking, conclusion to an unfinished life.

Word of his death spread quickly. Despite the winter season, two days after his death almost five hundred people gathered for the graveside funeral. Will had his father placed in the family plot beside his long-departed wife. He would rest eternally beside his beloved Constance, the wife of his youth.

The sky was overcast throughout the solemn ceremony. The air was moist and cold. There was a stiff breeze from the north. The onlookers huddled uncomfortably together for warmth and, despite their love and respect for William Newman, prayed that the vicar might quickly bring the service to a close. They were all greatly relieved when he leaned forward, picked up a handful of dirt, and then sprinkled it onto the casket. He lifted his right hand high and then proclaimed from the *Book of Common Prayer,*

> *"Forasmuch as it hath pleased Almighty God of his great mercy to take unto himself the soul of our dear brother here departed: we therefore commit his body to the ground; earth to earth, ashes to ashes, dust to dust; in sure and certain hope of the Resurrection to eternal life, through our Lord Jesus Christ; who shall change our vile body, that it may be like unto his glorious body, according to the mighty working, whereby he is able to subdue all things to himself."*

Following the proclamation, he led the people in a familiar hymn, and then concluded the service with an emotional and moving benediction. Finally, it was over. As the people dispersed in silence toward their horses and carriages, four African slaves stepped forward with shovels and began to return the remainder of the nearby pile of dirt to the grave.

Young Will Newman had just inherited a comfortable estate, including a small fortune in gold, silver, and banknotes. At the tender age of twenty years, he had become the owner of an established and lucrative family business. Instantly, he was the envy of the entire county. On the surface, it seemed like he possessed everything a man could want. He had a wealth of money, prestige, and a young, lovely, and very pregnant wife. But, deep inside, he felt as empty as a white-washed tomb. The only person whom he had ever loved with any measure of intimacy and depth lay buried deep in a muddy grave.

Will wondered if there was anything in Heaven or on earth that could resurrect his despondent, dead heart.

~

Six Weeks Later
February 15, 1753

"I GOTS the head in my hand! Just one mo push, Miss Mary!" exclaimed Venus, the Negro midwife. She peeked over the top of Mary's knees and smiled. Her crooked, yellow-white teeth gleamed against her shiny, dark brown skin.

Mary was clutching the headboard so violently that her knuckles had turned white. Digging her heels into the soft mattress, she writhed and wailed from the pain. She screamed, "Make it stop! Please, Venus, make it stop! Oh, God! I want my mother!"

"'Tis best you leave the Lawd out of this. He done did His part. Everythin' on you, now. You is the mammy. So, grit yo teeth and git to work! I gots somewhere else I gots to go. Dey's a 'spectin' me at the Mason house. Miss Stella's water done broke, and you is bein' a might bit slow."

Mary threw back her head and unleashed a high-pitched, wicked scream.

"Ain't but one way to make the hurtin' stop, and dat's to git this baby out. Now, when you feel the next squeeze a comin', bear down and push!"

Once more, Mary's belly began to tighten. Another contraction was overtaking her womb. Exhausted, Mary leaned her head forward, groaned, and pushed her feet downward into the bed. She gave a mighty howl of pain as the baby's shoulders erupted from between the stretched bones of her pelvis. And then, instantly, the pain subsided. She heard a splash of fluids as Venus pulled the infant from between her legs. She collapsed back onto the bed and closed her eyes, relishing in the bliss of painlessness. She turned her head to one side and wept quietly.

"It's a big old boy baby!" Venus declared victoriously. "He plump and fat and gots a head full of black hair! Lawd, just look at the size of dis baby. Somebody gon have to go and git him a biscuit!"

Venus cackled happily at the safely-delivered baby and at her own wit. She held up the purplish-tinted infant and then unceremoniously flipped him upside-down, dangling him by his feet. She slapped his backside twice. He coughed out a thick wad of mucus from his throat, gagged, and then immediately began to wiggle, scream, and cry. His face transformed from purple to dark red.

"Dat's what I wants to hear. All strong and healthy." She patted Mary on the knee. "You is almost done, Miss Mary."

Venus wrapped the newborn in a soft linen cloth and then plopped him, kicking and screaming, onto Mary's belly. She quickly tied and cut the umbilical cord. After a few seconds, she gently massaged the sides of Mary's abdomen and then pushed downward. Moments later, Mary's body expelled the afterbirth and Venus caught it in a large tin pan. It took her several minutes to clean up the entire mess. During that time, the baby finally stopped crying. Mary remained silent throughout the process. She lay still with her eyes closed and appeared to be asleep.

Once she was finished attending to Mary, Venus took the baby boy and washed him with a soft cloth that had been soaking in a pan of hot water. It took several minutes for her to scrub the blood and pasty, white substance from the folds in the baby's skin. Once he was clean to her satisfaction, she swaddled him in warm linen cloths and then presented him to his mother.

"Here is yo baby boy, Miss Mary. All ready fo his mama."

She placed the infant against Mary's breast. The tiny boy instinctive began to stretch his neck and nuzzle against her in search of a nipple. Strangely, Mary did not reach for the child.

"You gots to hold him, Miss Mary. He ain't gon' hold hisself."

Finally, Mary opened her eyes. She turned her head slowly and, frowning, scowled at the child. Still, she did not lift her hands to cradle him. She stared blankly at him for a few seconds and then looked away again.

"Miss Mary, take yo boy. He need you," Venus pleaded.

Mary mumbled, "Get it away from me."

"What?" asked Venus in disbelief.

Mary's head spun around. She glared angrily at the slave woman. "I said, get it away from me! Are you deaf, or simply a brown idiot?"

Venus cocked her head in confusion. "But ... Miss Mary!"

Mary screamed viciously, "Get out! Get out! Get out! And take that horrid little thing with you!"

The baby began to wail. Venus snatched him from his mother's chest and then ran, horrified, from the bedchamber.

WILL SAT CONTENTEDLY in his father's rocking chair and cradled the sleeping newborn in his arms. His felt that his heart might burst with joy. The little boy was absolutely perfect in every way. Only a few weeks before, when his father passed, he wondered if he might ever experience joy again. Indeed, he wondered if there was anything that might breathe new life into his wounded, lonely heart. Now, he was literally holding love and joy in his arms. Finally, he had something to live for. He was amazed that he had within him the capacity to love someone so instantly and so very much. Unfortunately, the musical dialect of the slave woman Venus invaded and shattered his blissful moment.

"Somethin' wrong with yo wife, Massa Newman. She don't even want her own baby!" Venus scowled and shook her head. Her face was etched with fear. "I's 'fraid she gots the devil in her. I ain't nevuh seen nothin' like it. You gots to do something'. Yo boy need to eat."

"Mary has refused to nurse him?" Will asked disbelievingly.

"Nurse him?" Venus echoed. "She won't lay one finger on him."
Again, she shook her head and then lifted her hands in front of her
chest in a prayerful gesture. "It be the devil, I knows it."

Will inhaled deeply. Obviously, something was very wrong with
his wife. It was not natural, at all, for a mother to reject her own child.
But, for the time being, he would have to take action to ensure the
health of his newborn son.

"I shall need to hire a wet nurse, then. Do you know of
someone?"

Venus nodded. "Yassuh. They's a girl, Coffey, over to the Dickey
place. She lost her baby to a fevuh a day or two ago. She still gots
milk."

"Good. Can you send for her? I will happily reimburse her
owner."

"Yassuh."

"Thank you, Venus, for everything. Thank you for delivering my
boy. You did a fine job."

She grinned proudly. "He a pretty boy, ain't he?"

"Yes, Venus. Yes, he is." He kissed his son gently on his tiny nose.
"He reminds me of my father."

∼

Two Weeks Later
March 3, 1753

MARY HAD NOT LEFT her bedchamber since giving birth. She wept
constantly. She refused to eat. She slept almost all of the time. Prefer-
ring to remain secluded and in darkness, she forbade Will from
opening the curtains inside her bedchamber. Visits from her mother
and sisters did nothing to improve her mood. She seemed overwhelmed by a melancholy that she could not escape. Through it all,
Mary refused to even look at her newborn son, much less hold him.
Each time Will presented the child to her, she rejected him and

insisted that Will take him away. Mary remained concealed inside a self-imposed prison of solitude and grief.

Mary's father, the wealthy and influential Spencer Kirby, hired a well-known and expensive surgeon named Dr. William Bull to travel out from Charlestown to examine his daughter and offer a diagnosis. Mr. Kirby spared no expense. The doctor arrived on Saturday morning and spent two hours that afternoon in Mary's bedchamber. He gave her a thorough medical examination and then interviewed her to assess the condition of her mind.

While the doctor was conducting his work, Will waited downstairs in the parlor with Mary's parents. The baby slept soundly in his cradle in the corner, having just been fed and changed by the wet nurse. The tension in the room was quite high. It was only mid-afternoon, and Will was already drinking. It was abundantly clear from the expressions on their faces that the Kirbys entertained little respect for their son-in-law.

Mrs. Kirby rose from her chair and sauntered to the window that looked out upon the front lawn and adjacent river. After surveying the lovely vista, she turned and walked quietly to the crib. She stood absolutely still and stared at her grandchild.

Spencer Kirby glanced at his wife, took a deep breath, and then declared, "I do wish that our daughter would come to her senses and re-join the world of the living. Perhaps, then, she might even be able to assist you in naming our grandson."

Will, reclining in his special chair, as always, took a sip from his glass of whiskey. "My son already has a name. It has been recorded in our family Bible."

Mrs. Kirby spun on her heels. "Oh? You have selected a name without our daughter's consent?"

Will never looked at the woman. He continued to stare into the fireplace and nurse his whiskey. "Your daughter has no interest in our son. Why, then, should she care what I name him? Or, for that matter, why should I even care what she thinks, at all?"

"It only seems appropriate to wait for her consideration and input," Mr. Kirby commented with an air of displeasure.

"Well, it has been over two weeks," Will observed with obvious disgust, still refusing to look at the Kirbys. "The boy needed a name, so I assigned him one, and I am quite happy with it."

There was a period of uncomfortable, tense silence. Mrs. Kirby took a step toward Will.

"Well?" she demanded. "Please tell us the child's name, so that we may address him, as well."

Will finally turned his head and made eye contact with the couple. "His name is Austin ... Austin Newman."

"Austin?" Mrs. Kirby echoed in disbelief. "What kind of name is that? Is it a familial name from one of your ancestors?"

"No. It is a noble British name, a shortened form taken from the title of the infamous Roman Emperor, Augustine."

She scowled disapprovingly. "I am familiar with the origins of the name, Austin, Mr. Newman. But, what I am having difficulty understanding is its application to our grandson. Is it not a worthy tradition to name one's firstborn son after the paternal grandfather? I thought that you might have chosen the name William, as a tribute to your own dear father."

"No," Will responded tersely. "All my life, I have suffered the confusion of a household containing two men with the same name. I figured that I might spare my son that frustration."

"But, how did you land upon such a name?" Mrs. Kirby inquired, sounding flustered.

"My son has been named in honor of Bartholomew Austin, a fine fellow and good friend who saved my life a few years ago. Had he not rescued me and brought me home after I received a grave injury out in the wilderness, I would never have fathered a son. So, my son's name is Austin Newman. It is done. I will not debate the subject."

Mrs. Kirby lowered her chin to her chest. "Very well."

Spencer Kirby's eyes met Will's. Austin's grandfather smiled slightly and nodded. Apparently, he approved of Will's choice of names. "'Tis a noble name, Will, and honorably chosen. We shall look forward to calling him thusly."

The creaking of the stairs captured their attention and ended the conversation. Moments later, Dr. Bull entered the room.

Mr. Kirby rose to his feet. "Tell us, Doctor, what is your assessment? Dare we have any hope of recovery?"

The surgeon walked across the room to Will's liquor table, fetched a snifter, and poured himself a generous measure of brandy.

"Mr. Kirby, your daughter suffers from a most severe case of the melancholy."

"We are already aware of that fact," Will responded sarcastically. "Surely, Mr. Kirby has not paid such a handsome sum for you to come out here and tell us what we already know."

"Indeed. Now, if you would allow me to continue ..." the doctor replied, obviously annoyed. "Hers is perhaps the worst cast that I have ever encountered. It is interesting, but I have begun to notice similar cases In young women immediately after giving birth. I have yet to conjecture a connection between the two events. Anyhow, there are several theories as to the cause of such maladies of the mind. Some believe it to be inherited and thus untreatable. Many afflicted with this disorder are institutionalized for the remainder of their lifetimes."

"Please, Doctor! No!" Mrs. Kirby swooned and then collapsed into a chair. She covered her face with her hands and began to weep.

"There is, however," the doctor continued, "a new avenue of thinking. Some claim that a melancholy such as this is brought about by an emotional conflict between what the afflicted individual wants and what they know to be right ... an internal war of right and wrong, if you will." He paused. "It is my recommendation that we approach your daughter's case from this viewpoint and begin immediate treatments."

"What kind of treatments?" Will asked, curious.

"There are only two of which I am aware. We must use a spinning stool to induce dizziness and, hopefully, rearrange the contents of your wife's brain back into their proper alignment."

"And the other?" inquired Mr. Kirby.

The doctor took a swift drink of his brandy. "Water immersion.

We must place your daughter under water and hold her there for as long as possible without resulting in drowning. It is believed that the mind's struggle in the face of potential death can reassign the patient's thought processes and, ultimately, return them to a normal state of mind."

"Do you attempt this treatment just a single time?" Mrs. Kirby inquired.

The doctor shook his head. "No. We must treat her by this method three times daily for a period of at least two weeks."

"Christ, Almighty!" Will swore out loud.

The doctor grimaced and nodded. "You may call upon Him, as well, I suppose. I fear that, in the coming weeks, we shall need all the help we can get."

$\sim$

Three Weeks Later

IT WAS DAWN. A pale, gray light bathed the barren winter landscape. A scratchy-voiced rooster crowed inside the barn, announcing the arrival of a new day. It was a cloudy, cold morning. The front door of the Newman house creaked quietly on its hinges. Soon, a ghostly figure appeared on the porch.

Mary Newman was a mere shell of the young woman she used to be. She stumbled weakly down the short staircase, clad only in her shift. Her skin was as pallid and as gray as the winter sky. Her formerly plump and curvaceous body was wasted and frail. Her breasts, which had once been ample, high, and full, sagged almost to the top of her belly. Her hair was a knotted, disheveled mop. In a manner of weeks, streaks of white had invaded her dark brown locks. There was no emotion displayed on her face, nor was there any life remaining in her eyes. Their once-brilliant shade of sparking blue had faded to an empty, pale, dull gray.

Mary slowly shuffled across the front lawn and approached the nearby bank of the Black River. Arriving at the water's edge, she stood perfectly still for a moment and watched the winter-swollen waters flow past her feet. The dark color of the water reminded her of that torturous tub where the surgeon submerged her multiple times each and every day. She thought about the horrible fear she suffered during those barbaric treatments. She considered, also, how many times she had considered simply opening her mouth, breathing in the water, and ending it all. But, for some unknown reason, she had continued to cling to life and hope.

But, Mary's hope was gone. She no longer desired to cling to her wretched life. She closed her eyes and stood still, listening to the water lapping at the riverbank and the dull, peaceful silence of the dawn. Somewhere in the distance, a doleful cow mooed as it called to her calf. Almost immediately, the calf answered with a high-pitched, excited cry. Mary smiled slightly at the irony of it. Oh, how she longed to feel the same concern about her own offspring.

After a short while, she opened her eyes and peered, once again, at the dark water that flowed swiftly past. Slowly, she reached down and grabbed the hem of her shift. She lifted it up and over her head and arms and then dropped it onto the ground beside her muddy feet. She stood naked and alone, with arms outstretched toward the heavens. But, she did not pray. She did not utter any words, at all. Instead, she just stood there for several agonizingly cold seconds.

Mary Kirby Newman then stepped forward slowly and deliberately into the cold, lonely waters of the Black River. She walked until the current grabbed her and knocked her off of her feet. She did not resist the pull of the water. She gave herself to it and allowed it to embrace her. As she disappeared into the current, her matted hair floated momentarily on top of the water, and then it, too, disappeared. Finally, her suffering and her guilt were gone.

5

STRONGER THAN BLOOD

Jackson's Creek — The South Carolina Backcountry
September 23, 1759

Will Newman rested his elbows on the top rail of his newly-constructed fence. He puffed lazily on his pipe and watched contentedly as his beloved son, six-year-old Austin Newman, wrestled with his dog in the small meadow adjacent to their home. The boisterous brown and white English Spaniel had the skinny lad pinned to the ground and was giving him a thorough licking around the neck and ears. The fuzzy dog's long, floppy ears dangled loosely over the little boy's face. Austin, his arms wrapped around the dog's wiggling body, giggled uncontrollably. It was a portrait of absolute, unbridled joy. Will could not help but smile.

"Do not stain your breeches! The grass will leave marks," he warned his son. "We have been invited to supper, and I do not want you to have the appearance of a pauper."

"Yes, Papa," Austin responded through a crescendo of giggles.

Will shook his head and grinned. Oh, how he loved his happy, wonderful, perfect little boy!

It was a soft, lazy Sunday afternoon. For Will, Sundays were always the loveliest of days. He adored the slow, restful pace of the Sabbath. As was customary, he performed his handful of necessary chores, mostly livestock care, early in the morning. Since there was not a meeting place of the Anglican Church anywhere in their vicinity, Will read for Austin from the *Book of Common Prayer*, along with a few selections from the Scriptures. It was their own simple version of "family church." They prayed their benediction around mid-morning and then the remainder of the day was theirs to enjoy together.

After feasting on some leftover smoked venison loin and roasted corn for their mid-day meal, the Newman men enjoyed a couple of fun but relatively fruitless hours of fishing in the lazy waters of Jackson's Creek. Then, after a restful afternoon nap, they ventured outdoors to hike the nearby woods and fields and explore their surroundings. Soon, they would depart for the home of Bat and Rachel Austin to enjoy what was always a very delicious and filling Sunday supper. Until then, Will was happy to relax, smoke his pipe, and watch his little boy run and play with his pup. Absorbed in the bliss of the perfect moment, he turned his face toward the sunshine, closed his eyes, and inhaled a deep, satisfied breath. He was a fulfilled, content man.

Much had changed in Will's life over the past six and a half years. In the months following his wife's suicide, he systematically sold off all of his newly-inherited businesses and properties. Then, in the early spring of 1754, he took his infant son, along with a hired wet nurse, and transported all of his earthly possessions to the west. He settled on his brand-new Royal land grant on Jackson's Creek, next door to the farm of Bat and Rachel Austin.

During those transformative years, Will also found victory in his life over strong drink. Finally recognizing his debilitating dependence upon distilled spirits, he had given up liquor altogether. He had not tasted a drop in over five years. At first, the removal of alcohol from his diet had been quite a shock to his system. He was sick for almost three weeks as he fought valiantly against the undeniable cravings for his once-beloved whiskey. But, eventually, he conquered the habit and put those years of drunkenness, emptiness, and emotional despair behind him.

Ultimately, the greatest change of all was in his lifestyle. There were no more businesses to run, no more deals to make, and no more properties to manage. He simplified everything. It was just himself, his son, and a modest one-hundred-acre farm. True, he was somewhat wealthier than most of his neighbors, but you would never have known that fact just by looking at him. Will invested the majority of the funds from his liquidation of properties and kept the remainder safely locked away in the Bank of Williamsburg. If he ever needed silver, he simply drew on those bank deposits. However, for the most part, he lived and toiled as an ordinary dirt-farmer alongside his humble neighbors. Over the past five years, Will Newman had become a respected and well-regarded member of the Jackson's Creek community.

Will turned and gazed proudly upon his frontier home. Typical of most dwellings in the region, it was an unpretentious little cottage. The small frame house, elevated on a brick foundation, had six windows and a large stone fireplace. A shallow porch protected the unfinished oak door. Certainly, it paled in comparison to the grandiose brick Georgian home that he had left behind in the lowlands. But, size and opulence did not matter at all to Will Newman. He had discovered everything that he needed right here in this tiny cottage beside Jackson's Creek. It was a house filled with love, happiness, laughter, and contentment. Truly, it was all that he and little Austin needed.

The unmistakable sound of a horse's hooves impacting hard-packed ground interrupted Will's thoughts. He turned and peered in the direction of the approaching horse. A rider soon appeared around the bend of the narrow road that led to Winnsborough. Will recognized the horseman as James Leslie, owner of a large farm to the northeast, and a very influential member of the regional community. Moments later, Mr. Leslie guided his mount from the road and onto the path that led to the Newman house. He smiled warmly as he rode into the yard. He quickly dismounted, tethered his horse to a small bush, and then walked over to greet Will.

"Good afternoon, Mr. Newman." He tipped his fancy black felt cocked hat. He wore an impressive dark green greatcoat over a butternut weskit and matching breeches. He had the appearance and attitude of a confident and distinguished gentleman.

Will courteously tipped his humble woven straw cocked hat in return. "Good afternoon to you, Mr. Leslie. What brings you out my way on this fine Sunday?"

The fellow peered seriously at Will. "I thought that I should stop by and inquire as to the nature of your loyalties, Mr. Newman. Where might they lie?"

"To King and Country, of course ... unless I receive a better offer." Will winked and grinned. Both men burst into laughter and then warmly shook hands.

"How have you been doing, Will?"

"Splendid, as always, Jim. It is good to see you. But, I am quite certain that this is not a social call. I cannot remember the last time I saw you this far west of Winnsborough."

The man took a deep, thoughtful breath. "I bring news which I believe may be of some interest to you."

"Oh?" Will responded, intrigued. "What manner of news?"

"It is regarding the recent Cherokee uprising. The governor has finally made a decision regarding our malcontent neighbors to the west."

Will's heart skipped a beat. Thus far, there had been no incidents of raids or violence in the immediate area. But, over the past several months, it seemed that the long and costly war against the French had begun to drift southward into the lower Colonies. The Cherokee, once friendly allies of the British, had recently risen up in anger and struck with great force against remote outposts along the western borders of the Carolinas, Georgia, and Virginia. There had been several bloody encounters and, on more than one occasion, outright massacres of backcountry settlers. The citizenry of the frontier had been placing intense pressure upon Governor

William Henry Lyttleton to formulate an appropriate military response.

"'Tis a serious matter, indeed," Will responded sullenly. "Come, let us sit and talk. I will fetch us some fresh cider. Austin and I just squeezed it yesterday."

"Thank you, Will. That sounds delicious."

They ambled toward the shade afforded by an expansive maple tree. Two wooden chairs and a table topped with a large stoneware pitcher and pewter mugs awaited them there. Will poured himself and Mr. Leslie mugs full of fresh, tangy, naturally sweet apple cider. He handed a dripping mug to his visitor and then sat down beside him. Once settled, he took a deep breath and prepared himself for what he fully expected to be bad news.

"So, tell me, Jim ... have there been any attacks near our region?"

The man nodded grimly. "Three days ago, fifteen people were slaughtered at a settlement just forty miles west of here. They were mostly women and children."

Will winced. "That is tragic, and frighteningly close. How will the governor respond?" He was uncertain if he truly wanted to hear the answer to his question.

"The militia has finally been called up. The armies of South Carolina will be massing at Congarees, just southeast of the Cherokee territories."

Will sighed. "When?"

"Three weeks hence. That gives us precious little time to recruit a company locally."

"Am I to assume that you are to be the captain?"

Mr. Leslie rolled his eyes as he took a hardy gulp of his cider. "I am, indeed. I have been tasked with organizing a company from this area and then marching it to join Colonel Richardson's Regiment."

"Richard Richardson, from Black River?" Will inquired.

"Yes. He is forming a regiment comprised entirely of men from Craven County." Mr. Leslie paused. "I am informed that you know him quite well."

Will shrugged. "I know him, but not all that well. He was an officer in our local militia back east. He is a very respected man in the river country. Honestly, though, I have not seen him in years. He and my father were close friends. He lived a short distance from our home."

"Well, he seems quite acquainted and impressed with you. I received a letter from him yesterday instructing me to approach you and offer you a position of leadership in my company. He informed me that you were, in his words, *a good soldier and a damned good man.*' I rode out as soon as possible in obedience to his request. So, here I am. I need you, Will. Your governor and your King need you."

Will's eyebrow arched in slight disbelief. "I find it curious that Mr. Richardson would mention me by name. But, I am quite honored."

Captain Lewis nodded. "As well you should be. As it stands now, I am in need of a sergeant. I wish I could offer you the rank of ensign, but that commission has already been purchased by William Mitchusson. I trust you understand."

"Of course. William is a good man. He will serve you well."

"So, can I count on you, then? Hardly any of these men around here have any military experience whatsoever. You drilled for years with the Craven County Militia. We need your expertise."

Will paused thoughtfully. "Might I humbly request that you allow me to provide my answer tomorrow? I am going for supper to the Austin home this evening. I would like to talk it over with Bat and see what he thinks."

Captain Leslie chuckled. "I can already tell you what he thinks. He signed my enlistment roll on Friday. But, go ahead and talk to him. I am quite certain that he will convince you to enlist in our most noble and worthy cause."

Will stood. "Very well. I shall happily give you my answer tomorrow. I have some errands to run in town. Whilst I am there, I will stop by your office to confer with you."

The captain drained his cider mug and then rose to his feet. "Excellent. I look forward to it, Sergeant Newman. Until then ..." He bowed slightly at the waist, returned his hat to his head, and then crossed the lawn to retrieve his mount. He nimbly climbed onto his horse and then guided it toward the road. As the captain departed, Will re-lit his pipe and resumed watching his son playing in the meadow.

~

Three Weeks Later
October 8, 1759

"Papa, please don't go!" begged Austin as he tugged on the hem of his father's coat. Huge tears crept down his dusty, tanned cheeks.

Will knelt down in front of the boy and wrapped both arms around him. "Son, I do not wish to go, but I have no choice. It is my duty. Uncle Bat and I must travel into the mountains and make sure that the Cherokee never bother our people again. Do you understand?"

Austin frowned and wagged his head in a negative response. He grumbled, "I don't even know what a cherkopee is."

Will cackled happily at his son's attempt to pronounce the tribal name. He pulled the boy closer and smothered him in a huge hug. "The word is Cherokee, Son. The Cherokee people are Indians to our west. Lately, they have been attacking settlers out on the frontier and hurting them. I worry that they might come here one day and try to harm us. So, Uncle Bat and I have to go and stop them. Now, do you understand?"

The boy shrugged slightly. Clearly, he was still not satisfied with his father's explanation. He wiped away his tears with the cuff of his long-sleeved weskit. "Where will I stay while you are gone?"

Will smiled lovingly at his son. "You shall remain right here with your Aunt Rachel. You are going to have a wonderful time playing with little Drury and John. You will be so busy and having so much fun that you won't even think of me. In fact, after I am gone for a couple of weeks, you won't even remember what I look like!"

Austin collapsed, sobbing, into his father's arms. He vowed, "I will never forget you, Papa. You are my family."

Will kissed him on the top of his head. He felt a tear forming in his own eye. He whispered softly, "I love you, Austin Newman."

The lad angled his head back and stared innocently into his father's eyes. His chin quivered with emotion. "I love you more." He hugged his father again. "Please come back soon, Papa."

"I will return as quickly as I can. Nothing could keep me away from you, little boy."

A scratchy voice interrupted their tender moment. "Sergeant Newman!"

Will reluctantly tore himself away from his son's embrace, stood, and then turned to face his commander. "Yes, Captain Leslie."

"Finish your farewells and gather your men. It is time to go. We have many miles to ride before making camp tonight."

"Yes, sir." Will took Austin's hand and placed it in the hand of Rachel Austin, Bat's lovely wife. "Please take good care of my boy. I have only the one."

She smiled. "You know that I shall. In exchange, I would be most appreciative if you would bring my husband back to me ... alive and with all of his parts intact."

Will perched his black fur-felt cocked hat atop his head and grinned playfully. "I will see what I can do. But, when it comes to your husband, you know all-too-well the difficulties with which I must contend."

Rachel smiled and nodded. "Indeed, I do. But, still, please make every effort to bring him back in one piece. He is not much of a husband, but he is the only one that I have."

Will patted her hand. "I will do my best."

Will leaned over and kissed his son on the top of his head. Walking away quickly and resisting the urge to look back, he climbed stiffly upon his horse and then joined the men of his company. Minutes later, over one hundred militiamen from the area surrounding Jackson's Creek began their journey westward toward the faraway Cherokee country.

～

December 3, 1759
Militia Encampment – Across the River from Keowee
Principal Lower Town of the Cherokee People

IT HAD BEEN the most miserable and frustrating eight weeks of Will's life. The Jackson's Creek Company had been one of the first to arrive at the muster point. He and his fellow militiamen languished at that location in a makeshift encampment for almost five weeks while the other companies and regiments trickled in from the east. Once assembled, the mass movement of the huge army to Keowee occurred at little more than a snail's pace. Due to the disorganization of the vast army and the complicated logistics involved in moving so many men, it had taken them almost a week to traverse a mere twenty miles.

Their arrival at Keowee had caused quite a stir amongst the natives. The size of the governor's army was frighteningly impressive. When the entire assembly of militia was mustered at Congarees, roughly ten miles from Fort Prince George, the English forces numbered almost fourteen hundred men. That was double the size of the population of the Cherokee town. Their presence in force evoked the desired effect. The Cherokee appeared quickly at the summit table. Now, as the governor negotiated with the chieftains, the men of his army waited and attempted to accomplish one primary goal ... to remain fed. It proved to be a most difficult task. There was little to be found in the surrounding forests that would suffice in feeding such a vast number of men.

Now, after two insufferable weeks encamped in the hilly Cherokee country, the men of the army were bored, exhausted, homesick, perpetually hungry, and thoroughly fed up with Governor Lyttleton's frustratingly slow peace efforts. They were deserting the governor's army by the dozens. Like many of the others who remained encamped in the hilly woods, Will was dangerously close to packing his belongings on his horse and simply heading home. But, he was a leader in his company. His sense of honor and duty, along with his good standing in the community, would not allow him to desert the King's cause.

Lyttleton's all-volunteer army included an amalgamation of men from every walk of life. There were privileged gentlemen who seemed to think that they were on an adventure resembling an outing for hunting foxes. They expected their every whim and wish to be granted by the common men who surrounded them. Conversely, the army also included a significant number of fellows who were little more than a worthless, criminal rabble. It seemed clear that they had joined in the campaign for no other purpose than to perpetrate perversity and mischief.

So, from one moment to the next, Will never knew what he might see in the army camp. One day he beheld the spectacle of a gentleman from Charlestown taking a bath surrounded by a cloud of frothy soap bubbles inside a makeshift bathtub hewn from a large log. The next day he witnessed a knife fight amongst a handful of backcountry ruffians over a half-pound of rancid salt pork.

There was no way to contemplate all the possibilities of absurd and unthinkable surprises that a new day might bring. And, as the level of boredom and hunger increased, so also did the conflict and angst amongst the soldiers. The men had traveled long and far, and many were itching to fight someone. If the Cherokee were not willing to pick up their arms, then there were some in the camp who were perfectly satisfied with fighting amongst themselves. Something needed to change ... and soon.

But, one thing was certain. Governor Lyttleton was not a man to be rushed. This was no war. Instead, it was a prolonged negotiation. The large army encamped within a stone's throw of the large Cherokee town was a vivid display of Royal English force. The governor intended to use them as his biggest bargaining chip in his ongoing negotiations with the Cherokee. His huge, hungry, loud army would have to be patient. They had no other option.

∾

It was a wickedly cold December evening. Will and Bat were just settling down to supper beside their large, glowing campfire when they received an unexpected guest. Their regimental commander, Colonel Richard Richardson, appeared out of the early winter darkness.

"Do you gents have any food to spare?"

Will sat upright and motioned to his old neighbor. "Sit down, Mr. Richardson. Yes, of course, we have plenty. We have a brimming pot of elk stew and some fresh, hot tea." He motioned to Bat. "Can you fill the colonel a bowl?"

"Certainly," Bat responded. He jumped to his feet and immediately began to search for a clean bowl.

"Thank you, William. I believe I will," responded Colonel Richard Richardson, commander of the Craven County Regiment. He joined Will beside the warm campfire. "I am grateful for your hospitality, gentlemen. It is mighty cold, indeed, and I am famished." He patted Will affably on the shoulder. "We have not had an opportunity to talk since you departed your home on Black River. I thought that a visit might be nice."

Will smiled and nodded. "It has been a long time."

"I regret that I never had the opportunity to convey my personal condolences regarding the passing of both your father and your wife." The colonel hesitated for a moment. "The news of your wife, especially, shook our little community to the core."

"That was a long time ago, sir. I have moved on. But, I do appreciate your kind words."

"And now you are living in the backcountry. Are you enjoying your new life out in the far reaches?"

"Yes, sir. I love it. I settled a Royal grant on Jackson's Creek, west of Winnsborough."

"And your boy ... is he doing well?"

Will grinned happily at the very mention of his son. "Quite well, indeed, sir. He is six years old now."

"Six years? My goodness, how quickly time passes. 'Tis a wicked truth, especially when you have more years behind you than in front of you. I can offer ample testimony. Now, please remind me ... what is your son's name?"

"Austin."

The colonel raised a curious eyebrow and cocked his head. "Austin," he repeated. "That is a curious name. Did it come down through your family?"

Will grinned. It was an all-too-familiar question. "No, sir. He was named after that no-good miscreant who is serving up your stew. He is Bartholomew Austin, my closest neighbor and dearest friend. He saved my life many years ago when we were mere lads. I figured that the least I owed him was to honor him in the naming of my firstborn."

"Most interesting. I shall have to hear that entire story someday, perhaps when this conflict is over and we have some more leisurely days on our hands."

Bat approached the colonel and handed him a hearty bowl of stew along with a very large pewter spoon. "Here you are, sir. I hope you enjoy it."

"Thank you, Mr. Austin." He sniffed the concoction and then gave an approving, surprised smile. "I wonder, though ... when did you fellows shoot an elk? I have not even seen one since our arrival."

"We did not shoot the elk," Will confessed as he ladled some of the stew into his own hand-carved wooden bowl. "Bat traded for it from a Cherokee woman."

"Indeed? How, exactly, did you manage that, Mr. Austin?"

"'Twasn't hard," Bat answered through a mouthful of meat and watery gravy. "The Injun women come across the river every morning with goods to trade."

"Really? I was not aware that such lines of commerce had been sanctioned." He seemed very surprised and suspicious.

"Well, I don't know how sanctioned they are. Be that as it may, every morning we trade for food, blankets, and other goods. The food is what has been most helpful. I fear we might have starved already if not for the Cherokee." Bat's face betrayed his disgust for their army's failure at logistics. "We have not, exactly, been receiving satisfactory rations on this little escapade."

The colonel shook his head angrily. "As well I know it. I wish there was more that I could do. But, one cannot manufacture food from nothing. This entire affair seems a bit ill-planned, at best. Still, I urge you fellows to exercise caution in dealing with the Indians."

"Why?" challenged Will.

"There has been talk that the pox is rampant in the Keowee town."

Bat cut a glance at Will. "We have not heard that. We will certainly remain vigilant."

"Good. We can ill afford an epidemic amongst the men of this dwindling army." Colonel Richardson sampled the stew and quickly nodded his approval. "It needs a tad bit more salt, but otherwise it is delicious."

Will handed the colonel his personal salt box. The hungry officer took it, sprinkled a pinch into his stew, and then returned the box to its owner.

"What in the hell are we doing here, Colonel?" Bat inquired quite suddenly and bluntly. "This is my first personal encounter with the Cherokee, and to be honest, they do not seem all that fearsome. In fact, the ones we have dealt have been downright friendly. I thought that the Cherokee were allied to the British, anyway. Now, all of a sudden, we are at war with them. What changed, exactly?"

"It is a rather long and complex story, I am afraid."

"I reckon we have nothing but time," Bat responded. "I would love to hear it."

"Well," the colonel began after swallowing a mouthful of stew. "The short version of the story is that it all started with a grand misunderstanding. Some Cherokee were returning home from a campaign with our forces in the north. While passing through Virginia, a local farmer accused the band of warriors of stealing some of his horses. One insult led to another and then, for whatever reason, the Virginian and his neighbors slew the entire lot of Indians. Over a dozen braves."

"Sincerely?" asked Will, aghast. "They just killed them all?"

The colonel nodded. "After that, in the name of honor and revenge, the Cherokee began to strike at remote settlements all up and down the frontier. Of course, the tally of deaths inflicted by the Cherokee have greatly outnumbered the original count of dead warriors. But I doubt that the Indians are actually keeping score."

"Go on," Bat urged.

"Over the past few months, there have been some limited negotiations. A cadre of chiefs went all the way to Charlestown to seek a truce, but Governor Lyttleton ended up taking them prisoner. It was a huge insult to the Cherokee." The colonel pointed toward the southwest. "The governor actually has them now down in his personal encampment. He is using them to help bargain with the Keowee chiefs. He is attempting to force a treaty of peace. I am of the opinion that he would like to exchange those chiefs for some of the Cherokee warriors that he considers the worst of the perpetrators of crimes against the western settlers."

"So, then, we are not actually here to fight?" Will asked, somewhat confused.

"We will fight if it comes to that," affirmed the colonel. "But, I believe that the governor would enjoy the opportunity to declare a victory without combat."

Bat tossed a large log onto the campfire. He declared hopefully, "Well, that would certainly suit the hell out of me."

The colonel chuckled. "I, as well, Mr. Austin." He inhaled a deep, tired breath. "Personally, I am weary of these mountains. I long to be back beside my river ... where everything actually makes sense. We have been here long enough, in my opinion. I am ready to abandon this place and go on home."

"Amen," Bat mumbled. "Amen to that."

~

Dawn – December 11, 1759
Militia Camp

WILL GAVE Bat a gentle kick in the backside. "Wake up, you miserable lout! Are you planning to sleep through the entire day?"

Bat groaned and then pulled his blanket snugly against his neck. Desperate for warmth, he scooted a bit closer to the fire.

"Are you still not feeling any better? You have rarely left the fireside in three days. You need to get up and move about. The activity will do you some good. Come and eat with me. I have cracked corn boiling and some hot tea. I heard that Jake Bingham might even have some sugar."

Bat did not respond. Will knelt beside him. He pulled back the covers and attempted to rouse his friend from his bedroll. "Come on, Bat. You cannot lay beside the campfire forever."

Bat rolled over slowly onto his back, clenching trembling fists beneath his chin. His face was red and sweat poured from his hairline. His teeth chattered uncontrollably. Another member of Captain Leslie's company appeared over Will's shoulder. It was James Asworth, a free black man who lived near Winnsborough.

James asked in his peculiar dialect, "What wrong wit Bat?"

"He has had a fever for days, and a raging headache. Now, he appears to be having a rigor. We just need to keep him warm, I suppose." Will reached down to pull up the blanket and cover his friend. "Surely, he will get over it in a day or two."

"Wait!" James warned. "Look at he face."

Will leaned closer to examine Bat's face. A dark, scarlet rash covered the skin around his mouth and spilled over onto his cheeks. He pulled Bat's collar downward. There were numerous distinct, red dots on his neck. He then lifted his shirt. The red marks covered Bat's chest and upper arms.

Will look at James. He was mystified. "What is it? What do the rash and marks mean?"

James frowned and then reached down and covered Bat with the blanket. He looked sternly at Will. "He got the pox."

"My God!" Will exclaimed. He carefully lifted the blanket and looked closely at Bat's rash. "Yes, I believe you are right! Why did I not see it before?"

"Dem pox'll go through this ahmy like shite through a goose. You gots to get him out of this camp rat now," James declared forebodingly.

Will nodded grimly. "I will go and speak to the captain."

⁓

"You ARE certain that it is the pox?" Captain Leslie demanded, frowning.

"Yes, sir. Absolutely certain."

"Caught whilst making his daily trades with the Cherokee, no doubt. We have confirmed that the disease is, indeed, ravaging the Keowee town." He stared at Will through tired, hollow eyes. "This is not our first case of the pox. We received reports yesterday of four sick men at the regimental infirmary. This morning, it was over twenty. Mr. Austin is, however, the first sick man in *our* company." He sighed deeply. "He must be removed from the encampment immediately, before he afflicts the men around him. You have not been feeling ill, have you?"

"No, sir. I doubt that the disease would affect me. My father exposed me to smallpox as a small child through variolation. I suffered a very mild case and recovered quickly, so I was told."

"Indeed? Well, then, you should be the one to transport him! Are you willing?"

Will nodded. "Of course, sir. That is why I came to you. I wish to evacuate him as quickly as possible."

The captain frowned ominously. "You will be traveling through harsh and unfriendly territory with an incapacitated man in tow. I am sorry, but I will not be able spare any men to assist you. Negotiations are coming to a head and the governor is feeling pressure from all sides. The period mandated by the legislature for this expedition expires in a few weeks. Something has to happen and soon. Either there will be a negotiated peace, or we will be forced to press an attack. Therefore, I need every single man under my command to remain here in the field. Surely, you understand my predicament."

"Yes, Captain. I am willing to take the risk alone. I will remove Bat from the camp and attempt to find a suitable place for him to recuperate before taking him home. It may take two or three weeks for the disease to run its course. I dare not return him to Jackson's Creek until he is well."

"Wise thinking. Very well, then. You must leave this encampment immediately, both for Bat's sake and for the sake of our army." He reached to shake Will's hand. "Good luck, Will, and Godspeed. Find a safe spot and hunker down. There may be snows coming. 'Tis the season. Hopefully, I will see you back home in a few weeks."

"I pray so, Jim. Thank you."

Will spun and then sprinted from the captain's tent.

~

Two Days Later
Deep in the Western Carolina Mountains

WILL'S luck had run out. The uncharacteristically pleasant December weather was gone from the Carolina mountains. In its place, winter made its presence known with a vengeance. The ominous gray sky had been spewing snow and ice for almost six hours. The fluffy, dry precipitation was several inches deep. The temperature was plummeting. Darkness was approaching. Will had to locate shelter, and soon, or he and Bat might not survive the night.

He glanced over his shoulder to check on his friend. Bat was unconscious. His limp body bounced awkwardly on a horse-drawn travois constructed from birch saplings. He lay beneath a thick layer of blankets that was topped with a waterproof elk hide. He had not wakened at all over the last two days. His current state of diseased oblivion had actually been something of a blessing. For several days, the poor fellow had been incessantly tortured by high fever. Now, his skin was covered with raised, hard, painful, fluid-filled pustules. His body had been racked with inescapable misery before the sleep of sickness liberated him from his prison of fevered pain.

Will's heart ached over the suffering of his friend. He mumbled, "I will find us shelter soon, Bat. I promise you."

He faced forward and tugged the collar of his coat tightly around his neck to keep the snow and ice from sneaking down his back. He clucked at his horse and then rode onward into the pummeling snow. About a half-hour later, he guided the animal through a tight, rocky draw that was barely wide enough for the travois. His heart leapt when he saw what awaited him below at the bottom of a large ravine. It was an ancient Cherokee hut nestled beneath a thick stand of pine trees. A tiny creek flowed past the cabin. Its crystal-clear water bubbled happily over the large rocks that lined its bottom. The structure appeared to be abandoned. The woven birch walls were intact, but a portion of the roof along the southernmost wall had collapsed inward.

Will had miraculously managed to find some shelter in the Cherokee wilderness. He was not at all worried about the hut's state of disrepair. He could repair the roof and had plenty of hides to hang as a covering over the open door. Soon, he and his friend would be dry and warm beside a blazing fire. The discovery of the abandoned dwelling was quite a blessing, indeed. If Will could manage to get them some fresh meat, they could hole up at this location for weeks. That would provide plenty of time for the pox to run its course before they returned to their homes on Jackson's Creek.

Will carefully eased his mount forward and down the steep hillside. Once safely in the bottom of the ravine, he maneuvered his horse so that Bat's travois was parked beneath the shelter of a low-hanging pine branch. He dismounted quickly, removed his flintlock rifle from its leather case, and then carefully moved forward to check the hut. He was reasonably convinced that it was empty, but he still needed to exercise caution. He cocked the rifle, stooped over, and then slowly entered the open door. He was relieved to discover that the shelter was, indeed, empty of both man and animal.

He inspected the hut to ensure that the dirt floor was dry. There was a single wet spot beneath the hole in the roof. Having never been inside an Indian shelter before, he was interested to note that there was a small hole in the very center of the conical ceiling, obviously for venting smoke from the room. A five-foot-wide, deep, stone-lined, ash-filled fire pit was cut into the floor in the very center. There was even a small pile of abandoned firewood stacked haphazardly against the far wall.

Will uncocked and lowered his rifle. He grinned happily. "This will do fine, indeed!"

~

One Week Later

BAT AND WILL RECLINED beside the glowing fire pit as they enjoyed their supper. The flames burned hot and high, filling the Cherokee lodge with ample warmth. All of the smoke generated by the interior fire concentrated in the apex of the ceiling and eventually escaped through the six-inch hole in the center of the roof. But, even though the hut vented quite well, the air inside remained smoky. One could not walk upright inside the tent for any amount of time. The air at the lower levels was much more breathable. Therefore, both men tended to remain low to the ground.

Bat was attacking his slab of roasted venison. As he chewed, he produced ecstatic moaning and grunting sounds. He slurped the juicy meat, belched, and drank thirstily from his pewter mug. The ice-cold creek water was sweet and refreshing. Clearly, his appetite had returned. It was yet another sign of his rapidly recovering health. Will, on the other hand, was eating much more slowly. He chewed his food deliberately and in a much more gentlemanly fashion.

"Slow down!" Will scolded him. "There is plenty of meat. She was a large, fat doe, and will last us many days."

"I cannot help myself," Bat responded unapologetically. "I feel as if I have not eaten in a year!"

"Well, it has been well over a week since you last ate," Will acknowledged. "But, you mustn't attempt to make up for all that lost time in a single meal." He playfully tossed a small stick at his friend.

"Your fever lingered much longer than I expected. But, now all of your lesions seem to be scabbing up quite nicely. I believe that I can declare with a measure of confidence that you are well on the mend."

"How much longer do you think we should remain here?" Bat inquired through a sloppy mouthful of meat. "I want to go home."

"About one more week. We must not return until all of your scabs have healed and fallen off. Only then will it be safe. But, you need not worry. I will get you home in one piece, and with all your parts intact." He grinned. "I believe that was the exact assignment that your wife imparted unto me before we left Jackson's Creek."

Bat laughed heartily. "She did, didn't she?" He smiled at the memory of his wife. "My God, I am ready to see that delicious woman."

"I am ready to see my boy, as well. But, we must be patient. It will not be long now," Will promised. "I am truly glad to see that you are so much improved. I was sick with worry for those first couple of days. I almost lost you, old friend. Your fever raged to the point that I feared your blood might boil. I finally had to cover you with packed snow to cool you down."

Bat smiled thankfully. "I am most grateful that you did."

"Well, I could not, in good conscience, allow you to languish here and die, could I? You did save my life once, after all."

Bat stopped chewing and swallowed hard. He wiped his lips with his shirt sleeve. "So, the deed has been returned. I reckon we are just about even now, huh?"

Will shrugged. "Even? I am not sure that I could ever think of it that way. There is no tally to keep." He paused and then stared, somewhat embarrassed, into the fire. He seemed to be searching his mind for the right words. "Bat, I would lay down my life if I had to in order to save yours. I hope you know that. You are like the brother that I never had. In my heart, we *are* brothers ... but by choice, not by birth. I believe ours is a bond that is stronger than blood."

Bat inhaled deeply and thoughtfully as he stared at his friend. He smiled and then nodded resolutely. "I agree, old friend. It is stronger than blood."

PART II

A TASTE OF WAR

6

CHOOSING SIDES

Jackson's Creek – Fairfield District, South Carolina
June 5, 1763

I t was a perfect day. The air was pleasantly cool for early June. The sky was a cloudless, brilliant sapphire blue. The late afternoon sun cast a dull orange hue over the tall forests to the west. Numerous cooking fires burned throughout a nearby meadow, unleashing the tantalizing aromas of smoked meat and assuring the promise of a coming feast. The atmosphere was jubilant. Almost all of the citizens of Fairfield District had come to witness an event that most believed would never occur. One of the district's handsomest and most eligible widowers was to be wed.

Like most weddings at Jackson's Creek, the ceremony was taking place out of doors. Friends of the groom constructed a beautiful arbor festooned with woven vines and vibrant wildflowers. The ladies of Jackson's Creek decorated the entire area with colorful cloth, festive flowers, ribbons, and bows. As was their custom, the people in attendance brought their own seating with them. Just before the ceremony began, the fastidious minister organized the mismatched chorus of benches, stools, and chairs into tidy rows. Now, every seat was filled as the outdoor congregants waited anxiously for the vows to be sworn and the marriage declared.

Will Newman stood beside the minister dressed in a brand-new corn yellow linen weskit and matching breeches. A contrasting moss green linen greatcoat completed the fashionable ensemble. His dark hair, tinged on the temples by just a touch of gray, was pulled back tightly into a braided queue and tied with a brown silk ribbon. He looked every bit the country gentleman and squire. Soon, he would have a lovely bride with whom he might share the blessings of his wonderful life in the South Carolina backcountry.

Will's heart pounded in his chest from anticipation. He could barely breathe as he watched his bride approaching him down the aisle. As he waited for her to arrive at the makeshift altar, he could not help but compare this wedding day to his first. Deep in the recesses of his mind he traveled back in time to that traumatic day. It was hard to believe that eleven years had passed. His first marriage, doomed from its inception, had been forced up him. It was a loveless union forged for the purposes of business and status. Will entered into that arrangement out of obligation to his father. But this time it was different. On this idyllic day, he was marrying for love.

Will cut a quick glance at his ten-year-old son, Austin, who was seated on the front row of benches. Austin grinned broadly and shot his father a quick wink. Will smiled and winked back. The handsome, wiry, towheaded lad was the one and only joy that he had found within his tragic first marriage. It was painfully true that he had never loved Mary Kirby, but he desperately loved the son that she had given him. His son's unconditional love was worth every moment of heartache and pain that Will had suffered during those dark days of his life.

The bridegroom quickly refocused his mind and thoughts back onto the present. He fixed his eyes upon the gorgeous woman who was approaching him, locked arm-in-arm with her proud, smiling father. As Will gazed into her glistening, dark brown eyes, he knew deep down in his soul that everything was going to be different this time. This marriage and this bride were nothing like the first.

Elizabeth "Lizzy" Harrison had the appearance of an angel. She wore an exquisite French silk damask gown decorated in a flower print. An elegant lace bonnet adorned her head. Tiny wisps of her dark brown hair, accented with yellow flowers, peeked from beneath the lace near her temples. She carried a simple homemade bouquet comprised of local wildflowers. Every eye was trained upon her. She was breathtakingly beautiful.

Will had fallen in love with Lizzy the moment he first laid eyes on her. Her father, Edgar Harrison, was a relatively new resident to Jackson's Creek. His family was part of a recent wave of Irish settlers moving into the South Carolina backcountry from Virginia and Maryland. Will and Lizzy met in a chance encounter on the highway to Winnsborough. Mr. Harrison's wagon had been disabled due to a cracked wheel hub. Will happened to be passing by on his way into town. He stopped to assist the travelers in making a temporary repair. However, he found it very difficult to focus upon the task of repairing the broken wagon wheel. His eyes and mind were much too occupied by the brown-haired, brown-eyed goddess occupying the front seat.

Edgar Harrison instantly noticed Will's keen interest in his daughter. He did not hesitate to make an introduction. Will found the young woman to be attentive, graceful, charming, well-spoken, and confident. It was clear, also, that she cared very deeply for her father. Will's heart was taken captive. By the time the Harrisons' wagon was repaired, he had reached a life-changing decision. Whether she knew it or not, Lizzy Harrison would be his bride.

Even though Will had been convinced of his love for Lizzy since the moment of their meeting, she had not been persuaded thusly. She had actually proven a most difficult prize to attain. Her love and attention did not come easy. It was not that she was disinterested in the notion of marriage. She simply did not have the time or energy for such endeavors. In addition to her father, she also had charge over three boisterous, messy younger brothers. Hers was a life filled with cooking, cleaning, gardening, mending, and laundry. Because of her family commitments, she had never possessed the spare time nor the inclination to enter into courtship.

The Harrisons were a tight-knit family. They had been on the move for many years. In 1758, they fled oppression and poverty in Ireland for a new beginning in America. That new beginning came in the form of a four-year indenture in Virginia. Tragically, Lizzy's mother perished during the traumatic sea voyage from the port of Cork, Ireland, to the Colonies. In the absence of her mother, and as the oldest child in the family, Lizzy assumed total responsibility for the care of her father and siblings. Even after fulfilling their family indenture and settling their new homestead on Jackson's Creek, Lizzy had assumed that nothing would change and that her life would remain focused upon running their home.

Ultimately, Edgar Harrison had been Will's greatest ally in pursuing courtship with his daughter. At just the right moment, he gave Lizzy a gentle nudge out of the family "nest." He encouraged her to open her heart and eyes to the overtures of the handsome, well-regarded farmer. Her father's permission to seek self-happiness was exactly what she had needed. She immediately made clear her willingness to consider courtship with William Newman.

And finally, the magical day had arrived. The two would become one. It did not bother Will, at all, that Lizzy was twenty years of age. That was considered an oddly mature age for an unmarried woman in the backcountry. Indeed, in some places she might have even been regarded as something of an "old maid." But, for Will Newman, who was ten years her senior, she was absolutely perfect. He had already once been married to a spoiled child. He had no desire whatsoever to repeat *that* mistake.

Soon, the love of his life arrived at his side. Lizzy's father hugged her and kissed her cheek and then placed her hand in Will's. He patted Will affectionately on his shoulder. The couple then turned and faced the Presbyterian minister. Will would have preferred that an Anglican Vicar officiate the ceremony, but there were none of those to be found in the backcountry. Indeed, it seemed that lately a vicar of the King's church was becoming something of a rarity. Will had finally resolved himself to a more ecumenical point of view, especially since his new bride was of the Presbyterian faith. Ultimately, he did not really care who officiated the service. He just wanted to be married to this perfect specimen of womanhood.

The wedding moved quickly. Will's delight and excitement were so overwhelming that the ceremony seemed abbreviated to him, much in contrast to the torturous and agonizing duration of his first wedding. But, this time, is was over before he even realized. Barely a half-hour passed before the vows were sworn and the rings exchanged. The Scriptures were read. The various prayers were prayed. And the deed was done. Will and Lizzy were married. All that remained was the clerical proclamation that they were now husband and wife.

Will's heart leapt with joy when the minister closed his Bible, smiled, and then declared, "By the powers vested in me by God's Holy Word and by our Lord and Savior Jesus Christ, I now pronounce you husband and wife." He smiled at Will. "Young man, I believe that it is time for you to kiss your lovely bride."

Will wrapped his arms around Lizzy's narrow waist. He felt the curve of her shapely hips as his pinky fingers brushed across them. It sent a pulse of undeniable passion through his veins. He drew her close to him, tilted his head slightly, and then kissed her softly but passionately on the lips. In her own hunger for him, she reciprocated. It was the first time that their lips had ever met. It was a perfect moment. A celebrative cheer erupted throughout the crowded lawn. Several seconds passed before they released one another from the embrace and then turned to face their friends and neighbors. Immediately, well-wishers and loved ones descended upon them. It was time for the feasting, libations, and celebrating to begin!

~

Twelve Years Later
August, 1775

LIFE HAD CHANGED DRAMATICALLY in South Carolina over the past decade. The coastal aristocrats seemed hell-bent on rebellion against

King George III. In contrast, many of the backcountry folk, including Will Newman and Bat Austin, remained loyal to their Sovereign. They had no personal qualms with the King. Indeed, they quite enjoyed and appreciated the protection afforded by the mighty British Empire.

But, the lowcountry elites dominated South Carolina's chaotic political system. The Royal government had become ineffective and was no longer regarded as valid by many South Carolinians. Some of those opposed to British rule had gone so far as to organize a "shadow" government. A gathering of their representatives met on July 6, 1774, and formed the *"Committee of Ninety-Nine."* Six months later, this committee held elections and seated South Carolina's First Provincial Congress. As was usual, the wealthy lowlanders dominated this representative body. The backcountry, where most men loyal to Great Britain resided, was effectively silenced.

Even as the newly-elected Congress met in Charlestown and plowed a steady pathway toward separation from Great Britain, many people in the backcountry chose a very different path. Tory pastors preached fiery sermons in support of the King. Alternative, Loyalist committees and local governmental structures formed. A significant resistance began to grow against the heavy-handed methods of the rebellious coastal elites.

Philosophical and political lines were drawn. Tensions brewed. The rhetoric and policies of both sides, complicated by the Colonial notions of honor and pride, magnified the differences between the two opposing viewpoints. The real tragedy was that, throughout South Carolina and the nearby colony of Georgia, this emerging conflict gave every appearance of becoming a civil war amongst neighbors. And that civil war was encroaching dangerously close to peaceful Jackson's Creek.

~

Dusk – Saturday, August 10, 1775
Jackson's Creek, South Carolina

IT WAS A SWELTERING, humid night ... quite typical of mid-summer in the South Carolina backcountry. Barn swallows swarmed overhead, gobbling up mouthfuls of the tasty insects that filled the steamy summer air. Millions of fireflies hovered over the fields of corn that surrounded Bartholomew Austin's home. Crickets chirped amongst the roses that grew beside the porch. A chorus of bullfrogs croaked their deep, throaty songs in the pond down in the south pasture. The atmosphere was filled with all of the sights, sounds, and wonders of an unspoiled American frontier.

Will Newman and Bat Austin reclined lazily in two large willow chairs on the Austin family's front porch. Both men were enjoying their after-supper tea and contentedly puffing their pipes. They reveled in the peace and quiet of the night. Since their children were all away from the house enjoying their Saturday evening activities, the two middle-aged fathers had the entire porch all to themselves. The only unwelcome guests were the pesky mosquitoes that buzzed near their ears. A pewter five-candle stand sat on the low table between them, bathing the porch with the warm, dancing glow of soft candlelight. Inside, they could hear the sing-song voices of their wives chatting happily and, most likely, sharing some juicy gossip as they worked together to wash the evening's dishes. It was a perfect place and a perfect finish to an evening filled with family, friendship, and conversation. But, as was becoming all too common, South Carolina politics and talk of revolution dominated their discussions.

Will sighed, somewhat dejected from their talk of recent events. "I just hope this new governor is the answer. Perhaps he can get things straightened out in Charlestown."

"Lord Campbell?" Bat declared incredulously. "I would not bet on it. Frankly, I do not see him as having any impact, at all. How can one man speak with power and authority when he is surrounded by an army of political enemies? Besides, I doubt that he is little more than the political manservant of someone higher up. Truth be told, his father probably purchased the office for him and in so doing filled the King's treasury."

"He will certainly have the King's army on his side," Will reminded his friend.

Bat growled a scoffing grunt. "That is all well and good. But, I do not foresee the British army taking up arms against good English folk here in the south."

"They did so in Massachusetts, and with a vengeance. Do not disregard Lexington, Concord, and the siege of Boston." He shook his head in disbelief. "And who can forget the carnage at Bunker Hill? English colonists actually engaged in open warfare against the King's army! I could never have imagined that ten years ago."

"This is, most assuredly, *not* Massachusetts, old friend. That could never happen here. Prudence dictates that one cannot force compliance by the barrel of a musket. Without the willing support and consent of the governed, there can be no effective government." Bat sighed. "And Lord Campbell will never hear a single word of support from the Loyalists out here in the backcountry. Our voices are and will continue to be drowned out by the self-indulged, loud-mouthed malcontents along the coast."

A voice in the darkness invaded the privacy of their conversation. "Are we arguing politics or simply discussing current events tonight, Father?"

Austin Newman, a rugged, handsome young man of twenty-two years, leapt up the steps onto the porch. He was accompanied by his best friend and Bat's oldest son, Drury Austin, age twenty-three.

"The specifics of our conversation are none of your concern, young man," Will retorted. "Where have you two troublemakers been for so long? I was worried that we might have to send for the sheriff to go out and find you."

"We have not been causing any trouble, Papa," Austin assured him. "After supper, we enjoyed a little stroll down along the creek. We walked for quite a distance and then stopped by the meeting house to speak with some friends."

"Friends, eh? Were there any of the female persuasion?" Bat teased.

"Perhaps one or two, but none of interest to us," his son, Drury, replied.

Bat peered past Austin and Drury into the darkness behind them. "Where is your brother, then? He has missed supper again and greatly troubled his mother. I have not seen John since early in the afternoon."

Drury grinned. "I believe that John *is* interested in a young maid we encountered down at the meeting house."

Bat raised one eyebrow. "Oh? She is a respectable young lady, I hope."

"Quite, Father. You need not worry. Besides, she will not be around after tomorrow, anyway. She is visiting from Charlestown with her father. He is a Presbyterian preacher."

Bat was confused. "What do you mean? What preacher?"

Drury nudged his friend. "Show him, Austin."

Austin reached inside the lapel of his coat and removed a handbill, which he gave to his father. "We have some distinguished guests at Jackson's Creek, Papa."

Will removed his reading spectacles from his pocket. He held the paper closer to the candles so that he might read its message. His lips mouthed the words as he digested the information on the handbill.

"Well, what does it say? If you are going to wag your lips like a feeble-minded old man, you might as well make some sounds and inform the rest of us," teased Bat.

Will tossed the paper onto Bat's lap. "It says that a delegation has come out from Charlestown to represent their rebellious Provincial Congress. I reckon they intend to sway the local folk hereabouts to their way of thinking."

"Anyone we know?" Bat asked before examining the paper himself.

"We know one of them quite well. Richard Richardson."

"Our old commander!" Bat marveled fondly. He began to read the handbill. "It has been a long time since I saw the colonel. 'Twill be nice to reacquaint with him."

"Joseph Kershaw from Camden is here, as well," Will added.

Bat grunted. "Another rebel!" He shook the paper, obviously irritated. "It says here that there will be a message from the Reverend William Tennent at the meeting house tomorrow afternoon entitled, *'The Justice of Our Revolutionary Cause.'*" He lowered the handbill to his lap and stared questioningly at Will. "Should we go?"

Will peered incredulously at his old friend over the top of his spectacles. "Of course, we should go! I want to attend, if only to see the colonel. It has been years since we last spoke. Besides, I do not fear any Whig preacher's words. My mind and my politics are steadfast."

"Even if he intends to advocate outright revolt against our King?" Bat confirmed.

"That matters not to me. Richard Richardson is an old friend. I refuse to let politics come between us. Grown men can disagree on such matters. Surely, old *friends* can."

Bat shrugged. "We can only hope."

~

Dusk - The Following Evening
Jackson's Creek Presbyterian Meeting House

THE POLITICAL GATHERING was finally over. It had been a two-hour civic marathon. After the Reverend Tennent unleashed a fiery hour-long sermon outlining his numerous grievances with Great Britain, the other visiting dignitaries then conducted an interactive session that extended the gathering by another half-hour. Afterwards, John Phillips, one of the founding elders of the congregation, offered a half-hour rebuttal in favor of loyalty to England.

Meanwhile, the men packed inside the tiny hewn-log church building suffered. The cramped, crowded space was humid and stifling hot. The men trapped inside were thoroughly miserable. It seemed that everyone, no matter their political persuasion, was greatly relieved when the adjournment was announced.

The gathering of over eighty men filed swiftly out the two exits to seek relief in the cooler evening air. It took only minutes for Will and Bat to locate Richard Richardson. They enjoyed a warm reunion. Will and Bat both took great pleasure in introducing their adult sons to their former commander.

Mr. Richardson reached forward and shook the hand of a smiling Austin Newman. "My God! This cannot be little Austin! Son, the last time that I saw you, you were nothing more than a scrawny, towheaded toddler. Who is this strapping young man who stands before me?" He cut a smiling glance at Will. "William, where did all of the years go? I suddenly feel like a very old man."

Will grinned happily. "I ask myself the same thing every day, Colonel."

Mr. Richardson waved his hand dismissively. "None of that 'colonel' business, Will. Our military days are long behind us. You must call me Richard."

"Of course," Will acknowledged rather uncomfortably. Philosophically, he could not fathom referring to a man so many years his elder by nothing more than his given name.

Mr. Richardson continued, "And I have heard that you have remarried and fathered another child. Is this true?"

"Yes, sir. My lovely wife, Elizabeth, and I were blessed with another son almost eleven years ago. His name is William, after my father. He is presently at home with his mother."

The old fellow beamed with pleasure. "And after you, as well! What an honor, indeed. Your father was a treasure to this world. How I miss my old friend!" He turned to Bat, smiling. "And how is life treating you, Bartholomew? Obviously, you have been blessed with some handsome sons, as well."

"Indeed I have, sir. They have their beautiful mother to thank for their good looks. Otherwise, they would have been completely out of luck."

Mr. Richardson cackled with delight. "Many years have passed since I was nourished by your delicious elk stew up in the Cherokee mountains. I have not tasted anything like it since. Isn't it amazing how true hunger adds to the flavor and memory of a good meal?" He smiled warmly. "I was most happy to hear that you survived the pox." His smile descended into a frown. He shook his head grimly. "Many of your comrades and their families were not so fortunate, I am afraid. It seems that the Cherokee won that battle without firing a shot. They sent the pox home with our army and wiped out a goodly portion of the populace of Charlestown. It was nasty, nasty business."

Bat nodded. "I, too, would have been counted amongst the lost if not for my friend, Will. He stumbled upon an old Cherokee lodge out in the middle of nowhere. We wintered there and he gave me care for many weeks. I owe him my life."

Richard nodded knowingly. "A debt that has been and, no doubt, will continue to be repaid more than once throughout your lifetimes. Truly, there is no greater blessing than that of a devoted friend. You men are most fortunate to have one another."

"Amen to that," Bat affirmed.

Drury nudged his father respectfully. "If you gentlemen will excuse us, Austin and I are going to head on back. We depart for Camden early tomorrow."

Bat nodded. "You boys go ahead. I will see you in the morning."

"Yes, sir."

The two young men tipped their hats and then bade their farewells. They turned and headed swiftly toward the fence where their horses were tethered.

Richardson patted both men on the shoulder. "You have both raised some fine young men." He motioned to a bench. "Come, gentlemen. Let us sit down and talk some treason."

Will shot a quick glance at Bat. His friend bore a look of unfettered incredulity. Both of his eyebrows were raised high in shocked disbelief. Neither of them could fathom such open, unabashed use of that most dangerous word, "treason." They slowly followed their old commander to a nearby stone bench and sat down, one on each side of him.

Richardson immediately sought to discern their political positions. "I rather think the good Reverend Tennent did a fine job of promoting our cause. What is your opinion?"

Will drew a hesitant breath. He answered diplomatically, "I suppose that depends on one's definition of 'our cause,' Richard."

The older gentleman scoffed slightly. "Why, it is the cause of independency, of course! Surely, you boys felt the temperature in that room. It was hot with patriotism!"

"It was hot with the scorch of August humidity," Bat retorted boldly. "But, I detected no great fervor for revolt against our Sovereign."

"Come now, gentlemen! You must have recognized the avid responses of those men!" Richardson protested. "They strongly favored the minister's proclamation."

"It was my impression that most of the men favored John Phillips' rebuttal," countered Bat. "I quite think that most of the men of Jackson's Creek remain loyal to Great Britain."

"I saw roughly half of the attendees in favor and the other half opposed," Will interrupted diplomatically. "This community is divided, Richard, as is all of South Carolina."

"But, certainly you gentlemen must regard our cause as one that is just," Richardson almost pleaded.

Will inhaled deeply and considered his words very carefully. "Richard, I must confess that I am struggling to do so. What you regard as just many others regard as oppressive."

"Whatever do you mean?" Richardson's face was flushing red. Beads of nervous sweat formed on his brow. Clearly, he had expected a different response from his former soldiers.

Bat answered, "From our perspective, sir, the coastal planters are ramming this notion of revolution down our throats. We have very little voice in your so-called congress. Your committees, inhabited mostly by lowland lawyers and planters, are handing down one directive after another. They simply expect us to fall in line and do as they say. But, in all honesty, Colonel, I have no quarrels with our King." He paused, and then added, "And I would never consider taking up arms against my country, England."

"But, America is your country, now," Richardson protested, his voice less confident than before.

"There *is* no such nation or country," Bat countered. "We are free Englishmen, citizens of the American Colonies of Great Britain, and subjects to His Majesty, King George III. To proclaim any different is, indeed, treasonous."

Mr. Richardson appeared thoroughly perplexed. "But, the King dishonors us all and inflicts great injustice upon us at every turn!"

"And your Whigs inflict injustice upon avid Loyalists, as well," Bat snapped back curtly.

"Not true! Not true, at all!" objected Richardson.

"What about our friend, Robert Cunningham?" Will countered. "He has been jailed twice for failing to comply with the directives of your Committee of Safety, when all he truly desired was to be left alone."

"And then there is Thomas Brown, from Augusta," added Bat.

"Who?" asked Richardson, confused.

"He is a planter from just across the river in Augusta, Georgia. Only two weeks ago your *Sons of Liberty* dragged him from the home of a friend here in South Carolina, scalped him, tarred and feathered him, and then tied him to a pole and roasted him alive! It was ghastly!" Bat declared with great emotion.

"That is tragic, indeed, and an unnecessary and unwise course of action for those men to pursue. They should not take a life in such a wanton fashion. We are not yet at war."

"Oh, but he didn't die," Will corrected the man. "That would have been a blessing. No, he survived the entire experience of torture and has been teetering on the brink of death ever since. But, we have heard recently that he is expected to live ... as a roasted, hairless, mutilated man." He paused to allow his old friend to digest the information. "You say that King George has inflicted injustice upon us. But, I have never heard of him doing anything so cruel and inhuman as that."

"But, fellows, you must understand ... incidents like that are rare, indeed, and not representative of our cause. That is not the type of behavior that we wish to display."

Will shook his head. "But that is how your politics are viewed by humble men out here in the backcountry ... men such as ourselves. I will say it again, Richard. I have no conflict with my King, and I will not take part in any effort that would subvert his God-given sovereignty over the Kingdom in which we reside."

"Then, you are steadfast Tories, both of you. Your opinions remain unyielding."

Will and Bat looked searchingly at one another. Will nodded slowly and answered, "Yes, sir. Neither of us will willingly take part in a rebellion against Great Britain." He paused. "But, the fact that you maintain a different conviction in no way causes me to disrespect you or hold you in anything but the highest regard. We may each harbor differing political viewpoints, but I do hope that we shall always remain friends."

Richard Richardson stood and smiled at the two men. "That goes without saying, Will. Above all else, we are gentlemen. And gentlemen can agree to disagree, even on the gravest of matters. Nothing that lies before us could ever undo the brotherhood forged in our common past."

"I am glad to hear that, sir," Will responded, standing.

"I, as well," added Bat. He stood and shook the fellow's hand. "I just hope that we never find ourselves on the opposing sides of a battlefield."

"That shall never happen," declared Richardson, shaking his head profusely. "South Carolinians must cease taking up arms against one another. Our political divisions, no matter how deep they may be, must never result in warfare amongst ourselves. Should that occur, there would be no winners. All would lose."

Will smiled thinly and nodded. "On that, Richard, we can wholeheartedly agree."

~

One Month Later

THE FERVOR of the American Revolution continued to reach down from the north and spread throughout South Carolina. Only one month after the delegation of Whigs visited the villages of the backcountry to issue their appeal for the cause of independency, the genteel southern colony remained on the brink of civil war. The Committee of Safety in Charlestown continued to demand loyalty from the backcountry farmers and planters. Their heavy-handed tactics and insistence upon compliance with their cause intensified. This resulted in motivating many of the more indifferent residents to become more Loyalist. Tempers were raw, and battle lines were being drawn.

Then, the unthinkable happened. William Henry Drayton, a wealthy planter and lawyer from Charlestown, deployed to the backcountry with a Whig militia army numbering almost a thousand men. This, of course, elicited a military response from the Loyalists in the region. Thomas Fletchall, a wealthy planter from Fairforest, rallied the men of the backcountry. Over twelve hundred armed Tories answered the call. This army, staunchly loyal to King George III, was encamped at Ninety-Six, four miles north of the Saluda River. Their encampment was not within sight of the Whigs, but the members of the "invading" army from the lowcountry knew that they were there. They were two impressively large armies, each numbering over a thousand men, and prepared to meet in battle. Tensions were high.

Many of the Whig soldiers were eager to press an attack and get on with the business of revolution. It would have been a bloody affair, indeed, if two unskilled armies of such magnitude engaged one another in frontier battle. As luck would have it, Providence ensured that no such battle would occur. Torrential rains descended upon the region, thoroughly soaking the encampments, armaments, gunpowder, and fervor of the soldiers. For many days, the men of both armies huddled inside their tents and makeshift shelters as they attempted to remain warm and dry.

Truth be told, the wealthy planters on both sides had no real taste for bloodshed. Instead, they decided to enter into a series of negotiations. Colonel Drayton, acting on behalf of the Committee of Safety in Charlestown, sought a treaty of neutrality with the backcountry Loyalists. His goal was to keep them from joining the British cause if the King ever deployed troops to South Carolina. The committee representatives saw this standoff as an opportunity to neuter their backcountry enemies without having to actually fight them. The Loyalists, for the most part, simply wanted the Whig militias to depart the backcountry and leave them alone to pursue undisturbed, independent lives on the frontier.

As the leaders from each side met in the comfort of their warm marquee tents, sipping tea and whiskey and seeking to negotiate a peaceful resolution to the potentially explosive standoff, the men of their armies languished in their rain-soaked, mud-filled encampments. They were sick of the weather and weary of the slow pace and apparent unconcern of their leaders. A common complaint arose within both camps. Men began to declare that it was time for their commanders to either *"shite or vacate the privy."* Something had to change, and soon.

~

September 16, 1775
Loyalist Encampment at Ninety-Six District

AT LONG LAST, the rains had ceased. The dreary, cloud and rain-filled skies had finally given way to azure blue heavens and ample sunshine. The spirits of the men were on the mend.

Will and Austin Newman huddled beside Bat, Drury, and John Austin near a tiny campfire. It was a pitiful little fire, indeed, but to them it was a lifesaving conflagration. Starting their humble fire had been no simple affair. It had required almost two hours of non-stop effort to finally establish a viable flame. Once the fire was hot enough to consume their rain-dampened fuel, the five men surrounded the tiny blaze, seeking to draw every possible measure of warmth from its embers. Slowly but surely, their wet, cold-numbed members began to revive.

The five men of the Newman and Austin clans had come out on the previous Sunday as part of a small band of one hundred militiamen commanded by the fervent Loyalist Robert Cunningham. They had been encamped longer than any of the other men in the field. Indeed, well over half of the citizen-soldiers had only arrived within the past two days. The newcomers seemed quite animated and excited about their little military adventure. But, the fellows from Jackson's Creek were done. Regardless of the warmth and sunshine, they were eager to pack up their belongings and return home. They had already invested a week in this venture and, thus far, it seemed as folly.

"Is there anything left to eat?" Austin inquired, famished.

"Most of our rations have been spoiled by the water," Drury responded. "I found only one sack of rice not tainted by mold and a two pound sack of sugar."

"Get the water boiling, boys," Bat ordered. "It is not much, but it will warm our insides for the journey home."

"You expect to return home today?" Will confirmed.

Bat nodded. "My sons and I are going home this day, no matter the outcome of these negotiations. The weather has cleared. It is a good day for travel. I plan to sleep in my own warm, dry bed tomorrow night. I suggest that you and Austin do the same."

"If you go, we go," Will confirmed.

Bat smiled. "Good." He nodded to his son, John. "Johnny, you and I will start packing our gear. Drury is on breakfast duty. We depart mid-morning."

"Austin and I will pack our things and then attend to our horses," Will declared. "We will saddle your mounts, as well."

Bat nodded. "Sounds good."

The men scattered and attacked their tasks with eager enthusiasm. They had just sat down to their hot breakfast of extra-sweet rice when their commander, Robert Cunningham, rode into the camp. He approached the Newman and Austin men, immediately noticing the disassembled state of their tents and equipment.

"You fellows going somewhere?" he inquired with a stern look.

Will stood and faced his captain. "We must return home today, Robert. Both of us have farms waiting for us. We still have corn in the field. We cannot linger here another day."

Cunningham nodded. The stern expression remained on his face. "Well, you might as well go on home. It seems that our time here has been wasted, anyway."

"What has happened?" inquired Bat, disturbed.

"That drunken bastard, Fletchall, allowed Drayton to walk all over him at the negotiating table. We told him our demands and instructed him as to what actions were necessary. We practically gave him a roadmap to follow. But, by God, he just cowered down and let them have their way! No doubt, he was more interested in swilling rum than he was in securing a true peace."

"You did not attend the negotiations?" Will asked, somewhat confused. "I thought that was where you had gone for the past two days."

"No. Thomas Brown and I thought it best to stay away from the gathering. We suspected that the entire meeting today was a ruse to capture us. I suppose, now, that I should have taken the risk."

"What was the outcome, then?" asked Bat.

He spat angrily on the ground. "A weak-arse treaty has been struck. It is rather wordy, but the long and short of it is that as long as we do not fight or render direct aid to British troops deployed in South Carolina, then we will not be molested ... at least not without the consent of their rebel Congress."

"It sounds as if we may have accomplished our goal," Will interpreted optimistically.

"Not even close," Cunningham retorted. "That treaty is not worth the paper upon which it is written. You mark my words. They will be coming after us. All it takes is a proclamation from their committee in Charlestown. This settles nothing. It will be open season upon all who refuse to associate with their rebellion."

"I hope you are wrong," Will declared.

"As do I. But, I am not. You can be certain of that." Cunningham tipped his cocked hat. "Good luck to you, gentlemen. I wish you safety in your journey back to Jackson's Creek. I must go and make the announcement to the other men. I daresay that most are as anxious as you to depart." He spat again. "We must get back to our homes before the rebels burn them to the ground with our families inside." He turned his horse and then guided the animal toward the opposite side of the camp.

"You heard him, boys." Will declared somewhat dejectedly. "Eat up. We have many miles to travel before sundown."

7

ALL MEN LOYAL TO THE KING

Throughout the autumn of 1775, all of South Carolina remained unsettled. The tentative peace that had been forged at Ninety-Six was actually doomed from the start. Though the Loyalists had no idea of it at the time, Governor Lord William Campbell had fled Charlestown on September 15 for the safety of a British warship in the city's harbor. Even as the Tories negotiated at Ninety-Six for peace and security in the backcountry, their Royal governor had all but abdicated his office in Charlestown. Though he made a feeble attempt to govern from aboard ship, such efforts were nothing short of ineffectual. Indeed, most considered them laughable. The Whigs controlled all of Charlestown and the coastal lowlands. Theirs were the loudest voices in the colony, and they were clamoring for war against England.

Meanwhile, though the backcountry seemed somewhat peaceful on the surface, tensions remained high. Neighbor divided against neighbor throughout the Ninety-Six and Camden Districts. Though most of the folk around Jackson's Creek were loyal to King George, there remained a handful who cast their lots with the Whigs. There was no open conflict, but the men representing the two opposing sides began to treat one another with disdain and suspicion. The once-peaceful region became strained as both sides acknowledged the likelihood of a coming war.

Unbeknownst to the Loyalists at Jackson's Creek, the revolutionaries in Charlestown had already hatched a plot to undo the fragile treaty of peace formed at Ninety-Six. In the days following that near-violent standoff, the very vocal and headstrong Robert Cunningham drafted a letter to Sir William Henry Drayton that revealed his true sentiments regarding the Ninety-Six peace agreement. Cunningham informed the avid Whig that the terms of the treaty did not apply to him, personally, since he was not party to crafting the language of the document. Drayton presented the letter to the Committee of Safety in Charlestown and the Provincial Congress promptly issued a warrant for Cunningham's arrest. Within weeks, he was captured and taken to Charlestown to await trial for treason.

Another action taken by the Whigs, though supposedly innocent in intent, nevertheless served as the spark that would eventually ignite open conflict in the backcountry. Drayton, shortly after his negotiating triumph at Ninety-Six and while still encamped there, met with a group of Cherokee chiefs escorted to the conference by an Indian agent named Richard Pearis. The chiefs appealed to Drayton for supplies of gunpowder and lead, which they claimed they needed for hunting. Drayton, representing the Committee of Safety, perceived their dire need for munitions as an opportunity to sway the Cherokee to become allies in their cause. Even if they could not be recruited as actual combatants, Drayton hoped that they would at least remain neutral and not openly side with the British if and when fighting commenced in South Carolina.

In October, 1775, a train of wagons departed Charlestown bound for the lower Cherokee villages. The wagons in that train contained one thousand pounds of gunpowder and two thousand pounds of lead. The agent in charge was Richard Pearis, the same fellow who had arranged the meeting between the Cherokee chiefs and Drayton.

It was a "perfect storm" of political manipulation combined with foolish blunder. The fact that the rebels had imprisoned Robert Cunningham would not be well-received amongst Loyalists in the outer districts. It was an insult that would surely deepen the political divide. But, the notion that the Whigs were supplying the Cherokee Indians, the decades-long foes of the residents of the backcountry, with munitions would be regarded as nothing short of a declaration of war. It was a powder keg, both realistically and metaphorically, and it was about to explode.

∽

Friday Evening – November 10, 1775
Isham Dansby's Farm

IT WAS ALMOST an hour past dusk. The night was cold and silent. There remained only a hint of the sun's faded purple glow peeking over the western hills. An almost-full moon hovered above the tree-tops to the east, bathing the gray autumn landscape with its brilliant silver light. Millions of tiny white stars and a wide, purple-pink strip of galactic dust painted the expansive night sky. As darkness covered the land, the temperature dropped significantly. A thick layer of fog hovered over the creeping waters of Jackson's Creek, spilling over the banks and blanketing the bottomlands and fields.

As the early evening darkness deepened, several of the young men of Jackson's Creek quietly made their way toward one of their favorite clandestine meeting places. It was a small clearing deep in the woods on Isham Dansby's farm. The hidden location was well away from the nearest road and concealed by ample timber. For many years, young men and teenaged boys had gathered at this magical spot to drink whiskey, rum, and ale, smoke their pipes, converse, and just "be boys." It was the closest thing to a secret club that one might find in the 18th Century backcountry.

Austin Newman, Drury Austin, and John Austin arrived at the meeting place just before dark. They built a roaring campfire, lit their clay pipes, and awaited the arrival of more of their friends. A half-hour later, Abel Phillips appeared out of the woods. He sported a huge smile and carried two bottles of dark amber-colored whiskey.

Abel was the son of the Elder John Phillips, one of the leaders of the Jackson's Creek Presbyterian Church. No doubt, the two bottles of spirits had been liberated from his father's ample supply. Moments later, Daniel Dansby arrived. He brought with him a large wooden platter covered with a linen napkin. The mouth-watering aroma wafting from beneath the cloth was fruity and sweet. The other boys could smell it from across the clearing.

"What do you have on that slab of wood, Daniel?" demanded Drury. "I trust that it is a tasty morsel to satisfy our raging appetites."

Daniel grinned proudly as he snatched the napkin away to reveal the delicious victuals that lay beneath. He announced, "Spiced apple fried pies. A dozen of them. They are freshly-made and still warm."

"What?" exclaimed John, licking his lips hungrily. "Where did you get them?"

"Mother cooked them for us. She instructed me to share them with you fellows. So, here they are. Just make sure that I get two of them."

He placed the platter on a nearby tree stump, right next to the open and partially-consumed bottles of liquor. Immediately, the young fellows tore into the sweet, tasty fried pies with great gusto. They washed the sweet treats down with copious amounts of strong whiskey. It was not long before the platter was empty and all of them were feeling a bit light-headed.

"That was absolutely delicious," Drury declared. "Daniel, your mother is quite the cook. Her pastries are always perfect. Please express my gratitude for her wonderful pies."

The other fellows echoed Drury's sentiments.

Daniel grinned and then unleashed an unexpected, thunderous, resounding burp. After the laughter of his mates died down, he responded, "I will let her know that you enjoyed them, but will be careful to leave out any reference to Mr. Phillips' fine whiskey." He glanced down the path that led toward the creek. The fog that had spilled over the edges of the water shrouded the trail with a thick, wall-like mist. "Is there no one else coming tonight? I had hoped that more of the fellows would come out to spend time with us."

Austin removed his pipe from his mouth and blew a perfect ring of blue-white smoke. "I doubt it. All of the boys I spoke to earlier today already had commitments for the evening. So, I reckon we are it." He smiled mischievously. "Tonight, we are few in quantity but superior in quality."

"Too bad for them," John responded as he took another swig from a whiskey bottle. His speech was slightly slurred and quite slow. "They missed out on some delicious pies, that much is certain."

The young men all laughed at their friend's drunken, haphazard enunciation.

"You had best lay that bottle down, little brother," warned Drury. "Papa will give you a taste of his ramming rod on your back if you wake up with a foggy head and sour breath in the morning. He will know for certain that you have been drinking."

"I reckon I am a grown man and can damned well do as I please," retorted John. "I am twenty-two years of age, by God!"

Drury raised an eyebrow. "You're still not old enough to escape the wrath of Bartholomew Austin. You will have to be married and with your fourth or fifth child on the way before you can pull that off."

The young men laughed out loud. They were all very familiar with the fury sometimes displayed by the headstrong and tempestuous Bat Austin. He was a well-known disciplinarian and constantly maintained careful watch over the words and deeds of his sons.

After a short while, the laughter died down as the young fellows stared contemplatively into their campfire. After a little more time and some light conversation passed, they all relaxed and reclined on soft beds of leaves and forest debris. They lay on their backs and stared at the brilliant stars that peeked through the leaf-bare branches overhead. They relished the peace and quiet of the perfect evening. Conversation was not always necessary for them to enjoy one another's company. They were pals, and young men who are such good friends have the amazing ability to enjoy time with one another without a proliferation of words. Finally, however, Daniel

Dansby broke the magical silence with a most disturbing announcement.

"I need to tell you boys something before you find out through the gaggle of local gossips. I know how the women-folk of Jackson's Creek can talk." He paused and considered his words carefully. "I have joined Captain Robert Allison's company of militia."

The other young men simultaneously sat up and stared in disbelief at their friend. There was a prolonged and uncomfortable time of silence.

Finally, Abel Phillips exclaimed, aghast, "You did what?"

Daniel sat up slowly and stared solemnly at his friends. "I joined Captain Robert Allison's company of militia. I began my drills and training last week."

"Daniel, how could you?" pleaded Abel. "His is a rebel militia company! Are you saying that you have aligned yourself with those outlaws from Charlestown?"

"I have not aligned myself with anyone in Charlestown," Daniel retorted. "I simply joined the militia."

"You joined the wrong militia!" Austin scolded him. "Those men stand in opposition to our King! Did you not understand that before you joined their ranks?"

Daniel stared at the ground in front of him and nodded slightly. "Yes, I fully understood what I was doing."

"But, why?" John pleaded. "Why would you swear your allegiance to a rebel commander?"

Daniel inhaled a deep, resolute breath. "Because I am opposed to the policies and actions of England. That is why."

His four friends sat in stunned silence. Their minds reeled. All of their families ... the Newman, Austin, and Phillips clans ... were staunchly loyal to Great Britain. The young men could not fathom any other political position. Their entire world was predicated upon allegiance to King and country.

"I ... I do not understand," Austin stammered. "I thought you to be a patriot like the rest of us."

"I am a patriot!" Daniel barked. "That is why I have pledged my service."

"But, if you stand against the King, then you are most definitely not a patriot. That, by definition, makes you a traitor!" declared Drury. His face distorted in shock and anguish. He could not believe that he was declaring such a thing to one of his very best friends. "If this coming conflict erupts into war, you could be held accountable for your actions. The King's men could hang you just for joining that militia company, Daniel!"

Daniel stared angrily at Drury. "Men do not always share the same politics, Drury Austin. What you regard as patriotism, some might consider oppression. I believe down deep in my heart that England oppresses us. The King's taxes are an undue burden upon us. He has sent his soldiers to slaughter our brethren in Massachusetts. Now, there is a Continental Congress meeting in Philadelphia to consider the future of this land. I believe, as does my father, that such a future should not include allegiance to England."

His friends gasped yet again.

"Surely, you do not mean that!" John hissed, shaking his head.

"I do, indeed ... with all my heart," affirmed Daniel.

"Your father made you do this, didn't he?" Austin accused. "He has made you cast your lot with the rebels."

"My values were imparted to me by my father, as your fathers have imparted their values unto you. But, I did not make this decision out of any compulsion or mandate from my father. I chose this on my own. I made up my own mind. In the end, I have measured King George and found him wanting. So, I chose a path that is different from all of yours." He swallowed hard. His heart was filled with raw emotion. He attempted to speak without crying. "I had hoped that you fellows would respect my choice to follow my conscience."

The other young men stared at one another searchingly. This was a disturbing, distressing moment for all of them. They had never been confronted by a close friend who openly and publicly confessed their opposition to the Crown.

Austin responded, "Of course we respect you, Daniel. You are our friend. And you are quite right ... a man must act as his conscience dictates. To do otherwise would be a grave dishonor. We were simply surprised, that is all ... and a bit confused. Your revelation has shaken us. You must give us some time to digest your news."

"I am afraid that I do not have very much time," Daniel answered quietly.

"What do you mean?" Drury inquired, concerned.

"My company is departing at dawn. Our militia has been called out."

"Where?" demanded Drury.

"I do not know. We are going west, I think. But, that may only be a rumor. I am reasonably certain that it is a training exercise. Still, I had hoped that I might go with your blessing. It would mean a lot to me." A tear formed in his eye. "This may be my last opportunity to enjoy fellowship with you lads ... at least for a month or two."

Austin inhaled deeply and shook his head. "Because of your allegiances, and the declarations that you have made this night, I am not certain that I can give you my blessing. But, I promise that I will keep you in my prayers. Whether we hold the same political views or not, I refuse to allow our differences to undo our friendship. It means too much to me."

"Do you truly mean that?" Daniel inquired hopefully.

Austin nodded. "Of course I do." He paused and then frowned. "I just hope that we never have to face one another on some distant battlefield."

"That could never happen!" Daniel retorted, shaking his head.

"Oh, it could happen," interjected Abel. "My father speaks of it every day. The political strife and divisions are growing throughout all of South Carolina. The drums of war are beating loudly. It is just a matter of time before the two sides clash. What will you do then? Would you train your musket upon one of us and pull the trigger?"

"Never!" Daniel promised.

Abel prodded him further. "But, what if you have no choice? What if you are given the order by your captain? What if you and I were to meet one another on the battle line with bayonets fixed? Would you run me through?"

Daniel closed his eyes and covered his ears with his hands. His face was blood-red. "I cannot bear to think of it! I will be no party to such a thing!"

Austin punched Abel angrily in the shoulder. "That is enough, Abel. You have gone too far. Perhaps you should consider how you might answer your own question. Would you run Daniel through?"

Austin turned and placed a reassuring hand on Daniel's knee. "Let us all pray that none of us will never have to make such a choice. And let us put an end to this tragic, depressing talk. We must speak of good things. For all we know, this could be our last night together, and I do not want us to regret a single word spoken around this fire." He scanned the eyes of his other friends. "Agreed?"

The young men all smiled grimly and nodded.

"Good," Austin declared happily. "Now, pass me that whiskey. Let us toast our good friend and, no doubt, good soldier Daniel Dansby."

∼

November 11, 1775
Saturday Evening – Will Newman's Home

IT WAS AN UNUSUALLY cold autumn night. A toasty fire burned happily in the bedchamber fireplace, casting orange flickers of dancing light onto the ceiling and walls. Tiny wisps of smoke leaked from the front of the fireplace, staining the whitewashed wall above the mantle with streaks of gritty soot. The room smelled of smoke, beeswax, and orange blossom water.

Will and Lizzy lay naked and spent, snuggled together beneath a soft wool blanket on their thick goose-down mattress. Will rested flat on his back with his eyes closed. He wore nothing but a contented smile on his face. His left arm cradled his wife. Lizzy nestled happily against her husband's muscular shoulder.

"That was nice," Lizzy whispered softly. "It has been a while. I have missed our time together very much."

Will grinned. "I am happy to be of service. I was beginning to wonder if you still had any more use for me, Mrs. Newman."

Lizzy punched him playfully in his rib. "I suppose that I could say the same about you. It is not as if you have been filled with romance in recent days, Mr. Newman. It seems that your mind is always elsewhere."

Will sighed. "I am very sorry if I have appeared disinterested. I assure you it is not the case. It is just hard to find time for us to be alone. The farm keeps me busy. I have my militia drills and political meetings. And, to top everything off, we have entirely too many young men and boys running around this place. It is enough that we have our own two sons with whom we must contend. But, lately it seems that Bat's boys have all but taken up residence here, as well. There is never a moment of solitude in this little house."

"I am glad they are all such good friends," she declared quietly. "I never really had any friends like that. They are blessed. We are blessed." She paused and kissed his shoulder. "We have a wonderful life here on Jackson's Creek, don't we?"

"Indeed, we do," Will affirmed. "I would not trade a single moment of it."

"Nor would I," Lizzy responded.

She playfully stroked the thick curly hairs that covered his chest.

"Goodness, Will Newman! You are becoming as fuzzy as a bear," she teased. "I do not recall all of this hair on your chest when we first wed."

Will grinned in the darkness. "I had none in those days. You are the one who has made me sprout all this fur, my dear."

She raised up on her elbow and stared at him, somewhat confused. "How so?"

"You made a man out of me, Darling. My chest was as slick as a catfish's belly until you got hold of me. But, with all of the fine loving that you have unleashed upon me for the past twelve years, my manhood took root and produced a bumper crop of manly chest hairs."

She slapped him playfully across his flat, muscular belly. "Well, I hate to be the bearer of bad news, but lately I have noticed that most of them are various shades of white and gray." She plucked a spindly, dry hair from the center of his chest. She held it in front of his face. "This white one is the color of your ornery old Billy goat. So, I suppose they might be better described as '*old*' manly chest hairs."

Will laughed out loud. "I can live with that." He reached across with his other arm and pulled her close. Once again, she snuggled against his chest. "I will happily grow old beside you, Lizzy, and cherish every minute of it." There was a moment of sweet silence as she reveled in the embrace.

Lizzy sighed wistfully. "I pray that we shall have the opportunity to grow old together. Sometimes I have my doubts."

Will turned his head to look at his bride. He studied the tiny lines on her face and stared deeply into her perfect eyes. "Whatever do you mean, my love?"

She shrugged. "I just worry. There is so much violence throughout the colony, and now there is the endless talk of war. You go and make your drills with the militia each month. Everywhere I look I see more and more armed men." She shuddered. "I cannot stand to think of it all. And I certainly cannot bear the thought of losing you."

He hugged her firmly. "Oh, my darling ... nothing is going to happen to me."

Lizzy's voice became slightly stern. "You cannot make me such a promise as that. You do not know what the future holds."

"Of course, I can. I am not going to war with anyone, that much is certain."

"What, then, did you intend to do down at Ninety-Six back in September? Did you go down there to shuck corn?" she snapped. "You were camped in the field with an army, William!"

"But, it was just the militia, Lizzy."

"Just the militia, indeed. Every one of you were under arms and prepared for battle. It was only a miracle that kept the lot of you from going at it. If just one fool on either side had pulled his trigger, the whole matter would have ignited like a keg of fresh gunpowder." She shook her head angrily. "I shall never understand the natural inclination that you menfolk have toward war and fighting."

Will shook his head. "I have no such inclination toward war, and I certainly do not care for fighting."

"You cannot deny your nature, Will. Twice in your life you have packed your baggage and gone to war," she challenged.

"No, I have not." He shook his head. "'Tis true, I went in service to my King, but I have never fired a single shot in battle." He groaned. "My entire experience with the militia has been nothing but frigid cold, wet clothes, boredom, and hunger. Believe me ... I have no desire whatsoever for war."

Lizzy threw back the covers and reached for her shift that lay across the corner bedpost. She angrily pulled it over her head, concealing her nakedness. "Why, then, must you answer every single time that you are called?" she pouted. She climbed down from the bed and walked toward the fireplace.

"I go in service to my country when called, Lizzy. I must honor my King."

"Why?" she demanded almost angrily. "What does King George have to do with you? What has he ever done for you?"

"He gave me this land. He gave my father his land," Will answered with deep conviction. "But, even so, he need not have done anything for me. He is my Sovereign, and I owe him my allegiance. It is a conviction that my father held and something that he passed on to me. I am a citizen of Great Britain and a free Englishman. I will always rally to my King."

"Men are slaughtering one another in Massachusetts, Will. It is only a matter of time before this rebellion makes its way down south. When these men from Charlestown decide to make war against those loyal to King George ... what then? If they raise up armies from amongst the citizens of South Carolina to fight against England, what will you do? Will you fight against our neighbors? Will you not go to war?"

Will sat up in the bed and fluffed the pillows behind him. He leaned back against the headboard and crossed his arms defensively. "It depends upon the circumstances. But, if some of my neighbors in South Carolina rise up in defiance of England, then I suppose I will go to war if needs be. My honor demands it."

She grunted defiantly. "You will make war ... at your age?"

"At my age?" Will echoed defiantly. "Good God, woman! It is not as if I am some old, feeble man! I am quite capable of comporting myself in battle, I assure you."

She wagged her finger at him. "You see? There it is! That undeniable lust for violence and war! You are just as infected with it as any other man!"

"It has nothing to do with 'lust for violence,' as you say. It is entirely about honor, Lizzy. I am speaking of duty and country. If there is a rebellion that threatens our home and our way of life, then, yes, I will go to war and defend it."

Lizzy stared stormily at the floor. "Bat says exactly the same thing. He uses all the same words that you do. You men toss around such noble verbiage in order to justify your lust for violence."

Will rolled his eyes. "How do you know what Bat says?"

"Rachel talks to me, Will. We speak every day. She and I fear all of the same things. She is horrified about the future and what it means to her husband and to her sons."

"Well, I can assure you that Bat is no more anxious for war than I. I quite imagine that his sons are more likely to romanticize the notion of war. Such are the ways of young men. They believe themselves immortal and indestructible." He paused. "Our Austin, no doubt, harbors similar sentiments."

Lizzy stared numbly into the fireplace. "And I suppose that when you march off to war you will take your son with you?"

"Austin is a grown man with a mind of his own." Will paused and then added, "And the boy is your son, as well. Try not to forget."

Lizzy turned to face her husband, placed her hands on her hips, and then rolled her eyes. "For the love of God, Will! I am barely ten years older than Austin. I am more like an older sister than I am a mother to him."

"Darling, you are the only mother he has ever known. Before you came into our lives, he knew nothing but menfolk, horses, and dogs." A tear escaped Will's right eye. "Lizzy, he loves you as his mother. He has told me so, over and over again."

Lizzy's lip began to quiver. "And I love him as my own, as well. That is why I cannot bear the thought of either of you going off to fight and die in some senseless war!"

She collapsed onto the floor in front of the fireplace and wept. Her shoulders and back heaved from the intensity of her sobs. Will jumped from the bed and ran, stark naked, to her side. He knelt down and then swiftly lifted her from the floor. He turned and sat down in his well-worn padded wingback chair, cradling her in his arms. He did not say anything. There were no words that he could offer that would comfort or reassure her troubled soul. Will simply held her close and allowed her to have a good cry.

～

Sunday, November 12, 1775
Jackson's Creek Presbyterian Meeting House

THE CHILDREN of the Austin and Newman families filled an entire row near the back of the church. Their parents occupied the row immediately behind them. Rachel and Lizzy sat next to one another so that they might talk. Bat and Will sat on either side of them. Since the two men were physically separated and could not speak to one another, they sat in patient silence and observed the goings-on throughout the church house.

The young folk whispered amongst themselves as they waited for the service to begin. William Newman, age eleven, was seated next to little Mary Austin, also eleven. The two had been inseparable since they were toddlers and were the best of friends. They were chatting gaily and giggling. William's high-pitched laugh soon reached an unacceptable level, at which point Bat Austin leaned forward and gave the unruly lad a resounding thump on the back of his ear. The boy yelped in pain and immediately covered the wounded ear with his hand. The giggling and talking ceased.

Will Newman leaned forward slightly and made eye contact with Bat. He smiled and winked and then mouthed the words, "Good shot." Bat grinned and gave Will a subtle upward thumb in response.

The meeting house was unusually full. The incessant talk of war had apparently convinced more local folk than usual to seek answers and solace from the Lord. The tiny log building was packed with a standing-room-only crowd. Since its beginning in 1771, the little church had been the main gathering place for the people of Jackson's Creek as well as the epicenter of local community and culture. As talk of revolution increased in South Carolina, the weekly gatherings had steadily increased in number. Though no one would admit it, the people likely gathered for the sharing of news, gossip, and information as much as they did for religion and worship.

The Sunday meeting would begin soon. Meanwhile, the people sat and whispered quietly as they awaited the elder's announcement of the beginning of service. Since the church had no established, ordained pastor, the elders of the congregation shared in the work by leading the singing and preaching the sermons on a rotating basis. The Elder John Phillips, one of the founding leaders of the church, was on duty this week. He sat on a tiny bench beside the makeshift pulpit reviewing his notes and thumbing through the Scriptures.

John Phillips was a learned, well-spoken Irishman. He settled on Jackson's Creek in early 1771, accompanied by his two brothers and two married sisters and all their associated households. He immediately rose in prominence and very rapidly became an influential leader in the community. He had recently welcomed the arrival in Jackson's Creek of the Chesney and Miller clans, more of his distant kin from Ireland. Their presence further increased his power and influence in the region.

Finally, Mr. Phillips stood and approached the podium. He reverently placed his large, open Bible on the wooden stand and then cleared his throat. The people, seemingly oblivious to his more restrained call to worship, continued their whispers and murmurs. Phillips smiled, quite amused, and then rapped his knuckles soundly on the rough wood. The murmuring stopped immediately and everyone faced toward the front.

"Good mornin', friends," he declared in his thick native Irish brogue. "As we gather on this Lord's Day, we must acknowledge that a cloud of darkness and evil hovers over this beautiful land."

Heads bobbed up and down in agreement with the elder. Two of the more vocal men in the church responded with a loud, "Amen!"

The elder continued, "I have received some disturbing news this very mornin'. I regret to inform you that one of our brethren in the faith, Judge Robert Cunningham of the village of Ninety-Six, has been taken prisoner by rebels in Charlestown. He now languishes in chains inside their gaol. I am told that they intend to try him for treason. He could hang."

A wave of groans and murmurs erupted throughout the church. There was genuine anger at this news. Phillips raised his hand to calm the crowd.

"I have not mentioned this travesty of justice as a device to incite your emotions or inflame your tempers. I merely offer this information in order to provide a proper context for my message to you this day." He paused and inhaled a deep, thoughtful breath. "Brethren, we now live in the midst of sin and rebellion in our glorious colony of South Carolina. There are many who would speak of wagin' war here upon our own soil. Of course, this comes as no surprise to those of us who know the revelations of this sacred Book. Consider the words of our Lord in Matthew chapter twenty-four, verses six through eight:

6 And ye shall hear of wars and rumours of wars: see that ye be not troubled: for all these things must come to pass, but the end is not yet.

7 For nation shall rise against nation, and kingdom against kingdom: and there shall be famines, and pestilences, and earthquakes, in divers places.

8 All these are the beginning of sorrows."

Phillips continued, "Indeed, such rumors of war should never surprise us. Our Lord has reminded us of the ever-present desire of our sin-tainted human hearts to engage in conflict. Yet, I submit to you that this unholy rebellion against the lawful authorities stands against Scripture and against the commandments of our Lord God. This timeless, insightful Book speaks directly to the climate of rebellion that exists within this colony, where our Sovereign's governor has been forced from its shores to seek refuge on a vessel of the Royal Navy. Hear this, the declaration of the apostle named Peter ... a friend, indeed, to our Lord. He declared these words in the second chapter of his first letter to the church, verses thirteen through seventeen:

13 Submit yourselves to every ordinance of man for the Lord's sake: whether it be to the king, as supreme;

14 Or unto governors, as unto them that are sent by him for the punishment of evildoers, and for the praise of them that do well.

15 For so is the will of God, that with well doing ye may put to silence the ignorance of foolish men:

16 As free, and not using your liberty for a cloke of maliciousness, but as the servants of God.

17 Honour all men. Love the brotherhood. Fear God. Honour the king."

The men of the church erupted in emotion. They shouted and waved their hats in the air. Their patriotic fervor was stoked nearly unto a frenzy as they considered the powerful and timely words from the Bible. As the elder made his case, it seemed to them as if these two-thousand-year-old words had been lifted straight from the latest edition of the *Charlestown Observer*. Again, Elder Phillips held up both hands as a signal for the men to calm themselves. They quickly assumed a more reserved air and returned to their seats.

"We, however, must be a people loyal to Scripture, to God, and to our King. Indeed, this is the only righteous and just position that one can hold in light of our current climate of politics in the Americas. I point you to the explanation given by Paul in his letter to the church in Rome, found in the thirteenth chapter, verses one through four:

> *Let every soul be subject unto the higher powers. For there is no power but of God: the powers that be are ordained of God.*
>
> *2 Whosoever therefore resisteth the power, resisteth the ordinance of God: and they that resist shall receive to themselves damnation.*
>
> *3 For rulers are not a terror to good works, but to the evil. Wilt thou then not be afraid of the power? do that which is good, and thou shalt have praise of the same:*
>
> *4 For he is the minister of God to thee for good. But if thou do that which is evil, be afraid; for he beareth not the sword in vain: for he is the minister of God, a revenger to execute wrath upon him that doeth evil."*

Elder Phillips stepped from behind the pulpit. He looked toward the ceiling and held his right hand upward, as if it were pointed toward the Lord. It was a dramatic pose. "Of course, the 'he' to whom the apostle Paul is referring to is none other than our God-appointed Sovereign, King George III of Great Britain. Those who serve him and do good should not fear the Lord. But, for those who resist him, the sword of wrath and justice awaits."

The elder lowered his gaze toward the congregants. "Friends, we have heard this day the testimonies of our Lord Jesus Christ, and of the Apostle Peter, and of the Apostle Paul. All three affirm the holiness of our God-ordained government and our God-ordained King. Brethren, it must never be questioned ... ours is the cause that is just. Ours is the course that is Scriptural. By remaining true to our Sovereign King and to the government of Great Britain, ours is the choice that is righteous!"

Though the women remained silent and dignified, the men erupted from their benches in thunderous applause. Men throughout the room shouted, "Hear, hear!" They stomped their feet and waved their hats in the air. Clearly, the people of the Jackson's Creek congregation were unwavering and fervent supporters of King George III.

Suddenly, in the midst of the frenzied affirmation of Elder Phillips' words, one of the front doors of the log cabin church burst open. The heavy portal swung inward and slammed against the wall with a mighty boom. A young, rugged-looking man stepped into the church. He was dressed for cold weather. His clothing was dirty and unkempt, giving the appearance of having been in the field. He carried a rusty, beaten Brown Bess musket strapped across his back. The people of the congregation, startled by the loud interruption to their worship, spun around on their benches and stared silently at the unexpected visitor.

Mr. Phillips demanded, "What is the meaning of this intrusion, young man? We are in the midst of our Sabbath worship."

The young fellow reached up and, as a sign of respect, removed his straw hat. "Beggin' your pardon, Reverend ..."

"I am not an ordained minister," Mr. Phillips corrected him. "I am merely a fellow servant of the Lord, just like the other worshippers gathered here."

The fellow seemed quite confused. He stammered, "Right. Uh ... beggin' your pardon, rev... uh, vicar ... I mean ... mister. Major Joseph Robinson has sent me here to summon all men loyal to the King. The rebels are attempting to incite the Indian savages against the back-country."

A gasp erupted throughout the room, followed by excited murmurs. Mr. Phillips stepped down from the speaker's stand and approached the fellow in the center aisle. "Explain yourself, young man. What evidence have ye?"

"Sir, I serve in Captain Patrick Cunningham's company. Last night we captured a train of wagons headed into the Cherokee country. They contained a ton of lead and a thousand pounds of gunpowder. The Indian agent, Mr. Richard Pearis, has sworn before a judge that the munitions were intended to incite the savages against us. Charlestown would have the Cherokee wage war upon our farms and homes."

A wave of anger swept across the room. The congregants became quite animated. The people were genuinely disturbed.

Elder Phillips responded, "But, if you have intercepted the munitions, then the crisis has been averted, has it not? Why summon the militia now?"

"Because the rebels are out. The Whig leader, Andrew Williamson, is gathering men in an attempt to reclaim their powder and lead. They intend to take it by force and then deliver it to the savages. Major Robinson is calling all men loyal to our King to join in the defense of their country."

Mr. Phillips nodded. "Thank you, sir, for your information and summons. You have done your job well."

"Thank you, sir." The fellow nodded politely, re-donned his hat, and then swiftly exited the room. A gentleman standing near the door closed it behind him.

Elder Phillips turned and marched back toward the speaking stand. He climbed the two steps up onto the tiny platform and re-occupied the pulpit. "Ladies and gentlemen, it seems that war is now upon us. I know that this is not Boston, but our situation is dire nonetheless. Because of this disturbing news, I must immediately declare our meeting suspended. Gentlemen, I encourage you to return to your homes and arm yourselves. Gather provisions for a week in the field. All those who will serve the King and defend our homes should return to this meeting house within the hour. Now, who will be our captain? Who will lead the men of Jackson's Creek?"

John Phillips' brother, James, rose to his feet. "I will lead them, brother."

The elder nodded reverently and proudly. "Very well. Captain James Phillips will command the soldiers of the Jackson's Creek Company. Go, then, to your homes and make your preparations. Arm yourselves, and spread the word as you go. You are dismissed."

The people of the congregation rose to their feet. The room exploded in emotion and animated conversation. As the people began exiting the building, the Newman and Austin children turned and faced their parents.

Austin stared searchingly at his father. "Are we going, Papa?"

Will nodded. "Yes, Son. If this is true, then we have no choice. The rebels have gone one step too far. We must protect our homes. Do you not agree, Bat?"

His friend nodded grimly. "This provocation cannot go unanswered. My boys and I will answer the King's call."

Rachel and Lizzy said nothing. They simply leaned toward one another and embraced. Both women had tears streaming down their cheeks.

"Come, then. We must gather our gear and rations, and quickly so," declared Austin. "We do not have long to prepare."

The members of the two families filed solemnly out of their aisles and headed toward the doors.

8

STARTING A WAR

The Newman and Austin men departed home mid-afternoon on Sunday. The soldiers of their rapidly-organized company joined the Loyalist militia force encamped at Nineteen-Mile Creek, about five miles west of Jackson's Creek. Unfortunately, John Austin, Bat's younger son, developed a raging case of the flux on his first night in camp and had to return home the following morning. He was heartbroken at the notion of missing out on a fight, but was well-aware that he was in no condition to travel with the army. Drury escorted his little brother home and then returned to camp just before nightfall.

Men continued to trickle into the encampment over the next three days. By November 16, the combined Loyalist militia force grew to almost 1,800 men in the field. Major Joseph Robinson then broke camp and led his imposing army southwest along the highway toward Londonderry. One day later, he received a report that an enemy force was massed at Ninety-Six. Robinson, determined to keep the rebels from establishing a foothold in the backcountry, turned northwest in pursuit. If the campaign went according to his plan, his Loyalist army would occupy Ninety-Six and drive the rebels back toward the coast. As his men marched, they readied their arms, equipment, and minds for war.

Mid-Morning - Sunday, November 19, 1775
Village of Ninety-Six, South Carolina

ROBINSON'S ARMY arrived at Ninety-Six eager for action, but quickly discovered that there were no rebels in the town. Instead, they learned that the enemy had taken up a position on the nearby plantation of Colonel John Savage, a local Whig. Peering across the fields to the west, they quickly spotted a makeshift fort surrounding a cluster of buildings and barns. Militiamen were moving in and around the fort. The enemy had established a secure and well-defended position and, it seemed, was ready for action.

The Loyalists quickly secured the town, occupied the courthouse for their headquarters, and then proceeded toward Savage's plantation. They marched proudly, advancing upon the enemy's position with their colorful Union Jacks unfurled and drums beating. The men sang songs celebrating Great Britain and its King as they marched. Major Robinson wanted the rebels to know that his army was in good spirits and that he meant business.

Robinson's men deployed in a large circle completely surrounding the fort and then dug in for a siege. The opposing forces waited and watched one another nervously. Every man encamped at Savage's plantation, regardless of his politics, wondered if this would be the place where a shooting war might actually erupt in the backcountry.

Noon – Near Ninety-Six

WILL and Austin Newman stood ankle-deep in soupy mud beside Bat and Drury Austin. They stared curiously at the odd-looking enemy fort. The Whig position was little more than a cluster of outbuildings connected by haphazard palisade walls. It was rather ramshackle in appearance. Still, despite its odd presentation and diminutive size, the rebel fortress bristled with men and guns. It would, by no means, be an easy objective to conquer and occupy.

"Well, at least it has stopped raining," quipped Drury, glancing up at the cloudless sky. He then looked dejectedly at the water and mud that surrounded them. "It would be down-right disheartening to contend with water from above and from below at the same time."

"As if that matters now," griped Austin. "I am already soaked to the bone. My bollocks have shrunk and shriveled from three days of non-stop rain."

"'Tis a crisis, indeed," Austin's father declared with a stoically serious look on his face. "Your pitiful little marbles were barely noticeable to begin with."

Bat grinned from ear to ear. Drury could not help but laugh out loud.

Austin sighed. "I can already see what this siege is going to be like for me. I shall be fighting against both sides. I'm just as likely to take a shot in the arse from my own army as I am from a Whig."

Will patted his boy affectionately on his shoulder. "Now, Son, you know that I am just teasing you. I love you, Austin," he paused. "Even if you do have tiny little tallywags."

Bat and Drury burst into hearty laughter. Will immediately joined them. Austin stood silently and suffered their merciless teasing and humiliation.

Captain James Phillips appeared unexpectedly at their side. "What is so funny, gentlemen?"

"Young Austin was just informing us as to the rain-shrunken state of his diminutive bollocks," Bat explained.

The captain smiled. "Poor lad." He nodded to Austin. "'Tis of little consequence right now, young man. No matter if you cannot find your bollocks. They will be of no use to you here, anyway. Perhaps your wife can help you find them when you return home."

"The boy has yet to take a wife," Will responded in a forlorn tone. He shook his head, feigning disappointment.

The captain grinned mischievously. "Well, then, maybe we can find you a pair out here on the battlefield. Then, you might be able to get yourself a fine wife!"

Everyone except Austin laughed uncontrollably. When they finally calmed themselves, the captain pointed toward the fort.

"You fellows had best move back a few yards, lest all of you wish to get your bollocks blown off. Our spotters have seen a few swivel guns inside that monstrosity."

"Swivel guns?" echoed Drury. "What are those?"

"They are tiny little cannons that you can mount on a wall or post. They have a bore size around an inch and a half ... perfect for shooting a big load of grapeshot or loose lead. Hell, you can even shoot nails out of the cursed thing."

Drury gulped. "Christ, Almighty!"

"Exactly," the captain responded. "So you had best stay further back. They likely have a few sharpshooters with rifles, as well."

"Do you think there will actually be fighting, Mr. Phillips?" Bat inquired.

The captain shrugged. "That all depends on those fellows over yonder. All they need to do is depart in peace and return to their homes. That is our only demand. The major will send a contingent to convey his terms very soon. So, do not be alarmed when you see a parley flag."

"If there is a fight, how many men will we be facing?" Will asked.

"Major Robinson estimates the enemy strength to be five or six hundred men. We outnumber them roughly three to one."

"Five hundred men behind walls and timber cannot be disregarded out of hand," Will warned. "'Twould be a costly venture to attempt to take that fort under enemy fire."

"Indeed," Captain Phillips declared. "Which is why we must make every effort to avoid actual conflict. Let us pray that these Whigs will pursue a sensible solution and go home."

"Amen to that," Bat mumbled.

Captain Phillips turned to Bat. "Where is your boy, John? I have not seen him in a couple of days."

"I had to send him home. The lad had a flaming case of the flux on our first night in camp. His arse was on fire. There was no way he could continue."

The captain scowled. "Oh, my. That is bad. Did he have fever?"

"No fever. I suspect it was merely some bad food or water. Hopefully, he is better by now. But, I would not expect him to join us any time soon. He probably cannot stray far from a privy."

The captain nodded. "Well, I sincerely hope that it is nothing serious." He turned and pointed toward a small ditch and tree line one hundred yards behind them. "Right now, I want you fellows to fall back to that ditch with the remainder of the company. Cut some logs from the thicket and build walls and barriers. Construct barricades that you can hide behind and still shoot. You should plan on staying here for a few days, so make your camp comfortable."

"Yes, sir," Will responded.

"Remain in our area and do not wander. If the enemy sends out patrols, things could get interesting after dark. I do not want one of you to be hit by a stray ball. I will be around to check on you at dusk."

"Yes, sir," Will responded again.

"Good luck, gentlemen." The captain turned to his right and headed toward a gathering of officers.

"Let us go," Bat encouraged. "Perhaps there is less mud back yonder."

The four men turned and trudged slowly and carefully toward their company area.

∼

3:00 PM - Sunday, November 19, 1775
Jackson's Creek, South Carolina

Lizzy Newman lifted the hem of her pinner apron to her forehead
and wiped away the bead of sweat that lingered there. She could not
believe that, despite it being mid-November, the autumn air
remained warm and humid enough to actually cause her to break out
into a sweat. She placed her hands on her hips and stretched the
aching muscles in her back, glancing apprehensively at the blustery,
gray sky. She was certain that rain would arrive by day's end. She just
hoped that her linens would dry before it started. She turned to her
best friend, Rachel Austin, and smiled.

"You did not have to help me with my chores, Rachel. I am
perfectly capable of hanging out my own wash."

Rachel grinned as she shook out a pillowcase and then hung it on
the drying line. She took two clothes pins from her mouth and
secured the item to the thin rope. "It is a pleasure, believe me. I
needed to get out of my house and find some fresh air. Lord knows
that John Austin has thoroughly infected my home with his putrid
foulness."

"How is your son?" Lizzy inquired as she stretched a sheet across
the clothes line.

"Oh, he is much better now. He spent almost three whole days in
the privy. He has been able to rest comfortably for the past day. But,
Lord help me, the vapors that escape that boy!" She waved her hand
in front of her nose. "His bowels continue to belch a horrid stench. I
have opened every window and attempted to cleanse the air, but the
odor lingers in my nose. I can still smell it right now, even as we stand
here in the open field." She shook her head. "We may have to burn
the house down when his father gets home."

Lizzy laughed, entertained by her friend's colorful descriptions.
"Well, if that truly is the current condition of your home, then you
can count me out for Sunday supper."

"One whiff of the inside of my house, and you would have
precious little appetite, anyway. Trust me."

The two women worked together to stretch the last blanket across
the line and then applied a handful of clothes pins. At long last, both
of their laundry baskets were empty.

Lizzy clapped her hands victoriously. "Tea?"

"That sounds wonderful," Rachel responded. "A biscuit would be nice, as well. I did not eat much this morning."

"I baked a batch of shortbread sweets yesterday. We should have several left, I hope. Our youngest children may have already finished them off."

"Oh, let us pray not," Rachel wished out loud.

Lizzy and Rachel trudged wearily back toward the house, empty laundry baskets in hand. It had taken Lizzy almost the entire morning to wash and rinse all of her bed linens. With Rachel's help, she was able to hang them on the drying line in less than a half-hour. Washing bedding was a labor-intensive task. Lizzy was tired and ready for a break. As she walked up the stairs onto the porch, she glanced through a nearby window at her son, William. As always, Mary Austin was by his side. Lizzy and Rachel paused to watch their children. The two youngsters were playing a game of jackstraws in the parlor floor. The women could not help but smile. The inseparable boy and girl were the very picture of joy and friendship.

Rachel leaned toward Lizzy's ear and whispered, "I can see those two getting married someday."

Lizzy nodded and grinned. "'Twould not surprise me, a'tall."

She had entertained the same thought on multiple occasions. But, obviously, she was in no rush for romance for young William. Both he and Mary were only eleven years old. For now, their common interests centered upon games, toys, and farm life. And she was not anxious for him to grow up. Indeed, in her heart of hearts, she wished that he might remain her little boy forever.

Lizzy had just placed her hand on the doorknob when the sound of horses caught her attention. She and Rachel turned to look at the highway to the east. A dozen men were riding swiftly westward and appeared to be headed in their direction.

"I wonder what this is about," Rachel mused. "Men rarely travel together in such numbers unless theirs is an official matter."

Lizzy kept her eyes on the riders. "I do not know. Most of our men-folk are away with the militia. I doubt that those men are from around here."

"They could be from Camden town," Rachel mused.

Lizzy shrugged. She hoped that they would pass on by, but her hopes were soon dashed. The entourage of horsemen turned down the lane and approached the Newman home. They reared their animals to a stop a few feet from the porch. The men were unkempt in appearance and clad in linen hunting frocks and jackets of various colors. Their breeches were dirt-stained and torn. They bore the appearance of having been in the field for some time. Just as the riders arrived, William and Mary, curious about the presence of visitors, stepped out of the house to join their mothers on the porch. The man at the head of the group, obviously the leader, tipped his rather dusty cocked hat to the women and children.

"Pleasant afternoon to you all."

Lizzy curtsied. "Good afternoon to you, kind sir. God save the King."

Several of the men in the group chuckled sarcastically. A shudder went down Rachels' spine. Clearly, these men were not Loyalists.

"We do not represent King George, Madam. I am Captain John Anderson of the New Acquisition District Militia. We represent the Committee of Safety and the South Carolina Congress in Charlestown. And who might you be?"

"I am Mrs. Elizabeth Newman, wife of William Newman."

The captain stood high in his stirrups and quickly inspected the farm. "What a lovely place you have, Mrs. Newman. Is Mr. Newman hereabouts?"

Lizzy's eyes narrowed. "No, Captain. I am afraid that he is away on business right now."

The captain appeared curious. "Business? What manner of business?"

The hair on the back of Lizzy's neck bristled. "That would be no business of *yours*, Captain. But, please tell me, how might *I* help you? Furthermore, what business have you here in Camden District?"

"My company is part of a larger militia force under the command of Colonel Richard Richardson. We are currently encamped about four miles east of here, on the banks of the Wateree."

Lizzy's outlook brightened somewhat. She smiled at the mention of a familiar name. "I am well-acquainted with Colonel Richardson. He visited here a few months ago. He was my husband's commander during the Cherokee Campaign of 1759." Lizzy tilted her head toward Rachel. "This is Mrs. Rachel Austin. Her husband, Bartholomew, served under Colonel Richardson, as well."

The captain tipped his hat to Rachel. "The pleasure is mine, Mrs. Austin. So, they served under the colonel in 1759? Goodness, that was a long time ago! Nevertheless, we are grateful for their service in the defense of South Carolina. But, I am afraid that has little bearing upon our mission today."

"What, exactly, is your mission here today, Captain?" Rachel demanded. Her voice communicated a bit more force and authority than did Lizzy's.

The captain shifted in his saddle. "The colonel has dispatched us, along with several other companies of the regiment, to procure supplies and foodstuffs as provisions for his army." He smiled disarmingly. "As you can well-imagine, a force of over two thousand men can be quite difficult, indeed, to keep fed."

The captain snapped his fingers. One of his men, apparently his sergeant, immediately handed him a leather-bound book and a small piece of paper. The other ten militiamen dismounted and quickly scattered across the farmyard. Three of them made a beeline toward the barn.

"What is the meaning of this?" Lizzy protested, her voice crackling. "Where are your men going? They have no cause to go snooping about my home and farm."

The captain smiled. "We must requisition a portion of your livestock, I am afraid. They are merely going to scout the barn."

Lizzy became somewhat frantic. "You cannot have any of our livestock! That is our personal property!"

"During times of emergency, the congress has authorized the lawful procurement of provisions from the general population. But, you need not worry, Mrs. Newman. You will be reimbursed in full for your livestock." He waved the slip of parchment paper that he held in his hand. "I will give you this voucher, which your husband may present to the magistrate in Camden at the conclusion of our campaign. The district authorities will pay him in currency or coin for the animals."

"And what kind of campaign might you be pressing here in the backcountry?" Rachel inquired with an air of suspicion.

The captain stopped smiling. "It is a campaign to rid the land of its Tory brigands. We are tasked with arresting all such ruffians and bandits and taking them to Charlestown to stand trial."

"Stand trial for what?" demanded Lizzy.

The captain appeared incredulous. "Why ... for rebellion against the lawful authorities of South Carolina, of course."

Rachel chuckled. "Last I heard, the only lawful authority in South Carolina was floating on a ship in Charlestown harbor."

The captain sighed and then lowered his eyes. He paused, then shook his head in an air of arrogant disbelief. "Now, that is *exactly* the sort of treasonous talk that we are attempting to purge from this land."

There was a small commotion near the barn as the three soldiers exited the building. One was leading a cow, one was leading a large hog, and the last man was carrying three chickens in each hand. The captain observed the men and then quickly jotted a few words on his paper. As the soldiers secured the tethers of the larger animals to their horses, the captain leaned over the neck of his horse and extended the voucher toward Lizzy. She made no move to receive it.

"I suggest you take this document, and thankfully so, Mrs. Newman. You will see that I have noted your contribution of one beef cow, one hog, and a half-dozen hens, and that I have been most generous in my estimation of the weights of the hooved animals. You will be reimbursed generously, I assure you."

Lizzy stepped down from the porch. She leaned toward the captain and then timidly took the paper in her hand. As she turned to walk away, the captain held tight to the voucher. He gave the paper a slight tug, halting her movement. She lifted her eyes and glared hatefully at the man.

Captain Anderson gazed intently at the defenseless woman. His face erupted into a taunting smile. "I have a feeling that I may someday encounter your husband whilst he is about his business. Do you think that might be a possibility, Mrs. Newman?"

She maintained her blank, disdainful stare. "Perhaps."

"If that is the case, then I will be sure to tell him that you said, 'Hello.' Wouldn't that be nice of me?"

He suddenly released the voucher. Lizzy jerked her hand away from the man. She glanced at the paper to make sure that the officer's signature was on it. She smiled.

"That would be kind of you, indeed, Captain. Of course, if you do not meet my husband whilst you are visiting here in the Camden District, perhaps I could send him and some of his friends to pay you a visit down at New Acquisition. Would that please *you*?"

The captain leaned back in his saddle. He cackled, quite entertained by his confrontation with the two headstrong women. "I rather look forward to it, Mrs. Newman." He politely tipped his dusty cocked hat. "I bid you ladies a good day."

Both women declared simultaneously, "God save the King!"

The captain paused for a moment, smiled, and then shook his head. He seemed amused at their boldness. He and the other men turned their horses and then headed back toward the highway. They moved slowly, hampered by the creeping pace of the cow and the short-legged hog. It was several minutes before they disappeared from view.

Rachel turned to the children. "Quick! Both of you! Run to our house and fetch John! Tell him to come immediately, and to pack for travel!"

William nodded. "Yes, ma'am."

"Waste no time! Do not dawdle! Do you understand?"

"Yes, ma'am," William declared once again.

The two youngsters ran to the far end of the porch and jumped off. They immediately ran north toward the Austin farm.

"Why are you sending for John?" Lizzy inquired, perplexed.

Rachel's face was clouded with worry. "Did you not hear that man? Colonel Richardson has over 2,000 rebels encamped here in Camden District. They are pursuing men loyal to the King. Surely, our husbands and their commanders do not know of this new army in the backcountry. We must warn them! We must send John to find them!"

Lizzy's eyes grew wide. She lifted her hand nervously to her mouth. "Oh, my! Yes, we must."

∼

Mid-Afternoon
Near Ninety-Six, South Carolina

THE JACKSON'S Creek men were in a secure and easily defensible position. They had constructed six two-foot-high walls from three and four-inch saplings. The walls were arranged end-to-end in a slight semi-circular formation. The men included gaps in the walls for firing holes, giving them the ability to shoot at the enemy without exposing themselves.

Once their defensive walls were in position, the men began to set up tents and start cooking fires. The Austins and Newmans elected to build lean-tos from saplings and small limbs. They covered the rooftops and backs of their lean-tos with spruce boughs. They also placed thick layers of the spruce and pine needles on the ground beneath their bedrolls for more comfortable sleeping. It took less than two hours for them to have their gear secured and their sleeping quarters weatherproofed.

"This wood is wet," complained Bat. "Keeping our fires going will be difficult."

"I do not know what we can do about it," Will responded. "It has been raining for days. We shall just have to do our best to contend with the conditions. Tomorrow, we can spread our fuel out in the sunshine to dry throughout the daylight hours."

"There are ample chips in the field," Austin announced. "They have been drying in the sun all day. Would not they be better fuel for our fires?"

"Well, by God, he's right!" Bat declared happily. "Cow chips would burn nice and clean. Why don't you boys go and gather us a couple of arm-loads?"

"I did not volunteer to collect them," Austin protested. "I was only suggesting."

"Surely, you do not expect us to go and pick up the shite," his father scolded him. "We are entirely too old to be doing all of that bending. It was your idea, and a fine one, at that. Now, you young fellows get up off your arses and go get us some chips!"

"You do not think the men in the fort will open fire on us, do you?" Drury asked, obviously worried.

"I sincerely doubt anyone will open fire on you lads picking up dried manure," Will reassured him. "You and Austin can take my canvas tarp and use it to collect the chips. Wear your muskets on your backs, but do not even give the appearance of being hostile. We don't want to start a war over manure. Do you understand?"

"Yes, Father," Austin promised.

"Yes, sir," Drury agreed.

Will nodded triumphantly. "Go, then. Bring back a nice, big load. If it works well, we shall send you out for some more." He glanced over their barricade at the field. "We need to accumulate a good supply before anyone else gets the same idea."

AUSTIN LEANED over and grabbed two large, flat, dry cow chips. He deposited them on the collection tarp. He complained, "This is not very glorious duty, is it?"

Drury grunted. "Picking up shite is definitely not what I foresaw as part of my service to the King. I hope this is not a harbinger of things to come."

"I shovel enough shite at home," Austin griped. "Picking up chips out here in the wide open, in full view of both armies ... it's just not dignified! We are likely being laughed at from both directions."

"Oh, I don't know," Drury countered. He pointed. "Look. There are more men out in the field to the west."

Austin looked in that direction. Sure enough, almost a dozen men were feverishly collecting dried chips from the expansive pasture.

"I reckon I do not feel so bad, after all," Austin mumbled. "But, I am still not happy about it."

Suddenly, they heard a voice call from the direction of the rebel fort. "Austin! Drury!"

Both young men stopped immediately and peered toward the sound of the voice. They saw a figure silhouetted over the top of one of the walls. The individual was waving both arms excitedly at them.

"Who is that?" Drury wondered out loud.

Then, the call came again, "Austin! Drury! It's me! Daniel!"

Austin's face erupted into a huge grin. "By God, that is Daniel Dansby!"

"No!" Drury objected. "Surely it is not."

"Yes, it is! Look! He is coming out to us."

Sure enough, the fellow who was calling them leapt over the top of the palisade wall. Another young man followed closely behind. Both of them ambled toward Austin and Drury. Soon, they could see Daniel's face. He was grinning from ear to ear. Neither of the approaching men carried a rifle or musket. However, Daniel had a pistol tucked into his waist belt.

"I thought that was you fellows!" Daniel exclaimed. He broke into a trot and ran, happily, into the embrace of his pals. The three young men hugged and celebrated as if they had been separated for ages, yet they had only been apart for a little more than a week.

"I never even considered that you might be here," Austin proclaimed, grinning.

"I have been encamped here at Ninety-Six for most of the week. It has been horrible duty ... cutting down trees and doing construction in the pouring-down rain. I should have kept my arse at home."

"Who is your friend?" Drury inquired.

"This is Eli Fowler, from Camden. Eli, these are two of my very best mates ... Drury Austin and Austin Newman."

The young men all shook hands.

Eli had an amused look on his face. "One fellow with Austin for a given name and another with Austin for a surname? There must be an interesting story behind that set of circumstances!"

Austin grinned and rolled his eyes. "It has been a source of confusion in my life for as long as I can remember." He patted Drury on the back. "You see, our fathers have been best friends for a few decades. So, as the first son of William Newman, I was blessed with the given name of Austin."

"It truly is as simple as that," affirmed Drury.

"It is good to meet you both," Eli declared.

"You, as well," affirmed Austin. He turned to Daniel. "I hope you boys will not get into any trouble for coming out here."

Daniel shook his head. "Not to worry. Captain Allison said it was fine. I told him it was only you fellows. No one is doing any shooting, so he saw no harm in us coming out for a visit."

"Thank God, no one is shooting," Drury declared.

Daniel looked over the shoulders of his friends. "There's a hell of a lot of King George's men over there."

Austin raised his eyebrows as he nodded. "Too many to tangle with. You fellows had best go home."

Eli frowned. "I do not think our colonel has any plans to leave. He seems pretty hell-bent on holding this fort."

"Surely, no one really wants a fight," Drury declared optimistically. "I know our commanders do not. They just want you gents to leave Ninety-Six in peace, forget about that load of lead and powder we captured, and then we can all go back home."

"What lead and powder?" asked Daniel.

Austin stared coolly at his friend. "One of our militia companies intercepted a wagon train of lead and gunpowder sent out from Charlestown."

"Headed where?" asked Daniel.

Drury answered, "To the Cherokee. They were attempting to stir them into attacking along the frontier."

"Horse shite!" growled Eli.

"It is true," Austin assured him. "The Indian agent in charge of the wagon train swore a document, before a magistrate, to that effect."

"There *must* be some kind of misunderstanding," Daniel declared hopefully.

Drury shook his head. "No. It was, most assuredly, a provocation." He wiggled his thumb over his shoulder. "Why do you think almost 2,000 men are surrounding you now? We want to keep you Whigs from getting the munitions back and sending them on to the Cherokee."

Daniel wagged his head in disbelief. "I simply cannot believe that our government has done such a thing. Ours is a just cause. We certainly have no desire to stand beside the Indians. I assure you, someone has made a mistake."

"Well, if it was a mistake, then these two armies encamped, facing off, and preparing to kill one another is a crying-arse shame," Drury answered curtly.

Austin sought to diffuse the tension between the friends. "Let us just hope that our officers can get this whole mess straightened out so that we might all return home safely."

Daniel smiled warmly and reached out to shake hands with his friend once more. "That sounds good to me."

Eli, staring past Drury and Austin, suddenly gave Daniel a swift elbow in his side. "Uh-oh. This does not look good. This gentleman appears less than pleased."

Drury and Austin turned and quickly spied Captain James Phillips approaching them. He seemed to be very angry. Seconds later, he arrived beside the cluster of young men.

"What is the meaning of this gathering, Mr. Newman?"

"I ... uh ... I do not understand your question, sir," Austin stammered.

"Why are you and Mr. Austin conferring with these two enemy soldiers? No one has given you leave to initiate a parley. You have no authority to represent our army."

"This is no parley, Captain," Drury assured him. "And we are not trying to represent the army. We are just talking. This here is Daniel Dansby, our friend and neighbor from Jackson's Creek."

The captain nodded curtly to Daniel. "Yes, I know who Mr. Dansby is, and am quite familiar with his lawless, rebel father."

Daniel wagged his finger at the captain. "Now, you just wait one damned minute! I'll not allow you to insult my father, Mr. Phillips."

"Oh, really?" the captain responded sarcastically. "What, exactly, are you going to do about it?"

Daniel looked down at the ground near his feet. He attempted to compose himself. He finally looked up and smiled at the officer. "Nothing, sir. I will do nothing today. I will offer no insult or reproach in response to your own. My father has taught me to act with more respect and dignity than a King's boot-licker."

Suddenly and swiftly, the captain whipped his pistol from his waist belt and pointed it at Daniel's head. He instantly pulled back the hammer on his flintlock. His hand was trembling. Beads of sweat erupted on his brow and upper lip. Shouts of alarm immediately erupted within the Whig fort. Soldiers began to deploy along the walls. Dozens of guns were aimed in their direction. The Loyalist militiamen sounded the alarm, as well, and began to take up positions behind their defenses.

"Captain Phillips!" Austin pleaded. "Calm down, sir. There is no need for violence. Daniel was just teasing ... and we were just talking. But, I can see now that this was not an appropriate thing for us to do. Let us simply part ways and avoid an unpleasant incident." He glanced at his Whig friend. "Daniel, you and Eli had best go on back to your fort. Now."

Daniel nodded subtly. The two young men turned to head back toward their compatriots.

"Wait!" exclaimed the captain. "I have not given anyone leave to depart this field." He paused. He eyed all four of the young men nervously. Finally, he gave a somewhat timid order. "Private Austin, I want you and Private Newman to relieve these two men of their weapons. They are now our prisoners."

"You are not serious," Drury declared.

The captain's chest swelled. "Excuse me, Private? My ears must be deceiving me. Surely, you have not questioned my order."

"Captain!" Austin pleaded. "There is no need to do this ... no need, at all. Daniel just came over to talk to us. Everyone could see that that this was a friendly gathering. Besides, our armies are not fighting. There is no need to take such a drastic action. It may cause more trouble." He paused. "It could even cause bloodshed."

"As your captain, I will be the judge of what actions are and are not appropriate! Now, do as I have ordered, damn you, or I will have both of you brought up on charges."

"Are you trying to start a war?" Austin challenged the officer loudly. "Because you are about to get us all killed."

The captain seethed. He appeared as if he might actually aim his pistol at Austin. "Private Newman, I will deal with your insolence when we return to our lines. Now, take their guns!"

Austin turned to the dumbfounded young men. "I am sorry, lads. I have no choice. I need your guns." He nodded to Drury. "Go and get the chips. I will take care of this mess."

"You sure?" Drury asked solemnly.

"Just go!" Austin barked angrily.

Drury ignored his friend's emotional reaction. He, too, was frustrated with the headstrong captain and understood why Austin was short-tempered. He turned and trotted toward the tarp full of dried manure, happy to depart the unpleasant situation.

Eli held his hands out to his side. "I am not armed."

Austin nodded. He lifted the lapels of the lad's coat and inspected beneath to ensure that he had no pistols. He then turned to his friend and held out his hand. "Daniel, I need you to dump the powder from your pan and give me the pistol."

Daniel exhaled in disgust. He glared at the captain with a gaze of burning hate. "This is horse shite and you know it, Austin."

"Yes, I know. But, right now I must follow orders. We can sort this all out when we get back over to our lines."

"Cease the chatter! Hurry it up!" barked the captain.

Daniel angrily whipped the pistol from his belt. He flipped the frizzen upward and then smacked the weapon against the palm of his other hand, emptying his priming powder onto the ground. He reluctantly surrendered the weapon to Austin.

"That is Papa's pistol. I will need that back when all this is done."

Austin nodded and then tucked the barrel of the gun into his waist belt.

"Hands up, gentleman," the captain commanded. "Lead the way. No tricks, if you please."

The two young men marched silently toward the Loyalist lines. Austin and his captain followed closely behind. Austin glanced to his left to check on Drury. He was dragging the heavy chip-filled cloth back to their camp. He was almost to the log barricades.

Suddenly, there was a dull thump as the ground erupted next to Captain James' feet. A half-second later, the report of a flintlock echoed from the fort behind them. Immediately, lead began to slam into the ground all around their feet as the rebel soldiers opened fire. Multiple booms erupted from the direction of the fort. The enemy began to fire in earnest. Lead rained down on the field. One ball came amazing close to Captain Phillips' head, clipping one side of his cocked hat and sending it flying into the air.

"Run!" the captain ordered. "The enemy has opened fire! Get back to the line!"

"How perceptive of you," Austin growled sarcastically.

Austin, Captain James, and their two prisoners broke into a sprint. In front of them there were muzzle flashes and clouds of white smoke. The Loyalists were returning fire toward the fort. Lead whizzed all around them from both directions. They continued to run through the barrage of gunfire. Thirty seconds later, they jumped over the nearest log barricade. Austin landed haphazardly on the ground beside his father. Will Newman fired his musket through a small hole in the log wall. He pulled his barrel out of the hole and rolled over onto his back. He stared angrily at his son.

He demanded, "Boy, what have you done?"

Austin shrugged, wide-eyed. "I reckon I have accidentally started the damned war."

9

STANDOFF AT NINETY-SIX

Late Evening- Sunday, November 19, 1775
Loyalist Siege Line – Ninety-Six, South Carolina

The November night air had turned raw and frigid. The wet ground magnified the cold that assaulted the Loyalist soldiers besieging Colonel Williamson's rebel fort. The men from Jackson's Creek sought refuge from the autumn chill by huddling near their large, cheerful, warming campfire. They also kept warm by sharing an unusually large and strong bottle of whiskey, courtesy of Bat Austin.

Austin Newman had already enjoyed a few swigs from the bottle and was feeling a bit light-headed. He sat in silent contemplation as he poked his finger through a large hole in the hem of his blue linen great coat.

Will Newman eyed his son curiously. "What did you do, Austin? Did you tear your coat? If so, Lizzy can repair it when we return home."

Austin shook his head. "No, sir. A rebel ball clipped me when I was making my run back to the line."

"Sincerely?" his father answered in disbelief. He rose and walked over to Austin and then knelt down to examine the damage to his coat. "I did not know that any of the enemy bullets came so dangerously close to you."

Austin nodded. He continued fingering the hole. There was a drunken look of disbelief and awe in his eyes. "The shots were landing all around us, Papa. Some of them chewed the ground around my feet. Captain Phillips had his hat blown off of his head. But, I did not realize that I had come so close to being hit until just now." He held up his coat for all to see. "That is how close I came to mortal injury, lads. It was no more than two or three inches from my thigh."

His father nodded and patted him reassuringly on the knee. "That was very close, Son. Still, you were not hit. You should count your blessings."

"Indeed. One inch is as good as a mile in a firefight," Bat Austin declared optimistically. "You were lucky this day, my boy. But, I would not recommend pressing that luck any time soon."

"I have no intention of doing so," Austin promised, releasing the coat and allowing it to dangle at his side. He received the bottle from Drury and took quick gulp before passing it along. He winced as the fiery liquid scorched his throat, then declared earnestly, "I plan to stay in camp and behind good cover for the duration of this siege."

Bat nodded and smiled. "As do we all! They are going to have to drag me out from behind these logs!" He pointed in the general direction of the enemy. "Those rebels over yonder likely cannot hit a bull in the arse with a bass fiddle, but I do not wish to give them any opportunity to try!"

The men around the campfire laughed at the slightly-slurred words of their slightly inebriated friend.

"Did Daniel or his compatriot suffer any injuries?" Will asked his son.

"Eli looked a wee bit hobbled when I saw him escorted away with the captain. I think he hurt his ankle when he came over the wall. But, I do not believe it was serious. The only thing wounded about Daniel was his pride." Austin peered in the direction of the courthouse, roughly a half-mile to their west. He could see candle and lamp light emanating from the windows of the stone building. "I sure hope those fellows are all right. The stunt that Captain Phillips pulled out there today was just ungentlemanly and unacceptable."

"I am sure they are fine," his father promised. "At least they get to sleep with a roof over their heads this night."

"It almost makes it worth going to jail!" joked Drury.

Bat shook his head. "Not really. I would hate to be surrounded by those cold stone walls on a night such as this. Out here, at least, we can have a warm fire and soft boughs beneath us."

The other fellows grunted and nodded. Their comfortable lean-tos and ample blankets would be much-preferred to the cold stone floor of the Ninety-Six courthouse gaol.

Will returned to his seat. He paused and sighed contemplatively. "Austin, I do not wish you to think badly of Mr. Phillips. He was just doing what he thought was the right thing to do ... what he considered his duty."

Austin shook his head and displayed a doubtful expression. "Are you sure that he was not just trying to be noticed by the major?"

"That could, indeed, be the case," his father acknowledged. "It would not be the first time that an officer attempted to conjure up some glory for himself, nor will it be the last. But, he is still your captain. You need to remember that. You must not disrespect him or undermine his authority in the field." He paused and cut his eyes at his son. "He informed me of some of the inappropriate things that you said to him out there today."

"Well, he *was* acting like a total arse," Drury testified on Austin's behalf. "Something needed to be said."

"He had it coming," Austin added confidently.

"Perhaps so, but not from either of you. You are not back home, and this is not a game. This is a military operation. Right now, you are a soldier in the King's army and you serve under Captain Phillips' command. He has the authority to charge you with mutiny, if he so desires. Did either of you know that? He could see you convicted and hanged for the offense."

Austin seemed dazed. He gulped slowly. "No, sir. I did not know that."

"Did you consider such a possibility, Drury?" Will demanded.

"No, sir. I did not."

"Well, then, now both of you know. Out here, he is not just one of the Phillips brothers. He is not simply a friend and neighbor and fellow churchman. He is our captain, and from now on you will address and regard him with the honor that he is due. Do you young men understand me?"

Austin drew in a deep breath. "Yes, Father."

Drury did not offer a verbal response. Instead, he simply nodded.

"Very well. I will report to the captain that we have discussed, at length, the unfortunate events of this day. In return, he has promised that he will consider the matter closed. Does that satisfy you both?"

Austin and Drury nodded contritely.

"Good," Will declared. "Then I will consider the matter closed, as well."

The campsite descended into an uncomfortable silence.

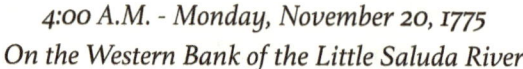

4:00 A.M. - Monday, November 20, 1775
On the Western Bank of the Little Saluda River

JOHN AUSTIN HAD BEEN RIDING HARD since the previous afternoon, with only occasional breaks to rest and water his horse. He was on a desperate mission. He had to locate the Loyalist army and inform its commander of the imposing Whig force that had invaded from the east.

Unfortunately for John, finding the King's army was proving to be a very difficult task. He checked first at the original encampment site on Nineteen-Mile Creek. That location was, of course, abandoned. But, just before dark, a local farmer informed him of the army's general direction. They were headed southwest toward Londonderry and following the main highway through the backcountry. John pressed on in pursuit. Two hours later, he stopped to satisfy his ravenous hunger at a rather shabby tavern in a tiny roadside hamlet. In the midst of devouring a lukewarm, mediocre supper and three pints of tepid ale, he accidentally discovered the destination of his comrades. He overheard a group of drunken men at a nearby table discussing the Tory army that had recently passed through their town. They revealed that the army was headed to the village of Ninety-Six.

Immediately after his supper, John cut cross-country in an effort to reach the remote western village more quickly. The overland route, however, proved quite treacherous. He had to cross several small creeks and ditches in the pitch-black darkness. The Little Saluda River, his biggest obstacle by far, was swollen by recent rains. After falling from his horse and receiving a thorough soaking while crossing the swiftly-flowing river, he finally decided to stop on the western bank, build a fire, dry his wet clothes, and get some much-needed sleep. With another four to six hours of travel remaining, he desperately needed the rest. His body had not yet fully recovered from the ailment that had recently assaulted his stomach and bowels. Despite being a strong and fit young man, he was still not in his best physical form.

So, John slept the deep sleep of exhaustion. He dozed for almost three hours, wearing only a dry linen shirt and wrapped in a warm cocoon of three heavy wool blankets. The shirt and blankets had been protected from the river by his waterproof goatskin bag, an item that his mother had insisted that he take along on the journey. As he slept, his once-vibrant campfire burned down to a barely-glowing, orange-red pile of ash-coated embers. His campsite grew cold and silent, as did the world around him.

In the middle of the night, a single, dull snap snatched him from his deep sleep. Startled by the unnatural sound, John attempted to sit up, but the blankets encapsulating his body bound him. Frustrated, he kicked against the heavy cloth and finally rolled over onto his back. At the exact moment that he freed himself from his blanket cocoon, he heard a metallic, high-pitched click. It was the unmistakable sound of a flintlock being cocked. He instinctively reached for his musket.

A harsh voice growled from the nearby trees. "Do not move! Stay where you are, or I will shoot! Slowly now ... put your hands up where I can see them."

John complied. He had no choice. He peered in the direction of the mysterious voice, but there was no light. The darkness of the moonless night was impenetrable. He begged, "I mean you no harm, sir. I only stopped here for some rest. I have been riding for many hours. My horse has given out, as well as myself."

A lone man stepped slowly from the cover of the trees. He appeared only as a shadow. He had his musket aimed at John.

"You are camping on my land, young fellow."

"I apologize, kind sir." John explained, "I had no knowledge of where I was. I fell in the water when I crossed the river a few hours ago and I had to build a fire and get warm. I simply camped in the first clean, dry spot that I could find."

The man stepped closer and kept his musket aimed squarely at the trespasser's chest. John's heart pounded thunderously. His mind raced. Should he reveal himself and the nature of his mission? If the musket-wielding man was a Whig, he might shoot John as a spy. Still, on the other hand, if he was a Loyalist, he could be a helpful ally. John decided to remain quiet about the reason for his travels and allow the situation to play itself out. He would let the mysterious man with the gun guide the conversation ... for now.

"Might I add some fuel to my fire?" John pleaded. "It is quite cold, and we could use more light. I do not know about you, but I prefer to see the person to whom I am speaking."

"I reckon that would be all right." The fellow waved the barrel of his musket toward John's small wood pile. "But, do not make any sudden moves. I know you have a gun hidden over there. Just leave it be."

"Yes, sir."

John reached over and grabbed a couple of handfuls of pine needles. He tossed them onto the bed of coals. The tinder quickly ignited, illuminating the clearing in bright yellow light. John added several small sticks and then topped off the fire with two large, dry limbs. The area was soon bathed in warm, dancing firelight.

The man took another step forward. At last, John could see his face. He was a plump, middle-aged chap and appeared to be quite ordinary. His cheeks were red and his eyes appeared hollow and tired. John imagined that he had been unwillingly roused from his sleep. Clearly, the man was inspecting and evaluating John. So, in an effort to make himself look as harmless as possible, John rubbed his hands together near the fire and flashed a huge, disarming smile.

John quipped. "I am grateful that you did not shoot first before introducing yourself. My mother would be most disappointed."

The man hesitated for a moment, and then responded with a somewhat reluctant grin. Seeing that the young fellow before him was dressed only in a nightshirt and clearly unarmed, he slowly lowered his weapon. He did, however, keep it pointed in John's general direction.

The gun-wielding man explained, "My wife, God love the woman, awakened me from a dead sleep. She was blabbering incessantly about a strange light down by the creek. I assumed you to be either lost or a traveler. I was not going to come here at all, but my wife would not give me peace until I put on my breeches and walked down to investigate."

"She sounds just like my mother," John declared honestly. Indeed, he could easily imagine his mother dispatching his father on a similar fact-finding errand if she spotted an unauthorized campfire on their land.

"Well ... I reckon the woman was right. She usually is, though I would never admit that to her face." He smiled mischievously. "As a landowner, I must remain vigilant at all times. One cannot be too careful these days. Recently, there have been Tories all over the backcountry. They have been murdering, robbing, stealing and making all manner of mischief."

John's heart sank. This man was a Whig. He would have to weigh his words carefully and remain discreet in his dealings with the stranger. He certainly could not divulge the true nature of his mission. He needed to think up a lie of some sorts ... something simple, sensible, and believable.

The landowner demanded, "What is your name, boy?"

"John Austin. And yours, sir?"

"Calvin Webster. Where are you from, John Austin?"

"I live on Jackson's Creek, southwest of Winnsborough."

The man's eyes narrowed. "You are a far piece from home, aren't you?"

"Yes, sir."

"So, tell me ... where are you going, John Austin, and why are you so far from the nearest road? Are you lost?"

John's pulse increased. He had to think quickly.

"Well, I suppose I am truly lost. I have been at the village of Ninety-Six for the past two weeks taking care of my father's business. I received a message yesterday that my mother has taken ill and began my return journey immediately. I thought that I might save some travel time by getting off the highway. But, I fear that has been a dismal decision on my part. I have suffered one setback and difficulty after another. My plan now is to head south and back to the highway at first light."

The man nodded. "I think that would be wise. You know, there is a reason why the roads are placed where they are. They always follow the easiest route according to the lay of the land."

John nodded. "Indeed. My father has taught me the same thing. But, I suppose I thought that I knew better. It took this night and a few swollen creeks and muddy ditches for me to learn my lesson and to understand how wise my old Papa truly is." He shook his head in mock disgust. "It has been a costly lesson, indeed, both in time and in comfort."

The fellow grinned. "Is that not always the way it is between fathers and sons? We try to teach you wisdom earned from our time-proven life experiences, but you youngsters always insist upon learning the hard way." He chuckled lightly. "What manner of business do you and your father operate?"

"Papa is a farmer, as most men are at Jackson's Creek. But, we have a barn lot full of hogs to sell ... two dozen of them, in fact. Papa wants to rid himself of them before the cold sets in. There are already far too many hogs roaming our woods in the winter. I was representing him and following up with a prospective buyer at Ninety-Six." He chuckled. "Papa is getting along in the years and does not like to venture far from his own bed. So, any business travel usually falls to me."

John cursed himself in his mind. His lie was getting a bit too elaborate. He was creating far too many details to recall with any measure of accuracy. Amazingly, however, the fellow smiled warmly and nodded. He seemed satisfied with John's explanation. He released the hammer on his musket from its cocked position and then inserted his arm through the leather sling, allowing the weapon to dangle loosely over his right shoulder. The caution was gone from his eyes. His formerly suspicious scowl had been replaced by a friendly smile.

"Very well, then. I wish you safety in your travels, John Austin. I shall now return to my house and make the report to my wife that all is well down here on the banks of the Little Saluda."

John exhaled silently in relief. "Thank you, sir."

The fellow tipped his straw hat. "Until we meet again."

John offered a friendly wave. "Yes, sir. Until we meet again."

The farmer turned and began to walk back toward the woods. He took only three steps and then stopped suddenly. He hesitated for a moment, but did not turn around.

He declared questioningly, "You said that you have traveled to Ninety-Six?"

"Yes, sir," John answered nervously.

The man turned around slowly. "But, when I first woke you, you informed me that you fell in when you crossed the river. Now ... if you were coming from Ninety-Six, would you not be encamped on the far bank?"

John's face flushed red. He was livid at his own stupidity. It was a silly, stupid mistake. He searched his mind for a plausible explanation to right his error.

"No, sir ... I said I fell in when I *tried* to cross the river. The water was too high and fast for me. I did not make it across."

The man's face clouded in suspicion. His eyes narrowed. "No, that's not what you said, at all." His voice deepened. "Why would you lie to me, boy?"

"I did not lie to you, sir. I assure you," John protested, waving his hands in front of him.

"Yes, you did! You lied to me!" The man chewed his lip nervously as he stared at John. He searched his mind for the details of their conversation. Suddenly, he declared, "You said that you are from Jackson's Creek! That area is a hotbed of Loyalists! You are one of King George's men, aren't you? You are a soldier in the Royal Militia, no doubt! Good God! Only yesterday, I heard they were headed to Ninety-Six!"

The man suddenly snatched his weapon from his shoulder. For the briefest of moments, his hands became caught in his leather sling. Finally extricating his hands, he reached awkwardly for the hammer on his musket and cocked it once again. The man swung the barrel in John's direction. John rolled to his right to grab his own musket from beneath his pile of clothing and equipment. As John knelt beside his gear and fumbled for his gun, the man excitedly yanked his trigger and fired. Fortunately for John, he had neither brought his weapon all the way to his shoulder nor aimed it properly. The ball slammed harmlessly into the ground beside John's knee, unleashing a spray of stinging dirt and sand into his chest and chin. The fellow's eyes grew wide with terror when he realized that his shot had gone astray. He immediately began to search for a cartridge in his belt pouch, but his exceedingly large belly got in the way.

John knew full-well that the man intended to kill him. He had no choice but to defend himself. His hands trembled as he cocked his musket, took aim, and fired. But, unlike the frightened farmer, John did not miss. He heard a hollow thump as the .75-caliber ball from his Brown Bess slammed into the man's sternum, dead center of his chest. The lead expanded upon impact and chewed its way through soft organs and hard bone and then exploded through the muscle and skin of his back, unleashing a cloud of bloody mist and shredded tissue. The man's spinal column was shattered. The central nerve that commanded all motion and feeling throughout his body was severed.

The impact of the lead against flesh and bone knocked the man off of his feet. His numb, non-functioning hands released his still-smoking musket as he tumbled backward. He landed awkwardly on his back with a huge thud. His lifeblood drained out of him quickly, filling his throat, mouth, and lungs, and soaking the ground around him. He was dead in a matter of seconds.

John's mind reeled. He was almost outside himself in disbelief. He had just taken a man's life in combat. Dozens of questions, worries, and terrors filled his mind. What was he going to do now? How could he cope with this horrific event? What should he do with the body? He attempted to slow his breathing, clear his mind, and compose himself. He scanned his campsite and quickly formulated a plan.

First, he re-dressed, donning his stockings, breeches, weskit, shoes, and coat. He quickly collected his other belongings and then loaded his baggage onto his horse. He claimed his enemy's musket and tied it, as well, to his saddle, along with the dead man's shooting bag, belt, and belly pouch. Finally, once all of his personal gear was packed and loaded for travel, John dragged the lifeless body to the river's edge. He prayed a brief prayer for the man's soul and then unceremoniously rolled his body into the swiftly-flowing current.

Before departing, John inspected the area once more. He covered the huge pool of blood with pine needles, limbs, and sticks. He kicked dirt onto his campfire to extinguish the flames. Once the campsite was disguised and secure, he numbly mounted his horse. He pointed the animal toward the west, kicked it smartly in its haunches, and then rode swiftly toward Ninety-Six. As he rode, he replayed the incident over and over again in his mind. The face of the dead man filled his thoughts. His recent struggle between life and death overwhelmed his spirit. He clung tightly to his galloping horse and wept.

～

Mid-Morning – Monday, November 20, 1775
Loyalist Line at Ninety-Six, South Carolina

FINALLY, there was a temporary lull in the shooting. The fighting had been fierce since daybreak, with both sides exchanging hundreds of gunshots. Thankfully, despite the volume of powder and lead expended, there had been relatively few casualties. The distance between the two forces was simply too great for either side to aim and fire with effect. During the brief pause in combat, the eyes of every man on the battlefield focused upon a handful of swiftly-running Tories with torches in the open area between the fort and the siege lines. Those men stopped, on occasion, and touched their torches to the tall grasses surrounding the Whig fort. Will Newman and the other men from Jackson's Creek observed the strange activity between the cracks in their log barricades.

"What, exactly, are those fellows doing?" Will asked his captain.

Captain Phillips explained, "They are going to attempt to set the grass and fences on fire. The major hopes that, if we can get several fires started in yonder field, the ensuing smoke will provide cover for an attack upon Colonel Williamson's fort."

Bat cut his eyes nervously at the captain. "Major Robinson wants us to take that fort?" he clarified, obviously concerned.

The captain nodded. "Yes. That is his plan."

"Let me be certain of what you are saying. He wants the militia to storm the fort ... conduct an all-out assault?" Bat queried, his voice cracking in disbelief.

Captain Phillips hesitated. "In a manner of speaking. There will, however, be a rather unique strategy employed in the attack."

"Go on," Will urged.

The captain explained, "John Williams, a rather clever fellow from Camden, has supervised the construction of a mantlet. We will use that device when we press the assault."

"What is a mantlet?" inquired Drury, suddenly interested in the conversation.

"It is a rolling barricade, an ancient strategy from medieval times. The mantlet is a wheeled shield constructed of thick logs. Our men will conceal themselves behind this shield as they propel it forward. It will give them cover from the enemy's fire until they can approach close enough to toss incendiaries onto the enemy's defenses."

Bat appeared to grasp the idea in his mind. "So, men are going to hide behind a rolling wall, go right up to the fort, and then throw fireballs onto the walls? Is that the general notion?"

"Exactly. With any luck, at all, the burning of the fort will do the rebels in. Surely, they would prefer surrender rather than fighting a battle with no good cover for their defense." He paused. "We also believe they are quite low on water."

"How could you possibly know that?" challenged Will.

The captain cut a taunting glance at Austin, who had remained silent throughout the entire exchange. "We gleaned this important information from our prisoners. As it turns out, it was indeed a wise course of action to capture those two young men on the battlefield." He turned his attention back to Bat and Will. "Young Mr. Dansby has refused to talk, of course, but the lad from Camden revealed that they had no source of water inside the fort. They began digging a well yesterday morning, but, as far as he knew, they have not yet found water. So, time and a shortage of water may be very much on our side."

"Then, why the hell have we been doing all of this shooting?" demanded Bat. "We should not be wasting all of these munitions."

The captain shrugged. "We are shooting to unnerve them ... and because we have plenty of powder and lead to burn. Do not forget that we relieved the rebels of an entire wagon train of munitions. They, on the other hand, have precious little powder. It is a distinct possibility that they may run out of ammunition and have no other choice but to surrender." He paused and peered toward the enemy's fort. "But, in either instance, we must take direct action in order to force their hand."

"Why the rush?" Bat challenged. "If time is on our side, as you say, why do we not simply maintain the siege and force them to come to us for terms? Surely, when they run out of food, water, and powder they will be at our mercy."

"Major Robinson wishes to achieve a more decisive military victory. Utilizing the mantlet could prove a brilliant combat strategy and provide us with an opportunity to dominate this battlefield. It would be a great victory, indeed, if we could manage to actually capture the biggest rebel army in the backcountry."

Will leaned forward and peered through his peep-hole in the wall. He studied the frenzied activity of the torch-bearers. The enemy had begun taking potshots at them, so they were all moving a bit faster than before. "Well, it does not appear that our bullet-dodging, fire-starting brigade is having much success," he declared sarcastically. "I see no flames, and scant little smoke."

The captain glanced through a crack between two logs and grimaced. He groaned in frustration. "It is as I suspected. Everything remains too wet from the recent rains. It appears that this phase of the attack has been a failure, indeed."

Suddenly, Bat pointed toward their right and shouted, "Damnation! Would you look at that!"

One hundred yards to their right, an odd-looking contraption crept out onto the battlefield. It was comprised of a semi-circular wall constructed from upright saplings. It measured roughly twelve feet in width and about six feet in height. There was a sturdy wagon wheel mounted to each side.

"That is the mantlet," Captain Phillips confirmed.

Six men took cover behind the portable wall. Four of them appeared to be propelling the mantlet forward. The other two held bottles and grenades. The shooting from the inside fort increased in tempo and ferocity. The men could see splinters and shards of wood exploding from the logs on the front of the vehicle.

"They are chewing up that lumber pretty good," Bat observed. "I do not know how long that thing will be able to take such concentrated fire."

"It will hold," the captain declared optimistically. "You will see." He glanced up and down the line. "I suppose we should offer some suppressing fire. Perhaps we can reduce the damage to the vehicle. Let us give them a taste, shall we?"

Will looked at Bat and shrugged. "I reckon we can waste some more powder."

Bat groaned, "We might as well."

The men began to shoot at the fort. Of course, being almost a hundred and fifty yards away, their gunfire was neither accurate nor effective. They actually had to aim high and attempt to lob their shots onto the enemy's position. Still, they provided some much-needed covering fire for their comrades. Men up and down the line soon followed their example. It appeared to have the desired effect. Fewer shots were impacting the mantlet.

The strange-looking contraption continued to inch its way across the field. It took quite some time, but it finally approached to within fifty yards of the wall. If they could progress another twenty to thirty yards, the hurlers would have the opportunity to drop fuel and fire onto the wood of the fort.

Suddenly, a horrific boom echoed across the field. The concussion of the explosion shook the ground. The Jackson's Creek men stopped firing and peered in the direction of the loud report. A huge cloud of billowing smoke hovered in front of the enemy's fort.

"What the hell was that?" Will exclaimed, rubbing his left ear.

"Damn! That was one of the swivel guns," Captain Phillips answered dejectedly. "And look … it has damaged the mantlet."

The heads of all the men spun, once again, in the direction of the rolling barricade. The left wagon wheel was tilted slightly and the outermost log on the left side appeared shredded.

Moments later, another huge boom traversed the field. They saw the lead and steel fired from the tiny cannon impact the wood of the mantlet. It lifted the vehicle up slightly and then deposited it back onto the ground. This time, the damaged wheel was sheared completely away from the frame. All of the logs on the contraption appeared damaged and separated. Clearly, the mantlet was done. It would never move again … not in its present condition. Moments later, smoke began to belch from the back side of the immobile device.

"Our men must be setting the thing on fire!" Will exclaimed.

Captain Phillips sighed. "They do not want to leave it for the enemy to claim. It would appear that our assault has failed."

The men previously concealed behind the wall suddenly darted into the open, all of them running full-speed back toward their line. Muskets began to bark from inside the fort, attempting to drop the men as they ran. The Loyalist troops returned fire, once again providing cover for their comrades. It took an agonizingly long minute and a half for the attackers to reach safety. By that time, the mantlet was fully engulfed in flames.

Once again, the deadly swivel gun boomed, belching fire and grapeshot in the direction of the burning vehicle. The mantlet disintegrated in a mighty explosion of smoke, embers, and shattered wood. The upright saplings collapsed backward and the remaining undamaged wagon wheel tumbled lazily onto the pile of burning lumber. A mighty cheer and three loud "Huzzahs" erupted from inside the fort. The rebels screamed and celebrated and waved their hats in jubilant triumph.

Will turned, quite disgusted, and peered into the eyes of his captain. "Well, so much for that. I reckon Major Robinson forgot about those little cannons, huh?"

Captain Phillips sighed and rolled his eyes in frustration. "As did we all, I am afraid."

&

4:00 PM – Monday, November 20, 1775
Ninety-Six, South Carolina

JOHN'S HEART leapt with joy when he spotted the small village of Ninety-Six. After many long and grueling hours, he had finally reached his destination. As he neared the town, he spotted two militiamen standing near the roadway. They were sentries. The two men alerted quickly at John's presence. They both stepped into the center of the highway and held up their hands as a signal for John to halt. He eased his exhausted mount to a stop in front of their makeshift barricade.

One of the sentries, a middle-aged man, declared, "This area is under military control. There is a siege to the west. We cannot allow you to pass through the town."

"I do not intend to pass through the town," countered John. "I have an urgent message for Major Robinson."

The two sentries glanced at one another. Their eyes were filled with suspicion.

"Who are you?" asked the second fellow, a younger lad.

"I am John Austin of Jackson's Creek. My father and brother are here with the Loyalist militia under Captain James Phillips."

"So, you have come for a visit, then?" asked the older man.

"No, damn it! I just told you! I have an urgent message for the major! Now, please tell me where I might find him!"

The older gentleman considered John's request and then turned to his companion. "Davey, take this fellow to the courthouse. Stay with him and keep an eye on him until someone up there dismisses you. All right?"

The younger fellow nodded nervously. "Yes, Papa."

"That's a good boy. Now, off with ya, then." He glanced at John. "Just follow my son down to the courthouse. He will take you to the major."

John nodded and then tipped his hat. "I am most grateful to you, sir."

Young Davey ran down the highway toward the Tory headquarters. John urged his horse to a trot and followed the excited boy.

MAJOR JOSEPH ROBINSON, the Loyalist army commander, sighed deeply as he walked toward the door of his office in the front room of the courthouse. He paused for a moment and stared at the half-mile-distant Williamson's fort. He turned and looked searchingly at John Austin.

"You are certain of this? You are absolutely positive that there is another rebel army deployed in the backcountry?"

John was seated beside a small office side-table. Overwhelmed with thirst, he simply nodded as he took another huge gulp of ale. He quickly wiped his mouth on his sleeve so that he might address the major verbally. Before he could speak, a loud belch escaped his throat.

"Sorry, sir." His face flushed red from embarrassment.

The major waved his hand dismissively. "It is quite all right, son. Now, please ... elaborate. Tell me everything you know."

"Yes, sir. A scavenger party hit one of our neighbor's homes two days ago. They confiscated livestock for feeding their soldiers. The sergeant in charge revealed there was an army of over two thousand men encamped near the Wateree a few miles south of Camden. He said that Colonel Richard Richardson was in command."

"Two thousand!" the major echoed in disbelief. He scowled. "Richardson, you say? What the devil is that old bastard doing in the field in command of an army? He is seventy years of age if he is a day!"

"I do not know, sir. But, as soon as she understood what was happening, my mother sent me to find you and deliver this message. She thought it most important."

Major Robinson grinned. "Well, she was definitely right about that. Your mother may have just saved our ever-livin' arses." He walked over to John and patted him firmly on the shoulder. "You have done a fine job, young man. Tell me again, what is your name?"

"John Austin, son of Bartholomew, from Jackson's Creek."

The major nodded. "I am grateful to you, John. Now, tell me, do you need anything?"

"Just some food, sir. But, I figure I can eat when I get to my company. Hopefully, my father and brother will have some rations to spare."

The major nodded. "Very well, then. Go and join your father and friends."

"Thank you, sir."

John drained his mug of ale and then placed the empty vessel on the table. He rose to his feet, grabbed his hat from a peg beside the door, nodded to the major, and then departed the courthouse quickly.

~

Dusk – On the Loyalist Line

THE CELEBRATION over John's arrival had finally ended. The Austin and Newman men were now stoically silent. They listened intently as John shared his news regarding Richardson's huge army, as well as the account of his harrowing journey to Ninety-Six. He spared no detail, especially when it came to his deadly shootout with the rebel farmer. John's voice broke as he told about rolling the man's lifeless body into the river. He appeared on the verge of tears.

"You did what you had to do, John. There was no wrong or shame in it," Bat reassured his son. "It was either his life or yours. You defended yourself. You were brave, indeed. I could not be prouder." He wrapped his right arm around John and squeezed him in a manly hug.

"I know that I had to do it, Papa. But, I simply cannot believe that I have killed a man. I see his face in my mind all the time." He stared blankly into the campfire. "I fear that I shall always see his face. He will forever haunt me."

"The faces of the dead never leave us, John," Will confirmed. "As much as I want to remember the happier times that I shared with my father, the one image that never escapes me is that of him drawing his final breath as I held him in my arms." He paused thoughtfully. "But, you do eventually move on. With time, the pain and horror of it becomes ... duller. And you will, someday, release yourself from the guilt."

"I hope so, Mr. Newman," John declared.

The group of men sat quietly around the campfire for a moment. It seemed that no one had anything else to say after Will's solemn, philosophical declaration. However, Drury Austin, ever the light-hearted prankster, was not about to allow the irony of the situation to go unnoticed.

He growled in disgust. "Well, let us not dance around the matter any longer. It must be said!" He glared at his younger brother. Jealousy filled his eyes. "I cannot believe what has happened! We have been in the field for over a week. We have shot a hundred pounds of powder and lead. We have been arse-deep in mud, dropping shite in a hole in the ground, growing mold on our bollocks, eating food that would make a goat puke, and little Johnny here is the first among us to actually best a man in battle!" He playfully tossed a stick at his brother's head. "It is not fair!"

There was an uncomfortable moment of silence as each man considered the inappropriate nature of Drury's teasing. But, when John's face broke out into a huge, toothy grin, all of the men burst forth in jolly laughter. Drury's banter was just the medicine that they needed to lighten the mood. For the next half-hour, the men joked, teased, and told stories. It was very good for the five of them to all be together once again.

Eventually, however, Austin stood and stretched. "I hate to abandon such good company, but I must visit one of those smelly holes about which Drury has so eloquently spoken. My evening constitutional calls."

"Be sure to burn a candle when you are done," chided Drury.

The men all chuckled at the young man's wit. As Austin turned to walk toward the latrine, he spotted movement in the field. There was a man walking from their line toward the besieged fort. He carried a one-candle wooden lantern and a white flag of parley.

"Look!" Austin exclaimed. "We have a man under white flag headed toward the enemy."

The fellows clamored to their feet and rushed toward the nearest log wall. They watched, mesmerized, as the man ambled slowly toward the enemy. Soon, another fellow emerged from a small gate on the near side of the fort. He, too, carried a white flag.

"Well, how about that!" Will declared. "It looks as if John's news has awakened a sudden urgency in our major to press for terms." He turned to his best friend. "What do you think, Bat?"

Bat's eyes narrowed as he observed the two men talking in the center of the battlefield. He drew in a deep, thoughtful breath. "I suspect that we will be leaving this place, and very soon. I doubt that Major Robinson has any desire to tangle with Colonel Richardson's imposing army."

Will stared solemnly at the two men and their white flags. "Do you think we are done?"

Bat chuckled lightly. "I will bet you a week's wages the major is about to declare some sort of victory and then send us all home." Bat cut his eyes at Will. His best friend nodded grimly in agreement.

10

OUR FIGHTING IS DONE

Monday Evening - November 27, 1775
Gathering of Loyalists - Jackson's Creek Meeting House

Captain James Phillips stood alongside his brothers, Robert and John. Together, the Phillips brothers presided over an emergency meeting of all the Loyalist men of Jackson's Creek. The looks on their faces were grim. The news that they had just shared was chilling. Colonel Richard Richardson and his rebel army were rounding up all men who remained opposed to independency from Great Britain, and they were, in all likelihood, coming for the Loyalists at Jackson's Creek.

"How many men does Colonel Richardson now command in the field?" inquired a stunned Bat Austin.

"Four thousand," responded Captain James Phillips tersely. "Richardson and his army are scattering throughout the backcountry, arresting all Loyalists and transporting suspected leaders in chains to Charlestown. They are squashing any and all resistance to their unlawful rebellion." He paused and then cut his eyes questioningly at his brothers.

John Phillips nodded grimly. He cleared his throat and took a single step forward. He stared forlornly at his friends and neighbors. His eyes were hollow and sad.

"There is something else that some of you men need to know. It is most disturbing, I am afraid. Somehow, Richardson has accumulated a list of all men of Jackson's Creek who took up arms at Ninety-Six. He carries warrants for your arrest."

The room erupted in shouting and frenzy. Men stood and waved their fists in anger. Some who had served at Ninety-Six appeared frightened and frantic.

"But, that makes no sense!" Will Newman objected over the din in the room. He stood. "Why is Colonel Richardson insisting upon pursuing *us*? We received terms at the end of the hostilities. All enemy reinforcements sent into the backcountry were bound by the conditions of our cease-fire." He stomped angrily. "We have that agreement in writing!"

The other men in the room shouted their obvious agreement with Will's proclamation. They were angry, desperate, and loud. The Phillips brothers waved their hands in an effort to calm the men and gain their attention.

"Gentlemen, please! Mr. Newman has posed a valid question that deserves an answer," Robert begged. He turned and addressed Will directly. "Apparently, the rebel Committee of Safety in Charlestown does not consider that agreement applicable to Richardson's army."

"And why the hell not?" Bat Austin demanded in frustration.

"Because, Mr. Austin, they were already in the field on November 2, a full three weeks before the cease-fire agreement," Robert explained. "It is their position that, since his army was not actually deployed to reinforce Williamson, then Colonel Richardson is not bound by the terms of Ninety-Six."

"So, they are claiming a technicality," Will barked angrily.

John Phillips nodded. "Indeed."

The room fell eerily silent as the forty men gathered at the church digested the unthinkable news. It was an inescapable truth. The Whigs were purging the backcountry of all men loyal to the King, and they were coming, specifically, after the Loyalists of Jackson's Creek.

"What, then, must we do?" asked Will Newman. He nodded to Captain Phillips. "James, you led us at Ninety-Six. What are your plans?"

The captain responded confidently, "I have decided that I will not remain here and allow myself to be arrested and hauled away to the gaol in Charlestown. Instead, I intend to make my way to Florida."

"Florida?" echoed several of the men, obviously dumbfounded by his declaration.

"Yes. East Florida, to be precise. Major Robinson is making his way there now. He has plans to organize a regiment of South Carolina Loyalists and then return at an appropriate time in the future to liberate our Colony from the grip of these rebels."

"When will you go?" asked one of the militiamen from the back of the room.

"I and all who will go with me depart at dawn tomorrow. We must not tarry. Raiders from Richardson's army could appear at any moment." He pointed toward a young man seated on the front row and invited him to stand. The fellow rose to his feet and faced the group. "Alexander Chesney, whom some of you know, has agreed to guide us to his father's estate in the north. We will take refuge there, acquire provisions and guides, and then travel west through the Cherokee and Creek lands. We will work our way around all rebel-controlled areas and eventually make our way to East Florida."

"That sounds like a long and perilous journey," Bat observed.

"True," responded the captain. "But, as I said before ... I refuse to remain here and suffer the indignity of arrest. I am no criminal. I am a Patriot, and I faithfully and steadfastly serve my King. If you share my convictions, then I invite you to join me in this expedition. If you choose not to do so, then I will not consider you disloyal, nor will I consider you unfaithful to our cause. Each man must make a decision in accordance to his own conscience and circumstance. But, should you decide to join us, you do so with the understanding that I remain your captain. I will be in command of the company from Jackson's Creek. Do all of you understand?"

The men grunted and nodded.

"Good," declared Robert Phillips, stepping forward to join his brother. "Then, we should declare this meeting adjourned. I encourage you to return to your homes and talk things over with your wives and families. If you elect to make the journey with my brother to East Florida, then you must make preparations posthaste."

Will stood. "Wait one moment, Robert. What about you and John? Are you gentlemen going to Florida, as well?"

Robert answered, "Yes, Will. I intend to go. But, John has decided to stay here and serve as an advocate for all who elect to remain at home. Since he has not actually taken up arms against the rebels, they hold no indictment against him ... not yet, anyway. John believes that he can best serve our cause by staying home."

Will nodded and then sat back down. He glanced at Bat. His best friend returned a stormy, anguished look.

"Very well," Robert declared. "If there are no further questions or comments, you are dismissed. God save the King!"

The men answered loudly, "God save the King!"

The meeting disbanded quickly. Most of the men bolted toward the door, eager to make their preparations for the sojourn in Florida. Will and Bat, along with their sons, lagged behind to hold their own private conference.

"What will *we* do, Papa?" Austin whispered quietly. "Are we going with Mr. Phillips to Florida?"

Will cut a searching glance at Bat. "What do you think, old friend?"

Bat scowled. "I have neither the desire nor the fortitude for such a rigorous quest. I also have a wife and home for which I am responsible." He groaned. "Aw, hell ... truth be told, I am just too damned old for all of this. I am staying home."

"And what of us?" asked Drury. He nodded toward his brother, John.

"Yes, Father. What of us?" echoed John.

Bat patted his younger son affectionately on the shoulder. "You fellows must decide for yourselves whether to stay or go. You are grown men, now. Either way, I will respect your decision."

Drury turned to his best friend, Austin. "What will you do?"

Austin did not hesitate. "I am staying here with my family. My home is my first responsibility. I have no desire to journey all the way to Florida and join the King's army there."

"I agree," Drury declared. "I am staying home, as well."

"I am with you fellows," added John.

Will summarized the groups' decision. "So, then, we are agreed. The Austins and Newmans will make their stand here at home."

"Together, as always," added a grinning Bat.

Will smiled. "Together."

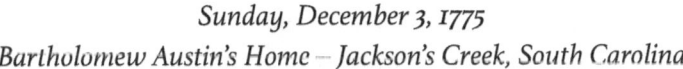

Sunday, December 3, 1775
Bartholomew Austin's Home – Jackson's Creek, South Carolina

IT WAS time for the weekly Austin and Newman family supper. Each Sunday afternoon, when their schedules allowed, Lizzy Newman and Rachel Austin labored together to prepare and serve a feast for their combined families. On this particular week, the gathering was being hosted by the Austins. As was their custom, they dined promptly at 5:00 pm and then enjoyed an evening of fellowship, games, and entertainment.

All heads remained bowed as Bat led the gathering in a traditional mealtime blessing. The ample table was filled to overflowing with two haunches of roasted venison coated with salt and cracked peppercorns, four plates stacked high with boiled red potatoes, and two wooden bowls of thick porridge composed of ground corn and wheat flavored with elderberries, blackberries, and hickory nuts. Four plump loaves of fresh, steaming-hot bread filled a single platter in the very center of the table. Dessert was roasted and mashed pumpkin flavored with butter, molasses, pecans, and ground cinnamon and nutmeg. The aromas that filled the house were simply mouth-watering.

After subjecting the ravenous pioneers to his customarily long-winded and frustratingly rambling prayer, Bat finally tied his thoughts together and brought his divine appeal to a close. He uttered in a most elegant and dramatic fashion, "For this wonderful bounty before us, O Lord, we are truly grateful. We beseech you that you might bless this delicious food to our bodies as you prepare our bodies for your eternal service. We pray this together and in one accord in Jesus' Name. Amen."

"Amen," echoed the members of the Austin and Newman families.

Bat then declared, "God save the King."

Everyone echoed, "God save the King."

Immediately, the throng of hungry folk reached for the various bowls, plates, and platters scattered across the familiar oak table. They served themselves and then passed each dish along to the next person. The two families enjoyed one another's company so much that, at first, conversation and laughter seemed to overshadow the actual practice of consuming the delicious food. The two tight-knit families relished in their togetherness. However, as soon as the eating began in earnest, communication subsided as everyone focused on the tasty task at hand.

"This venison is delicious, my dear," Bat declared, licking his lips after partaking of a generous bite of the juicy meat. "It is so tender, mild, and moist."

"You have our John to thank for that," Rachel responded. "It is from the young doe that he shot last week."

"That venison has been hanging for six days, Papa," explained John. "With the cold weather that we have endured of late, the meat aged and tenderized perfectly."

Bat grinned. "Indeed, it did, son. I reckon, then, that the both of you are to be commended for this wonderful roast. It is a delicious treat."

"Just make sure you leave some of that venison for the rest of us, if you please," Rachel urged. "I prepared plenty for all, so long as no one takes more than his fair share." She pointed her fork authoritatively at the large bowl near Bat's right elbow. "There is ample porridge in yon bowl. Make sure you serve yourself a hearty helping. It will satisfy your hunger nicely. I find that honey sweetens mine just right."

Bat gagged. "Woman, are you truly trying to fill me up on corn and nuts? I think you know me better than that." He feigned shock and offense. "And are you implying that I am in the habit of taking more than my allotted share of meat?"

Will chuckled sarcastically. "You have always filled up on meat, no matter what else is offered at the table. It has been so from the moment I met you. And I have rarely, if ever, seen you partake of corn or porridge. 'Tis a wonder those wretched bowels of yours function, at all."

Lizzy dropped her fork loudly onto her plate. "William Newman! How dreadful! You will not speak of such uncouth things at Rachel's supper table! Do you understand me?"

Will's chin dropped to his chest in shame. "Yes, Mum. Sorry, Mum."

Will contorted his face in a desperate attempt not to laugh. Then, with consummate timing, Austin unleashed a barely discernable farting noise with his lips. Almost immediately, Drury emitted an identical noise from the other side of the table. Will could not maintain his composure. He began to giggle and then all the other men around the table immediately joined in. Uncontrolled laughter filled the room. Rachel and Lizzy shook their heads and covered their embarrassed smiles with their hands.

Rachel leaned toward Lizzy and whispered, "Whatever are we going to do with these insufferable men?"

Lizzy grinned and then whispered back, "Love them forever, I suppose."

IT WAS ALMOST DUSK. The house was eerily quiet, despite being filled with souls from two entire households. Everyone was lost in the bliss of after-supper satisfaction. Lizzy and Rachel sat at the kitchen table, which was covered with bolts of cloth, needles, and thread. They were sewing, talking quietly, and enjoying one another's company. Little William and Mary played dominoes quietly in the floor near their mothers. The three young men: Austin, Drury, and John, were in the adjacent parlor partaking in a friendly game of cards. Bat and Will sat contentedly beside the stone fireplace. Bat occupied his favorite rocking chair. Will perched comfortably on top of a short three-legged stool. They each lazily puffed on their clay pipes and enjoyed a cup of tea as they pondered and discussed the politics of the day.

"Have you heard anything else about Colonel Richardson and his army?" inquired Will. He lifted his blue onion-patterned china cup to his mouth and then took a satisfying sip of his fragrant, sweet tea.

Bat made a circle with his mouth and lazily blew a series of perfect smoke rings. "I heard some talk in town yesterday. Rumor has it that he is currently quartered in Camden and preparing to enter the Cherokee country."

"Why would he go there? Is he pursuing our friends?"

Bat shook his head. "No. Richard Phillips informed me that our Compatriots are still hiding somewhere on Chesney land on the Pacolet River. They plan to make their way into North Carolina and then head west through Indian country." He paused and then cut his eyes at Will. "Actually, I heard that the colonel is after Patrick Cunningham and his company of men."

"And he thinks they are in the Cherokee country?" Will asked disbelievingly.

Bat hesitated and then made a somewhat disgusted face. "They are, actually."

"What?" exclaimed Will, sitting upright. He gazed at his friend through eyes of dismay. "What are our comrades doing in the Indian lands?"

"Taking refuge from Richardson. Mr. Cunningham is still in possession of the remainder of the confiscated munitions. He has rather ambitious plans to press the fight against the rebels."

Will seemed thoroughly disgusted. "But, to seek refuge the Indian country! That is almost unthinkable! Is he somehow attempting to ally himself with the Cherokee?"

Again, Bat shrugged. "Perhaps. I think it more likely that he is simply trying to outrun Richardson for now. His is the only militia unit remaining in action. Everyone else has either been arrested or fled to Georgia or Florida."

Will frowned. "I have been hearing about numerous arrests of late. Camden, it seems, has been emptied of all men loyal to the King. Many others, fearing reprisal or execution, have simply surrendered themselves to the rebel army. I am a bit mystified that we have not yet received a visit."

"'Tis only a matter of time, I am afraid," Bat prophesied.

Will stared grimly at his friend. "What will you do if they come for you?"

"I do not know. But, it would be foolish to resist. I reckon I will do as I am told and see how everything plays out."

Will nodded. "As will I."

Suddenly, somewhere in the distance, a chorus of hounds unleashed a frantic din of angry barking and mournful howls.

"I wonder what has disturbed your dogs," Will mused.

"Likely, one of them saw a rabbit run across the pasture. It only takes one bark to get them all going. Most of the time, they have no notion as to why they are barking ... they simply join in with the rest." He chuckled softly. "They are daft animals, to be sure. Once they get all worked up, they usually end the excitement with a huge fight."

Drury's voice echoed from the parlor. "Papa! Come quick!"

"What is it, Son?"

Drury popped excitedly around the corner. "There are men out front!"

"Who are they?" demanded Bat, sitting upright in his chair.

"I am not certain. They do not look familiar to me."

"How many?"

"I counted eight, all on horseback."

Bat pulled himself up from his rocking chair. "Why, pray tell, would a group of mounted men be out so late on a Sunday evening?"

Rachel rose from the table and approached Bat nervously. "Husband, it must be Richardson's men!" A tear formed in her right eye and then leaked out onto her cheek. "They have come for our livestock ... or worse!"

Bat smiled lovingly at his wife. He cupped her cheek with his hand. "Let us not jump to any conclusions, my dear. You must not always assume the worst in every circumstance."

"Two men have dismounted!" Will called from the front parlor. "They are approaching the house!"

Seconds later, there came a loud rapping on the front door. Bat scanned the expressions of his friends and family members. Clearly, they were all concerned.

"I will answer," Bat announced. "The rest of you should be about your business." He strode determinedly toward the door.

A muffled voice called from beyond, "Mr. Austin? Are you home? I must speak to Bartholomew Austin!"

Bat opened the door and stared at the two men who were standing on his front porch. Both were dressed for travel and cold weather. They were armed with muskets and pistols. One of the men, a slightly older chap, carried a scabbard and sword on his left hip. Clearly, they were military.

"I am Bartholomew Austin. Welcome to my home. How might I be of service on this lovely autumn evening?"

The fellow reached up and tipped his hat politely at Bat. He spoke with a pleasant Scottish accent. "Mr. Austin. I am pleased to make your acquaintance. I am Captain Lewis McKenzie of the Craven County Militia. This is Levtenant Angus Clinkscale, my adjutant. Might we come in for a moment and have a word?"

"What is this regarding, Captain McKenzie?"

The captain hesitated slightly. "I am here as a representative of Colonel Richard Richardson."

Bat's countenance fell. They were, indeed, rebels from the east. He stammered, "Yes ... please ... of course. Do come inside."

"Thank you, Mr. Austin." He paused. "But, before we do... would you kindly allow my men to take refuge in your barn? Darkness is falling, and we are all a bit chilled. We need a place to stay for the night. Some shelter from the cold would be most appreciated."

"Of course. Your men will find ample fodder and water for the horses in the barn. But, for their personal shelter, I would recommend you use the small cabin near my east pasture. It has a fireplace and is well-stocked with wood. We keep it prepared for travelers and guests."

"Very well. I am most grateful for your generosity." He turned to his aide. "Levtenant, will you please see to the men and then return here once they are settled?"

"Are you certain, Captain?" The younger fellow cut a suspicious glance at Bat.

"Get along, Angus. These fine people pose no threat to me."

"Yes, sir." The officer nodded and then quickly departed.

"Please, come on inside, Captain," Bat invited. "Are you hungry? Would you like some tea?"

The captain smiled warmly. "I am quite famished, to be honest, and a spot of tea would be delightful."

"Come along, then. My wife will be happy to fetch you some supper."

The captain removed his cocked hat and cloak as he entered the home. Little Mary Austin took his garments and hung them on a peg board near the door. The captain stepped into the warm front room and was immediately assaulted by the prying eyes of every member of the two gathered families. They all stared at him and remained completely silent.

The captain smiled, amused. "What is happening here? Is it some manner of a party? I almost feel like the guest of honor."

Bat chuckled nervously. "No, Captain. 'Tis no party. It is merely our typical Sunday gathering." He pointed to his family. "This is my wife, Rachel, and our children: Drury, John, and Mary. The other folk are the Newmans, our life-long friends and closest neighbors. We often take supper together on Sunday afternoon."

"Newman, you say?" He turned to Will. "Would you, perchance, be Mr. William Newman?"

Will stepped forward and shook the captain's hand. "Yes, Captain. I am William Newman." He pointed to his family members. "This is my wife, Lizzy, and our sons, Austin and William, Jr."

The captain smiled warmly. "'Tis a pleasure to meet you all."

Bat grabbed two ladderback chairs from the dining table. "Come and join us by the fire, Captain. We have nothing but porridge and bread left over from the meal. I am sorry that I have nothing else to offer you."

"A bowl of porridge and a slice of bread sounds wonderful, Mr. Austin. I have not had hot food in almost three days."

"Come, then. Sit down and warm yourself. That is what chairs and fires are for," invited Bat.

The three men sat together near the hearth. Bat reclined, once again, in his rocking chair and Will returned to his stool. Everyone else sat at the table or hovered within earshot, anxious to glean whatever information they could from the surprisingly friendly Whig. The men enjoyed small talk for a while as Rachel and Lizzy ladled porridge from the warming pot and carved slices of bread. Soon, the young lieutenant returned from his errand and joined them. He reported that the soldiers had fed and sheltered their mounts and were in the process of occupying the cabin. The ladies then served both of their guests a generous portion of leftover grain porridge, a large wedge of bread, and a pewter mug full of steaming tea.

The two soldiers nodded gratefully. The captain declared, "Thank you, ladies. You are most kind, indeed."

The two ravenously hungry men devoured their hot, filling supper in a matter of minutes. Afterwards, they continued to thaw their hands and feet near the toasty fire as they relished in the luxury of a cup of fresh tea. Bat shared a generous portion of his pipe tobacco with each man. Soon, the four gentlemen were all sipping tea and smoking their clay pipes.

After a few minutes of relative silence, Will could stand the suspense no longer. He demanded bluntly, "What brings you gentlemen to Jackson's Creek on such a chilly Sunday evening? The timing of your visit seems a bit odd."

The captain inhaled a deep, reticent breath. He considered carefully the words he was about to speak. Finally, he answered, "I assume that you are aware of the presence of our army and our mission here in the backcountry."

Will glanced briefly at Bat. He then turned his attention quickly back to the captain. He nodded. "Yes, Captain. Rumors say that you are rounding up all Loyalists, especially those who took up arms against Williamson at Ninety-Six."

"Yes, that is the essence of our work here," Captain McKenzie affirmed. "I believe that both of you were party to that unfortunate confrontation."

"We were," Bat responded unashamedly.

"And your sons were there, as well?" confirmed the lieutenant.

Will inhaled deeply. Reluctantly, he responded, "Yes."

Bat added somewhat sternly, "I would remind you that we departed that field of battle under formal truce and cease-fire. The commanders reached terms amicable to all ... terms which included our unmolested return to our homes. So, you must understand our confusion and dismay when we learned that the colonel and his army have acted in violation of those terms."

The captain smiled thinly. Some of the friendliness vanished from the face. "I have no knowledge of nor do I hold a personal opinion with regard to any negotiations or agreements reached at Ninety-Six. I am just a soldier and, as you both know from your own experiences, compelled to do my duty as ordered by my superiors. It is within that role of obedient soldier that I have been dispatched on my mission here. That mission was prescribed by none other than Colonel Richard Richardson, himself. I believe that both of you know him."

"We do," Will affirmed. "Mr. Richardson and I were once neighbors. He and my deceased father were very close friends. As a matter of fact, Bat and I both served under the colonel in the Cherokee uprising in '59."

The captain nodded thoughtfully and drew deeply on his pipe. "The colonel has informed me thusly. He dispatched me here today to invite you and your sons to our encampment headquarters. He wishes to speak to all of you as friends and former comrades."

"All of us?" Will asked, confused.

Captain McKenzie reached his hand toward Lieutenant Klinkscale. The young officer reached inside the lapel of his great coat and produced a folded piece of paper. He handed it to the captain.

"These are my instructions." He scanned the paper. "I have been ordered to escort Bartholomew Austin and his son, Drury Austin, as well as William Newman and son, Austin Newman, to Colonel Richardson at his headquarters in Camden town." He folded the paper. "The colonel wishes to speak to the four of you with all expedience."

Bat stole a slightly relieved glance at Will. Both of them were thinking the same thing. Young John Austin had not been included on the list.

"So, then ... this is something of a social invitation?" Bat clarified.

Captain McKenzie turned toward Bat and looked deeply and honestly into his eyes. "Not exactly. Please understand. Colonel Richardson harbors no ill will toward any of you. He merely wants to have a personal conference with the four of you. Of course, if you decline his congenial summons, we retain the option of compelling you to accompany us."

"I see," responded Bat. "Then, it would behoove us all to go willingly."

The captain nodded. "Candidly, Mr. Austin, yes. It would in your best interests to respond positively to his friendly invitation. The colonel has spoken fondly of you both. I believe that he has your best interests at heart. From our brief conversations, I know that he wishes to ensure your safety and protect you from any unnecessary unpleasantries."

Bat looked at Will. Will smiled and nodded to his friend. Both men stood. Immediately, Captain McKenzie and Lieutenant Klinkscale stood, as well. Bat extended his hand to the captain.

"Very well, then, Captain McKenzie. We will be happy to accompany you gentlemen to Camden. Should we leave our arms at home?"

"No, Mr. Austin. That would be unwise. I rather think that you fellows will need your weapons for your return trip. One never knows what dangers he might encounter out here in the wilderness." He smiled, much more warmly this time. "We shall depart at first light, if that is agreeable. That should leave you plenty of time to return home before nightfall."

"Thank you, Captain," Bat responded.

Rachel and Lizzy appeared in the midst of the men. Rachel retrieved the iron pot from the fireplace crane. Wrapping a thick potholder around wire handle, she handed it to the lieutenant. Lizzy gave the captain a basket covered with a linen napkin.

Rachel explained, "Please take the remainder of the porridge and bread to your men, Captain McKenzie. In addition to the bread, there are a few boiled potatoes in the basket, as well, along with a small bowl of salt. I am certain that your soldiers will sleep better with their bellies full of hot food."

The captain bowed slightly at the waist. "You are most generous, Mrs. Austin. My men will be very pleased, indeed." He nodded to Bat and Will. "Gentlemen, until tomorrow."

"We will meet you at the barn at dawn," promised Bat.

The Whig militiamen moved swiftly toward the door and made a quick exit. Bat slowly closed the door behind them as they departed. As soon as they were out of earshot, the entire household erupted in frenzied conversation. John scurried to meet his father.

"Why was I not on the list, Papa? What does it mean?"

Bat placed a reassuring hand on his son's shoulder. "It means they do not know about your presence at Ninety-Six."

John's lip trembled. "But, what about the incident that occurred on the way?"

"Clearly, they know nothing of that, either. So, you must not worry yourself."

John nodded, relieved. "Shall I go with you all tomorrow, anyway?"

"Most definitely not! They did not ask for you, so there is no reason why you should volunteer to go. Like I always say, a man deals with trouble when it presents itself. He does not go in search of it. I want you to remain here and take care of things until your brother and I return."

Will appeared at Bat's side with his family in tow. "We are heading on home. Austin and I have preparations to make." He glanced at the women. "Besides, I do not think that any of us remain interested in fun and games this evening. Our rebel brethren have ruined the mood."

Bat nodded dejectedly. "Of course. I sincerely hate that our unexpected guests have aborted our Sunday fellowship."

Will inhaled deeply. "Well, it certainly was an interesting visit, was it not?"

Bat chuckled. "A bit too interesting for my taste. And now I get to sleep with a squad of rebels in my old cabin!" He shook his head disbelievingly. "Light all your lanterns and travel safely. Drury and I will be waiting for you in the morning."

"Very well." Will turned and took Rachel's hand and then gave it a gentlemanly kiss. "Supper was wonderful, as usual. We are always grateful for your hospitality. Will you folks do us the honor of dining at our house next Sunday evening?"

Rachel smiled grimly. "Yes." She paused. A single tear crept down her cheek. "I hope so."

~

Noon – The Following Day
Col. Richard Richardson's Headquarters – Camden, South Carolina

COLONEL RICHARDSON'S steward stepped through the door into his office. "Begging your pardon, Colonel. Captain McKenzie is in your parlor. He has with him a group of gentlemen from Jackson's Creek."

The colonel's face brightened. "Excellent. Please send them in."

Moments later, Captain McKenzie entered the room. Will, Austin,

Bat, and Drury followed closely behind. The captain bowed politely and then made his report to his commanding officer.

"As requested, Colonel, I have escorted these four gentlemen from their homes at Jackson's Creek."

"Did the miscreants give you any trouble?" The colonel looked past the captain and winked at Will. Will smiled back at him.

The captain remained quite serious. "Quite the contrary, sir. They were hospitable beyond description. Mr. Austin generously fed and housed my men last night. The visit to Jackson's Creek was amicable in every respect. I only wish that all of our encounters with Loyalists in the backcountry were of such a noble fashion."

"Well, these here are honorable gentlemen, Captain. Such deportment was exactly what I expected." Colonel Richardson nodded to the captain. "You are dismissed, Lewis. Thank you for your service. Well done."

"Thank you, Colonel, sir." Again, Captain McKenzie bowed slightly at the waist. As he turned to leave the room, he nodded to Will and Bat. "Gentlemen, it was a pleasure, indeed. I hope that we might meet again someday." He shook their hands and then departed quickly.

Colonel Richardson stepped from behind his desk and gave Will and Bat each a warm handshake. "Welcome, and God bless you both. It is damn good to see you again."

Will smiled warmly. "It is good to see you, sir, despite these awkward circumstances."

The colonel sighed. "Indeed." He motioned to four ladderback chairs that sat in a line in front of his desk. "Please sit, gentlemen. We have much to discuss."

The two men and their sons obediently seated themselves. Colonel Richardson returned to his handsome, plush leather-upholstered desk chair.

"William, Bartholomew, boys ... there is no need to dance around the subject at hand. We must get down to business. I assume you agree."

All four men nodded.

"The Loyalist resistance in the backcountry is done, gentlemen. The movement has been defeated. There remains only one group of criminals on the loose and unaccounted for. We will soon apprehend them, as well. Meanwhile, the South Carolina Congress has entrusted me with the task of rooting out the last of the armed resistance. Unfortunately, some of the more violent and unsociable characters have required incarceration in Charlestown. Thankfully, however, most of your compatriots have been reasonable and have sworn their oaths to South Carolina and returned peacefully to their homes."

He paused and stared at the four men. They maintained their silence and simply stared back. The atmosphere was quite uncomfortable.

"All right, then. Let us continue." The colonel picked up a document from his desk. "I have a report here that says all four of you were involved in the recent insurrection at Ninety-Six."

Will rubbed his chin and, for a brief moment, pondered his response. Finally, he answered, "I find your verbiage quite interesting, Colonel. From our standpoint, those who oppose England are the real insurrectionists."

The colonel smiled, seemingly entertained. "Ours is a quandary of semantics, I suppose. Nevertheless, all of you were there, under British flag, and in the company of Captain James Phillips. Is that correct?"

Will nodded. "Yes, sir."

"And you all elected to return home after the supposed cease-fire agreement?"

"There was no 'supposed' about it," countered Bat. "The officers reached a formal agreement under flag of parley. They all signed it and bound themselves to it."

The colonel nodded. "I understand your position, Bartholomew. But, please tell me ... what about the remainder of your company? Our patrols at Jackson's Creek did not locate anyone else that our intelligence identified in Captain Phillips' command."

Will squirmed uncomfortably in his chair. He decided that there was no need to attempt to conceal the truth. The other men of their company were long gone. "It is my understanding that they have departed South Carolina altogether. They have elected to join a Loyalist force in another locale."

"In Georgia or East Florida, perhaps?" inquired the colonel, smiling smugly.

Will lied, "I cannot say with any certainty."

Colonel Richardson nodded. "As you wish." He sighed. "Since you chose not to accompany him, might I assume that you did so with the intention of living and working with an attitude of peace?"

Will looked at Bat. His friend nodded slightly.

"Yes, sir," Will answered. "Our company of comrades are gone. There is no fight to continue, so far as we can see."

Colonel Richardson smiled. "That warms my heart, William. Obviously, I have no desire to send you fellows to Charlestown." He scowled and shook his head. "That prison is nasty business, believe me."

Bat squirmed in his chair. "Well, Colonel, I reckon we have no desire to go there, either."

"It seems, then, that we find ourselves in one accord. Therefore, my proposal to you is simple. I will administer to the four of you, right now, your oaths of neutrality. Then, once you add your signature to those oaths, you will be free to return to your homes. I will send you away with the satisfaction and peace of knowing that we need never face one another on the battlefield." He paused and searched the faces of the four men seated in front of him. "What say ye? Is my proposal agreeable to you?"

Bat and Will sat silently for a moment. They each glanced at their sons. Both young men were wide-eyed with fear.

Will nudged Bat. "What do you think, old friend?"

Bat cleared his throat. His voice trembled slightly as he spoke. "I think the colonel has extended us a very generous offer, and that we should accept it in gratitude."

Will nodded resolutely. "I agree."

Colonel Richardson slapped the palm of his hand victoriously on his desktop. "Wonderful! Then let us get to it." He handed Will and

Bat each a small handbill-sized slip of paper. "I believe that both of you can read. Is that correct?"

Will nodded. "Yes, sir."

"Good. William, if you would please share your copy with Austin. Bartholomew, please share yours with Drury. I need you all to stand, raise your right hands and then read, in unison, the wording on that document."

Bat and will scanned the oath quickly, and then nodded.

"Proceed," the colonel urged.

The four men stood to their feet, raised their right hands, and then began to read:

"I do swear before Almighty God, that I will not for the future be of any aid, or contribute assistance of any kind to any person or persons whatsoever, who are of a contradictory inclination to the common cause of American Liberty. Furthermore, I do hereby declare that I will not lift arms against the Americans in their present contest with Great Britain, nor do anything by word or action that we know to be against the American Cause. I hereby swear my allegiance to South Carolina, its Congress, and its lawful Committees. So help me God."

The colonel nodded happily. He handed a turkey feather quill to Will and pushed his ink jar forward on his desk. "Please sign your names on the bottom of your documents. I will add them to the others in my file."

The four men quickly signed their names. Colonel Richardson picked up his pounce pot and shook a generous measure of ground cuttlefish bone onto the wet ink. He then carefully returned the excess powder back into the concave top of the pounce pot. He placed the papers inside a desk drawer and then stepped out from behind his desk. He shook the hands of all four men. His face beamed with pleasure.

"Gentlemen, I cannot describe for you how happy I am. I was most hopeful that you would depart my office today as friends, not as enemies."

"We, too, are pleased, Colonel," Will affirmed honestly.

"Good. Now, I beseech you to return to your homes and pursue your lives as you see fit, within the bounds of your oaths. I pray you do so with all success and prosperity." He paused and gave the four men a stern look. "But, make no mistake. This war is over for you fellows. Do not test my resolve. If you ever renege on your oaths and take up arms against independency, then our government and our armed forces will respond with all severity."

"Yes, sir," acknowledged Bat. "I believe we understand fully."

"Good. Be gone with you, then. I have several other appointments this day which are sure to be much less pleasant than this one."

They all shook the colonel's hand one last time and then immediately departed his office. Minutes later, they were mounted and headed back toward home. They rode in silence for quite a while. Finally, Drury spoke.

"So, that is it, then? Is our resistance truly over?"

"Yes, Son," Bat confirmed. "We swore our oaths. We are men of our word."

"But what of our oaths to King and country?" challenged Austin.

"There may come a day when we will be confronted with a different path," his father explained. "But, for now, we will honor our word to Colonel Richardson. We are not soldiers. We are farmers. So, let us return home and live in peace. We must pray that this conflict will remain far from us. Jackson's Creek will be our refuge. Our fighting is done."

"That sounds good to me," declared Will.

PART III

TORIES

11

MUSTER AT CAMDEN

Wednesday – February 16, 1780

Austin just wanted to eat and enjoy his supper in peace. But, as usual, the meal was headed toward relational disaster. He did not want to become angry at his parents, but they would not stop pestering him. He was growing weary of their incessant harassment. It seemed that an all-out confrontation was inevitable.

Lately, Austin's home life had become an endless torment of interrogation and humiliation. The fundamental issue, in the eyes of his parents, was that he was twenty-six years old and unmarried. His unwed condition at such an advanced age was almost unthinkable in the South Carolina backcountry. Indeed, some considered it scandalous. To make matters worse, his parents bore his brazen bachelorhood as a humiliating badge of shame. Lately, Austin could not even enjoy a family supper without suffering the indignity of their marital badgering. Will and Lizzy Newman wanted their son to be married. They also wanted grandchildren. And they did not hesitate in the least to verbalize with annoying regularity those two soul-burning desires.

"Have you seen Drury and Elizabeth's new baby girl?" mused Lizzy, Austin's step-mother. "Elizabeth brought her over for a visit today at tea time. Oh, my, that little one is a cherub! She has the fattest, pinkest cheeks! I could just squeeze them and kiss them all the long day." She paused and cut her eyes at Austin. "That makes baby number three for Drury and his wife, you know. They have only been wed for three years, and already they have three little ones to show for it. Is that not wonderful?"

"Humph!" grunted Austin sarcastically. "You would think that they might need to come up for some air on occasion." Visibly annoyed, he pinched off a chunk of bread and jammed it into his mouth. "She came for tea, you say? 'Tis a wonder the woman can move about, at all, seeing as how she has been spraddle-legged and flat on her back for three straight years."

"Austin Newman! I will not tolerate such crass vulgarity at my supper table," Lizzy shrieked angrily. She attempted to calm herself by taking a sip of tea. She paused for a moment, and then offered a response to Austin's lurid observation. "Drury and Elizabeth are simply going about the business of young married folk. It is God's way and nature's way. One day, you will understand ... sooner than later, *hopefully*. That is, if you *ever* get married."

Her mocking emphasis upon the words "hopefully" and "ever" was unmistakable. Her speech dripped with displeasure and judgment. Somehow, Austin chose not to respond to his step-mother's cold, calculated dig. He merely stuffed a forkful of roasted potatoes into his mouth as he stared sullenly at his plate.

"I already know who I am going to wed, Mama," declared William, her sixteen-year-old son, in a disgustingly cheerful voice. The compliant lad was obviously fishing for affirmation in the midst of the parental displeasure being unleashed upon his older brother. "I already asked Mary Austin to marry me. She said she would."

"Is she aware that you still do not comb your own hair in the morning or pick out your clothing to wear each day?" Austin accused mockingly. He then mumbled sarcastically, "Your mother still cuts your meat for you. I am surprised that she does not feed it to you and then wipe your lips after. Hell, she may even still accompany you to the privy and wipe your arse, for all I know. Surely, Mary needs all of the facts before she agrees to be wed to a spoiled infant."

Unbeknownst to his parents, under-table combat ensued immediately. William viciously and subtly kicked his big brother in the shin as he shot him a contemptuous look. Austin promptly kicked William back and then mercilessly stomped the lad's toe with the heel of his shoe. They kicked one another twice more, increasing the force with each strike. It was amazing that they could deliver such extreme blows to one another without moving the upper portions of their bodies. These were maneuvers that the two of them had perfected through years of practice. Each of them successfully inflicted pain and fresh bruises upon the other. Finally, they declared a silent cease-fire and then resumed their normal above-table interactions.

Lizzy, oblivious to the secret combat beneath the dining table, shot a contemptuous look at Austin. She then turned her head, smiled proudly at William, reached toward him, and caressed his baby-smooth cheek in her hand. "Pay no attention to your brother's harsh and unkind words, William. He is simply jealous of you. Your announcement comes as no surprise to me, my love. We have always imagined you and little Mary together in wedlock. I pray that it will someday be so."

William declared with confidence, "Oh, it will! We are getting married. We have decided."

"Austin, do you simply not fancy any of the young lady-folk hereabouts?" Will Newman interrupted, refocusing the conversation back onto his older son. "I realize that the pool of potential mates here in Jackson's Creek is quite shallow. There are relatively few unmarried girls in your age range. Is that the problem? If so, I could send you to Charlestown on business, or perhaps up to New Bern. You could even journey to Richmond, if you like. You have never visited Virginia. Surely, you could secure a bride of your liking there."

"Father!" Austin exploded, furiously slamming both of his fists on the table. The dishes and cutlery jumped and rattled from the force of the blow. Will's wine glass tipped over, spilling its contents onto the tablecloth. "Are you listening to yourself? Have you actually considered your words before giving them release from your mouth? You act as if finding a mate is akin to riding into town and purchasing a saddle or a new pair of shoes!" Austin folded his napkin and threw it contemptuously onto his pile of unfinished food. "Surely, you of all people should know the dangers of being wed in an untimely manner and against your own wishes."

Austin cursed himself silently. Lizzy gasped. The room became deafeningly quiet. Will slowly lowered his fork and then placed it on the table beside his plate. His bottom lip quivered almost imperceptibly. Austin felt a sudden pang of panic and dread. He had gone too far. In his desire to retaliate against the shame being heaped upon him by his parents, he had done nothing short of stabbing an emotional dagger into his father's long-wounded heart. He regretted his words before they had even escaped his lips. But, it was too late to take them back. Words could not be unsaid. The damage could not be undone. All that he could do was apologize.

He immediately begged, "Papa, I should not have said that to you. I am so very sorry. Please, please forgive me."

Will took a handkerchief from his pocket and dabbed it against his right eye. He stared silently at his plate for a moment and then cast a sorrowful glance toward his wife. Lizzy stared at him in dismay. She instinctively reached across the table and took her husband's hand in hers.

"Papa," Will pleaded frantically. "I beg of you. Please forgive me. I should not have disrespected you so."

Will slowly reached over and placed his free hand on top of Austin's. "No, Son. It is I who should be asking you for forgiveness. I have disrespected you. Your words stung, 'tis true, but you were absolutely entitled to say them. Of all people, I should know better." He smiled at Lizzy. "*We* should know better." He took a deep, thoughtful breath. "I know in my heart that God has a plan for you. Someday, you will find the woman of your dreams, just as I did. And when you do, you will know it beyond any doubt. Meanwhile, until that day comes, we will wait with you, and patiently so. And we will try to restrain our tongues. I promise." He turned to his wife. "Right, Lizzy?"

"As you wish, Husband." Lizzy Newman sounded neither enthusiastic nor pleased. However, as always, she would submit to her husband's desires.

Austin nodded humbly. "I am grateful to you for your words." He swallowed hard. "You know how much I love you both ... at least, I hope you do."

Will smiled and nodded. "I think we have a pretty good idea." He picked up his fork again. "Now, let us put this unpleasantness behind us. We are going to eat, enjoy our meal, and talk of other things. Agreed?"

Austin nodded enthusiastically. He returned his napkin back to his lap, picked up his fork, and pried a wedge of chicken from the bone. He was just about to take a bite of the tender bird when the sound of a galloping horse reached his ears.

"I believe we have company," declared Will.

"'Tis odd to have a visitor at suppertime," remarked Lizzy.

"I will see who it is." Austin wiped his lips, placed his napkin on the table, and then rose to his feet. He heard the approaching horse come to an abrupt stop. Next, came the sound of someone running up the front steps.

"Austin! Uncle Will! Open up! Hurry!"

"It is Drury," Will declared, puzzled. "He sounds distressed."

Austin walked toward the front door. A heavy fist pounded urgently against the wood.

"I am coming!" Austin yelled. He grumbled, "Good Lord, what can be so important?"

He opened the door. Drury pushed his way inside. The young man's face was blood-red and he was breathing excitedly. Despite the chilly winter air, sweat poured from his brow.

"Have you heard, Austin ... Uncle Will? Have you heard the news?"

Will stood instantly. "What news? Is something wrong?"

Drury's face beamed. "No! Something is *very* right!" He stared wide-eyed at his friends, but said nothing else.

"Well ..." Austin prodded him. "Do not just stand there like a mute idiot. Tell us. What could be so urgent that it possessed the power to tear you away from your baby-making endeavors?"

Drury rolled his eyes at his friend. "I have no time to console your jealously, Austin Newman. If you do not wish to hear what I have to say, then ..."

Austin exhaled in frustration. "Oh, for God's sake! Spit it out, would you?"

"The Regulars have arrived!"

"What do you mean?" demanded Will.

"General Clinton has invaded from New York by sea. He has landed an army in South Carolina!"

"Where?" Will asked excitedly.

"Simmons Island, south of Charlestown."

Will cut a quick glance toward Austin, then refocused his attention upon Drury. "How many men?"

"I cannot be certain. Some say they number 5,000, but others report there are as many as 10,000 troops."

Will's legs felt jelly-like. He could not believe this incredible news. Numbly, he collapsed into his chair. All he could say in response was, "Good Lord."

Austin looked stunned, as well. He mused, "I reckon this changes everything, doesn't it?"

Drury grinned broadly. "Indeed, it does! The King's army has arrived! Soon, those rebels will pay a dear price for the way that they have mistreated us. Once General Clinton gets hold of them, they will regret having trod us all underfoot such as they have done these past five years."

Austin turned and faced his father. "What must we do now?"

Will pondered his son's question, then answered, "Nothing. We wait and see what happens."

∾

Three Months Later: Sunday – May 14, 1780
Jackson's Creek Meeting House

JOHN PHILLIPS STOOD to address the congregation. "Before we dismiss for the day, Elder, I have an announcement." The church folk all turned and stared at him. "It is most important news, indeed."

The elder in charge of the gathering responded, "Of course, Mr. Phillips. You are recognized."

John Phillips held his hand across his chest in a most gentlemanly pose and bowed slightly. "Thank you, kind sir. I must report to you all that I received important news by messenger early this morning. The long siege at Charlestown has ended. The city has fallen to the army and navy of Great Britain."

His unexpected announcement reverberated throughout the meeting house. The congregation fell silent. Everyone seemed overwhelmed by a sense of both awe and disbelief. Austin turned slightly to steal a glance at his best friend, Drury. Their eyes met. Drury flashed a huge, excited smile.

"When?" inquired Bat Austin. "How?"

"Two days ago," explained Mr. Phillips. "Lincoln surrendered his entire force of over 5,000 men, both Continentals and militia, along with all their weapons, artillery, and a harbor full of ships. The British now control the entire city, its port, and the surrounding district."

"But, what does that mean to us out here in our district?" asked one of the parishioners from the back of the room.

"It means, sir, that those of us loyal to the King may now go about our business without fear of reprisal. The oppression that we have received at the hands of the rebels is over. There will be no more sanctions, mistreatment, or incarcerations of Loyalists. The rule of law and English justice has returned to South Carolina. We may now rely upon the British army to protect our rights and freedoms."

Mr. Phillips smiled victoriously. He knew all too well the fury and injustice visited upon Loyalists by the rebels in Charlestown. He had been arrested and bound in chains for almost an entire year because of his refusal to swear an oath to South Carolina administered by the leaders of the rebellion. His ankles and wrists still bore the scars of his cruel captivity at the hands of the Whigs.

"What about the rebels still on the loose here in the backcountry?" inquired Will Newman.

"Emissaries of the British army are currently *en route* to Camden and Ninety-Six to receive the surrender of the rebel garrisons at both locations. The deed will be done by week's end."

"Then, it truly is over?" another fellow asked hesitantly.

Mr. Phillips frowned and then shook his head. "No, it is by no means over. This insane war rages on. As you well know, things have not been going very well for our cause in the north. I believe that this is why the King's generals have chosen to come here and open a second front in the battle against this unlawful rebellion. They are counting upon all men loyal to the King to rally to their cause. I trust that many of you will answer the call to serve."

"But, surely, there will not be open warfare down here like there has been in the north," Will Newman predicted. "I can scarcely imagine the notion of huge armies slaughtering one another in our very own fields and forests."

Mt. Phillips shrugged. "One cannot predict our future with any certainty. Now that the rebels no longer enjoy control of the colony, they will likely launch some form of resistance. No doubt, other rebels from the north will make incursions into the Waxhaws, and perhaps even into *our* district. Therefore, we must prepare ourselves. Since our defeat five years ago, there remain no active Loyalist militia companies within the borders of South Carolina. You should expect that to change immediately. I anticipate a call from British command to re-inaugurate the militia as a mitigating force against bandits and raiders here in the backcountry."

"Will your brothers return to take leadership?" inquired Bat Austin.

"I have not heard from Robert or James in many months. Therefore, I cannot speak to their plans. I quite imagine they have their hands full with the rebels down in the Georgia backcountry. In light of their absence, it is my intention to travel to Camden tomorrow and seek a commission from the Crown to organize our very own regiment here at Jackson's Creek. Once my commission is in hand, I will appoint junior officers and then we will begin recruiting. I expect that our military services will be required almost immediately to provide security here and along the frontier."

Austin glanced at Drury again. A huge, excited smile still filled the young man's face. He gave Austin a subtle nod. The room, however, remained deafeningly silent. Clearly, most of the people were overwhelmed by the news of British victory.

Mr. Phillips smiled. "I can see that I have given you all much to ponder. Might I suggest that we dismiss at this time? Hopefully, by the next Sabbath, I will have my commission and instructions from the British command, as well as a more definite plan." He paused. "God save the King!"

The congregation answered him rather reservedly, "God save the King."

The elder in charge of the meeting called the group to prayer. He droned on for several minutes, but Austin did not hear a single word that he uttered. He was far too excited to listen. Finally, the fortunes of this war of rebellion had turned. He and his neighbors would no longer be subject to the humiliation of the Whigs. At long last, he and his mates would have the honor of taking up arms and taking the fight to the enemy. Austin Newman had every intention of joining John Phillips' Jackson's Creek Regiment.

Three Weeks Later - June 3, 1780

AUSTIN KICKED the sides of his mare, urging her into a full gallop. He could not contain his excitement. He had to tell Drury first. John Phillips was back from Camden, and he had in hand a commission from General Lord Cornwallis. Mr. Phillips was now a Lieutenant Colonel and commander of the Jackson's Creek Regiment of militia.

Soon, Austin and his best pal, Drury, would be joining the fight against the rebel revolution!

Austin rounded a sharp curve in the Winnsborough highway. The familiar lane that led to Drury's house appeared to his left. He effortlessly guided his mount through the break in the tall pine trees and then rode swiftly down the wagon-rutted road that led to Drury's house. As he reared his horse to a stop on the front lawn, he spotted another horse tethered to a bush near the porch. Austin quickly tied his horse to the same bush and then darted through the open front door of the house. The scene inside was not as he expected. He discovered Drury's wife, Elizabeth, sobbing uncontrollably. She was being consoled in an uncomfortable embrace by her brother-in-law, John. It was disturbing for Austin to see her in another man's arms, even if it was Drury's little brother.

"What is going on here?" Austin demanded. "John, what have you done?"

"I have done nothing, you daft prick!" John retorted angrily. "This is entirely the fault of that idiot brother of mine."

Austin glanced down the hallway and then stepped toward the door that led into the kitchen. Glancing inside, he saw nothing out of the ordinary. "Where is Drury? What has happened? Has he been injured?"

"No, Austin. He is gone! The man has left me!" wailed Elizabeth. Immediately, she exploded in uncontrolled, wailing sobs. She buried her face in John's chest. Her body shuddered as she gasped for air.

Austin glanced, confused, at John. "What? Elizabeth, surely you jest. Where has he gone?"

"To join the army," was her muffled reply.

Austin felt faint. "No, he has not!" he objected strenuously. "We were going to join the local regiment together. We agreed a long time ago."

John patted the tormented young woman reassuringly on her head. "Well, apparently my big brother's plans changed. Ever since the British arrived back in the winter, he has not been in his right mind. He has been a bit too eager to go and fight. I reckon he could stand it no longer. He departed before daylight this morning."

"But, where did he go?"

"He headed northwest into the Upper Ninety-Six District. He went in search of a fellow named Zechariah Gibbs. Apparently, this Mr. Gibbs is organizing a new militia regiment."

Austin was stunned. He felt betrayed. He detected tears forming in his own eyes. "I do not understand, John. Why did he not wait for me? John Phillips just received his commission as lieutenant colonel. Our regiment is forming as we speak. We will be with the army in Camden in a matter of days!"

John shrugged. "You know Drury as well as I. He has always been an impulsive, impatient, selfish bastard."

"Where are the children?" Austin asked, suddenly aware of the absence of two toddlers and a baby.

"They are with my parents. Mother will be bringing them back in a bit. The baby will need to nurse soon."

Austin shook his head angrily. "How could he just up and leave his wife and family like this? Did he not make plans for their care? Where will they go? Who is to watch over them?"

"Papa and Mama are working on that right now," John answered sullenly. "I suspect that they will be moving back home. My parents have plenty of room in their house. Besides, Elizabeth cannot keep up this entire farm by herself."

"What about the crops that are already in the field?" Austin demanded.

"Papa will see to those, as well. He may have to hire men."

Austin noticed that Elizabeth was no longer crying. Indeed, she appeared to be asleep. "Is the girl all right? Her eyes are closed."

"Mama gave her a tonic of opium about an hour ago, along with a wee dram of whiskey. It is supposed to help her sleep. I think it has finally worked. Wait here."

John gently rose to his feet, all the while supporting the weight of his sister-in-law. He effortlessly scooped the tiny young woman into his arms and then carried her down the hallway toward her bedchamber. He returned in a matter of minutes.

A wide-eyed John exhaled in relief as he re-entered the parlor. "I think she will sleep for a while, now. She needs it, God bless her heart." He walked over to a small liquor table in the corner and poured two generous glasses of whiskey. He handed one to Austin. "Christ, Almighty, this is a mess. If only Drury would have only waited for two more days, then we could have all gone away together."

Austin took a sip of his whiskey. "Indeed. I would like to take a whip to his arse."

"As would I," John affirmed, throwing his head back and downing all of his whiskey. He immediately poured himself another shot.

Austin, meanwhile, was doing the best he could to control his emotions. He had never experienced such a deep and unexpected betrayal in all of his life. He felt as if someone had pierced his chest with a sword.

"So, what will you do now that my brother has jilted you?" asked John somewhat teasingly.

Austin shrugged. "I will join the militia. I have already given verbal commitment to Colonel Phillips. What about you?"

John grinned. "I am going with you, of course." He held up his glass in a toast. "God save King George."

Austin, grinning happily, tapped his glass against John's. "God save King George."

They drained their glasses.

∼

Friday – June 9, 1780
Mid-Afternoon
Militia Camp – Camden, South Carolina

THE AIR WAS thick and hot. The road-weary men from Jackson's Creek had been traveling since daybreak. They stared in awe at the immense field crowded with tents, campfires, men, and horses. The South Carolina Loyalist encampment was impressive, indeed. Over 1,000 militiamen and officers inhabited the field and surrounding pine forests. To the west, several dozen men on horseback were practicing maneuvering and fighting with swords. At the northern end of the field, there was a firing range. Musket fire cracked with regularity as the men practiced shooting at various targets. A thin haze of gray-white smoke hovered over the shooters. Over one hundred men marched in formation in a large, open drilling field in the center of the camp. The entire place buzzed with every manner of military activity.

"Good God, there be a lot of us," declared Hugh Campbell. "Just look at them tents! Sweet Jesus, they's 'nough linen in this field to float a damned fleet full of ships."

"What the hell would you know about ships?" teased his friend, George Rogers. "You have never been on the water in anything bigger than a dugout canoe. I would even venture to guess that this is your first time east of the Wateree."

"I reckon I knows enough!" retorted the toothless, backwoods Campbell. "'Bout as much as you do, you uppity little lobcock."

The group of backwoods men exploded in laughter and jeering. Though exhausted from travel, they remained a happy, excited, and expectant group of men. All were eager to serve their King. But, they were equally as excited to be together on this great adventure.

"That will be enough of the idle talk and vulgarities, gentlemen," Captain James Miller chastised his men. "We have little time for frivolous banter. Colonel Phillips has very high expectations for this regiment, and I want my company to stand tall above the rest. That will require discipline, hard work, and attention to detail. Understood?"

The grinning men nodded. A few answered, "Yes, sir."

"I need all of you to get your tents up and your campsites secured. Get your cooking fires laid and prepare for the evening. It will be dark in a few hours. Men with mounts need to see to the welfare of their animals. If you expect to serve as a dragoon, you will need a healthy horse." He pointed to his right. "There is hay for fodder and a water barrel for our regiment's horses in that nearest stand of pines." He rested his hands on his hips and sighed. "I want everything to be neat and orderly when I return in one hour. Questions?"

Hugh Campbell raised his hand. "My breeches are 'bout worn clean out, Cap'n. When does we get some new 'uns and one of them fancy red uneeforms?"

Captain Miller rolled his eyes. Clearly, Hugh Campbell was destined to be the dimwit of his newly-inaugurated command.

"Private Campbell, you are a volunteer in the civilian militia. You are not counted amongst the Regulars. Only the British army is issued government uniforms. You will wear the clothing that you brought with you. Now, if your garments are in disrepair, I suggest you practice your sewing skills." The captain paused and scanned the faces of his men. "Are there any sensible questions?"

The men, most of them smiling, shook their heads.

"Very well. Get to work. I will go and consult with Colonel Phillips. We will arrange a training schedule. Work begins tomorrow. I will inform you of your assignments later this evening. God save the King."

His men responded mindlessly, "God save the King."

∿

Dusk – Three Days Later

AUSTIN NEWMAN WAS COMPLETELY SPENT. His weary back and legs ached from three straight days in the saddle. A squad of dragoons from Colonel Banastre Tarleton's British Legion had been training him and the other horsemen from Jackson's Creek in the fine art of cavalry combat and field tactics. Austin was quite proud to be training alongside these heroes of the British cause. Tarleton's men were all battle-hardened soldiers. Their recent victory over the rebel Buford in the Waxhaws was the talk of the entire camp.

Needless to say, serving under Tarleton's dragoons was not for the faint of heart. They displayed no mercy toward their trainees. Their drill and training regimen was intense and demanding. One skill that they insisted the local militiamen master was the use of blades in combat. Austin had just endured an entire afternoon of practicing with his newly-acquired saber. He had mercilessly slaughtered dozens of melons, pumpkins, and squashes that were perched as targets head-high atop wooden posts. The newness and intensity of the strenuous activity awakened and tested muscles in his arms and back that had long gone unused.

But, finally, the day's work was done. Austin reclined upon a soft bed of pine needles and wool blankets next to the tent that he shared with John Austin. His head rested comfortably atop his rolled-up linen greatcoat. His eyes were closed and he existed in a blissful state of semi-sleep. Still, he could hear John puttering about the camp, stirring the campfire, and making all manner of unnecessary and obnoxious noises. He wondered how his friend, who was also a horseman and learning the skills of the dragoons, could possibly possess so much energy.

Suddenly, a most unpleasant odor assaulted Austin's sense of smell. "Good God!" he exclaimed, sitting up and covering his nose with his hand. "Has something died in this camp?"

"No, you have caught a whiff of your supper," declared John as he danged a ladle filled with gray fluid near Austin's face. "I was just giving you a little nose sampling."

"What in God's Name is it?" Austin demanded, pinching his nose shut with his thumb and forefinger.

John grinned. "Stewed beef, supposedly. I procured a potful from the regimental mess. Though, one would be hard-pressed to find any beef in it ... or any meat, at all, for that matter." He squinted as he examined the liquid in his ladle. "To be honest, it more closely resembles grain porridge smothered in a mysterious and very greasy gravy."

"That stuff does not smell like any concoction of beef that I have encountered before," declared Austin, scrunching his nose. He peered at the sampling of stew. "Reckon how long the critter was dead before the cooks butchered it?"

"I cannot offer an educated answer to that question. But, suffice it to say, this is all that is available for our supper tonight. Do you want some, or not? I have added plenty of salt and a bit of cracked pepper-corns. In all likelihood, that is all that you will taste when you eat it. I hope."

Austin shook his head. "No, thank you. I think I will just have some more of your smoked venison, if you please."

"We need to slow down on that dried meat, Austin. At our current pace, we will run out of it before the end of the month. I had hoped to save it for when we go into the field."

Austin suddenly felt guilty for having consumed so much of his friend's jerked meat. "Oh, all right, then. Pour me up a bowl of your putrid sludge." He reached into his haversack and fished out a small wooden bowl and matching spoon. He handed the bowl to John. "At least we have ample ale to wash it down."

"Amen to that!" chimed a nosy Hugh Campbell. He followed his affirmation with a deep, thunderous burp.

John rolled his eyes. "As if you need ale to drown the flavor, you foul, filthy bastard. That is your third bowl of stew. I have been count-ing. You actually seem to enjoy the stuff."

Hugh licked his lips. "I cain't help meself. It tastes just like my old grandmammy's fricassee. It takes me back to my childhood."

"So, the old crone specialized in simmered shite, did she?" mocked Hugh's friend and tent-mate, George Rogers.

Hugh shot the man a nasty look. "No. That was your own mama, I reckon. She dropped you right out of her huge arse. 'Tis a big, fat, stinky turd you are."

The men of Captain Miller's company exploded with laughter. Even George could not help but smile at the insult. Their banter was not malicious. It was the type of jest and mocking that typified life in an army encampment. Deep down, Hugh and George were insepa-rable and lifelong friends and would gladly lay down their lives for one another if called upon to do so.

"Here ... eat your stew," John urged Austin.

Austin rose slowly to a sitting position. He crossed his agonizingly stiff legs and then half-heartedly accepted a steaming bowl of very unappetizing stew from John. He took another whiff and then quickly turned his offended nose away.

John grinned. "I know it does not smell like Aunt Lizzy's home cooking. But, you do need some food in your belly. You have been working hard. Just hold your nose and put it down quickly, then pray that it does not come back up. 'Twould be a great injustice to have to taste it twice." He placed a pewter mug of ale on the ground near Austin's knee. "At least the ale is good and stout, even if it is warm." He patted Austin playfully on the head and declared in a mock Irish brogue, "Now, if you act a good wee boy and eat all your supper, you might get a dram of whiskey for your dessert. And before you ask, we have no biscuits."

Austin grinned. "The liquor almost makes it worth eating this swill."

John grabbed his own bowl and then sat down next to Austin on the bed of pine needles. He began to shovel huge spoonsful of the stew into his mouth. Austin took a more reserved approach to the meal. He managed to choke down only a single, timid bite. He decided to mitigate the foul taste with conversation and drink.

"Have you seen any sign of your brother?" He followed the question with a large gulp of ale.

John shook his head. "I have asked all over this camp and can find no one who knows the whereabouts of Gibbs and his regiment. And, as to be expected, no one has even heard of Drury Austin."

"Perhaps they are out on patrol, or at one of our other camps."

"I doubt they are on patrol. Drury's regiment is only three or four days older than ours. Surely, they are training in drill and tactics as are we." John sucked down another mouthful of the unpleasant stew.

Austin took another gulp of ale. "I hear there is another sizable encampment to the north at Rocky Mount. They are much closer to the action. The rebels have been acting up in the Waxhaws and further north near Charlotte Town. Perhaps Drury is there."

John nodded. "Or at Ninety-Six. I heard that there is a garrison of a few hundred men there, as well." He smiled. "We had some interesting times out yonder back in '75, didn't we?"

"Interesting is a good word for it." He paused thoughtfully. "Well, surely, we will cross paths with Drury before long," Austin encouraged his friend. "Or, better yet, after two or three months of boredom, all of us will simply return home. I cannot imagine that the rebels will be causing much trouble in our region anymore. They have been whipped, for certain."

"Perhaps." John sighed. "I just wish Papa and Uncle Will were here with us," he declared somewhat forlornly. "Do you think they will come to their senses and join us soon? It is just not the same being in an army camp without them."

Austin shook his head. "My father has absolutely refused to join the militia. He informed me in no uncertain terms that he was too old for fighting a war. I can understand his position. He has a stiff knee that torments him for hours when he awakens every morning. Were he in this camp, it would take three of us to get him up off of the ground and extract him from his tent." He chuckled at the thought of his father attempting to soldier at his age. "Papa remains true to the cause, but he is not willing to pick up a weapon and join a regiment. Besides, I reckon he has also grown quite accustomed to his own bed and to sleeping beside his wife."

John declared proudly, "I suppose it is up to us young bucks to get the work done this time." He glanced quickly around the camp. "It seems that most of the men here are about our age. How old is Uncle Will, anyway?"

"He is forty-seven, same as your father."

John nodded. "I reckon I had long forgotten they were exactly the same age." He paused and pondered for a moment. "I miss them both."

"I, too, miss them terribly."

John grew sullen and quiet. "I only hope that I get to see my Papa and Mama again."

Austin reached over and gave him a friendly punch in the shoulder. "Do not start with the morbid talk. We have only just begun our time with the army! We have yet to meet the enemy in battle, and already you are thinking about dying."

"Well, 'tis a war, Austin, and a bloody one, at that. Men will die. Some of our mates will die." He looked around the camp and observed his friends. He dropped his bowl on the ground beside him. "Suddenly, I am not hungry anymore."

Without hesitation, Austin added his bowl to John's. "I was not hungry to begin with, especially for that nasty slop."

A deep, familiar voice interrupted their conversation. "You fellows had best fill up on that nasty slop whilst you have the chance."

Both Austin and John turned to greet Captain Miller. They declared simultaneously, "Good evening, sir."

"Good evening, boys. Is the stew not to your liking?" He removed his leather gloves and then sat down beside them. John offered their captain a mug of frothy ale. He nodded and smiled. "Thank you, Mr. Austin."

John grinned. "My pleasure, Captain."

"We both noticed that this stew tastes unlike any flavor or variety of beef that either of us has ever eaten," Austin confessed.

The captain leaned forward and whispered, "Perhaps there is good reason." He glanced surreptitiously over both shoulders. "Do not tell anyone, but I believe there may be a mule missing from the quartermaster's pen ... and a particularly old and skinny one, at that."

The look on his face was intensely serious. Austin and John stared at him in disbelief and then shifted their stunned gazes toward one another. Austin, in particular, appeared to be quite disturbed.

He growled, "Damn it, John! I told you that snotty shite did not smell right!" He felt the fluids in his stomach rising in his throat. He gagged and appeared to be on the verge of vomiting.

Captain Miller's serious look disappeared in an instant. He shook his head and chuckled, enjoying a hearty laugh at the expense of the two naïve young men.

"I am only jesting, boys. Worry not. There is no mule meat in your stew. It is, indeed, beef of some sort. But, I am reasonably certain that it remained on the hoof well beyond its years."

"Well, from the taste of it, it might well have been stewed mule," Austin confessed, joining in with the captain's laughter.

"Nevertheless, you fellows need to eat up. You will need your strength. You have a big day ahead of you tomorrow."

John's interest was piqued. "What is happening tomorrow?"

"Those of you on horseback will be joining in with some of Tarleton's men and moving up to Rocky Mount. You will be detailed under the command of Colonel George Turnbull. The colonel has suffered some losses in his personnel. His ranks have been reduced by a large number of desertions. It seems that quite a few of our fellow Loyalists in that region felt the need to return to their farms and crops. Turnbull needs us to bolster his strength, especially in regard to mounted troops." The captain's face became quite serious. "The Whigs have been causing some trouble up in that region as of late. There have been some raids resulting in loss of life and property. There is even talk of a new enemy encampment that is filling with rebels from the north. I anticipate that you boys will see some action."

"Sincerely?" John inquired in awe. "What about the rest of the company?"

"Colonel Phillips has insisted that we stay here for a while and continue training the remainder of the regiment. But, I suspect we will be joining you fellows in a matter of weeks, if not days."

"Then, we are headed into the fray," John declared forebodingly. He glanced at Austin.

"It appears so," the captain confirmed. He stood. "Get your accoutrements and affairs in order, boys. See to your horses. Your animals are vital to the war effort. You will depart at dawn. God save the King."

John and Austin echoed hollowly, "God save the King."

12

AN ACT OF MERCY

Two Hours Before Dusk
Saturday – June 17, 1780
Hugh White's Mill – Upper Fishing Creek, South Carolina

The Jackson's Creek horsemen enjoyed only one night at the well-supplied British encampment at Rocky Mount. Their brief stay included a hot, filling meal, cold ale, and a peaceful night's sleep. The following morning, Colonel Turnbull sent them in search of Captain Christian Huck's long-range patrol with a satchel full of dispatches and orders to join his command. Huck was a captain of the dragoons in the British Legion. He had recently been deployed with a sizable detachment of men on a mission of pacification in the region around Fishing Creek, near the border with North Carolina.

As Austin Newman and the squad of newly-trained horse soldiers proceeded northward out of Rocky Mount, they noticed that most of the area residents made a determined effort to avoid contact with them. Some exhibited fear. As they traveled deeper into the back-country, they encountered outright disdain from many of the rural settlers. Austin, John, and friends began to wonder if they should have stayed back closer to home in the outpost at Camden. Clearly, the people of this remote region had no affection for strangers, especially those of a Loyalist persuasion.

Austin Newman and his five compatriots from the Jackson's Creek Regiment, though unfamiliar with the land and roads in the region, were able to find Captain Huck's trail with relative ease. All they had to do was follow the painfully visible pathway of destruction. They counted no less than six burned homes along the road to Upper Fishing Creek. Numerous barns and other structures had also been destroyed. The men were particularly disturbed to discover evidence of a burned-out church.

After some investigation, a local farmer informed them that the particularly large pile of torched lumber constituted the remains of the Lower Fishing Creek Presbyterian Church. Huck's men had destroyed it one week previous. The same farmer also accosted them with a brief but intense rant about a murder supposedly perpetrated by men from Huck's detachment. According to this very odd and outspoken fellow, the reason that Huck ordered the young man executed was simply because the boy was caught reading the Holy Bible in a barn. He further informed them that the dead lad's name was William Strong.

Of course, such an outlandish claim seemed absurd to Austin and his friends. They assumed that the man's report was nothing more than hearsay birthed in rumor and gossip. There must have been a valid reason for the King's soldiers to claim the life of a local resident. Surely, the young fellow was a combatant of some sort, or had taken some manner of provocative action against the dragoons. Austin determined that he would make inquiries about the killing as soon as was practicable, if only to satisfy his own curiosity. But first, they had to check in with their new commander and deliver Colonel Turnbull's dispatches.

Two days later, the group of six men reached the Loyalist encampment. They provided their credentials for the sentries posted near the roadway and then found their way to Captain Huck's headquarters to make their report and deliver the documents. Somehow,

Austin was elected by his fellow soldiers to serve as leader and spokesperson of their little band. Reluctantly, he tossed the colonel's messenger satchel over his shoulder and then approached the open doorway of the headquarters tent. He rapped firmly upon an exposed tent pole to announce his presence.

A gruff voice from inside the tent barked, "I thought I left instructions that I was not to be disturbed! Oh, hell! Enter at your own risk, damn you!"

Austin hesitated at the sound of the harsh and perplexing command. After a brief, disconcerted pause, he slowly stepped inside the large, two-pole marquee tent. To his right, he spotted a surprisingly young officer reclining on a cot. Was this the infamous Captain Christian Huck? The fellow had his arm draped across his face, apparently in an effort to shield his eyes from the daylight. Austin hesitantly cleared his throat to announce his presence in the room. The captain sat up quickly. He studied Austin with a gaze of impatience and displeasure.

"Just who the bloody hell are you? You dare to wear a green coat, as if that gives you the appearance of one of my dragoons? Speak, man!"

Austin stood up straight and stiff. "Private Austin Newman, sir, of Colonel John Phillips' Regiment. I bear dispatches from Colonel Turnbull." He extended the satchel toward the captain. "And my coat just happens to be green, sir. 'Twas not my intention to imitate anyone."

"I have never heard of him."

Austin was thoroughly confused. He was quite confident that his face betrayed his bewilderment. He stammered, "Uh ... excuse me? You ... uh ... well ... you have never heard of Colonel Turnbull, sir?"

The officer shouted angrily, "No, you provincial moron! John Phillips! Who the bloody hell is John Phillips?"

Austin was beginning to dislike this foul-mouthed man. "He is my commanding officer, Captain, sir."

Captain Huck rolled his eyes in frustration. "Christ, Almighty, you are a daft idiot! I know that he is your colonel. But, who is he? Where is he from?"

"Jackson's Creek, five miles west of the Wateree, and just south of Winnsborough, sir."

"Humph!" grunted the captain. "A South Carolinian, eh? Well, I have never heard of any of those places. It sounds like the crotch of hell to me, and dangerously close to the arse." He pointed impatiently toward a small desk to his left. "Leave the satchel and then be on your way. Get on back to your dimwit colonel and your inbred regiment."

"But, sir, I and my mates have been assigned here ... under your command."

"Horse's arse! By whom?"

"Colonel Turnbull, sir." Austin reached into the breast pocket on his coat and produced a folded document. "I carry orders for myself and five of my compatriots. We have been instructed to join with your dragoons for the campaign."

The captain shook his head vehemently. "I absolutely will not allow a gaggle of backcountry idiots who just happen to own horses to muck up my highly-trained dragoons. You may return from whence you came. But first, leave your horses with my quartermaster. The real dragoons will need them."

Austin felt his face flush red. He began to sweat. There was no way in hell that he was leaving his fine horse with the army and then walking back to Rocky Mount.

"But, Captain, our men have all been in training this past week with one of the officers from your Legion."

"Which one?" inquired the captain, suddenly interested.

"Lieutenant Mayfair."

The captain's face registered a display of pleasant surprise. Indeed, he almost seemed impressed. "Mayfair is a good man, and one hell of a swordsman."

"I agree," Austin affirmed. "And he has attempted to transfer some of that knowledge and experience to us. It has been quite the challenge, but my mates and I have taken to it quite well, I assure you. He and the colonel felt confident enough to send us out to join your patrol."

Captain Huck examined Austin's orders and then abruptly dropped the document onto the disarrayed pile of papers on his desk. "Very well, then. You will be assigned to Lieutenant Anderson's troop. Do you have pistols? A good dragoon needs a pistol, blunderbuss, or carbine."

"Only one amongst our group has a pistol, sir. We have little use for them back home. The rest of us have fowling guns."

The captain displayed a disgusted and angry face. "Fowling guns! I might have known. Excellent for ducks, geese, and rabbits, but abysmal in battle. You might as well be throwing rocks at the enemy." He sighed impatiently. "Very well, then. Find the quartermaster's tent and requisition pistols for your men. We have confiscated quite a few over the past week. He should have an ample supply in storage. And each of you should roll at least a dozen cartridges tonight."

"Yes, sir."

The captain continued, "Anderson's troop is quartered in the southwestern portion of the camp. See to your animals and then pitch your shelters. But, do not get too comfortable. We will be departing early in the morning. We have a rebel camp to pillage. We shall not return for two or three days hence."

Austin felt his pulse quicken. "Then, we are going to meet the enemy?"

The captain opened the satchel and began to examine the dispatches from his commander. "If fortune favors us, yes. I desire greatly to stain my blade with the blood of these damned traitors."

Austin squirmed uncomfortably. "Yes, sir."

After a long, awkward period of silence, the captain glanced impatiently at Austin. "Why, pray tell, are you still here?"

Austin was even more confused. "I was awaiting your leave, sir."

"You have it. Be gone. Get out of my sight."

"Yes, sir!"

Greatly relieved, Austin turned and almost sprinted out of the tent.

~

Later That Evening

"SURELY NOT!" exclaimed John Austin, suddenly jerking his pipe from his mouth. "That cannot be true, Joseph! You are jesting us. We have heard from everyone that the battle at Waxhaws was a great and noble victory."

The Jackson's Creek men stared in shocked disbelief at their new friend, Joseph Huber. They had taken an instant liking to him. Joseph was a most affable and talkative lad from New York and an experienced dragoon in the British Legion. For almost two hours, he had captivated the South Carolina boys with his colorful and entertaining stories. But, his latest revelation regarding the victory over General Buford was troubling, indeed.

John placed a tentative hand on the young man's arm. "Joseph, you must explain. Are you saying that the men of the British Legion executed the rebels as they waved the white flag of surrender?"

Joseph's head hung low. He nodded almost imperceptibly. "It was not as if we intended to do it. We were simply angry and frightened and vengeful. It all happened so fast."

"But, why would seasoned soldiers commit such an atrocity?" asked a disturbed Austin Newman.

"Because we saw Colonel Tarleton go down. He had his horse shot from beneath him. We could not see him moving, and feared that he was crushed and dead. So, we pressed the attack. Even when they stopped fighting and dropped their weapons, we kept on killing."

He paused and stared, empty-eyed, into the campfire. Clearly, he was reliving the battle in his mind. A tear escaped one eye and crept down his cheek.

He continued, "I remember striking this one lad with my saber. It was only after I ran him through that I realized that his hands were empty of all weapons." He closed his eyes as he remembered the traumatic moment. "I can still see the lad clutching at the sword in his chest. There was so much blood." Joseph opened his eyes. "I came to my senses very quickly. But, as I surveyed the battlefield, I saw that many of my fellow Legionnaires did not care who was or was not surrendering. They continued slashing and stabbing and slaying the enemy soldiers. Some were even putting the bayonet to men who lay wounded and helpless on the ground."

"Christ, Almighty!" hissed Austin in disgust. "What of Captain Huck? Was he also executing the surrendering and wounded?"

Joseph stared numbly at Austin. "He was, indeed. I saw him working over several unarmed men with his sword. He carved them up with great precision and skill." Joseph closed his eyes again. "I can still hear those men screaming and begging for mercy."

"That is evil unlike anything that I have ever heard," hissed John in a cautioned whisper.

"It was ... unfortunate," Joseph countered. "But soon, we realized that the colonel was actually unharmed and very much alive. He was only stunned. It was then that every man in the legion came to his senses. But, by that time it was too late. We were instantly filled with regret over what we had done. We immediately halted the attack and began offering aid and quarter to the enemy wounded."

"I simply cannot believe that the officers of the illustrious British Legion took part in such a vicious, uncivilized slaughter," marveled Austin. "And to think that our Captain was right there in the midst of it!"

Joseph offered a half-hearted smile. "Please understand, we are not all evil. He ... Captain Huck ... is not evil. He is simply a bit misguided sometimes." His smile expanded into a genuine grin. "In fact, there are times when he can be most entertaining."

"Like when, supposing?" inquired John sarcastically. He sounded unconvinced.

Joseph chuckled. "Like yesterday. We had this big public meeting on the Upper Fishing Creek. For days, we put out handbills and advertisements. People traveled many miles to come and hear the captain's appeal for peace. But, in the end, it turned into one of the most amusing displays of insult and vulgarity that I have ever experienced."

John gulped. "Vulgarity? In public?"

"Oh, yes." Joseph laughed out loud. "Captain Huck started out with an air of tact and diplomacy. But, before long he was ranting and cursing at those poor souls. It was foul, I tell you. I would have been embarrassed by it all had it not been so funny!"

"How did the people react to his words?" asked Austin.

"With disgust, for the most part." He chuckled and then shook his head. "And then it really got interesting when the blasphemy kicked in."

"Blasphemy?" exclaimed Austin. "Did he proclaim the name of the Lord in vain?"

"Worse," responded Joseph. "He pretty much declared that the Lord was his enemy."

John displayed a skeptical look on his face. "Now, I know that you are full of shite."

"I swear!" pledged Joseph Huber, raising his right hand in the air as a token of his sincerity. "I have never heard such bold and blasphemous statements in all my life." Once again, he stared into the fire as he recalled the captain's words. But, this time, there was a huge smile on his face. "I shall remember it 'till my dying day."

"Tell us. What, *exactly*, did he say?" Austin demanded impatiently.

Joseph opened his eyes. "Well, Captain Huck stood up, big as life, on a platform in front of the gathering of farmers and Whigs. He railed on and on about the evils of the rebellion and the futility of their cause. He harangued those folks, I tell you. He called them horrible names. He threatened them. It was something to behold! Then, when he really got excited and bold, he declared, *'Even if you rebels were as thick as trees and Jesus Christ Himself were to command you, I would still defeat you all.'*"

"Horse shite!" Austin exclaimed.

Joseph chuckled and shook his head. "As God is my witness."

"And the people just stood there and listened to him say all that?" asked John, flabbergasted.

"They did, indeed. You could tell that it did not sit well with them, though. Some of them looked pretty displeased. But, still, they kept listening. And that was not even the worse thing he said!"

"Go on," John begged. "Please tell us!"

"Well, just a little while later he swore, *'God Almighty has become a rebel! But, even if there were twenty gods fighting for the rebel cause, I would still conquer them all!'*"

There was an audible gasp among the men from Jackson's Creek. They all looked at one another in fear and disbelief. They were greatly disturbed by the captain's words, so much so that they even feared having heard them repeated.

Joshua Ginn, a fellow militiaman and neighbor who lived near Austin and John confessed, "After hearing all that, I feel as if I need to go somewhere and pray."

Joseph Huber chuckled. "Obviously, our Captain Huck does not hold religion in very high regard. I heard it was because he lost all of his land and fortune in Philadelphia because of some of the Presbyterians in the city. Since then, he has had little use for the things of God or the church. And he holds people of a Presbyterian persuasion in especially lowly regard."

"Why, pray tell?" Austin demanded. His shock and displeasure with the captain was quickly and progressively intensifying.

"Because most of the Whigs in Philadelphia, especially the ones who were the roughest on him, were all Presbyterians. After suffering at their rebel hands, he has had no use for them, at all." He paused. "I imagine that is why we burned that church to the ground last week."

"We passed by that site during our travels," remarked John. "We wondered why you fellows destroyed a church."

Joseph shrugged. "'Tis to be expected, I suppose. The pastor was a rabid Whig. He had several churches in his charge throughout the region and developed quite a reputation for stirring up the rebels in his district. Captain Huck went after him and burned his church in the process."

"You speak of the man in past tense. Did you kill the pastor?" inquired Austin, aghast.

"No. He is still alive, I reckon."

Austin exhaled in relief. "Good. I am glad the captain showed some restraint in his dealings with a minister of the Gospel."

"Oh, it was not because he showed any restraint. He would have killed the man, for certain. We simply could not find him. The old rebel preacher gave us the slip and made his escape into North Carolina," Joseph explained. He stared thoughtfully into the campfire. "Like I said, our captain hates Presbyterians."

"But, *we* are Presbyterians ... the entire lot of us from Jackson's Creek," Austin protested. "Indeed, we all attend the same church back home."

Joseph's eyes widened in surprise. He stared in disbelief at every man in their group. "Is this true?"

The men nodded.

"And still, despite your religious inclinations, you serve the King of England?"

The men nodded again. They seemed perplexed by the young man's incredulous reaction.

"I have never known any men of your denomination who supported the King." Joseph chuckled and shook his head. "But, if I were you, I would avoid mentioning it in the presence of Captain Huck."

"Do not worry!" exclaimed John. "Whilst we are near him, we shall abstain from discussions of a religious nature altogether."

"I think that would be wise," Joseph affirmed.

The men sat in silence for a while, drinking ale and puffing their pipes as they pondered the complex politics of their day. There remained, however, one more question in Austin's mind that demanded an answer. At first, he considered letting the matter go altogether. But, it seemed to him that Joseph Huber was a kind and honest lad. Surely, he could provide a rational explanation for the killing of the young man named William Strong.

"Joseph, when we stopped to investigate the burned-out church, that farmer also told us about a young fellow who had been murdered on a nearby farm. He claimed that the lad was unarmed and non-belligerent. What do you know of that?" Austin stared expectantly at his new friend.

Joseph grimaced. "That was some nasty business. I was actually amongst the ones who discovered the boy."

Austin desired to probe the matter further. "So then, you found him concealed in a barn?"

Joseph nodded. "I assumed that the lad was just frightened by all the commotion and hiding from us. He was sitting behind a pile of hay and clutching his Bible to his chest. Well, it was not actually a Bible. It was the Psalter in Gaelic ... you know ... the kind that the Scottish Presbyterians use for singing. He was mumbling on in the language of the Scots and quoting passages from his book, no doubt."

"But, why was he killed? Did he pull a weapon on you when you found him? Did he make an aggressive move?" demanded John.

Joseph's chin dropped to his chest. He gently shook his head. "No. The boy was not belligerent. He took no offensive action. He did not say a word to us, other than uttering his Scottish ramblings. He merely clung to that book as if his life depended upon it. He was greatly upset when one of my comrades took it from him."

"What happened after that?" inquired Austin. He was quite disturbed and growing more so.

Joseph inhaled deeply. "We gave the book to Captain Huck. He took one look at it, saw the Scottish writing, and then ordered the sergeant to run the boy through."

"But, why?" demanded Austin. "I do not understand."

Joseph glanced over both shoulders to see if anyone else was listening. Once certain that their conversation was a private one, he whispered, "I told you already. It was because the boy was a Presbyterian." He stared silently into the darkness for several seconds. "And Captain Huck ... well, he hates Presbyterians."

Austin looked at John, who was staring, glassy-eyed, at Joseph. John's head slowly cocked to one side in an expression of complete and utter bewilderment.

~

The Next Morning
Hill's Iron Works

THE ATTACKING force was an impressive one, indeed. Over two hundred dragoons and a small contingent of infantry surrounded the rebel camp on three sides. Austin Newman and the Jackson's Creek men were among those battle-ready dragoons.

Austin, perched proudly atop his horse, scanned the enemy camp from his place of concealment in the thick forest. To him, the name given to the rebel outpost seemed somewhat less than accurate. All of the Loyalists referred to the place as 'Hill's Iron Works.' They described it as a facility where the Whigs were processing metals to produce weapons and ammunition. But, upon seeing the location first-hand, Austin was quite impressed with the vast array of other activities ongoing within the rebel encampment. In addition to the iron smelting and refining facilities, there were also two impressive mills. One was a large sawmill and the other a gristmill. Both were located on the bank of the swiftly-flowing Allison Creek. Dozens of temporary shelters surrounded the larger buildings. Altogether, the camp actually had the appearance of a small village.

Soon, the Tory dragoons would dispatch these rebels encamped at the iron works. They had the double-advantage of surprise and swiftness, thanks to the fact that the majority of their troops were on horseback. With any luck, the Loyalists would kill or capture the entire garrison. But, until the order came, they remained hidden in the surrounding woods and awaited their captain's order.

Austin glanced at his mates. He was barely able to make out the features on their faces in the dull glow of the pre-dawn. He wondered if they were as frightened as he. His heart pounded loudly inside his chest. His pulse was so strong that he could hear the faint, high-pitched, fluidic whooshing sound of blood coursing through the arteries in his neck. The prospect of hand-to-hand combat was terrifying to him. Austin attempted to slow his breathing and calm himself.

True, Austin Newman had already served with the Loyalist army at Ninety-Six back in 1775. But, in his own mind, that had not been actual combat. He merely hid behind log barricades for a few days and lobbed blind shots into an enemy fort. He could scarcely even see his targets. But, on this day, it would be starkly different. This promised to be a close-quarters fight with blades. It would be cruel, primitive, and bloody. Austin tentatively reached across his body and felt the handle of his saber. He ran trembling fingers across the cool metal wire that was woven tightly around the saber's grip. He closed his eyes and tried to imagine plunging the shiny blade into the heart of another man. His body trembled involuntarily at the thought.

He opened his eyes and peered once more toward the enemy's position, straining to see any possible threats. There were dozens of tents and lean-tos surrounding the four large industrial structures. Numerous smoldering cooking fires were spaced amongst the rebel militia's sleeping quarters. A large number of horses and mules were housed within a large pen on the northern side of the camp. Everything appeared quiet and peaceful. There was no evidence of alarm. It appeared that everyone was asleep, except for a handful of pickets and lookouts. The slumbering Whigs had no notion of the impending attack.

Austin leaned in close to John. He whispered, "It looks pretty quiet, does it not?"

John nodded and grinned. "I think everyone is asleep, including most of the sentries. What a stroke of luck! I reckon they will soon get a very big surprise."

After a brief period of silence, Austin confessed ashamedly, "John, I am frightened."

John sniffed and then wiped his nose on his coat sleeve. He cut his eyes at Austin and smiled. "As am I. You are not alone in your fear. 'Tis a weighty thing to kill a man. But, worry not. You will be fine. We should remain close together and lag back just a bit. There is no need to be in front of the line in the midst of our very first fight."

Austin nodded, somewhat relieved. "I agree. A most excellent plan."

Suddenly, a cry erupted from somewhere to their right. Then came the muffled thunder of hooves pounding against the loamy, composted soil of the forest floor. The men nearby all drew their swords and screamed their battle cries. Instantly, they spurred their horses into motion and galloped toward the enemy encampment. Austin, John, and their mates from back home followed suit. Per their agreement, they delayed momentarily and allowed the more experienced troops to lead the way.

Austin held tightly to the reins with his left hand and brandished his saber in the right. He became slightly disoriented as he rode through the thick trees. Numerous branches and limbs assaulted his upper body. One particularly low branch caught him just below the eye on his right cheek. It slashed a deep gouge into his skin. He felt the sting of the wound and immediately sensed the warm flow of blood trickling down his face. He also tasted the metallic tang of blood on his lips. Assuming it to be minor, Austin ignored the injury and pressed on. Soon, he emerged from the trees into the open ground beyond.

The scene that greeted him within the enemy encampment was nothing short of mayhem. He could see dozens of men in the distance, most of them sparsely clad, scattering madly into the woods. Inside the camp, there was very little in the way of actual combat. There were scant few gunshots. Near the western edge of the battlefield, a handful of dragoons attacked fleeing men with their swords. But, that was it. It was barely a battle, at all. Captain Huck's dragoons had routed the sleeping enemy and taken captive their encampment in a matter of minutes. Most of the rebel militia did not even fight back. Instead, they made a frantic escape into the surrounding woods.

Austin's heart beat wildly, fueled by the large doses of adrenaline that still coursed within his veins. He searched the area for enemy soldiers, but there was no one left for him to fight. The only inhabitants of the camp who remained were negro slaves. Several dozen of the filthy, shabbily-clad laborers stood, hands up in surrender, outside their primitive lean-to shelters. A squad from the dragoons took charge of them and almost immediately began marching then onto the nearby roadway. These slave laborers would, no doubt, soon be conscripted into the King's army.

Austin quickly returned his saber to its scabbard, thrilled that he had not been called upon to actually use it. He turned to John. "What do we do now?"

John shrugged. "Hell if I know. We stay put and wait for orders, I reckon."

At that exact moment, Lieutenant Wallace Anderson, their squad commander, approached from their left. He barked, "What, exactly, are you men doing?"

Austin turned his horse to face the officer. "Awaiting instructions, sir. This is our first action, and we are unsure as to what we must do next."

The lieutenant's eyes narrowed with concern. "You are bleeding pretty badly, son. Were you wounded in the fight?"

Austin reached up for the first time to feel of his cut. It was quite deep and bloody. He was disturbed to discover that blood had run down his neck and thoroughly soaked the collar of his relatively new homespun shirt.

"No, sir. I got nicked by a stiff limb on the way through the woods."

"It looks deep. It may require some stitching. Have the surgeon see to it when we return to camp this evening."

"Yes, sir. I will, sir. Thank you."

"Very well. What is your name, young man?"

"Austin Newman, sir."

The lieutenant pointed toward the north. "Mr. Newman, we need skirmishers to check those woods. I saw numerous rebel militiamen fleeing into the trees. Your orders are to pursue and engage the enemy and either kill or capture them. 'Twould be splendid if you secure me a prisoner or two. Take the rest of the new fellows with you. But, do not wander off too far. There could be an ambush waiting for you out there." He paused. "I appoint you as acting corporal in charge of the squad."

Austin's heart began to beat loudly again. He could feel the heat in his face as it flushed red. "Yes, sir."

"Move quickly. You will want to join us in plundering the camp. There is much booty to be had. It appears they fled with only the shirts on their backs. After we claim our prizes, we shall tarry only long enough to burn the iron foundry and mills."

Austin nodded, "Yes, sir."

"Get to it, then." The lieutenant whipped his horse around and then headed toward the sawmill.

AUSTIN and his friends were spaced thirty yards apart and making their way slowly through the thick woods. Each man had his pistol drawn and at the ready. They had gone roughly a quarter-mile from the iron works. Thankfully, the undergrowth thinned as they entered a large stand of virgin timber, but the woods became darker and more foreboding. Huge, towering trees formed an interwoven canopy overhead, allowing scant light to pass through. The ground was covered with a thick layer of gray-brown compost, produced by the accumulation of many years of fallen limbs and leaves. The woods were dark, dank, and silent. There was no sign of the enemy, other than a few places where the ground cover had been disturbed by the feet of fleeing men.

After they had progressed another quarter-mile, John angled his horse in Austin's direction. He approached his friend and drew his mare to a halt.

"Spooky as hell, is it not?" John observed. "This place is too quiet for me."

Austin nodded. "Indeed. Nary a bird or squirrel or any other critter is moving about."

John continued to scan the woods. "I have seen no sign of rebels, other than churned-up ground. What about you?"

Austin removed his hat and wiped his brow. "Same here. Reckon we should head on back?"

"I think so. I figure we are at least a half-mile from the enemy's camp. 'Twould be a shame to get cut off out here and then wander into a rebel trap."

"Agreed." Austin scanned to his left and right. "Signal our friends to the east. I will inform the fellows to the west."

"Yes, sir, Colonel Newman, sir." John winked and grinned.

"That's Corporal Newman, you lobcock." Austin winked back at him.

John turned his horse and then went to inform the two fellows on their right flank. Austin headed in the opposite direction. He guided his horse over a stretch of rocky ground that dropped off into a shallow draw. He heard water flowing nearby. He soon discovered a bubbling spring near the top of the draw. It filled a shallow, rock-lined, crystal-clear pool. The spring was a most fortuitous discovery, as all the men were running low on water.

Austin halted his horse and dismounted. He untied his two canteens and quickly knelt beside the pool, anxious to collect a personal supply of clean, fresh water. While his horse drank, he submerged both canteens and filled them. The task required only a couple of minutes. Once done, Austin lashed the canteens to his saddle. As he was preparing to climb back onto his horse, Austin caught a glimpse of something white in the center of a large, three-trunk oak that stood only a few yards north of the spring. He was not sure what he saw. He only knew that it appeared out of place. The pale color was odd for the deep woods.

Leaving his horse beside the water, he pulled his pistol and crept silently toward the enormous split tree. His heart leapt when, once again, he saw a brief flash of white. He immediately became convinced that it was cloth ... a shirt, no doubt. His heart leapt into his throat when he spotted a human eyeball peering at him from between two of the converging tree trunks.

"I see you in there!" Austin shouted as he cocked his pistol. "Come out with your hands held high."

"Please, do not shoot," begged a high-pitched, Irish voice. "I ain't armed."

"Come out so that I can see you! Hurry it up!"

Two small, pale hands appeared amongst the cluster of tree trunks. Then, slowly, a frightened, shaking fellow emerged from his hiding place. He was a mere lad, and a skinny one, at that. The boy had a tangled mop of blazing red hair and was naked except for his stained linen shirt and off-white stockings. The stockings were not gartered and had collapsed into heaps around his ankles. He was covered with streaks of mud and debris. His legs were pitifully thin and white as goose down. He appeared to favor one of them.

The lad begged, "Please do not hurt me, kind sir. Like I said, I ain't got no gun."

John and the other fellows had heard Austin's shouting and come quickly to his aid. They appeared quickly, pistols cocked and ready for action. The men looked quite disappointed when they laid eyes upon the bony, half-naked boy.

John released his pistol to half-cock and swiftly tucked it back into his belt. He smiled victoriously. "You have captured an enemy soldier, I see."

"Not much of one," chided their friend, George Rogers. "That frail, knock-kneed lad looks like death's head upon a mop-stick."

"He is old enough to pull a trigger, I reckon." Austin released the cock on his pistol and lowered it. "Come closer, boy."

The young fellow limped slowly toward Austin. His hands remained in the air.

"You can put your hands down, son. We mean you no harm."

The boy complied. Though completely helpless, his gaze remained defiant. Clearly, he was not pleased with his situation.

"What's your name, boy?" Austin inquired.

"William Armstrong."

"How old are you?"

"I just turned fifteen."

Austin rubbed his chin thoughtfully. "You look familiar. Where are you from, William Armstrong?"

"Camden District. My father has a place a couple of miles north of Winnsborough."

Austin studied the lad. Suddenly, he remembered where he had seen him.

"Your father is Ephraim Armstrong, is he not?"

The boy's eyes grew wide with surprise. "Yes, sir. But, how in the blue blazes could you know that?"

"Because I am from Jackson's Creek, William. My name is Austin Newman. My father, William Newman, has done business with yours. In fact, I believe that I went to your home once. My father paid a debt that he owed to yours and then your mother fed us a fine meal. That was maybe three or four years ago." He grinned. "I thought I recognized that hair of yours. I have never seen such a shade of red quite like it."

"Well, I certainly do not remember you," the boy retorted defiantly.

"'Tis no surprise," quipped John, grinning. "He has a most disagreeable and forgettable face."

The other fellows laughed and, seeing that there was no real danger, deactivated and stowed their weapons.

Austin turned to his friends. "There is excellent water in yon spring. 'Tis sweet as sugar. You fellows fill up your canteens and jugs. I am going to see to young William. It appears that he has been injured."

The men nodded and complied.

"Come, William. Sit down." Austin pointed at a large, flat boulder near the spring. "What has happened to your leg?"

The boy hobbled toward the rock and then sat down. "I tripped on a vine in the woods as I fled the attack. I twisted my knee pretty bad. I think I heard somethin' pop."

Austin knelt down and gently lifted the boy's right leg. He examined the injured knee. It was very swelled, indeed. He squeezed the knee gently. The lad winced from the pain.

"The joint 'tis fat and soft, to be sure. It could use a good, firm wrap. I would bind it for you, William, but I have no spare cloth with me. Nevertheless, 'twould be wise for you to rest up and stay off of it for a while."

"To what purpose?" challenged William. "I know that I will have a stretched neck before the day's end." Tears filled his eyes. "I have heard all about your Captain Huck. He is a vile and bloodthirsty man. I hear tell of how he disposes of his prisoners."

Austin patted the lad on his uninjured knee. "No one is going to hang you, William. You have my word." He paused thoughtfully. "Was your father with you in the camp?"

"No, sir. I joined the militia on my own. Papa forbade me to go, so I ran off. He does not know where I am."

"Do you have any close mates in your rebel regiment?"

His chin dropped to his chest. "I thought so. But, they all ran off and left me after I tripped and fell. They are all still runnin', I reckon."

Austin smiled. "Were they all buck naked and dressed in their shirt-tail same as you?"

William tried to suppress a grin, but he could not. He nodded.

"Well, these things happen, William. Most men quite naturally care more for their own arses when the lead starts to fly. They were simply frightened. Try not to hold it against them." Austin peered toward the north. "Are there any farms or cabins nearby?"

"I think there is a big plantation on the far side of these woods. 'Tis no more than a half-mile or so from here. I believe that is where ever'one was headed."

Austin nodded and then smiled. "Worry not. You will be with your comrades soon. I will see to it."

John approached, gulping delicious, cold water from his gourd canteen. He winked. "What are we going to do with this dangerous prisoner?"

"We are going to let him go."

John's countenance became serious. He shook his head. "That is a bad idea, Austin. The lieutenant said specifically that he wanted prisoners."

The other men from their group gathered around to listen to the exchange.

Austin explained, "This boy is no soldier, as you can see. He is a good Presbyterian lad from Camden district. And we all know what Huck will do with him if we take him back, do we not?"

The men all looked at one another and nodded grimly.

John answered bitterly, "The bastard will string him up, no doubt."

"Exactly," Austin agreed.

"So, what is your plan, then?" asked George Rogers. "We cannot stay gone all the long day. Huck will leave us behind, for certain. And, right now, we are missing out on the plundering of the camp. The other fellows are going to get away with everything of value."

Austin considered the situation for a moment and then quickly reached a decision. "You boys head on back. I am going to take young William north to the edge of the woods and then send him on his way." He grinned. "Grab a little something from the rebel tents for me. More than anything, I could use some tobacco."

John nodded. "I will see what I can find. Make haste and be cautious."

"I will." He extended his hand to John. "I will be along shortly. I promise."

John shook Austin's hand. "We will be waiting for you."

The five men mounted their horses quickly and then trotted southward back toward the iron works. Austin reached down and took the lad by the arm and helped him rise to his feet.

"We must move quickly, William. We both have places to be."

THE DARK CANOPY of the forest ended at an open pasture. Beyond the trees, Austin could see a large, white plantation house. He halted his horse roughly one hundred yards from the edge of the field.

"William, this is as far as I go. You are on your own from here."

Austin dismounted and then gently helped the lad down from the tall horse. He untied a small gourd canteen from the side of his saddle and then handed it to the boy.

"This should help hold you over until you can get some new gear. Now, go and join your mates."

"I do not know how I could ever repay you, Mr. Newman. I owe you my life."

"'Twas the Christian thing to do, William. We Presbyterian brethren have to watch out for one another, do we not?" He winked and smiled at the boy.

William grinned happily. "Perhaps we might see one another again someday. If so, I shall be honored to count you amongst my friends."

"I look forward to that day, Master William." They shook hands. "Be on your way. Good luck, William."

"Good luck to you, Mr. Newman."

The lad turned and, clutching his water bottle to his chest, hobbled through the trees toward the plantation house. Austin quickly mounted his mare and then turned the animal southward. He rode through the woods as swiftly as he could. A half-hour later, he rejoined his friends just in time to help them set torches to the buildings and other structures at the rebel iron works. No one spoke a word about their young prisoner.

13

HUCK'S DEFEAT

July 10, 1780
British and Loyalist Headquarters – Rocky Mount, South Carolina

I t was a typical South Carolina summer. As was usual, the heat and humidity were oppressive, draining strength and will from both man and beast. Austin Newman and his friends sought a meager measure of relief from the scorching mid-day sun in the shade of a cluster of thick pines. They each reclined upon their great-coats, which were spread across soft beds of fluffy pine needles. The men wore only their breeches and shirts. Since there were no women in or near the army encampment, modesty and decorum were of no particular concern.

Per the orders of Lieutenant Anderson, the men had been resting throughout the day and taking occasional naps. They needed to get as much rest as possible during daylight hours, since they would all be confined to the saddle throughout the coming night. The Jackson's Creek horsemen were scheduled to depart at dusk on a mission, along with over one hundred other dragoons and mounted militia-men. Their patrol would be traveling in the cool of night, as had become standard procedure for the Loyalist army over the past two weeks.

Most men at the army encampment, especially the New Yorkers, found it quite difficult to rest in the stifling southern heat. Considering the fact that, in addition to the high temperatures, swarms of mosquitoes and gnats were determined to feast upon every living creature in the backcountry, it almost seemed fruitless to even attempt to sleep. Still, the men had to make an effort. The six mates languished in various states of tortured slumber. None amongst them wanted to suffer the brutal chastisement of the officers that always came when a soldier fell asleep in the saddle whilst on duty.

John Austin interrupted their futile efforts at sleep with a most surprising announcement. "I will not be going on patrol with you fellows tonight."

"And why not?" demanded George Rogers, sitting up on his makeshift pallet.

"I have been assigned to messenger duty. I will be making the run to Camden after supper. Do not be jealous, George. I will not be getting any extra sleep. I will be traveling throughout the night, same as you."

George shrugged and then lay back down. "I reckon you are going to miss all the fun, then."

"What do you mean?"

"I hear tell we are going after a few of the big fish in the Rebel ranks. The colonel got word that three of the leaders from Fishing Creek have come down from North Carolina to check on their families and crops. Supposedly, they have been doing a little recruiting in the backcountry, as well. Captain Huck intends to capture them."

"How is it that you always know so damned much?" inquired a closed-eyed Austin Newman.

"I have some very good sources in the headquarters," George answered proudly. "After all, information *is* my specialty."

"That is odd," declared John. "I always thought that horse manure was your stock and trade."

The other fellows all snickered and laughed. They knew all too well that George Rogers was a world-class purveyor and, on occasion, author of gossip.

Their friend and fellow horseman, Joshua Ginn, commented, "One thing is certain ... 'twill be a pleasure to get out of the horrid squalor of this army camp. These past three weeks have been nothing but tortured, sleepless boredom. And ever since the battle at the iron works, I have had naught to do but look upon all of your hideous faces."

"You must have been studying your own self in a looking glass," teased George. "I once heard from your mother that, when you were born, the midwife accidentally threw away the baby and kept the afterbirth."

George's uncouth insult resulted in a wave of groans and laughter.

Austin, quite annoyed, cleared his throat loudly. "How about we all practice the art of silence for a change? We need our sleep. Remember, we have to go to work tonight. Eight or ten hours in the saddle will be no joy, I assure you."

George answered in a high-pitched, nasal voice, "Yes, sir, Corporal Newman."

All of the fellows, including Austin, exploded in laughter.

~

The Next Morning
Near Fishing Creek - The Home of John McClure, American Officer

Austin's blood boiled with indignant rage. The conduct of his officers and sergeants was an offense to him. Their actions were devoid of honor and most definitely did not resemble the behavior of true gentlemen. Deep down in his heart, Austin was beginning to wonder if the cause that he served was a just one. For, how could a just cause result in such unjust treatment of unarmed civilians?

The overnight journey to Fishing Creek had already been disturbing enough. As the patrol made its way northward, Captain Huck ordered his men to appropriate supplies and horses from each homestead and farm they encountered. They roused a dozen families from their sleep and then confiscated all of their horses and food-stuffs. It did not seem to matter whether the victims were Tories or Whigs. Captain Huck had plundering on his mind. In wartime, the plunder and appropriation of property to support the war effort were to be expected. Indeed, in the South Carolina backcountry, such actions were practiced with great enthusiasm. But, since arriving at their destination, the behavior of Huck and his men had devolved considerably. He now authorized the beating and torture of prisoners.

The Loyalist patrol had finally located the home of the rebel officer John McClure. Captain Huck greatly desired to take this particular man into custody. Upon their arrival, the captain dispatched his soldiers to search every building and potential hiding place on the property. When his men entered the house, they discovered James McClure, the younger brother of John, and another fellow named Edward Martin. Both of the young men were arrested, along with Mary McClure, wife of John. They were captured in the process of melting pewter plates and then using the molten metal to cast musket balls. Of course, John McClure was nowhere to be found. Captain Huck, foiled in his effort to apprehend the elusive Whig, immediately lost his temper and cast aside all pretense of propriety. Then, the most unthinkable drama began to unfold.

Austin, like most of the other men assigned to the patrol, stood at a distance and watched the brutal, bloody interrogation of the prisoners. He was aghast at the indecent and heartless acts being perpetrated by Captain Huck and some of the other officers and sergeants. He wanted no part in their dishonor.

George poked his elbow into Austin's side. He hissed, "Are you believing this?"

Austin shook his head slowly. He replied, "Truly, these are not the actions of honorable gentlemen."

"No, they ain't," growled their friend, Joshua Ginn.

James McClure appeared to be no more than twenty years of age. His face was bruised and bleeding from a vicious beating at the hands of two Tory sergeants. Despite the brutal treatment, the lad refused to divulge any information regarding the location of his brother. Likewise, his compatriot, Edward Martin, had been beaten until he was almost unconscious. And, like McClure, he had bravely held his tongue and refused to talk. But, as bad as the beatings of the two young men had been, the most unthinkable atrocity was yet to come.

Captain Huck shouted angrily, "Bring that rebel bitch to me!"

Austin, George, and Joshua exchanged disturbed, disbelieving looks. Instantly, two of the New York Volunteers pulled a screaming Mary McClure from her cabin. Her bonnet was gone. One of the soldiers dragged her mercilessly by the hair of her head. Her short gown was ripped apart in the front, exposing her stays and the tops of her pale, white breasts. The soldiers threw her onto the ground at Captain Huck's feet. She rose to her knees. Amazingly, the woman did not weep. She bravely repressed the urge. Instead, everything in her countenance reflected an attitude of bold defiance. A gaggle of terrified children watched from just inside the doorframe of the house. All of them were whimpering and crying. The oldest one, a young teen-aged girl, sobbed uncontrollably.

Her mother barked, "Hush, children! I will be just fine. I know how to handle the likes of such miscreants as these." She turned and faced Captain Huck with a steely gaze.

Austin gasped when the captain drew his sword. He brandished the weapon tauntingly in front of Mary McClure's face. She glared at the man with eyes of hatred. Huck placed the flat side of the blade of the sword on her shoulder and then slowly walked all the way around her. As he walked, he gently brushed the blade across the back of her neck and then rested it on her other shoulder, maintaining downward pressure against her collar bone. As he came back into her field of view, he gave the blade an almost imperceptible flick, slicing off a six-inch long section of her silky auburn hair. The severed hair landed on her shoulder and then slowly slid off and fluttered to the ground. Unblinking, Mary McClure maintained her icy, defiant stare.

"I have only one question for you, Mrs. McClure. If you answer it truthfully, I will allow you to live. If not, you will suffer the same fate that awaits these two traitors to the Crown." He pointed his sword at the bruised, bloodied young men. "Of course, they are to be hanged."

Mrs. McClure casually brushed the remnants of hair from her shoulder and then spat on the ground at Captain Huck's feet. The captain smiled. He appeared to enjoy the challenge.

"Your husband, John McClure, has taken up arms against his lawful Sovereign. He is to be apprehended and tried for his treason and crimes. I am counting upon you to reveal his whereabouts so that we might dispense British justice and bring order, once again, to this horrid backcountry. Now, tell me, woman ... where is he? Where has your traitorous husband gone?"

"Oh, is that all you want to know?" she replied sarcastically. "He has returned to his regiment, of course."

"And where might that band of honorless brigands be located?"

"I do not know their whereabouts, Captain. Obviously, my husband would not divulge such information to me."

"Perhaps." He ran the tip of the sword around the contour of her ample breasts. "But, as can be plainly seen, you are a woman. And women are notorious for their gossip and talk." He placed the tip of his sword under her chin and forced her head upward. "Surely, you know something, even if that information did not come directly from your husband. Therefore, I will ask you one more time. Where is the rebel John McClure?"

Mrs. McClure did not respond to his insulting inquiry. Instead, she asked him a question. "What is your name, sir?"

"I am Captain Christian Huck of His Majesty's British Legion." He bowed mockingly. "At your service."

She chuckled sarcastically. "Until my dying day, I shall never forget that name. It is dripping with insult and irony, for a true Christian would never behave in such a manner as you have this day. Rest assured, I will be most satisfied to share your name with my husband at the earliest opportunity."

He returned a mocking smile. "Why wait, Mrs. McClure? Let us go now and visit him together. You could make your introductions in person. I would be most honored."

Her smile disappeared and her eyes narrowed. "You will meet him soon enough, I reckon. But, be warned. When you do see him, his will be the last face that you ever behold ... just before he guts you like a wailing sow."

Captain Huck, greatly insulted, instinctively swung his sword and slapped the flat of the blade fiercely across her right cheek. The impact of steel against flesh elicited a high-pitched pop. Mrs. McClure yelped with pain, tumbled sideways, and landed face down in the powdery dry dirt. She lay there for a brief moment and then rose, once again, to her knees. The left side of her face was covered in red-brown dust. She pressed her right hand tightly against her cheek. A tiny trickle of blood leaked from between her thumb and forefinger. The razor sharp edge of the blade had penetrated her tender skin.

Mrs. McClure, tears of pain trickling from her eyes, remained defiant. She declared, "Sir, that will be a dear blow to you!"

Captain Huck's chin quivered slightly. Clearly, he had not expected such resistance, bravery, and fortitude from a mere woman. He stole a glance at the observers who surrounded him. He was disturbed by the shame in their eyes. Indeed, some of his soldiers seemed to be staring at him with gazes of anger, if not hatred. Despite his position of power, Captain Christian Huck had been humiliated and defeated in the very midst of his own men. He instantly returned his sword to his scabbard and then turned his back toward Mary McClure. He pointed at the two male prisoners.

"Bind these men and bring them with us. They will both die a traitor's death. We shall hang them after tomorrow's breakfast."

"And what of the woman and children?" inquired Lieutenant Anderson.

"Leave them. They pose no threat to us. But, fire the house and outbuildings. Do not leave a single stick or log on this farm intact. John McClure shall have no home to shelter him when he returns. Move quickly. We depart within the hour."

"Where are we going?" asked another of his junior officers.

"To the plantation of William Bratton. It is a mere ten miles to the north. Perhaps we will have better luck there." He turned to his men. "Secure the prisoners and prepare for travel!"

Austin and the fellows from Jackson's Creek turned and solemnly marched toward their horses. They were stunned. But, more than anything, they were ashamed.

"What do you think of all that?" marveled George.

"Honestly, I do not know what to think. I have never seen anything that compares to it." Austin confessed. "To see a man treat a woman in such a way!" He sighed. "I am beginning to wish that I was back home."

George nodded grimly. "I, as well. Surely, there are none of these goings-on at Jackson's Creek." He glanced over his shoulder at Mary McClure. Her weeping children were assisting her into the house. "That could just as easily have been my own wife."

"I should pray not." He frowned and stared thoughtfully at the ground near his feet. "The notion of someone treating my step-mother, or your wife, in such a way ..." He shook his head as his voice trailed off into anguished silence.

George placed a reassuring hand on his shoulder. "'Tis all right, Austin. Our families are safe. Worry not."

They turned to fetch the reins to their horses, but Lieutenant Anderson halted them.

"Stand fast, gentlemen! Corporal Austin, I want you to start a fire. Have your men construct torches. You fellows are ordered set fire to all the buildings. Move quickly. We have precious little time. The captain is anxious to depart."

Austin sighed and nodded reluctantly. "Yes, sir."

❧

Late Afternoon
The Home of William Bratton, Whig Officer

THE DISTURBING EVENTS at the McClure farm had been only the first act in a horrifying, unimaginable drama. Act two took place at the farm of William Bratton. Once again, the King's soldiers found no evidence of their quarry. Like McClure, William Bratton had already made his escape. Huck missed apprehending him by only a few hours. He, too, had received word about the approaching Loyalist patrol and fled his home early that morning. He did so with the assumption that an enemy army would not make war upon his helpless wife and children. But, he was sorely mistaken.

Captain Huck was almost outside his mind with rage when he realized how close he had come to capturing the rebel officer, only to have yet another enemy combatant slip from his grasp. Huck interrogated everyone on the premises in order to discover the location of the enemy encampment, but to no avail. No one would give him the intelligence that he sought. Finally, just as he had done earlier in the day, he focused his anger upon the wife of the fugitive.

Huck was in a blinding fury when he ordered Martha Bratton brought forth from her cabin. He instructed his men to position her beneath an expansive maple tree. He then ordered a noose placed around her neck. The rope was draped over a large limb. Several men pulled the rope tight until Mrs. Bratton was stretched and barely standing on the tips of her toes. But, even as she was threatened with hanging, she still would not reveal the location of her husband. Then, the truly unthinkable happened. Captain Huck, in a surge of rage, grabbed a reaping hook from a nearby bench and lunged at the woman. He placed the curved blade menacingly around Mrs. Bratton's neck. As he pressed the steel against her throat, he demanded that she reveal the location of her husband and his rebel encampment. Still, she remained silent.

Everyone present thought for certain that the incensed captain was going to slice the woman's throat. Austin Newman placed a trembling hand on the grip of his pistol. He prayed that he would not have to draw his weapon on his own commander in order to prevent him from murdering this helpless woman. But, he had resolved himself to do whatever was necessary, even if it meant that his own neck would replace hers inside the hangman's noose. Thankfully, Lieutenant John Adamson, a Loyalist from Camden, intervened. He actually grabbed Captain Huck's arm and pulled the rabidly enraged officer away from the helpless woman.

Suddenly coming to his senses, Captain Huck ordered Mrs. Bratton released. He sent her back inside the cabin and instructed her to prepare supper for himself and his officers. Since darkness was descending in the backcountry, the men would need to make camp soon. After receiving a report from one of his scouts describing a large field of oats on the nearby plantation of James Williamson, Huck ordered his men to go there, feed their horses, and make camp. He promised that he would join them before dusk.

Austin and his friends quickly mounted their horses and pointed them northward. They were anxious to put distance between themselves and the traumatic experiences of the day. Though they would never say so out loud, they were also anxious to remove themselves from the presence of Captain Christian Huck. Austin determined that he would seek another assignment at the first available opportunity.

～

Just before Midnight

AUSTIN AND GEORGE were on the first watch of picket duty. They occupied one of six two-man outposts positioned strategically around the periphery of the camp. Their post was southwest of the Williamson cabin, just inside the edge of the adjacent forest. The position overlooked the militia encampment, located in an open field directly in front of the cabin. The New York Volunteers were encamped about fifty yards to the north, on the small lane that led from the main highway to the plantation. Their double row of tents fit perfectly between the two split-rail fences that lined both sides of the tiny road.

It had been a long, frustrating, and disturbing day. Both Austin and George were anxious for their relief to arrive so that they might return to their tent and climb into their bedrolls. They were thoroughly exhausted and ready for a good sleep. While they waited, they sat cross-legged in the darkness and stared, mesmerized, at the dancing, glowing sky. It was filled with a brilliant, colorful display of the *Aurora Borealis* ... the Northern Lights. It was the first time that either man had ever witnessed the strange, captivating phenomenon.

"'Tis a beautiful sight to behold, ain't it?" marveled George.

Austin whispered, "Yes, indeed. I have never witnessed anything quite like it."

George grinned in the darkness. "Why are you whispering?"

Austin chuckled softly. "I do not know. The sky is just so beautiful. It almost seems holy."

"What is it called again?"

"One of the New York fellows told me that it was called the 'Northern Lights.' He said they see it up in their area from time to time ... once or twice every two to three years."

"Well, I have never seen it before down here in South Carolina," George declared.

"Neither have I."

George turned to his friend. "What do you reckon it means?"

Austin shrugged. "I suppose there is no meaning to it. It is just another manifestation of weather, like fog, sunshine, or rain."

George continued staring at the dazzlingly beautiful strings of dancing lights in the sky. "It is far too strange and beautiful to simply be the weather. This must mean something." He paused. "Maybe it is a sign or some manner of omen."

"An omen?" asked Austin skeptically. "What do you propose that it portends?"

"Judgment, perhaps, for what we have done." He pointed to the nearby corn crib that housed the two prisoners seized at the McClure house. "Maybe it is declaring God's judgment upon us for killing those lads tomorrow. They were only pouring musket balls, after all. We have done the same thing ourselves hundreds of times, but no one wanted to stretch our necks for it."

Austin elbowed George in the ribs. "George Rogers, when did you start thinking so much? It does not become you."

"I have been doing a whole lot of thinking as of late," George confessed. "The events of recent days have given me much to ponder."

"What do you mean?"

George did not respond immediately. He appeared to be weighing his words. "If I reveal to you some of my innermost thoughts, can I trust you to keep them in confidence?"

"Of course, George. You are my comrade, and a lifelong friend."

George inhaled deeply. "Recently, I have been questioning our cause, Austin." He paused and lowered his gaze toward the dark ground. "And my allegiance to it."

Austin considered his friend's confession in silence. It was a candid revelation, to be sure. Some might even consider it treasonous. But, Austin understood his friend's sentiment. He, too, had been questioning his own personal politics as of late.

"What manner of questions are troubling you, old friend?"

George glanced around to make sure no one else was listening. "Questions such as: Why am I loyal to a King I have never seen? Why should I be willing to risk my life for a cause I do not truly understand? Am I here because of the convictions of my own heart, or simply because of the convictions of my father's heart?" He paused and allowed his words to penetrate Austin's mind. "Does any of that make any sense to you?"

Austin draped his arm around George's shoulder. He leaned in close to his ear and whispered, "It makes perfect sense, indeed. For I have been struggling with those same questions, and many more."

George gulped. Though Austin could not see it, tears were welling in George's eyes. "Then, each of us has a decision to make, do we not?"

Austin looked back up toward the dancing lights in the sky. "Yes. Yes, I believe we do."

Two shadowy figures approached from the direction of their

camp. They were the soldiers assigned for the next watch. Austin gave George an encouraging slap on the shoulder.

"Come, George. Our relief is here. Let us sleep on our thoughts. Perhaps tomorrow everything will seem a bit clearer to us."

～

Minutes Before Dawn
July 12, 1780

GEORGE AWAKENED WITH A START. Somewhere in the distance, he heard the sharp crack of gunshots. At first, he thought that someone must be hunting. There were only a few shots at first, but the volume of gunfire increased rapidly. Then came a mixed chorus of angry, wailing, excited, and mournful screams. Suddenly, he heard a dull thump overhead. He looked up and saw two perfectly round holes near the peak of his tent. They were left there, without doubt, by a musket ball. It was an attack!

George rose and fumbled for his clothes. He tugged frantically at his breeches and clumsily attempted to clothe himself in the dull, purple glow of the pre-dawn. He glanced at Austin, who lay sleeping soundly beside him. The two militiamen shared a small bell-backed linen wedge tent provided for them by the British Army. He kicked violently against his friend's leg in an effort to wake him.

"Austin! Austin Newman! You must wake up! The Whigs are upon us!"

But Austin barely moved. The fog of sleep still had a firm grip on his mind and body. He tried to force his eyes to open, but the weight of exhaustion kept tugging them closed. Somewhere in the distance he heard shouting and several odd popping sounds. He wondered, *"What manner of strange dream is this?"* He groggily rolled over onto his side and then pulled his wool blanket snugly beneath his chin. A vigorous, violent slap across his face finally extracted him from his world of blissful slumber. His eyes flew open and then he sat up, pressing his hand against the sharply stinging flesh of his left cheek.

"Why the hell did you hit me?" he demanded.

"I had to do something to wake you! Get dressed, you fool! We are under attack!"

"What?" Austin asked, thoroughly confused. He fumbled with his breeches. "Where? How? Who?"

Outside, the gunfire increased dramatically. Another lead projectile tore through the side of the tent, this one much lower than the first. It passed between George and Austin and then slammed into Austin's tin British Army canteen. The impact unleashed a spray of water that soaked the bedding of both men. Shards of tin shrapnel exploded outward, tearing tiny slashes and holes in the cloth wall.

"Good God!" Austin exclaimed. "Did you see that?"

George grabbed Austin by the shoulders. "You must act lively, Austin! The enemy is trying to overwhelm us! 'Tis an ambush! We must get into this fight! Where are your weapons?"

"My pistol is here somewhere." Austin fumbled through his pile of belongings and soon located his pistol and leather cartridge pouch. "My musket is outside near the cooking fire."

George struggled to pull his black leather shoes onto his feet. "The pistol will have to do for now. Hurry! Get your breeches and shoes on." He grinned excitedly. "We cannot go into this fight naked, can we?"

Austin, his mind somewhat more alert, snapped into action. He quickly donned his breeches and shoes. He slipped the strap of his cartridge pouch over his shoulder. Outside, the din was becoming deafening. He heard the booms and cracks of dozens of flintlocks. Then came the unmistakable report of Brown Bess muskets only a few yards away. At last, some of the Loyalist troops were returning fire. Two more slugs tore through the walls of the tent. One came so close to Austin that he felt a hot breeze as the projectile passed in front of his face.

He touched the end of his nose and exclaimed, "Christ, Almighty! That one was close! I could smell gunpowder on that ball!"

"Focus your mind, Austin. You are unharmed. Are you ready to go out there?" asked George.

"Not really."

"We must go anyway. Our comrades are depending upon us. Follow me!"

George rose to his knees. He held his loaded and cocked flintlock pistol in his right hand. He threw open one flap of the tent door and immediately darted outside. He was trying to reach cover behind a nearby tree stump. He ran only three steps before a .69 caliber musket ball, fired from a Whig militiaman's French Charleville musket, impacted his face just above his right lip. The bullet drove his front teeth through his upper palate and deep into his sinuses. It plowed through his head and then exited the back of his skull, unleashing a cloud of blood, bone fragments, and brain matter all over the outside of his tent. His body went rigid for just a moment and then he tumbled forward into the soft grass of the meadow. George Rogers never moved once he fell. He was dead before he hit the ground. He lay awkwardly on his right side, his body folded at the middle and twisted in a grotesque fashion. Most of his head was gone.

Austin, kneeling just inside the doorway, witnessed George's grisly death. He froze from shock and stared in utter disbelief at the lifeless body of his friend. Feeling something wet and sticky on his face, he reached up with his left hand and plucked a bloody chunk of brown hair and skin from his right cheek. He gagged as bile rose into his throat. His stomach wretched. He instantly vomited a small pool of clear liquid onto George's bedroll, at the very spot where his friend's head lay the night before.

His stomach finally empty of its meager contents, Austin retreated back inside the tent and then lay flat on his back as he tried to make himself a lesser target for the enemy guns. In his heart, he wished that he could simply dig a hole in the ground and hide in it. He lay there for a moment and stared at the roof of the tent, mesmerized by the mass of dark, bloody goo that covered the outside of the shelter. Amazingly, even more holes appeared in the linen walls as enemy musket balls tore through the cloth.

Austin finally fought through his paralyzing fear. He realized that he had to move, or he would most certainly die. He rolled over onto his belly, turned his body completely around, and then slowly crept toward the open tent flap. He glanced, once again, at his dead companion. He closed his eyes and prayed, "*Oh, God, please watch over the soul of my friend.*"

He opened his eyes and scanned the field of battle, looking for a potential path of escape. The scene was mind-numbing. Dozens of his comrades lay dead, most of them within a few steps of their tents. He witnessed the smoke of muskets in the trees behind the Williamson cabin, as well as in the woods near the roadway where the New Yorkers were encamped. The surviving New York Volunteers had taken cover behind the split rail fences and were pouring concentrated fire at the enemy. They appeared to be putting up a valiant fight.

A loud shout came from the direction of the cabin. Austin turned and saw Captain Huck, who had been quartered overnight inside the Williamson home, running out of the front door of the house. The officer was clad only in his breeches and shirt. He sprinted quickly toward his horse and then jumped onto the saddleless animal. He rode onto the dirt lane, into the very center of the battle, waving his saber in the air and shouting in a bold effort to rally his men. He was hit by musket fire almost immediately. He tumbled awkwardly from his horse and landed head-first on the hard-packed earth of the road, where he lay absolutely still. Captain Christian Huck was dead.

Enemy militiamen suddenly emerged from the woods behind the cabin. Some had bayonets fixed onto their muskets. Others carried tomahawks and hunting knives. They descended upon the disoriented Loyalist soldiers with their blades. Some of Austin's comrades were only half-dressed and unarmed, yet they fell to the merciless assault of the Whigs. The enemy soldiers were everywhere. There were hundreds of them. And they were out for blood.

"This is madness!" Austin groaned. "I am doomed!"

He spotted several of his comrades, soldiers of the Camden militia, running for their lives toward the woods behind their tents. There appeared to be no enemy troops in those trees, since there was no smoke or evidence of musket fire. Austin did not hesitate. He knew that he, too, had to make his escape into those woods. He turned and crawled toward the back of his tent. The cloth of the rear bell was pulled tightly to the ground by wooden stakes. He whipped out his hunting knife and then cut a long slit in the back wall from top to bottom. He stuck his head through the hole and stole a quick glance toward the woods. He saw no one. He was roughly eighty yards from the tree line. It was a long distance to run under enemy fire, but flight was his only chance for survival.

Austin rose up on his haunches and then tore through the hole in his tent. He took off running, but immediately stumbled over a tent stake and fell face-first onto the ground. He landed hard and felt a wave of pain as his chin impacted a sharp rock hidden in the grass. Blood poured from a puncture wound on the right side of his chin. He ignored the pain and quickly jumped to his feet. Again, he ran, but his fear-stiffened legs felt as heavy as stones. They seemed unwilling to move. He forced himself to continue moving forward one step at a time.

He peered longingly at the line of trees in front of him and prayed that he might reach them unharmed. He heard lead from the enemy muskets whizzing past his ears. Some of the shots impacted the ground near his feet. He marveled at the fact that none of them had found their mark. After running for what seemed like an eternity, he found himself within ten yards of the forest. He only had a few steps left to reach the safety afforded by the thick timber.

"Run, Newman, run!" he encouraged himself. "Just a bit further!"

Finally, Austin passed the first tree at the outer edge of the forest. He celebrated the achievement in the depths of his soul. Still, he ran on, knowing that he was not yet safe. He realized that he remained within line of sight of the enemy. He needed to continue deeper into the forest where he might disappear into the shadows of the trees.

Austin managed only two more steps before the enemy's lead finally found his flesh. A rebel musket ball tore through the skin of his back, clipping the muscle located just below his left shoulder. It plowed through the soft flesh beneath his arm, scraping against the outer edge of one of his ribs. The bullet redirected slightly, following the curvature of the rib, and lodged into the hard muscle of his left breast. The impact of the slug knocked him off-balance, causing him to slam head-first into a small sapling. He reeled to his right and then tumbled sideways onto the leaf-covered forest floor. He rolled twice before coming to a stop against the base of a giant oak tree.

The searing pain in his back, the point of the bullet's impact, was almost unbearable. Austin sensed another dull, throbbing pain beside his left nipple. He gently felt of the sensitive area with his right hand and discovered a large, hard lump deep inside the muscle in his chest. Immediately, he knew that it was a musket ball.

He cursed himself, "Get up, you damned fool! You must keep moving!"

More lead screamed past him. Some of the rounds slammed into trees, but most fell harmlessly onto the leafy forest floor. Austin crawled around to the far side of the nearest tree, using it for cover from enemy fire. Somehow, he rose to his knees. He grasped the rough bark of the oak and then managed to stand. He leaned against the tree for a moment and recovered his balance. He attempted to lift his left arm and inspect beneath it for blood, but the arm would not move. It hung limp and numb at his side. He reached around his back with his right arm and felt a patch of warm, sticky blood. His shirt was soaked. He knew that it could possibly be a life-threatening wound, but he also knew that he had to keep running. Once they had the battlefield secured, the Whigs would dispatch pickets to search the woods for stragglers. From what he had just witnessed in the body-strewn Loyalist camp, it did not appear that the enemy militiamen had any intentions of taking prisoners.

Austin closed his eyes and prayed. "*God, make my feet move. Give me the strength to run. Deliver me from the hands of those who would kill me.*"

Then, he ran. He traveled roughly a quarter-mile toward the south, where he stumbled upon a small creek. Desperately hot and aching for water, he knelt in a shallow pool in the center of the creek and then plunged his head into the refreshing, cold fluid. He rocked back onto his knees, allowing the gloriously cool water to run down his chest and back. He then braced himself with his right arm and leaned forward to drink, sucking the water down his parched throat in frenzied gulps.

Once his thirst was quenched, Austin twisted his legs to one side and then sat down in the deep pool. Slowly, gently, he reclined backward and immersed his aching back and shoulder into the blissfully cool wetness. Black blood stained the slowly-flowing creek water. As the coagulated blood diluted, a cloud of crimson and pink surrounded him and then slowly meandered downstream, eventually thinning to invisibility. The coolness of the water brought some relief from the dull ache of the open wound and the embedded lead. As he lay there, Austin listened for sounds of fighting in the distance. The gunshots had finally stopped. It sounded like the battle was over.

A metallic click echoed through silence of the deep forest. A trembling, high-pitched voice commanded, "Get up! Show me your hands! No sudden moves! I swear to God I will shoot you!"

Austin's head instinctively spun in the direction of the unexpected voice. He stared into the eyes of a skinny, frightened lad. The boy's face was streaked with dirt and gunpowder. He was pointing an ancient, rusted fowling gun menacingly in Austin's direction. He looked strangely familiar.

Austin slowly sat upright and then raised his right arm in surrender. He confessed, "I am hit in the other shoulder, boy. I cannot lift my left arm. But, worry not. Except for my knife, I am unarmed. I humbly surrender to you."

The boy slowly lowered his weapon. He took three steps in Austin's direction. His face erupted into a huge smile of happy recognition.

"Mr. Newman?"

Immediately, Austin recognized the voice and the powder-stained face. It was William Armstrong.

～

WILLIAM GAVE the bandage strap a final, firm tug. Austin let go a groan of discomfort. Despite the wounded man's pained protest, William appeared quite satisfied with his work.

"I think I got the bleeding stopped, Mr. Newman. But, that ball is going to have to come out soon. I wish I knew how to help you, but I do not. I reckon you need a surgeon, or at least someone who is handy with a blade." He leaned over and inspected Austin's chin. "I do not think the cut on your chin is severe. But, it may require a stitch or two." He grinned mischievously. "It should not ruin your good looks, since you had none to begin with."

Austin smiled warmly. Without even thinking, reached out with his right arm and pulled the lad toward him. He gave him a strong, manly hug. "I cannot thank you enough for what you have done for me, Master William. Surely, you have saved my life."

William appeared thoroughly embarrassed. His face flushed red. "'Twas a debt that I owed you, Mr. Newman, and I pay my debts. Dressing your wound is the least that I could do."

"I hate it that you had to cut your blanket for bandages to patch me up."

William shrugged, obviously unconcerned. "I can get another blanket."

William stood and scanned the forest in the direction of the battlefield. There were no gunshots coming from the direction of the Williamson home. He could see no one else in their immediate vicinity. It appeared that they remained undiscovered. He knelt back down behind the large boulder that served as their hiding place.

Austin shook his head. "I still cannot believe that so many Whigs descended upon us without our sentries providing warning."

"It appeared to me that all your sentries were asleep."

Austin grunted and the shook his head in disgust. "Typical! That last watch is always the most difficult one. But, please tell me, how did you fellows field such a large army?"

"Word spread quickly about your presence here," William explained. "The local folk were already pretty worked up over the foul mouth and blasphemies uttered by your captain. Then, last night a slave from the Bratton place, a fellow named Watt, arrived in our camp with a message from Mrs. Bratton. He informed us of your location." He paused thoughtfully. "Old Watt told about all the horrible things done to Mrs. Bratton. He said that your captain almost hanged her, and that he put a blade to her neck. He said that one of the other officers had to restrain him. Is that true?"

Austin nodded, obviously ashamed. "George and I were sickened by it. But, there was nothing that we could do. I am glad that Lieutenant Adamson intervened. It was a brave act and the moral thing to do."

William frowned and shook his head. "Well, the news of Huck's abuse of that woman surely got our men riled. They traveled all the long night just to have their revenge."

"It appears that they got it. Captain Huck is dead as well as most of his command."

"Where is Mr. George?"

Austin's head hung low. "George Rogers is dead. He was shot in the head as he fled our tent."

William sighed. "I am truly sorry. Mr. Newman. He seemed like a jolly, happy fellow."

Austin grinned at his friend's memory. "He was that, indeed. And he shall be sorely missed by all who knew him."

Shouts emanated through the woods to their north.

"My comrades are coming!" William declared with urgency. "You must get moving. I fear what the fellows may do to a captive."

"I have nowhere to go," Austin confessed. "And I am not familiar with this area."

William pointed to his left. "Follow this little creek downstream. It flows westward to the Sandy Creek. You can follow the Sandy down to the Broad River. Surely, you can find help somewhere along the way. There are homesteads all over that area. If you could find a boat, you might even float down the Broad River all the way home."

"I do not think I could last that long, William. I am so weak."

"You have lost a lot of blood. That is the cause of your weakness," William confirmed. "My advice is that you find a homestead somewhere along the Sandy and get help. But, if I were you, I would keep my politics a secret. There are scant few Tories in these parts."

Austin smiled. "I will keep that in mind."

William extended his hand to Austin. "I have to go back now, Mr. Newman, before my captain comes looking for me. It was good to see you again, despite the circumstances."

"It was good to see you, also, William. Perhaps the next time we meet, neither of us will be hobbled or bleeding."

"Or trying to kill one another," William added, grinning.

"Or trying to kill one another," Austin echoed. "Get going, lad. God be with you."

William stood and cradled his fowling gun in the crook of his arm. He stared at Austin for a brief moment, smiled his friendly, boyish smile, and then marched swiftly toward the north. Austin took a deep breath, pulled himself to his feet, and then proceeded south-west along the bubbling creek.

~

Four hours Later

AUSTIN WAS DIZZY. His head pounded with each beat of his heart. He was scorching hot with fever. His mouth felt dry as dust. Despite stopping every few minutes to drink from the creek, it seemed that nothing could satisfy his thirst. He was disoriented, but somehow he still managed to keep the waters of the creek in sight. He stumbled onward, praying that he might soon find help.

Just ahead, he saw where the waters of the tiny creek emptied into a larger waterway. Suddenly, he smelled smoke. He continued onward. His heart leapt with joy when he caught sight of a tiny cabin in the middle of a lovely glade. A thin wisp of white smoke leaked from the top of the cabin's low chimney. It was inhabited!

Austin excitedly picked up his pace. He was almost running now, frantic to get to the cabin. He reached the edge of the trees and then stumbled into the open, grassy field. He spotted a woman near the cabin, standing beside a large iron pot. He raised his right hand high in the air and attempted to call out to her, but only a dull, dry moan escaped his lips. He thought he saw the woman begin walking toward him, but his vision was starting to fade. He heard a strange, dull roaring sound in his ears. For some reason, his legs stopped moving. He felt himself tumbling through the air. He saw the ground rushing toward his face. Then, the whole world turned black.

14

MONTAGUE AND CAPULET

Five Days Later

Austin opened his eyes slowly. He lay still for a moment, adrift in a fog of disorientation. He had no notion of where he was. He noticed smoke-stained rafters and crude shake shingles overhead, hinting that he was inside a log cabin. The pleasant odors of freshly-baked bread and roasted meat filled his nostrils. He heard voices. They were happy voices, intermixed with the laughter of children. He surmised that the place where he lay was a very nice place, indeed. It was a happy place. It felt like home.

Suddenly, he remembered his wounds. He reached across his chest with his right hand to feel the place where the lead was lodged in his muscle. There was a thick bandage covering the spot, but he could no longer feel the lump that had been there before. Obviously, someone had removed the musket ball. He slowly lifted his left arm. It actually moved! He experienced a flood of relief. He continued stretching the arm upward. He felt a stiff, dull pain in his shoulder blade, but other than that, everything seemed normal.

A pitchy, pre-teen voice exclaimed from somewhere nearby,

"Mama! He's awake! He's startin' to flop around in the bed and wave his arms!"

Austin whipped his head in the direction of that startling voice. A rather chubby brown-haired lad was perched atop a stool near his feet. The stout young fellow held a tomahawk menacingly in his right hand and glowered at Austin with a gaze of intense distrust. Austin was unsure why the boy appeared so resentful.

A terse feminine voice exclaimed, "Marshall Wilbanks! Put that horrid blade away! You are going to drop that thing and cut off a toe!"

The boy's bottom lip poked outward. He whined, "But, Mama!"

"Boy, do not talk back to me! Put that blade back on the mantle where it belongs and then go and fetch me a piggin of water. Supper is almost ready."

"Yes, ma'am," mumbled the boy.

Marshall climbed down from his stool and then waddled toward the fireplace. As he passed by Austin, he kicked the leg of the bed and simultaneously smacked the side of the tomahawk against the palm of his hand. It was a provoking, threatening gesture.

The woman barked, "Marshall! Do as I said and leave that man be!"

The lad instantly took off running toward the fireplace. After depositing the tomahawk safely atop the mantle, he grabbed a small piggin bucket and then darted out the door. Moments later, a kindly-looking, round-faced, extremely overweight woman appeared at Austin's bedside. She was not ugly, but neither was she pleasant to look upon. The woman had abnormally large breasts and it was painfully clear that she was not wearing any stays. Her bulbous mammaries stretched the cloth of both her shift and her worn, pale gray short gown to their limits. She wore a petticoat that was a slightly darker gray. Both of her outer garments were stained with age, food, dirt, and perspiration. A very wrinkled, off-white mob cap covered her greasy, sweaty head. She wiped her hands on a filthy linen dishcloth, raked the cloth across her wet brow, and then nonchalantly slung it across her shoulder.

"'Tis good to see you back amongst the land of the livin', young fellow," she declared, smiling, with her hands perched comfortably atop her ample, chunky hips. "'Twas a day or two that we wondered if you would survive the fever that had its hold on you."

"Water ... please," Austin begged, his mouth parched and dry.

The woman fetched a pitcher and poured several ounces of water into a horn cup. She gently lifted his head and then poured the refreshing liquid down his seared, aching throat. Austin thirstily drained the contents of the cup.

He mumbled weakly, "How long have I been here?"

"Today is Thursday, August 17. So, I reckon it has been five days since you appeared out of our woods." She chuckled and shook her head. "You near 'bout frightened young Eliza to death."

Austin echoed, "Eliza?"

The woman nodded. "My sister-in-law, Eliza Wilbanks. She was tendin' a pot of indigo dye when you showed up. She is the one who dragged you inside the house and first tended to you."

"Is she here now? I would very much like to thank her." Austin's throat seemed to be opening after drinking the water. The pain was diminished and his voice was much stronger.

"No, she is not here. She has been out in the west cornfield all afternoon huntin' for some decent roastin' ears. Our corn crop is near 'bout too dry for cookin'. 'Twill be pickin' time soon. She will be back in just a bit, though. By the way, I am Abarilla Wilbanks, wife of William. This is our homestead that you managed to stumble upon. My husband is gone right now to serve in Colonel Thomas Brandon's regiment in the fight against King George."

"*Well, isn't this wonderful!*" Austin thought. "*I have been taken in by a family of rebels. I must proceed carefully.*"

The woman continued, "Right now, it is just us women-folk and children takin' care of the farm." She paused and gazed at Austin through narrowed eyes. "You do not have any intentions of doin' harm or takin' advantage of a house full of women and children, do you?"

Austin laughed lightly at such an outlandish notion. "No, ma'am.

I cannot even lift my own head. I am not a threat to any living creature right now."

She smiled, leaned forward, and then lifted the blanket from Austin's chest to inspect the bandage beneath his arm. Her unnaturally large bosoms appeared to be on the verge of spilling over the top of her short gown. Austin quickly turned his head and looked away, horrified at the notion of what might escape from beneath the strained, threadbare linen.

"Your wound does not appear to be weepin' any blood or water. That is a good sign." She quickly tucked the blanket back beneath his arm and then inquired, "What is your name?"

"Austin Newman."

"Well, ain't that a fine, fancy name! I have never met anyone with the given name, 'Austin,' before."

The woman pulled a stout three-legged stool to his bedside and then sat down. It appeared that she intended to stay and visit for a while. She seemed to have a curious nature about her. Austin surmised that an interrogation was coming. He instantly attempted to formulate a story that might account for his presence in this place. But, it was difficult for him. His mind remained foggy from days of fever and sleep. He decided that his best strategy was to tell as few lies as possible. That way, it would be easier to replicate his account when questioned or induced to tell it again.

"Where are you from, Mr. Newman?"

"Camden District, southwest of Winnsborough."

She nodded. "Tell me ... how did you come to be a wanderin' about in our woods?"

"Well, I got shot."

The plump woman threw back her head and chuckled gaily. "I am already aware of your injuries, Mr. Newman. I was the one who did most of the doctorin' and cleanin' of your wounds. Though, Eliza was the one who did all the stitchin'. You should be glad of that. She is a fine seamstress. I would have scarred you up, for certain."

She reached above Austin's head and retrieved a pewter bowl

from the flat-topped bedpost. She lowered the bowl beneath Austin's nose. It contained a lop-sided, semi-flattened musket ball.

"I cut this out of your teat on the day that you arrived. It is one big chunk of lead. How it managed to get from the back of you to the front of you without scramblin' any of your innards, I shall never know. But, rest assured, you be one lucky man."

Austin nodded humbly. "I am grateful for your generous care. Will I be all right, then?" he asked with trepidation.

"I suspect you'll live." She returned the bowl containing the bullet to its original resting place. "Though, I doubt you will be goin' anywhere any time soon. 'Twill take some time to heal. I packed your wounds with moss and a mustard poultice. That should help. But, you will need to be still and rest for a few days, at least.

"I am truly grateful for your hospitality, Mrs. Wilbanks."

"Takin' care of an injured, wayward soul is the Christian thing to do, Mr. Newman." She stared intently into his eyes. She seemed to be searching his spirit for any hint of dishonesty or deception. "Where, exactly, were you when you got your wound?"

Austin answered honestly, "It was in a battle near a plantation somewhere to the north. Williamson's, I believe they called it."

Mrs. Wilbanks nodded knowingly. "True enough, there was a big fight up that way on Saturday. We heard that the Tories received quite a whippin' and that their commander was slain. The whole back-country is talkin' about it."

He nodded. "That would be the place."

"So, then ... you were in that fight?"

Austin nodded honestly. "Yes ma'am. I was there."

She seemed somewhat skeptical. "How, in God's Name, did you come to be all the way down here in Union County? Williamson's plantation is almost eight miles northeast."

Austin's mind reeled. He had been sticking to the facts up until this point. But, the time had come for a well-executed and plausible lie. He took a deep breath and then launched into what he hoped was a believable fabrication.

"I was a horse soldier serving amongst the dragoons. We were attacking in the field in front of the cabin. Right when I got hit, my horse also got nipped in the flank by a ball. It was just a cut, but it spooked her terribly. She took off running into the woods, with me holding on for dear life and bleeding all over the place. She refused to slow down, much less stop. All along, I was convinced that I was going to fall from the saddle and die, if I did not bleed to death first."

He took a deep breath and continued, "I have no idea how far she ran. I was leaning over to one side to dodge a low limb when I lost my balance and fell. Old Sadie never stopped running." He grinned a disarming, boyish grin. "She might be all the way back home by now. If so, I envy her. Anyhow, I found myself lost in the woods. I located a small creek and just kept following it downstream. It eventually led me here."

"But, how did you manage to get shot in the back?" she asked suspiciously. "The ball hit you just below the shoulder blade. That seems an odd place to be wounded when attacking an enemy."

Her last comment was a cutting one. Clearly, she was hinting at the possibility that Austin was a coward or fleeing from the fight.

"The battle was nothing short of madness and mayhem, Mrs. Wilbanks. Tories were all over the field and scattered up and down the road. There seemed to be militiamen in every tent and building and behind every tree. Lead was flying in every imaginable direction." He closed his eyes and gave the appearance of reliving the moment in his mind. "I had no idea which way to go or which direction to fire. I was confused. There was so much shooting and screaming." He opened his eyes. "It was my first real fight, Mrs. Wilbanks. I have never seen anything quite like it, and hope that I never will again."

The woman leaned forward and rested her elbows on her knees. Her eyes narrowed even more. "I can only imagine. Still, there is one thing that truly vexes me, Mr. Newman. You were wearin' a mighty good dressin' on your back when you stumbled onto our homestead. There is no way you could have put that bandage and sling on yourself. Who patched you up?"

Austin's heart leapt into his throat. He had not considered the matter of the bandages placed upon his wounds by William Armstrong. He decided to swing his account back toward the realm of truth, if only partly so.

"I encountered a young fellow by the name of William in the woods shortly after my fall. He was but a lad, no more that thirteen or fourteen years old. He washed my wounds in the creek and cut strips from his blanket for my bandages."

"And then this boy just left you there all alone in the woods?" she asked incredulously.

Austin nodded. "He seemed in a hurry. But, thankfully, he is the one who pointed me downstream. He said there was a homestead near the intersection of the little creek we were near with the Sandy Creek. He promised me that it was not very far."

Her eyebrows arched high in the air. She nodded, seemingly satisfied by Austin's account of events. "Your friend must know this area well if he knows the location of our cabin. Most likely he is a lad from a neighboring homestead. Did you not get his surname?"

"I cannot remember. If he told me, I must have forgotten."

She continued to peer deeply into his eyes as if searching his very soul for truth.

"What of your pistol, Mr. Newman? It was primed and loaded. There was no way that you could have loaded it yourself with your arm in a sling."

"*Christ Almighty!*" he thought. "*Will this meddlesome woman never be satisfied?*"

He smiled. "I fired it only once during the battle. Somehow, I managed to keep hold of it whilst atop my runaway horse. Young William loaded it for me after he tended my wounds. He did not wish to send me on my way unarmed."

Mrs. Wilbanks stared at Austin for a moment as she considered the details of his account. After a few seconds, her serious gaze transformed into a satisfied smile. Austin felt relief wash through his soul. Apparently, the time of intense questioning was over.

"It appears to me you owe a great debt to this young lad. Perhaps you will be able to thank him one day." She patted Austin's hand in a motherly gesture. "Lie still and rest. Sleep if you can. Your body needs time to heal. I do not want you out of this bed for at least two days, maybe three. I will have Eliza bring your supper when you wake up."

"That sounds good. The smell of your cooking is making my belly ache with anticipation. Once again, I sincerely thank you for everything, Mrs. Wilbanks."

She stood and then pushed the stool with her foot toward the nearby wall. "You are most welcome, Mr. Newman. Now, be still, close your eyes, and rest."

Austin needed no convincing. He was completely spent by her intense questioning. Lying was exhausting business. He closed his heavy eyelids. Sleep came quickly.

Austin felt a gentle shaking against his arm. He slowly opened his heavy eyes. Though disoriented at first, he quickly remembered his situation and whereabouts. He also felt the gnawing, aching hunger in his stomach.

A soft, feminine voice called his name. "Mr. Newman?"

Austin turned his head to the left, toward the sound of the lovely voice. He almost gasped when he saw its source. Sitting beside him was the most exquisitely beautiful woman he had ever looked upon. She was young, certainly no older than her mid-twenties. Her face was perfect. She had full, red lips and a diminutive nose. Her cheeks were pink. She had dazzlingly blue eyes. A wisp of dark brown hair dangled from beneath her linen bonnet. She smiled, revealing two perfect rows of straight, pearl-white teeth. Austin glanced downward. He could not resist. She wore a clean, tidy green linen short gown. Though she was wearing stays, it was clear the she was blessed with ample bosoms. She was ideal in every respect. Austin was instantly taken captive by her beauty and her genuine, heart-melting smile.

"Hello, Mr. Newman. It is wonderful to see you awake and free of fever."

Austin thought, *"Even her voice is perfect! My God, can this woman be real? Or is she a figment of my imagination ... a fantasy birthed inside my sick, fevered mind?"*

She reached toward him and placed her hand on his forearm. It was very soft and warm. Her touch felt real enough. He could smell her, as well. Her feminine scent was very pleasant. She smelled of mint and lavender. Perhaps this was no dream! Austin's heart raced inside his chest. The very touch of her hand upon his bare skin roused unfamiliar feelings deep inside his body. He felt a dull ache in his loins. He was so filled with delight that he could not will his mouth to form words or utter a sound. He merely lay there on the bed and stared at the beautiful young woman with a stunned, foolish gaze.

Her brow knit in an expression of concern. "Mr. Newman? Are you quite all right?"

Somehow, Austin compelled his voice to function. He stammered, "Yes ... of course ... yes, I am fine." He lied, "I was merely a bit disoriented. For a moment, I could not recall whence I lay."

She smiled warmly. Again, Austin almost gasped from her indescribable beauty.

"'Tis to be expected, Mr. Newman. Both your body and mind have suffered much. To be honest, I am quite surprised that you even survived your ordeal. Your fever was a wicked one, indeed. But, here you lay!" She smiled happily. "My name is Eliza Wilbanks. I am sister to William, the owner of this farm. You have already met his wife, my sister-in-law, Abarilla."

Austin nodded. "'Tis a pleasure to finally meet you, Miss Wilbanks. Your sister-in-law and I had an interesting and lengthy conversation earlier this afternoon."

"She told me all about it." Eliza leaned closer to him and whispered, "From all the information that she revealed to me, 'tis a wonder you had any time to nap. I expect that it took her the entire afternoon to complete such a thorough investigation."

Her proximity to his face was intoxicating. Austin's heart raced even faster. His breathing quickened. Eliza, suddenly aware of their uncomfortable and inappropriate closeness, drew away from him.

She reached to her right and pulled a small table close to his bedside. There was something on top of the table that lay concealed beneath a linen napkin. From the amazing aroma, Austin assumed that it was his supper. His mouth began to water profusely.

Eliza explained, "The rest of the family is about to take supper at the table. I volunteered to eat here with you and help you with your meal. Can you sit up?"

"I think so, but not without assistance."

"Then, we shall recruit some helpers." She clapped her hands. "Marshall, Hosea ... come and help Mr. Newman. He needs help sitting up so that he might eat his supper."

"What about me?" whined a forlorn, high-pitched voice.

"Yes, of course. Come along, Joseph. You may help, as well."

Instantly, three lads appeared by Austin's bedside. He recognized the tallest one immediately. He was the boy who had menaced Austin with his tomahawk. Thankfully, this time he was carrying no bladed weapons and the distrust that he had displayed earlier in the day seemed to have disappeared. The two larger boys helped support Austin beneath his arms. The youngest boy, who was no more than six or seven years of age, did not actually provide much help. He merely pushed against Austin's feet and made all manner of loud grunting and groaning noises. Still, despite the comical futility of his supposed contribution to the effort, he appeared quite pleased with himself once their guest was sitting upright.

"Thank you, gentlemen," Austin declared once he was seated and comfortable. "I am indebted to you all."

The three boys immediately and simultaneously responded, "You are welcome." Their good deed done, the hungry boys all darted back to the supper table.

Eliza removed the napkin from the table top, revealing two pewter plates filled with food. Each plate contained a thick slice of ham, several boiled new potatoes, and a mountain of green peas.

"Do you prefer your peas whole or mushy?" she inquired.

"Mushy, please."

She nodded and then declared, "As all good Englishmen do!"

Eliza added a quarter-inch thick slice of butter to Austin's peas. While the butter melted, she added a generous pinch of salt and then used the flat side of her knife to press and mash the peas. As she prepared his food, Austin experienced an uncharacteristic surge of boldness. He decided that he would perform a little interrogation of his own. He needed to know more about this lovely maiden.

"Have you lived here very long, Miss Wilbanks?"

"Only about six months. I came down from North Carolina after the winter broke."

"What part of North Carolina?"

"Bute County. My parents lived there for many years."

"I have not heard of Bute County. Where is it?"

Eliza chuckled. "Well, it is nowhere now! The state legislature did away with it last year. They divided it into the counties of Franklin and Warren. We lived in what became Warren County, up near the Virginia border."

"What brought you here?"

Eliza shrugged slightly. "I had nothing left to keep me there. My father died of the lung fever during the winter. My mother passed two years before. My brothers lived down here in the South Carolina backcountry. So, I packed my meager belongings and moved to join them."

"That is a brave action, indeed, for an unaccompanied young woman."

"Why, thank you, Mr. Newman. I rather think so, as well." She grinned proudly.

Austin was growing weary of the small talk. He decided to accelerate the conversation toward more personal matters. It was time to go fishing for more personal details.

"I suppose a suitor was here awaiting your arrival. A fiancé, perhaps?"

Eliza shot him an incredulous, seemingly shocked look. Both of her eyebrows raised high. "Mr. Newman, seeing as how we have only just met, I do not think it appropriate to discuss matters of such an intimate nature. Do you?"

Austin felt crushed. "No ma'am. I reckon not."

She had reduced the former pile of peas into a buttery, creamy mound of pale, green, soupy goo. She scooped a spoonful of the freshly-mashed peas, cradled her free hand beneath the spoon to catch any potential drips, and then slowly guided the large spoon toward Austin's mouth.

"Enough talk. Time to eat. Open wide."

Austin obeyed. She stuffed the spoonful of mushy peas into his mouth and then placed the spoon on the table so that she could retrieve a knife and fork to cut Austin's ham. She quickly and expertly carved him a hearty bite. Austin swallowed his peas and then happily received the forkful of smoky, tender meat. Next came a salty chunk of potato. Eliza continued the process, occasionally enjoying small bites from her own plate. They were so busy eating that they shared little in the way of further conversation. Austin was thoroughly famished and, once the meal actually began, had little besides food on his mind. He devoured his plateful of supper and, once finished, yearned for more.

"I must seem like a pig," he confessed. "I sucked down that meal with neither manners nor decorum. Even so, I feel as if I could eat another plateful."

"I rather think you have had enough for this evening, Mr. Newman. Your belly has not held food for many days. I fear that you might make yourself sick if you eat any more. However, a bit of whiskey might be good for your digestion. Would you like some?"

"Oh, yes, please. I have not tasted good whiskey in a month or more."

She grinned. "Well, I cannot promise that it is *good* whiskey. But, I assure you that it will be wet and have a fine, strong bite."

"That sounds wonderful."

"Can I get you something else? Is there anything that might bring you a measure of comfort?"

"Did you find my pipe? Was it amongst my belongings?"

"Indeed, it was. I shall be happy to fetch it for you. Though, I am afraid that your tobacco pouch was moldy. It appears to have gotten soaked. But, worry not. My brother has plenty of fresh leaf. I will fetch you some of that, as well."

"Thank you very much, Miss Wilbanks." He smiled a genuine smile of thanks.

She happily returned his smile. "My pleasure."

As she sauntered across the room to fetch Austin's pipe, he got his first glimpse of the entire Eliza Wilbanks. She did not disappoint. She was slender, well-breasted, and had wide, voluptuous hips. She walked with an air of dignity intermingled with grace.

Austin closed his eyes and thought, *"No, Eliza Wilbanks. 'Tis my pleasure."*

There was no doubt in Austin Newman's mind. His heart was won. He would have Eliza Wilbanks, and forever so. She would be his bride. But first, he had to win *her* heart.

∾

Three Weeks Later
Late Afternoon - Sunday, August 6, 1780

AUSTIN HAD BEEN LOOKING FORWARD to Sunday. It promised to be the pinnacle of his week. Thankfully, there was no work to perform, since the Sabbath was a day of rest. Austin was much in need of a Sabbath's rest, for he was dog-tired. For the past week, he had been working on the farm alongside the Wilbanks women and children, helping them bring in their crop of corn. He had just spent six straight days in the fields, laboring from dawn until dusk. Though he had recovered quite well from his wound, his body remained somewhat weak from the injury. He had not yet returned to his previous level of excellent health. Therefore, he was more than thankful when Sunday finally arrived. He was also thrilled at the prospect of a day full of free time to spend with the lovely Eliza Wilbanks.

It was obvious to everyone in the household that the fires of romance were burning bright between Austin and the beautiful young maiden. Abarilla took great joy in mentioning the fact as often as possible, much to the chagrin of Austin and much to the embarrassment of Eliza. But, the reality of the woman's observations was inescapable ... Austin and Eliza were falling in love. True, it was a very new and a very young love. But, it was real. Austin prayed that the depth of their affections might grow with time.

As there was no organized church in the area, it was the custom of the Wilbanks clan, staunch North Carolina Baptists, to hold an informal family service just before dinner on Sunday morning. Since Austin was the only male of age currently under the roof, Mrs. Wilbanks had insisted that Austin lead in the reading of Scripture and prayer. He happily granted her request. The women and children seemed to enjoy his efforts, especially when he told a story from back home that helped illustrate the meaning of the Scripture passage that he had just read for them.

After a cold dinner of pork sandwiches, fresh watermelon, and day-old fried apple pies, Austin and Eliza spent the afternoon lounging around the cabin and yard. The boys played their customary outdoor games. Abarilla went on a brief visit to a neighbor's home. Around mid-afternoon, Eliza and Austin each decided to take a Sunday nap. Austin slept for almost two hours on his soft pallet in the barn. He had been relegated to the outdoor sleeping quarters ever since he had recovered enough to walk. Everyone agreed that it was most inappropriate for a healthy young man to sleep in the family cabin in the presence of a very young and unmarried woman.

Abarilla returned from her visit while Austin was still asleep. After he awakened from his nap, he played outdoors with the boys while Eliza and Abarilla tidied up inside the house. Right before dusk, Eliza declared her intention to go for a walk. She seemed a bit moody. Indeed, her face appeared cloudy, as if she bore a troublesome burden. Austin could almost swear that she had been crying. Though she did not invite him, Austin volunteered to join her on her walk. He tried not to read too much into her sudden, stormy, aloof state. He would, as always, remain patient and allow her to explain and express herself in her own time.

They ambled along the banks of the beautiful Sandy Creek. It was an unusually pleasant afternoon for the month of August. A steady breeze blew from the northwest, bathing the landscape with its luxurious coolness. The backcountry was pristine and green, enriched by the moisture of ample summer rains. But, Austin paid little attention to either flora or fauna. His mind, heart, and eyes were all too occupied with the lovely Eliza Wilbanks. As they walked, neither of them uttered a word. Eliza was strangely silent. She appeared to have a great cloud of sorrow hanging over her. Austin grew more and more concerned.

Her behavior was especially troubling to Austin in light of the many deep and wonderful conversations that they had enjoyed over the past three weeks. Every day, they shared hours of lively discussions on every imaginable topic. They told stories about their homes, childhoods, and families. Austin talked of Jackson's Creek so much that Eliza felt that she could almost imagine the place in her mind. Likewise, Eliza described life in the Piedmont of North Carolina, raising tobacco on their family farm, and making trips to such exotic places as Williamsburg, Baltimore, and Richmond. They revealed to one another many of the fondest and most intimate details of their lives. Both of them enjoyed their talks, their meals together, and their quiet times sitting beside the fire in the evenings.

Still, in the midst of their joyful interactions, a subtle cloud of secrecy hung over their relationship. It appeared to Austin that Eliza was hiding something. He suspected that there was something in her past ... something deep and painful ... that burdened her heart. Despite his burning curiosity, he remained patient and prayed that Eliza would reveal her secrets to him when she was ready.

Austin was relieved when Eliza finally chose to break the uncomfortable silence of their afternoon stroll. However, her words sounded disturbingly cold and distant.

"We have been most grateful for your help on the farm, Mr. Newman. It would have taken us another week, or more, to accomplish the work on our own. You have been a blessing to our family."

"It has been an honor and a pleasure to serve you all, Miss

Wilbanks. Since you snatched me from the very jaws of death, I figured that helping you on the farm was the least that I could do."

Eliza smiled thinly. But, her smile did not seem genuine. Indeed, she seemed a different person than she had been over the past three weeks. It was most disconcerting to Austin. His level of anxiety grew. They walked in silence for a while longer. Finally, she spoke again.

"I assume that you will be leaving to rejoin your regiment soon. Your health is almost restored. Surely, you have been missed."

Austin shrugged. "'Tis likely they think me dead. To be honest, I am more inclined to remain here than I am to return to my regiment."

"Why so, Mr. Newman?"

Austin was twenty-seven years of age, but woefully inexperienced in the ways of romance. Still, it seemed to him that the moment was right for him to make a big move. It was time for him to take a leap of faith, hopefully one that would mark the beginning of a future with Eliza Wilbanks. He desperately desired that she become his bride. Austin abruptly stopped walking and then seized Eliza by the hand. She stopped and turned to faced him. They looked deeply into one another's eyes.

"I think you know why, Eliza."

Austin could not believe that he had called her by her given name. It was a brash, bold, and risky thing to do. His heart pounded inside his chest. It beat so strongly that he feared she might see the movement of the powerful muscle through his clothing. Eliza never looked away. She stared at him, but not in a warm way. Her gaze seemed almost icy.

She replied, "When we first met, you asked me about my courtship status. I believe it was a query you posed during our very first conversation."

He nodded. "Yes. I asked if you had a suitor awaiting you here when you moved to South Carolina."

Eliza shook her head hesitantly. "I had no suitor here. But, I once had a fiancé back home in North Carolina. His name was Allen Dunbar. He was the most amazing, kind, and lovely man. We were engaged to be wed for almost a year." Her eyes reddened and filled with huge tears. "Then, he left with the army."

Austin's heart ached for her. "Tell me, please. What happened to him?"

"He fell in a battle near Charlestown on the Stono River last June. One of his mates told me that he died by the blade of a British bayonet." She looked away from Austin and wiped her tears with a handkerchief.

Austin spoke softly and reverently. "I am very sorry for your painful loss, Eliza. Does your love for him still hold sway upon your heart?"

She sighed thoughtfully. "It did for a very long time. Ours was a love so deep and so real. I assumed that I would never love that way again. I doubted that my heart could ever open to another." She paused and swallowed hard. Her shoulders trembled. "Then, you came."

Austin's pulse quickened. He began to sweat, such was his excitement and joy. "I see. Might it be possible, then, for you to love me in the same way that you once loved Mr. Dunbar?"

Eliza burst into tears and then collapsed into his arms. She declared, "I fear that I already do. I love you, Austin Newman ... with all my heart."

He tried to comfort her. "There, there, my dear. Weep not. Why should you fear it? Yours is not a declaration of sorrow. It is a cause for great joy, for I feel the same! I have loved you since the moment I opened my eyes and looked upon your angelic face. My heart is yours, Eliza, and shall be until it lies buried with me in the grave."

Her entire body shook. She wept even louder. Austin pulled her face away from his chest. He cupped his hand beneath her chin, forcing her to look into his eyes.

"Why do you weep, Eliza? This is wonderful news to me. I have prayed that you might love me, and now you have declared it so. Our future is bright! Joy awaits us!"

She sniffed and then once again wiped her tears. She pulled away from him, separating herself entirely from Austin's embrace.

"I weep because I cannot be with you, Austin. We can never wed. Ours is a future that will never be."

"Why?" Austin demanded sharply. "Why would you declare such a hurtful thing after you have confessed your love for me?"

She blurted angrily, "Because you are a damned Tory! That is why!"

Austin was stunned. His mind reeled. He did not know how to respond. He stammered, "Why ... why would you say that? What would make you suspect such a thing?"

"Abarilla was bragging to our neighbor this afternoon about how she saved the life of a Patriot wounded at Williamson's Plantation. The fellow thought it curious, since there were scant few of our soldiers wounded in that battle, and only one killed." She paused and then glared hatefully into his eyes. "And he informed her that none of the regiments reported any of their soldiers missing."

Austin did not offer any response. He simply stared into the eyes of his beloved. Now, *he* was on the verge of tears.

"It is true, isn't it?" she demanded. "You are a Loyalist. You serve King George."

Austin was undone. There was no escaping the truth. The time for pretense was over. He could tell no more lies. He had to be completely honest and transparent with her. He responded with a single, powerful, heartbreaking word.

"Yes."

She collapsed into his arms again. This time, however, she pounded her fists in agonized frustration against his rock-hard, muscular chest.

"Why?" she screamed. "Why would you deceive us so? Why would you perpetrate such a horrible, shameful lie?"

Now, tears flowed down Austin's cheeks. He explained, "I lied so that I might survive, Eliza. I did not know what would become of me if I were discovered. If you had turned me in to the sheriff or to the militia, I most certainly would have hanged." He hugged her tightly against his chest. "But, I never intended to hurt you. I had no idea that I would meet someone like you. I had no notion that I would be wounded and near death and then wake up and discover the love of my life."

"Even so, we can never be together," she moaned. "You are a Tory. Your people killed my beloved Allen. My brother ... my family ... fights against you. I do not think I could ever reconcile it all, either in my mind or in my heart."

"You cannot allow politics to separate us, Eliza. I hold no deep personal commitment to the King's cause. Indeed, I would gladly walk away from King and country to remain here with you. I just want to marry you, stay here on this creek, and live out the rest of my days in your arms. I care not who is in charge of the government."

She shook her head adamantly. "It is not that simple."

"It is, indeed, that simple! Please, Eliza. Won't you put all those other things ... those worldly things ... aside and cast your lot with me? With us? We can be husband and wife. You and I can be forever." He dropped to one knee and grasped her hand. "I ask you here and now, Eliza Wilbanks. Will you do me a great honor and marry me?"

Eliza jerked her hand away and attempted to compose herself. "Do not do this now, Austin. You are charging at me like a bull. I cannot think!"

"Please, Eliza!"

She took several steps backward. Her countenance was frantic. Her breathing was rapid. She looked as if she were about to flee. She turned to walk away.

Austin stood. He begged, "Do not go, Eliza. Please ... not like this."

She called over her shoulder, "Leave me be, Austin. I must have time to search my heart and think."

"We can talk more after supper," he encouraged hopefully. "Everything will be all right. You will see."

"Stay away from the house tonight, Austin. Abarilla does not want you there anymore. Hosea will bring your supper to you in the barn."

"But, Eliza ..."

"I need my privacy, Austin. I need time. If you truly love me, you will respect my wishes."

She turned and ran, sobbing, toward the cabin. Austin stood, helplessly, and watched her go.

~

Later that Night

SOMEHOW, Austin had managed to fall asleep. It was an amazing feat, considering that his mind was tortured and his heart was in complete turmoil. He ate a cold, lonely supper and then, once darkness fell, he lay down upon his bed of soft hay. He had nothing else to do with his time. He tossed and turned for several hours before finally giving in to a shallow, fitful, restless sleep.

Sometime deep in the night an odd noise awakened him. He looked toward the door of the barn and immediately spotted a shadowy figure sitting on a barrel and leaning against the wall. Austin instinctively reached for his pistol.

"There is no need for weapons, Mr. Newman. I have no intention of harming you."

Austin stopped moving. He was confused. "I am afraid that you have me at a disadvantage, sir."

The man rose to his feet and stepped into the silver-blue moonlight streaming through an open window.

"I am William Wilbanks. Eliza is my sister. You are sleeping in my barn."

Austin gulped nervously. "I am honored to make your acquaintance."

The man chuckled sarcastically. "Well, sir, I am afraid that I cannot say the same. My wife was so greatly stressed by your presence here that she sent my son, Marshall, to fetch me. He rode all the way to my encampment to convince me to return home. I just arrived within the hour. I have conferred with my wife and sister and we have come to an agreement."

"I am listening," Austin confirmed nervously.

The man sighed impatiently. "Mr. Newman, if it were up to me, I would have sliced your throat while you slept. But, Eliza convinced me otherwise. I will not harm you, nor will I turn you over to the constable. I am going to allow you to leave here honorably. I expect you to be gone before daylight. I also forbid you to return ... *ever*." He paused to allow his declaration to sink in. "If you do come back to my home, I *will* kill you."

Austin growled angrily, "I love Eliza, you know. She loves me. I have asked her to marry me. I demand to speak to her."

"You are in no position to make demands, you Tory bastard! Furthermore, she has no desire to speak to you. As her brother and as the head of this family, I will not allow you to see her again, and I most certainly will not give her to you in marriage." He turned toward the door. "That is all I have to say to you, Mr. Newman. This is not a negotiation. If you are still here in the morning, I *will* shoot you dead. Have no doubt."

He stepped through the door of the barn and then quietly pulled it closed. Austin sat in the darkness in stunned silence.

15

THE BEGINNING OF HIS END

August 12, 1780
Early Evening
Loyalist Encampment – Rocky Mount, South Carolina

I t was the happiest of nights in the Jackson's Creek Regimental camp. Three dozen men imbibed enormous volumes of ale, smoked their pipes, and sang joyful songs of celebration and reunion. Only the most wonderful of events could bring about such a happy jubilee. After losing five of their compatriots in the massacre at Williamson's Plantation, the past month had been filled with darkness, sorrow, and grief. But this was a day of great joy, indeed, for a dear friend and neighbor had come for a long-awaited and much-welcomed visit.

Drury Austin arrived at the encampment late in the afternoon. A soldier in the Upper Ninety-Six Loyalist Militia, he had been dispatched by his commander, Major Zachariah Gibbs, on a mission as messenger to the British encampment at Rocky Mount. He traveled overnight from his regiment's remote outpost on the western frontier to deliver a satchel filled with maps, reports, and letters addressed to British command. Upon arriving in camp, he signed over his satchel to the proper authorities. Once his military mission was complete, he went in search of his friends. His unannounced arrival sent a shock-wave of delight through the fellows from Jackson's Creek. John Austin was especially thrilled to see his big brother. Surely nothing could equal the joy of such a cheerful reunion. Or so they thought ...

Joshua Ginn, the lone survivor of Williamson's Plantation, had just tapped a fourth hogshead of ale when a most unexpected voice interrupted the rowdy merrymaking.

"I do hope you lads have saved a drop or two for me."

The drinking and revelry ceased immediately. Every head turned toward the direction of the hauntingly familiar voice. The men of the Jackson's Creek Regiment stared, wide-eyed and dazed, at a dead man. Gazing back at them and sporting a grin of mischief was Austin Newman.

THERE WERE TEARS, hugs, and handshakes aplenty. No words could describe the joy experienced by the men upon witnessing the return of one of their own ... especially one who had long been relegated to the grave. The celebration grew in fervor and intensity to the point that it eventually began to draw in men from other nearby regiments. Word of Corporal Newman's miraculous return spread like wildfire. Every man in the Rocky Mount encampment wanted to catch a glimpse of the fellow who had miraculously returned from the dead.

Austin was quite surprised and thrilled to discover that Joshua Ginn had also survived the battle at Williamson's Plantation. He had assumed that, like George Rogers, all of his other Jackson's Creek compatriots had perished in the brutal attack. And he was absolutely stunned to see his best pal, Drury, in the camp. The two men enjoyed an emotional, joyful reunion. Suddenly, the fact that Drury had abandoned him and run off in the dark of night to join the army no longer seemed to anger Austin. He was just glad to once again be in the presence of his old friend. His close brush with death and the pain of his jilted heart had given him a renewed perspective on life and friendship.

It took almost an hour for Austin to greet all of his regimental mates, tell his captivating story, show his wounds, and then answer the barrage of questions unleashed upon him. Eventually, Captain Miller appeared. Word of Austin's return had reached all the way to the officers' quarters. He, too, had many questions. It took over an hour for Austin to give his commander a report on the battle, his unlikely escape, and his stay at the Wilbanks homestead. Austin spared few details. The only element that he chose to conceal from his captain was his love affair with Eliza. He decided that particular aspect of his experience was none of the captain's business.

Captain Miller seemed quite satisfied with Austin's report. He promptly informed his freshly-returned soldier that, since he was now horseless and the regiment had no other men attached to the British Legion, he was immediately relieved of his duty with the dragoons. Also, his field promotion to corporal was rescinded. He was, once again, a lowly private in the infantry along with the rest of the men of his regiment. Austin was quite relieved and pleased. He was more than happy to remain in the company of his friends.

The captain departed so that his men might return to their celebrating. The festivities continued into the wee hours of Sunday morning. Four hours and three more hogsheads of ale later, the men of the Jackson's Creek Regiment were done. Drunkenness and fatigue took hold of them. One by one they succumbed to inebriation. Each man slept on the ground wherever he fell.

~

The Next Morning

AUSTIN HAD A POUNDING HEADACHE. His eyes rebelled against the very presence of the morning sunlight. He greatly regretted his previous evening's overindulgence in rum and ale. Of course, he had not been alone in the consumption of copious amounts of alcohol. The fact that most of the other men of the regiment lay fully clothed and sleeping on the ground throughout the encampment was proof positive of their unbridled debauchery. Soon, no doubt, those men would also awaken with similar debilitating symptoms of a morning-after hangover.

Austin sought refuge from his pain in quiet and solitude. He reclined against a tall pine tree on a small rise overlooking the Catawba River. He had intended to sit and watch the lazy waters of the river, hoping that the picturesque view might somehow relax him and remedy his throbbing head. However, the sunlight reflecting upon the water elicited even stronger and sharper pains in his forehead. To combat the torturing brightness, he removed his neck sock and wrapped it around his head as a covering for his eyes. He sat in self-imposed blindness and sipped cool water from his tin canteen. He prayed fervently that the head-splitting pain would soon depart. He was actually on the verge of dozing when a familiar voice invaded his peaceful seclusion.

"Suffering the after-effects of over-jollification, are we?"

Austin pulled the wrap from his eyes and gazed upward at the smiling face of Drury Austin. He could not help but smile back. He motioned for his friend to sit down beside him. Drury happily complied.

"'Tis wonderful to see you again." Drury ruffled his pal's unkempt hair. "But I must confess, Austin, that I was nowhere near as glad to see you as were all the other fellows. I reckon I am the only one who did not think you dead." He chuckled. "The looks on their faces were priceless!"

For some unknown, inexplicable reason, Austin's anger at his friend suddenly rekindled within his heart. The thrill of their reunion was in the past. There remained words that needed to be spoken, and this might be his only opportunity. Despite his fatigue and headache, Austin could not restrain himself from confrontation.

"You should know, Drury ... you almost lost your own life a couple of months ago."

Drury cocked his head to one side in a confused gesture. "Whatever do you mean?"

"I speak of the day when you ran off to join the militia. If I had known where you had gone and found even the slightest opportunity, I would have gone there and killed you with my bare hands." Austin lifted his leg and gave his pal a swift, angry kick in the shin.

"Ouch! What the hell was that for?" Drury swung his legs out of range of Austin's boot. He gingerly rubbed his bruised leg.

"That was for the anguish and misery you caused your sweet wife, you bastard! You left the poor woman in utter distress. She wept for days. It was a pitiful sight to behold."

"Elizabeth knows my convictions. She understood why I was compelled to go and serve."

"Perhaps so," countered Austin curtly. "But she was not very happy about your swift and unannounced departure. She felt abandoned, Drury. Hell, she *was* abandoned!" He shook his head in disgust. "You should not have left her without even speaking a word of goodbye. It was most inconsiderate and ungentlemanly."

Drury waved a dismissive hand. "I am sure that she is fine. She has her family nearby."

"You are her family!" Austin fumed. "And do not even get me started on the manner in which you turned your back upon John and me."

"I did no such thing," Drury objected.

"Yes, you did! We said all along that we would serve *together*. We swore our oaths to one another. Then, on the very day Colonel Phillips came home with commission in hand to recruit a regiment, you took off on your own and joined the militia at Ninety-Six! Why, Drury? Why?" Austin growled in frustration. "Even now, I am still toying with the notion of shooting you in the leg. That might be what is required to teach you a lesson."

Drury removed his cocked hat and then placed it on the ground beside him. He sighed. "'Twould serve me right, I suppose."

"Indeed it would," Austin declared angrily. He was surprised by his friend's unexpected acquiescence.

The two men sat and sulked for a long and rather uncomfortable period of time. Austin stared stormily at the sparkling river. Drury interlocked his fingers behind his head and then lay back on the soft bed of pine needles that covered the ground. He nonchalantly stared upward into the branches overhead. After several minutes, Drury finally broke the strange, disconcerting silence.

"You know, Austin ... if you were to shoot me in the leg, the report of your pistol would probably hurt your swollen head more than the ball would hurt my leg. Besides, I doubt you could actually see well enough to hit your target. You appear a bit cross-eyed to me."

Drury gave his old pal a friendly nudge with his knee. Austin's frown slowly transformed into a smile.

Austin growled, "I still want to wring your neck."

"Yeah, I love you, too," Drury responded. "Are you quite finished with your scolding, Mother? I surrender. I hereby declare myself adequately reprimanded."

Austin exhaled a long, cleansing breath. "I suppose so, as long as you consent to writing a letter of contrition to your wife."

"I posted such a correspondence to her only yesterday."

Austin nodded. "Good. She deserves it. She is a good woman, Drury."

"I know she is. And I know that she deserves better treatment from her husband." He paused thoughtfully. "I pray that you might find a woman like her one of these days. You *are* getting a bit long in the tooth, you know. People back home are beginning to talk."

Austin leaned forward and rested his elbows on his knees. Immediately, his mind flooded with images of Eliza Wilbanks. He could almost smell the sweetness of her scent. He had only been gone from her for a few days, yet already it seemed as if months had passed since he last saw his beloved. His mind was transported back to those brief, happy days at her side. His heart ached as he wondered if she even thought of him. He shook his head to clear away the memories and pain.

"Someday, perhaps, I will find such a woman. But, I must not think of such things right now. Instead, I must focus my mind upon surviving this God-forsaken war."

Drury sat back up again. He patted his friend's shoulder. "You have suffered much, Austin. You bear the wounds of battle in the service of your Sovereign. Surely, it is an indescribable honor to make such a personal sacrifice for King and country."

Austin lowered his chin to his chest and stared at the dusty, needle-strewn ground between his legs. He wondered, *"Dare I confess my doubts and struggles to Drury? Oh, how I need to tell someone! But, how will he respond? He is such an avid Tory."* Austin decided to speak the words that were upon his heart. He inhaled a deep breath and prayed for courage.

"Drury, I once thought such things to be honorable. All my life, my father taught me to revere the Crown. He filled my heart with an indescribable love for England. All I ever wanted to do was serve in the name of my King." He paused. "But, lately, I have begun to wonder."

"Wonder about what?" Drury inquired in a confused, disbelieving tone.

Austin shrugged. "I sometimes wonder if I am doing the right thing. I wonder why I should lay down my life for a King that I shall never see with my own eyes." He turned and looked at his friend. "And, more and more, I wonder why I must be compelled to strive against and kill my neighbors."

Drury's face became cloudy and stern. "Austin, any amongst our neighbors who choose to rebel against England are traitors, indeed. They deserve to die, and by my own sword, if necessary. All those who rebel against King George are vile, evil, ungrateful scum."

"Not all of them," Austin retorted.

"Yes, Austin ... all of them!" Drury's indignance was growing.

As Austin stared at his best friend, a single tear escaped his right eye and then slowly crawled down his cheek. "What about the rebel who saved my life? Is he vile and evil?"

Drury shook his head. "I do not understand."

Austin inhaled deeply. He prayed for clarity in his words. He prayed that Drury might understand the evolving convictions within his heart.

"I have seen many horrible things since joining this army, Drury. My commander in the dragoons burned a Presbyterian church to the ground. He ordered a young lad executed for simply holding a Scottish prayer book in his hand. I saw that same officer beat and torture young boys for information." Tears began to flow down both of his cheeks. "I watched him ... that vile, insufferable man ... string a woman up by her neck and then threaten her with a blade to her throat." He stared, dismayed, at his friend. "He tortured a woman, Drury! Is *that* not evil?"

"Surely, the officer's actions were justified. There must be more to the events than you have described."

"No! There is nothing that can justify such wickedness! Drury, I have watched the men of our army commit horrible atrocities against the civilian population of our colony. I have seen them loot and pillage the homes of backcountry folk, regardless of their politics." His shoulders began to shake. "And I despised them for the things that they did. I was ashamed of them, and of my identification with them." He paused to take a breath and control his emotions. "But, then I experienced grace from my enemy. After that horrible battle, one amongst those vile, ungrateful rebels that you so despise rescued me in the woods. He bathed me in a creek. He bandaged my wounds. He even gave me a canteen of water. Then, he sent me on my way in peace. I ask you, does that kindly lad truly deserve to die a traitor's death?"

Drury did not hesitate. "Yes. If he has taken up arms against the King, then yes, he does."

"So, then, it is your opinion that any evil actions perpetrated by our own forces are always justified?"

"Yes ... if such actions are taken on behalf of our lawful Sovereign."

"That is a steaming pile of horse shite, Drury!" Austin exploded. "Nothing is so simple as that! Less than fifty miles from here there are Whigs encamped ... our brethren of South Carolina ... who hold to their convictions just as deeply as we. Why should we take up arms and slay them over their politics? And if we are honest with ourselves, we will admit that we do it all in the name of a King who would not piss on us if we were on fire." He shook his head. "It no longer makes sense to me."

Drury's face was red with anger. His expression was one of utter dismay. "The words that you speak are dangerous, indeed, Austin. Some would even consider them treasonous."

Austin retorted, "You have not seen what I have seen. You cannot understand."

Drury pointed his finger threateningly in Austin's face. "It matters not what one has or has not seen or experienced. If you speak evil against our King, then you risk the consequences of your words. You must continue to prove your loyalty and serve him faithfully."

"I was wounded for King George!" Austin shouted angrily. "I do not have a damned thing left to prove!"

Drury inhaled deeply and attempted to calm his emotions. "You had best get your mind right, Austin. I would not enjoy seeing you hanged as a traitor."

"And you had best remove your head from your arse and take a good look around you, Drury. This is South Carolina. This is America. It is not England. There are no kings in these woods."

Drury balled his fists in anger. But, before he could respond or take physical action, frantic shouting erupted in the camp. Both men turned to look for the source of the commotion. Several officers were prancing throughout the encampment, pointing and issuing orders. Dazed, hungover men struggled to gather their belongings. Some of the soldiers were in the process of taking down their tents.

"What the hell is going on now?" Austin wondered out loud.

"I do not know," Drury answered grimly.

A young soldier came running past them. Austin called to the lad, "What has happened? Why is everyone in such a frenzy?"

"The rebels are out of North Carolina!" the smiling boy exclaimed breathlessly. "Thousands of them! They are marching upon Camden.

We have been ordered to join General Cornwallis there. The officers say there is going to be a *huge* battle!"

The young fellow turned and ran on toward his destination. Austin stood. He reached a hand down to his friend and helped pull him to his feet. When Drury was fully upright, Austin held fast to his hand. Though Drury attempted to pull away, Austin refused to let go.

"Drury, you are the best friend I have ever known. No matter what occurs, nothing can change that."

"Let us hope so," Drury replied coolly as he looked away. He refused to look Austin in the eyes. Instead, he stared at the ground at his feet. "Take care of yourself. If what that boy says is true, this will be a battle unlike anything you have ever seen."

"You are not going?"

Drury, still looking away, shook his head. "I wish I could, but my orders are to return to my regiment today. I will be heading in the opposite direction."

Austin placed his free hand on Drury's shoulder. "We shall talk again soon, old friend. I need you to understand my heart."

Drury did not respond. He merely nodded. He tore his hand forcefully from Austin's grip, turned on his heels, and then marched angrily toward his tent.

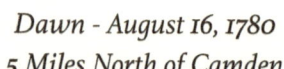

Dawn - August 16, 1780
5 Miles North of Camden

THE YELLOW-PINK GLOW of a brilliant sunrise erupted in the east over the tops of millions of dark green Carolina pines. The sun was barely up, yet the day was already steaming hot. Thick humidity hung low over the field in a dense, smoky haze. Without doubt, it was going to be a typical, sweltering summer day in central South Carolina. Tragically, for many of the men gathered in this field near Camden it would be their last sunrise ... their final summer day.

The field teemed with a carnival of humanity. Austin and his mates from Jackson's Creek had never seen anything quite like it. Indeed, they had never before witnessed so many human beings assembled in one place. The spectacle of the maneuvering armies was breathtaking. Thousands of troops were spread across the field. Colorful flags waved lazily in the light morning breeze. There were the anticipatory sounds of pounding drums and shrill fifes. To the east could be heard the wailing drone of bagpipes, the distinctive instruments of the Scottish Highlander regiments. Up and down the lines on both sides of the field, officers rode prancing horses amongst their men as they barked orders, delivered inspiring speeches, and made their armies ready for the impending battle.

The South Carolina Loyalists occupied a low knoll toward the rear on the left side of the British flank. To their far right, numerous regiments of British Regulars, including two battalions of curious-looking Scotsmen, stood in perfect boxes and rows. The colorful regiments were squared off against their distant enemies. The highway that led northward into the Waxhaws and southward into Camden intersected the very center of the battlefield. General Lord Cornwallis positioned his artillery on either side of the rutted dirt road. The barrels of his cannons pointed downrange toward the enemy.

To the north, the rebel army appeared to greatly outnumber the British force. Directly across from the Loyalist militia there were several smartly-dressed Continental Army regiments. Those men appeared to be well-trained and were maneuvering in orderly formations. However, on the far side of the road, the enemy's left flank did not look very organized, at all. Their militia regiments occupied that section. They were aligned in several semi-orderly clusters directly across the field from Cornwallis' most seasoned troops. The battlefield was flanked on both sides by swamps and thick pine forests. Should either side falter and retreat, escape into the dense, snake and bug-infested swamps would be most unpleasant and treacherous.

The Jackson's Creek Regiment was tiny in comparison to the fully-staffed regiments of British Regulars. Their diminutive unit of Provincials numbered a mere thirty-three men, including officers. They deployed with the Camden District Militia, which numbered only one hundred and twenty-eight men total. It seemed clear to most of the citizen-soldiers that General Cornwallis did not hold the Royalist militia in very high regard. Indeed, why should he? Almost half of the militiamen, like Austin, arrived at Camden without adequate weapons. Lord Cornwallis had become quite frustrated dealing with a so-called army that was so desperately lacking in arms. Somehow, however, the British commanders managed to assemble an odd assortment of muskets, fowling guns, rifles, and pistols for the South Carolina militia's use. Still, despite being more respectably armed, they had been assigned a position near to the rear of the British Army.

Austin Newman did not care about his regiment's lowly position on the battlefield. By his calculations, the rear of the formation was one of the safest places to be. As he watched the armies maneuver, he ran his fingers across the smooth, shiny steel of his new Brown Bess musket. It had a fairly new flint and sparked well. He touched the freshly-issued cartridge box hanging on his side. It was not an official British Army piece. Most likely, it had been made by a local merchant in Camden. But, Austin did not care. He was just happy to have sufficient arms and ammunition for the coming fight. He could not imagine facing the army arrayed before him with nothing but his old pistol. Still, he was very happy that he had managed to retain his trusty handgun. The pistol was loaded and tucked safely into his belt beside his tomahawk.

Austin glanced up and down the line on either side of him. All of the Jackson's Creek men, including Colonel Phillips and Captain Miller, stared, wide-eyed and open-mouthed at the spectacle of the two enormous armies as they slowly spread across the battlefield.

"This scene would be beautiful were it not so frightening," commented Joshua Ginn in a quiet, reverent voice.

"It is a glorious pageant, is it not?" marveled John Austin.

"Indeed," Austin responded quietly. He pointed at the enemy directly in front of them. "But, I do not like the way in which the lines have formed. Those appear to be Continental Army regulars directly in front of us."

John nodded. "I was thinking exactly the same thing." He pointed to the right. "And the enemy militia is lined up on our Regulars."

Austin shook his head grimly. "Both flanks are mismatched. That could be bad news for either side. Surely, General Cornwallis can see what we are seeing."

Austin turned and peered toward Lord Cornwallis and the other officers. The distinguished gentlemen occupied a small hilltop to the south, far behind the British force. His friends turned and looked at them, as well. The fancily-dressed British officers, most sporting tall ostrich feathers on their hats, were all perched high atop their horses and surveying the expanse of the battlefield. Cornwallis appeared to be using a spyglass.

"Why should His Lordship care about such trivial matters?" answered Joshua. "He just wants to win the coming battle. I doubt he is much troubled over the welfare of us lowly provincial privates." He shot a wry, sarcastic grin at Austin.

"Well, at least we are close to the rear," Austin declared. "If all goes well, we may not even be pressed into the battle."

Joshua nodded. "God willing." He craned his neck and peered toward the enemy soldiers in front of them. "I wonder when it will start. Do you think we will be able to tell?"

Seconds after Joshua verbalized his question, a series of explosions rocked the field. Though the British cannons were almost two hundred yards to their right, Austin and his mates still felt the concussions from the blasts. The English artillery had been loosed upon the rebels. The backcountry fellows watched in awe as the smoking projectiles arched across the sky and then finally impacted into the ground on the far side of the field. The first rounds fell well short of the enemy soldiers. Almost immediately, the rebel cannons answered and began firing back at the British.

John declared, chuckling. "I think we can safely assume that the fight has started, Joshua."

For a while, not much else happened. The artillerymen continued to exchange fire. Slowly, they walked their projectiles closer and closer to their targets. Then came movement on the far side of the rebel line. The militia on the eastern flank began to advance upon the British Regulars. Moments later, the British drums began to rattle a strange cadence that Austin had never heard before. However, Colonel Phillips seemed to know exactly what it meant. He strode proudly in front of his men and then faced them. He drew his sword.

"Regiment, shoulder your firelocks! Prepare to advance!"

The men of the regiment swiftly lifted their muskets to their left shoulders and then stood at attention. Colonel Phillips turned and faced toward the enemy. He held his sword upright against his right shoulder. Seconds later, the drum cadence changed vigor and tempo. Immediately, officers up and down the line began shouting at their companies. Colonel Phillips followed suit.

"Forward! March!"

The thirty-three intrepid men from Jackson's Creek, along with 2,200 fellow British soldiers, marched bravely toward an imposing enemy army numbering over 4,000 troops.

~

CHAOS. No other word could adequately describe the melee. Almost immediately, the enemy militia lines collapsed. They were quickly overwhelmed by the British Regulars. It looked like every enemy soldier not dressed in a Continental Army uniform was fleeing toward the north. The green-coated dragoons of the British Legion galloped through the gap in the line and pursued the retreating militiamen. Within minutes, over half of the enemy force was either taken captive or on the run.

However, things were not going quite so smoothly on the British left. The Continentals were pressing the fight against the Loyalist militia and steadily gaining ground. They overwhelmed the Royal North Carolina Regiment, the least trained troops under Cornwallis' command, and captured a great number of them. Colonel Lord Rowdon, commander on the British left, called in the South Carolina militia reserves to help hold the line.

Suddenly, the men of the Jackson's Creek Regiment found themselves thrust into the violent fray. They advanced with the other South Carolina provincials and maintained their ranks in a most professional manner. They got off two shots in good order before the bayonet-wielding Continentals charged them. When the enemy soldiers and their deadly blades appeared out of the smoke, they were only twenty yards distant. Their bayonets glistened in the hazy sunlight. Discipline and order evaporated as the Loyalist militia entered into desperate hand-to-hand combat against the more experienced Continentals.

Austin lost track of all his mates in the confusion of battle. Musket and pistol balls screamed past him. All around, men were engaged in personal combat, mostly steel against steel. Men fought with bayonets, swords, hunting knives, and tomahawks. Many had simply given up trying to load their muskets and fowling guns. Instead, they swung the heavy weapons as clubs or used them as shields to deflect the enemy bayonets. It was gruesome, primeval, and bloody. Men screamed, howled, and cried from rage, fear, and pain. Dozens lay upon the ground, all of them bleeding from wounds. Some lay still in death. The grass was on fire everywhere. The field reeked of smoke, blood, sweat, feces, and fear.

Austin stumbled forward through the blinding smoke in a frenzied attempt to locate his comrades. He gagged when he tripped over a severely wounded Continental soldier. The pitiful fellow lay flat on his back and had his hands pressed tightly against his belly. The shiny, wet tissues of his intestines squeezed between his fingers and around the edges of his hands. The lad was bleeding profusely from his mouth. He peered at Austin, his eyes begging for help. He attempted to speak, but his throat was so choked with blood that no words came. Austin made himself look away from the grisly spectacle of imminent death. He immediately fled the unpleasant scene.

Suddenly, a screaming bullet clipped the top of Austin's shoulder. The scorching lead severed the hemp strap that held his cartridge case. The untethered leather pouch immediately dropped from his side. Austin panicked. That case contained the pre-rolled cartridges for both his musket and his pistol. He could not survive a battle without ammunition. He instantly dropped down on his knees to retrieve the case. He opened the flap and fumbled for a cartridge, desperate to reload his recently-fired Brown Bess. He was in the process of priming his pan when he heard a ferocious, angry cry.

Austin turned to his left, toward the direction of the shrieking voice, and discovered a blue-coated Continental charging him with a bayonet-tipped musket. The man's bayonet was dripping with blood. The enemy soldier was only paces away. Knowing that he did not have time to load his own musket, Austin instinctively reached for his pistol. He whipped the weapon from his belt and simultaneously cocked it. He rolled to his left and flopped over onto his back as he took aim. But, Austin never got off his shot.

He observed in sickened dismay as the right side of the Continental's face and head seemed to disappear. Bone and flesh exploded outward as a ball exited his skull just in front of his right ear. The man's legs, no longer communicating with his shattered brain, ceased moving. Still, his momentum carried his dying body forward. He landed in an awkward pile on top of Austin. His body jerked in the violent spasms of death. Thick, black blood poured from the open cavity in his head. Some of it landed on Austin's face and invaded his mouth. Austin coughed and immediately sensed an urge to vomit. He quickly turned his head and then spewed the remnants of his breakfast onto the grassy earth beside his face.

The man finally stopped moving. He was dead, and Austin was pinned beneath him. He pushed frantically against the crushing weight. Then, quite unexpectedly, the dead body flipped to Austin's left, seemingly moving on its own. Austin, still in shock from the encounter, stared upward into the grinning face of John Austin. His friend held a still-smoking flintlock pistol in his right hand.

"That boy almost gutted you, Austin Newman!" John declared as he reached a helping hand to assist Austin to his feet. "I was afraid that your pistol might not be loaded, so I took care of him for you." He immediately began to reload his pistol. "Are you all right? Are you wounded?"

Austin quickly examined himself and felt for wounds. He was covered in blood, but it was all from the dead man. He breathed a sigh of relief. "No, I have not been shot. I think I am all right."

John pointed at Austin's face. "You have a pretty big knot on your forehead."

Austin immediately reached up to feel his injury. When he touched it, he winced from the pain. "I reckon that fellow's skull smacked me pretty hard."

"Well, 'tis a good thing that you have a hard head. You will get over that lump easily enough." He turned and surveyed the battle-field. "Look. I think the enemy is finished."

Amazingly, much of the shooting had stopped. The hour-long battle appeared to be over. The smoke and haze of gun and artillery fire were beginning to dissipate. The field was littered with hundreds of men, many of them dead or dying. Dozens of others were fleeing into in the thick trees and swamps to the east and west. There remained almost no combat on the field. The enemy was in a full-on, disorderly retreat.

"Do you *really* think it is over?" Austin asked in a broken, almost childlike voice. His eyes were wide with fear. His breathing seemed rapid and erratic. Clearly, he remained traumatized from his close encounter with the Continental soldier's blade.

John patted his friend on the shoulder and nodded. "Yes, Austin. It is over. We have taken the field. Still, you need to reload your weapon. Clear your mind. Everything is all right. You are still alive ... *again*." He smiled teasingly as he emphasized the last word. John pointed over Austin's shoulder. "And just look who is coming to greet you!"

Austin turned. His heart leapt with joy when he spotted a grinning Joshua Ginn trotting toward them. He, too, had made it through the fight. The three friends met and, ignoring the death that surrounded them, embraced in an unashamed celebration of their survival.

～

Four Hours Later

THE MEN from Jackson's Creek were completely spent, both physically and emotionally. They lay in the shelter of a small grove of oak trees at the southwest edge of the battlefield. It was the only available spot of shade in their vicinity, and they were desperate for a respite from both their exhausting duty and the blazing mid-morning sun.

They had been serving as stretcher bearers since shortly after the battle ended. It was bloody, heartbreaking, backbreaking work. Their first task was, of course, to evacuate all of the British and Loyalist casualties from the field. For hours, they carried their wounded comrades on canvas stretchers to the roadway and then loaded them into the crowded beds of awaiting wagons. Once filled with the wounded, those wagons made the jostling, unpleasant journey south to Camden where the British surgeons had established field hospitals.

"I cannot lift my arms!" moaned John. "I must have hauled over fifty men to those damned bloody wagons, and some of them were right big lads!"

Austin sat up, stretched, and scanned the field. "Boys, it is time for us to return to our work. Captain Miller said we were allowed only a half-hour for rest. We must help evacuate the rebel wounded."

"It is not as if they will be treated by our surgeons any time soon," remarked Joshua. "They will certainly go to the back of the line. More than likely, most will die whilst waiting their turn at Camden."

Austin stood, crossed his arms, and assumed an authoritative stance. "Even so, it is our Christian duty to make them as comfortable as possible. The very least that we can do is get them out of this hot sun. Some shade and water could, perhaps, save a few lives."

"You seem overly concerned about the comfort of our enemies, Austin. Do they really deserve such kindness?" remarked John sarcastically. "They are seditious rebels, after all."

"And what if those rebels had taken this field today?" Austin snapped angrily. "You could be the one lying wounded and bleeding out there on that hard ground. We need to help them, men. Come on! Get up! Let us make haste!"

"Stop telling us what to do, Austin! You have been reduced in rank, remember? Corporal Newman is no more. I will go when my captain orders me to and not a moment sooner," retorted John. "We still have some rest time coming to us."

Austin kicked Joshua in the foot. "Joshua, are *you* coming with me?"

Joshua pulled his cocked hat down over his eyes. "I am with John on this one. Let them lay there and cook. I don't give a damn."

Austin was filled with rage. "To hell with all of you, then!"

Leaving his friends staring after him in complete disbelief, Austin turned on his heels and marched determinedly toward the casualty collection point. There were dozens of soldiers there, many of them red-coated Regulars. Some were delivering rebel wounded to the wagons. Others were simply milling about and observing the process. Austin approached a haphazard stack of stretchers and quickly extricated one from the pile. He turned and walked northward toward the center of the battlefield, dragging the stretcher behind him.

Dozens of men were scurrying about. Most of them were inspecting the rebels and checking for signs of life. Others appeared to simply be searching for plunder amongst the bodies. Austin glanced to his left and noticed a strange commotion near the edge of the western swamp. A strangely-clad Scotsman, one of Fraser's Highlanders, was embroiled in an odd tug-of-war with one of the rebel wounded. The Scotsman was attempting to remove something from the rebel's hand, but the enemy soldier did not appear to want to let go. Suddenly, the highlander raised his right arm high in the air and then struck the wounded Whig across the face with the back of his hand. It was a vicious blow. The wounded fellow's arms fell limp to his sides. Austin gasped in disbelief. He dropped his stretcher and took off running toward the offender.

He shouted, "You there! Highlander! What do you think you are doing?"

The man stood and smiled. He waved an object in the air in a proud display of victory.

"I was just liberatin' this lovely lit'l piece o' gold from a dead rebel. 'Tis a fine, large locket." He pushed a button on the side of the object and it instantly opened into two halves that were connected by a tiny hinge. "Oh! And there be a lovely likeness inside! 'Tis the image of a fine woman." He reached down and pawed suggestively at his crotch. "I'll be a celebratin' Palm Sunday with this lovely lass tonight, if ya ken what I'm sayin'."

"This man is not dead!" Austin protested in disbelief, pointing at the wounded rebel.

The Scotsman shrugged. "True, but I am quite certain he will be soon, and the lad will not need any gold jewelry where he's a goin'."

Austin glanced down at the stricken man's ravaged torso. His taut belly and bony chest were filled with blood-stained puncture wounds. A large puddle of thick, congealed blood colored the ground beneath the diminutive man. His wounds were, without doubt, fatal. Indeed, Austin wondered how he could still be alive so many hours after the end of the battle. Unexpectedly, the doomed man spoke. His weak, broken voice sounded strangely familiar.

"Mr. Newman? Is that you?"

Austin slowly turned his head and gazed in disbelief into the pale eyes of the dying young man. He did not immediately recognize the smoked-stained, mud-crusted face, but he could never mistake the kindly, youthful voice. It was his young savior, William Armstrong.

"William? Oh, my God! William? Is that you, boy?"

The lad coughed. His body shuddered slightly. Blood oozed from the corner of his mouth. He responded with a timid voice, "Yes, sir." He smiled weakly. "I did not expect to see you here."

Austin exclaimed, "God help me! Oh, William! What has befallen you?"

William coughed again. "Lobsterbacks, I am afraid, with their wicked blades. No matter how many times I begged for mercy, they would not stop piercing me."

"You *know* this dead boy?" asked the Scotsman in disbelief.

Austin shot the man a hateful glare. "Yes. He is my friend."

Austin immediately removed his canteen. He gently lifted William's head and helped him take a few sips of cool water. He then soaked his handkerchief with water and used it to clean the boy's face. When he was finished, he almost wished that he had not done so. William's color was ashen gray. It was obvious that what little life he had left was steadily ebbing from his broken, tortured body.

"My locket," William begged. "I must have it. It contains my mother's one and only likeness."

Austin stood and faced the Scotsman. "Give back the lad's property."

"I will not!" the soldier protested. "'Tis mine by all custom and manner of war."

Austin exhaled, frustrated. He took a step closer to the man. "This dying boy wishes to look upon his mother's face once more. Be a gentleman and allow him that peace. Give it back to him. Now!"

The Scotsman chuckled sarcastically. "I don't give a bloody shite what the lit'l rebel bastard wishes!" He waved the locket tauntingly in front of Austin's nose. "This gold is mine. By the laws of war, I claim it as plunder."

Austin's mind reeled. What manner of man was this, that he would torture the broken soul of a helpless, dying boy by stealing from him? Where was his honor? Where was his decency? A flicker of rage burned hot within Austin's soul. He did not think. He simply reacted from emotion and exploding anger. He whipped his pistol from his belt, swiftly spun it around in his hand, and then viciously clubbed the Scotsman over the head with the butt of the gun. The blow elicited a deep, hollow thud inside the man's skull. The tall, red-haired fellow did not even realize what had hit him. His legs crumpled beneath him as he collapsed into an awkward, unconscious pile of flesh. Austin tucked his pistol back into his belt and then leaned over to retrieve the locket from the benumbed man's open hand. He turned, knelt beside his young friend, and reverently placed the heirloom inside William's waiting, bloody palm.

"There you go, my boy. You sweet mother is back with you. Hold her close."

William smiled. He held up the locket in his right hand and stared fondly at the tiny painting. Tears formed in both of his eyes. They trickled down his dirt-stained temples.

"There are so many things that I wish I could tell her, but I shall never see my sweet mother again ... or my brothers and sisters." He coughed again, spewing a fine mist of blood into the air. He chuckled quietly. Blood gurgled in the back of his throat. "Mr. Newman, I am beginning to think that I should have stayed home."

Austin smiled. "I have been harboring the same notion lately, my young friend."

"I feel myself going, Mr. Newman." William's face contorted into an emotional sob. He groaned, "Oh, God, I do not wish to die alone in this field."

Austin sat down on the ground and scooted close to him. He gently lifted William's head and cradled it in his lap.

"You are not alone, William. I am here with you. I, Austin Newman, am your friend. I will not leave you, I promise." Austin felt tears welling in his own eyes. "I only wish that I had known you better ... perhaps before the war."

William slowly turned his head so that his eyes might meet Austin's. His eyes were becoming hollow and gray like his skin. His breathing was shallow. Austin knew that William did not have long to live. Still, the lad managed to coax a smile from his weak, dying muscles.

William whispered, "I wish that I could have known you *after* this bloody war. What a merry time we could have had."

Then, the boy went limp. Every muscle in his body relaxed in death. He sank, lifeless and heavy, into Austin's tender embrace. William Armstrong, a brave young Patriot from Camden District, was dead. Austin wept without shame as he stroked the boy's curly, unkempt hair. A few minutes later, a harsh, unpleasant voice interrupted his tender moment.

"Who the hell is that?" demanded John.

Austin did not even bother to look at John. Through his tears, he answered, "This is William Armstrong. He saved my life at Williamson's Plantation. He was a good friend."

"Well, he is gone now," John declared matter-of-factly. "God rest his misguided rebel soul."

Austin gently moved William's head to the side and laid it back on the ground. He stood and faced John with a look of disgusted defiance.

"As am I, John ... gone, I mean. I am gone. I am done. I want no more of this bloody mess. I do not wish to kill any more of my fellow Americans." He looked forlornly at William. "You fellows enjoy your war. I am taking this boy back home to his mother. I will see you when you return home to Jackson's Creek."

"You are not serious!" John exclaimed.

Austin did not respond. He bent over and picked up William's limp, lifeless body. Cradling the boy in his arms, he walked slowly toward the crowded, rutted road that led to Camden.

PART IV

TURNCOATS

16

REVELATION

Jackson's Creek, South Carolina
September 10, 1780

Austin reclined comfortably in his father's woven willow porch chair with his left leg dangling lazily over the wide arm. A floppy-eared pup, a third-generation descendant of his very first dog, snoozed happily on his lap. Austin gently stroked the soft skin and hair on the dog's neck and ears. He sipped from his cup of steaming hot tea as he watched the sun rise over the freshly-cut eastern cornfield. The setting was peaceful and serene ... a far cry from the battlefields that he had endured during his months in the Tory army. He sighed contentedly. He was in the happiest, most comfortable place that he could imagine.

The door swung open and his father stepped out onto the front porch. Immediately, Austin felt his peace evaporate. He loved his father, but in recent days the man's intrusive interrogations and moral pontificating had become something of a nuisance. After his traumatic wartime experiences, Austin simply needed a little time of respite to rest his body and heal his soul. But his father seemed to have little patience for either of those endeavors. Instead, he remained adamantly fixated upon duty, King, and country. He insisted with great frequency and vigor that Austin return to Royal service in the Jackson's Creek Regiment. His tone was often condescending and preachy. To Austin, his pestering was becoming quite insufferable. Austin inhaled a deep, preparatory breath and awaited the inevitable.

Will Newman ambled slowly across the porch and then crossed in front of Austin. He balanced a cup of tea on a saucer in his right hand and carried a small coal tong in his left. The tong held an orange, smoking coal from the fireplace. He sat down in his wife's willow chair. He placed his saucer and teacup on the tiny table that sat between the two chairs and then lay the coal tong across the top of his teacup. He retrieved his clay pipe and leather tobacco pouch from his pocket, quickly filled the pipe, and then lit it with the smoldering coal. He blew on the coal to keep it hot and then carefully balanced the tong on the corner of the table.

"You are going to drop that ember, catch you chair on fire, and burn the house down," Austin warned. "These willow chairs are as dry as kindling."

"I will put it out in just a bit. I may need to re-light my pipe, and I do not wish to go back inside to retrieve another coal. If Lizzy sees me, she may attempt to put me to work preparing breakfast." He shot his son a playful grin.

"I imagine she might," Austin affirmed. "Lord knows little William is of no use to her. He is more interested in eating than he is in cooking."

Will chuckled quietly and nodded. "As are we all."

Once again, the porch grew silent. Will puffed his pipe. Austin closed his eyes. The sun had finally crept high enough to shine directly onto the porch. Austin basked in the luxurious warmth of its comforting glow. As he rested, he hoped and prayed that his father would remain silent and allow him to simply sit in peace. But his hopes were soon crushed. Will Newman was a conversationalist. He had little tolerance for silence.

"I want to thank you again for your assistance on the farm,

Austin. You were a big help with the corn crop. It would have taken William and me another week to harvest the south field."

Austin smiled contentedly but kept his eyes closed. "I enjoyed the work, Papa. It is nice to have a job where no one is shooting at you."

Will paused for a moment, then replied, "I reckon it would be." He retrieved his cup and took a drink of tea. "They say the war is going well, though. That bastard, Washington, and his rabble in the north are being whipped at every turn. And it appears that Cornwallis has the local rebels well under control. I predict that this unpleasant conflict will be over before the new year."

"I doubt it." Austin kept his eyes closed and continued to stroke his fuzzy puppy.

Will hesitated for a moment and then announced, "I heard that John has returned home from the camp at Camden. According to his mother, the regiment is on a one-week furlough."

"That's nice."

Will rolled his eyes in silent frustration. Still, he pressed on. "Rachel told Lizzy they will be returning to camp on Wednesday to prepare for an upcoming campaign."

"Is that so?"

"Colonel Phillips will need all of his men to return to duty. No doubt, the rebels will want to avenge their great loss at Camden."

"No doubt."

Will became utterly frustrated. He was not interested in hearing Austin's noncommittal, transient responses.

"Damn it, Austin! Will you not talk to me? When are you going to come to your senses? It has been three weeks since you returned home. You have been sulking and brooding about this farm for long enough, Son. I know that your heart was broken over that dead boy, but it is time for you to pull yourself together and move on. You must return to duty. You are a soldier in the service of the King. You need to act like one."

Austin lowered his leg from its perch atop the arm of the chair. He gently placed the puppy in the seat beside him and then turned to face his father.

"Are you throwing me out, Papa?"

"No, Austin. Of course not. This is your home. It will always be your home."

"Even if I do not return to militia service?"

Will's face displayed his discomfort and displeasure. His skin flushed red. He shook his head. "I had hoped that we might avoid any such unpatriotic unpleasantries." He reached his hand across the table and placed it on Austin's arm. "Do you not understand, Son? I am worried for you. What will you do if the authorities come looking for you? Where will you go if they issue a warrant for your arrest?" Tears formed in his eyes. "They have commenced to hanging men for desertion, you know."

Austin shrugged. "Well, if you are turning me out of my bed, I suppose that I could go and seek refuge amongst the Cherokee or the Creeks."

"I did not say that I was turning you out!" Will growled in frustration. "Lord help me! Why must you be such a headstrong, defiant young man?"

Austin's eyes twinkled with mischief. His face erupted into a huge grin. He patted his father's hand reassuringly. "I was only teasing you, Father. You can rest easy tonight. I will be returning to duty with the regiment on Wednesday."

Will's eyes grew wide with surprise. His face displayed a look of total happiness and satisfaction. "Are you being sincere, Son?"

"Yes, sir. I have been in correspondence with Colonel Phillips for the past couple of days. He has agreed to forgive my unauthorized absence if I am willing to extend my enlistment by one month." Austin grinned and slapped his father playfully on the arm. "He said that it would be much easier than having me hanged."

Will sighed happily. "Oh, Austin! I am thrilled by this news. But, I must confess that I am also a bit bewildered. After our conversations these past few weeks, I had wondered if you would ever return to serve the King."

Austin's smile evaporated into a scowl. "Please understand me, Father. I am not going back to the regiment to serve King George. I am going to serve alongside my friends. I am going to stand with *them*. But, once my enlistment is up, I am done. I will be returning home permanently at the end of January. I will no longer serve a cause in which I am not wholeheartedly invested."

Will inhaled deeply and nodded. "I can respect that."

"Good. Then, might we have a bit more peace and quiet on this porch? I would like to make the most of my final Sunday at home. 'Twill be four long months before I get to look upon these lovely fields again."

Will stood. "Of course. But first, I must go and tell Lizzy this news." He pointed at the lop-eared puppy. The dog was asleep and lying completely upside down with his head dangling off of the front of the chair. His long, skinny tongue hung loosely down the side of his pink jowls. "I will leave you in good hands. Cesar will take fine care of you."

Austin stroked the pup. "I must warn you, Papa ... I may not leave this chair until dinner time."

Will leaned over the chair and gave his son a firm hug. "You just sit and rest here as long as you like. We will be inside if you need us." He clung to his son, refusing to release their embrace. "I love you, Austin."

"I love you, too, Papa."

Will stood, wiped a proud tear from his cheek, and then strode happily into the house.

~

Cowpens, South Carolina
Four Months Later - January 18, 1781

"Christ, Almighty!" moaned John Austin. "There be ghosts in this field. They do not even look like real men."

"They are real enough," Austin responded in a soft, reverent voice. "God be with them all."

The Jackson's Creek soldiers could scarcely believe the scene that greeted them when they stepped out of the tree line. It was the catastrophic aftermath of a great battle. The signs of the tragic conflict were everywhere. Austin stared, heartbroken, at the over-whelming scene of death and destruction. The bodies of over one hundred scarlet-coated British soldiers were scattered throughout the field. Two dozen dead horses lay sprawled amongst them. All of the remains of the dead, both man and beast, were covered by a thin coating of frost and light snow. The layer of white gave the frozen corpses a strange, ghostly appearance. As Austin took in the deathly scene, he thanked God that he had not been involved in this partic-ular fight.

It had been a humiliating defeat for the British and their Tory allies. Austin actually heard Colonel Phillips use the word, "disaster," to describe the previous day's action at the Cowpens. The debacle occurred when Lieutenant Colonel Banastre Tarleton led his force of over one thousand tired, starving men against a well-positioned rebel army under the command of General Daniel Morgan. The cunning Morgan had actually drawn Tarleton into a perfectly-executed trap. When the battle was over, over three hundred of the King's soldiers were either dead or wounded. An astounding six hundred more were taken prisoner. Only a handful of the British Legion dragoons, Tarleton included, escaped capture by taking flight into the surrounding woods.

It was yet another devastating loss for the British. Only three months prior they had suffered a similar humiliating defeat at King's Mountain, a crushing blow to the Loyalist cause in South Carolina. Hundreds of Loyalist militiamen had been slain on that remote South Carolina ridge. Over seven hundred were captured. Combined with this disaster at the Cowpens, the decisive losses threatened to crush the British offensive in the southern Colonies.

The rebellion was definitely picking up momentum in the south. Many Loyalists were beginning to turn coat and join the Whigs. For most, it was a practical matter of strategic alignment with what appeared to be the winning side. As Austin surveyed the battlefield and considered the seismic shift that had occurred in the war, he wondered if he, too, should consider joining their ranks. After all, he was no longer committed to the Tory cause. He harbored neither love nor respect for King George III. He served in the King's militia only to stand by his good friends. But, a day was approaching when loyalty to friends might no longer be a valid cause to continue the fight. Austin had to think of the future and consider the very real possibility of the successful establishment of a United States of America.

Captain Miller stepped in front of his men. He pointed toward the cluster of small marquee tents in the center of the field and announced, "Our wounded are being housed there. The rebels were kind enough to render aid and give them temporary shelter. Those men are now our mission. As soon as Colonel Phillips arrives with the wagons, we shall load the wounded officers and then escort them back to our surgeons in Camden."

"Just the officers?" asked Austin with an air of sarcasm.

"For now. The officers, because of their importance and rank, must be evacuated first. The enlisted men will follow in the next caravan."

Austin rolled his eyes and simultaneously shook his head. Inside, he seethed with righteous indignation. More and more, it seemed the British Army was infinitely more interested in the welfare of their commissioned officers than they were the welfare of the common soldiers. For Austin, it was simply one more reason to reject the British cause.

"So, then, our militia is now relegated to clean up work?" Joshua Ginn asked in disbelief. "Why has Tarleton not seen to his own wounded? Everyone admits he is the one who is responsible for this God-forsaken mess."

"You are exceeding the limits of your station, Private Ginn," Captain Miller warned sternly. "But, if you must know ... Colonel Tarleton is with Lord Cornwallis in fevered pursuit of the rebel army. They have the bastards on the run and are now in North Carolina. Since we are among the limited forces remaining in this region, care for the our wounded has fallen to us. I assume you have no objections to ensuring the welfare of our comrades in arms."

Joshua shook his head. He appeared thoroughly chastised. "No, Captain."

"Very well, then. Now, let us get to work."

The twelve-man detail from the Jackson's Creek Regiment trudged slowly through the snow-covered grass toward the casualty tents.

~

Later that Night

It was bitterly cold. To combat the fierce northerly winter wind, Austin and John pitched their shared wedge tent as a lean-to, facing south, with one wedge open toward their campfire. They cut pine branches and layered them on the sloped back and ends of the tent as extra insulation against the biting wind. They also lined their fire pit with several heavy rocks. The rocks would absorb the heat from the fire and then radiate it slowly throughout the night. They would place smaller heated rocks beneath their blankets to help keep their feet warm. Though it was the dead of winter and well below freezing, the two seasoned soldiers would still sleep warmly and soundly.

Austin and John sat cross-legged and stared numbly into a blazing campfire. Their bellies were full of stewed beans seasoned with pork. Such a hearty, filling meal was a rare treat in the field. They sipped hot tea and smoked their pipes as they pondered the events of the day. They had seen many disturbing sights. The pitiful state of the wounded men housed inside the rebel tents was the most distressing of all. It was hard to put the images of the broken, agonized men out of their minds. Indeed, even as the two friends sat and relaxed by their fire, they could still hear their tortured screams and moans.

John angled his head and looked in the direction of the casualty tents. "'Twill be hard to sleep tonight with all that racket."

Austin drew deeply on his pipe and then exhaled a thick cloud of smoke through his nose. He coughed softly and then nodded. "I doubt that I will sleep, anyway. All the better for you. I can keep the fire going."

John stared, concerned, at his friend. "Austin, are you well? You have not seemed yourself in recent days."

Austin shrugged. "I am the same as ever, I suppose."

"I do not think so. Something about you has changed."

Austin stared into the fire. "I do not know what else to tell you, John. I am the same old me."

John sighed deeply. He appeared frustrated. It was clear that he wanted to say something else, but for whatever reason, remained hesitant to speak. Austin glanced at John. Their eyes met. Austin could sense his friend's reticence.

"John, if you have something to say, just go ahead and say it," Austin urged.

"I am worried about you, that is all."

"'Tis useless to worry. Doing so accomplishes nothing."

"All right, then ... I am *concerned* about you, particularly your state of mind."

"Why in the hell would you say something like that?" Austin demanded, offended.

"I received a letter from Drury last month. He urged me to keep an eye on you. He said that you were not thinking straight."

Now, Austin was the one growing frustrated. "How in the hell would your brother know anything about my thinking or my state of mind? I have not seen him since August."

"He informed me that you made some disturbing confessions to him during our brief time together at Rocky Mount." John hesitated for a moment. "And he insinuated that your loyalty to the cause might be wavering."

Austin did not offer any response. He revealed no expression on his face. He leaned forward, retrieved the copper pot from its perch near the fire, and then poured himself some more tea.

"Your silence only confirms my concern, Austin. Tell me ... why have you not reenlisted like the rest of us? Everyone serving in our regiment, except for you, has signed on for another tour. You do not have much time remaining in your current enlistment."

Austin nodded. "Just two more weeks."

"*Then* will you reenlist?" John asked hopefully.

Austin inhaled deeply and then turned to face his friend. "No, John. I no longer wish to serve. I am going home. I was ready to desert after Camden, but my father counseled me to fulfill my commitment. And here I sit, doing just that. But, in two weeks, that goal will be accomplished. I will be done for good."

John was aghast. "But, Austin ... surely you remain loyal to our King and to England! How can you not continue to serve and fulfill your greatest honor as a subject of our great Sovereign?"

Austin turned and stared deeply into John's eyes. "The answer is quite simple, old friend. I no longer consider myself loyal to King George. I am not here to serve him. I am here to stand by you and Joshua and all our other mates. But, hear me well ... in two weeks I will have fulfilled all the requirements of my enlistment in the militia. After that, I refuse to take up arms in the name of the King."

John grinned uncomfortably. "You are jesting. Is this your idea of a joke?"

"No. Not at all. This is the most thoughtful, deliberate decision that I have ever made in my life. I have invested much reflection and soul-searching in recent days. I have searched my mind and heart and arrived at the only course of action that my conscience will allow. I am going home. I am done with this war."

John's face clouded with rage. "You cannot simply claim neutrality in this conflict, Austin."

"What do you mean?"

"I mean exactly what I said! You cannot remain neutral. If you are not on the side of England and the King, then you are *against* England and the King. There are only two choices. There is no middle ground. You have to take a stand."

Austin clenched his teeth. The muscles of his jaw tightened. "Do not give me any ultimatums, John Austin. If you demand that I choose a side, you might not like my response."

Austin turned away from John and inhaled a deep, cleansing breath. How *could* he explain his heart to his friend? How could he help him understand that his convictions had changed long ago ... that every single day he was living a lie? The simple truth was that his loyalty no longer lay with England. And after the horrible defeats at King's Mountain and the Cowpens, the future of America appeared clear to him. Britain was destined for defeat. It seemed a certainty. The Continental Congress declared independency in 1776. Now, four years later, the fledgling, struggling nation was taking root and growing. Its armies were winning. Though the British would never admit it, Cornwallis was on the run. The United States of America would be a nation of its own, and those who did not choose the side of liberty were certain to suffer gravely in the future.

John's face flushed red. "Austin Newman, you could never cast your lot with those damned rebels!"

Austin looked fondly at his friend and smiled. "Actually, John, I believe I could. And therein lies my dilemma."

John angrily hurled his tin mug into the darkness beyond their tent and then shot to his feet. He stood, legs wide apart, and glared furiously at Austin. His fists were clenched so hard that his knuckles turned white.

John hissed, "Then I suppose we have nothing else to say to one another, *old friend.*"

His final two words dripped with bitter sarcasm. John angrily kicked a cloud of dirt into the campfire, turned, and then stomped away into the darkness.

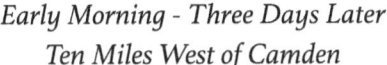

Early Morning - Three Days Later
Ten Miles West of Camden

THE SKY WAS CLEAR. After days of frigid winter cold, the prospect of a sunshine-warmed thaw thrilled the souls of the men in the convoy. But, when that blessed sunshine did appear, it would inflict a great price. The frozen roadway would thaw and return to its natural state as a thick, muddy quagmire. Wagons would become stuck in the cement-like mud. Then, the hapless militiamen would suffer the exhausting work of extracting them. Such was the life of a lowly foot-soldier in the American Colonies.

Until the thaw came, the small convoy of evacuation wagons crept slowly along the frozen, deeply rutted roadway. It was a frustratingly slow process. The convoy had been traveling for three straight days and yet it still remained ten miles short of its destination. Most of the men in the escort doubted that they would reach Camden before nightfall. They feared that, for the fourth night in a row, they would have to suffer sub-freezing winter temperatures inside their tiny wedge tents.

There were three wagons in the convoy, each one holding eight wounded officers and sergeants. The escort numbered forty men. Twenty were mounted soldiers in Lieutenant John Fanning's Independent Company of Scouts. The remainder, comprising the infantry element of the escort, were from the Jackson's Creek Regiment. Of course, Colonel John Phillips, his son, David, and brother, Robert, all enjoyed the luxury of riding on horseback. They did not have to suffer exhaustion and wet, mud-encrusted feet.

Austin trudged determinedly along the side of the roadway, keeping pace with the third wagon. He tugged his coat tightly around his neck in an effort to keep the invading cold at bay. The sun was still below the horizon and a heavy frost remained on the ground. Austin look up at the lovely purple-pink sky and prayed for the sun to come quickly. He desperately wanted to feel his toes once again. He also desired to feel the satisfaction of food in his stomach. The escort patrol had run out of rations two days prior. The men had been surviving on squirrels, rabbits, and hickory nuts for the past three days. More than anything, it was the prospect of a hot meal that compelled Austin to continue marching toward Camden.

He felt a poke in the back. It was the barrel of Joshua Ginn's gun. Much like Austin's father, Joshua had been blessed with the gift of gab. To Austin it seemed more like a curse. He did not particularly enjoy conversation, especially after his recent and bitter conflict with John.

"Hey, Austin."

Austin exhaled, aggravated. "What do you want, Joshua?"

"Albert Doak says we need on be on the lookout for bears. He says they are all over this part of the county. Pass the word along. A bear would make for a big mess of meat and a fine supper."

Austin rolled his eyes and shook his head. "You will not find any bears in these woods, you moron."

"And why not? Albert says they are all over these parts."

"They are. But the bears are all holed up and sleeping for the winter. The only way you or Albert will see one is if you go cave hunting, find a sleeping bear, and then curl up beside it."

"Oh. I had not thought of that," Joshua confessed.

"No, I reckon you didn't."

"What about a deer or an elk?" Joshua mused hopefully. "One of those would be a fine kill. Just one big, fat doe would feed damn near all of us."

"Good luck sneaking up on a deer in the presence of this loud mob. They can hear us coming from a mile away. And if they do not hear the wagons grinding in the frozen mud and rocks, surely they will hear all our mindless, annoying chatter."

Austin turned slightly to observe his friend and see if he perceived the insult that he had just unleashed upon him. However, Joshua appeared as clueless as ever. Austin smiled and then turned his attention back to the road. An unexpected gunshot erupted somewhere near the front of the column. Austin immediately jerked his flintlock from his shoulder and held it at the ready.

"Reckon what that was?" Joshua wondered out loud. "I bet somebody shot a deer critter!"

Suddenly, a barrage of gunfire erupted from the woods that lined both sides of the roadway. Several of Fanning's men on horseback tumbled, wounded or dead, from their mounts.

Austin turned and shouted, "Ambush! Take cover!" He dove

beneath the rear wagon in the convoy. Joshua followed closely behind him.

Austin scanned the area. "Do you see John anywhere?"

Joshua shook his head. "No. He is up by the first wagon, I think. He's been walking up front for a few days now." He looked at Austin. "Say ...why ain't you two talking lately? I have not heard a word betwixt the two of you for the last three or four days."

Austin stared incredulously at his friend. "Are you daft? We are under attack! This is no time for idle talk! Keep your eyes on the woods!"

Joshua nodded. He peered toward the trees to their southwest. "What must we do? Should we make a run for it?"

"No. We stay here and wait for orders."

Chaos ensued. Deadly, concentrated fire poured into the column. Dozens of bullets impacted the wagons, splintering and shredding the thick lumber. More men in the escort fell. The Tories were being decimated. Some of them returned fire, but their only targets were occasional muzzle flashes in the darkness of the trees. They simply could not see their foes. Moments later, enemy cavalry emerged from the tree line. Fifty mounted soldiers descended upon the column from two directions wielding pistols and swords. A wave of infantry followed. There was nowhere for the Tories to go or to hide. They were completely surrounded.

"There are so many of them!" Joshua wailed, terrified. "How do we fight them all?"

Austin inhaled a deep, resolute breath and then placed his musket on the ground in front of him. "We cannot fight them, Joshua. This battle is lost. We must surrender."

Austin crawled from beneath the wagon and held his empty hands high in the air. Joshua followed his lead.

"Will they shoot us?" Joshua asked worriedly.

"Not if we comply with their commands. Just stand still and hold your hands up."

Joshua followed Austin's instructions. Up and down the length of the convoy, Loyalist militiamen lifted empty hands in surrender.

Enemy militiamen descended upon them and quickly stripped them of their weapons and equipment. Austin leaned forward and peered toward the front of the convoy. He saw and heard John shouting in the face of a Whig militiaman. John was not holding a weapon, yet his posture and attitude remained boldly defiant. Suddenly, the obviously perturbed Whig swung his musket around with a sweeping move. He smashed the buttstock of the weapon against John's left jaw. Immediately, John crumpled and fell to the ground. He lay perfectly still.

"Well, it looks like John has finally surrendered," Joshua announced. "God help us all when he wakes up."

~

Early Evening

AUSTIN SUDDENLY FELT a great fondness for his confiscated wedge tent. He longed to be curled up beneath the folds of the little linen shelter. As tiny and threadbare as it was, it still offered a measure of protection from the wind and frost. But, alas, there were no warm, protective shelters in Austin Newman's immediate future. He was now a prisoner of war.

All totaled, thirty Loyalist soldiers survived the surprise attack unharmed. The remaining ten men were either dead or wounded. Immediately after the skirmish ended, the rebels searched the three wagons in the convoy, obviously hoping to find arms or plunder. Instead, they discovered British casualties. They removed several dead bodies, piled them on the side of the road, and then placed the men wounded during the skirmish inside the wagons alongside their comrades.

Most of the Tory prisoners were crowded together at the edge of the woods near several small campfires. Rebel guards kept watch over them. The captives warmed their hands and feet by their fires and attempted to forget the gnawing pain in their empty stomachs. As was customary, the officers were separated from the enlisted men and kept in a separate area. They were positioned on the opposite side of the wagons. They enjoyed only slightly better conditions than their men. Their primary advantage in captivity was a half-filled bottle of whiskey presented to Colonel Phillips by the Whig commander.

A handful of men considered criminals or troublemakers by the Whigs were placed in restraints. They were tied securely with ropes to the wheels of the wagons, maintained in isolation from the other men, and kept under double guard. Of course, John Austin was numbered among that group. He was tied while unconscious to the wagon wheel nearest to the spot where he fell. After he awoke, he unleashed an endless stream of curses and protestations upon his captors. Austin was actually glad that his foul-mouthed friend was far removed from the rest of the men.

A small cluster of Whig officers were engaged in a conference at a campfire between the second and third wagon. They were arguing loudly over the difficulties caused by taking such a large group of prisoners. The presence of the three wagons filled with wounded British officers seemed mind-boggling to them. They were baffled as to what they should do with sixty enemy prisoners, half of which were incapacitated or dying.

Austin decided that he would execute a clandestine reconnaissance mission. He stood to stretch and then moved to one of the other fires. He intentionally positioned himself as near as possible to the enemy officers so that he might eavesdrop on their conversation. Joshua soon joined him. Their captors did not seem very concerned about the movement of the prisoners as long as they made no sudden moves and remained near the fires.

"What are you doing, Austin? Why did you move over here? We had a bigger fire over yonder," whispered Joshua.

"I wanted to get closer to the officers' parley. I need to know what they are saying."

Joshua nodded. "Smart." He stole a glance at the enemy officers. "Do you recognize any of them?"

"The tall fellow looks very familiar, but I cannot place him."

"Hell, Austin! That there is Richard Winn!"

Austin's eyes widened. "You mean *the* Richard Winn, the father of Winnsborough?" A look of realization washed across his face. "Now I know why he seemed so familiar to me. My father has had business dealings with him. I think I have even been to his plantation."

"I have been there, as well. He is a powerful man back home. He is the Colonel of the rebel militia in Fairfield District. The other fellows are all from our area, as well. I know a couple of them."

Austin frowned. "So, then, we have been captured by an army of our neighbors."

"It would seem so." Joshua gave Austin a nudge. "And listen ... it appears there is a disagreement amongst them."

They sat very still and listened to the officers deliberating. The words being spoken by some of the Whig leaders were not very reassuring at all. In truth, they were terrifying. Austin and Joshua were particularly disturbed by a violent proposal made by one of the young captains.

"Why are we so worried about the welfare of these prisoners? I say we hang all the officers and then just shoot the rest of them," growled the unpleasant fellow. "Those sons of bitches in charge of this mob, the Phillips brothers, are the worst ones of them all. I know them all from back home. They don't believe their own shite stinks." The fellow spat on the ground. "It's high time we put that lot in their place."

Colonel Winn removed his hat. He closed his eyes thoughtfully and shook his head solemnly. "Captain Gentry, we are not going to execute any of these men. Many of them are our neighbors. Half of this group is from our district. One day, this conflict will end and we will need to live in harmony with our former enemies. That will be a most difficult endeavor if we have the blood of our neighbors on our hands."

"What, exactly, do you propose, Colonel?" asked another of the officers.

"I propose nothing, young man. This is not a democratic gathering. I give the orders in this regiment. I will make my wishes known and you will all accommodate them. Have I made myself perfectly clear?"

The men all looked at one another and then slowly nodded. They answered with a quiet, simultaneous, "Yes, sir."

"Good. Then, here it is. Tomorrow morning, I will dispatch a small detail as escorts for the wagons of wounded men. They will proceed under white flag to Camden and deliver the Lobsterbacks to their surgeons."

"And what about the rest of us?" asked the villainous Captain Gentry.

"We will escort the uninjured Tory prisoners to our encampment on the Pee Dee. They will be processed and sent to appropriate prisons. The officers, especially, could be quite valuable in a future prisoner exchange."

Joshua cut a concerned gaze at Austin. He whispered, "So this is it, then. Our war is over. We are headed to the gaol."

Austin did not respond. He simply frowned and nodded.

AUSTIN SLEPT FITFULLY. He fought against numbing, tooth-chattering cold throughout the entire night. The ground sapped all warmth from his body. The only parts of him that remained warm were the portions of his body that were facing the fire. So, like all of the other cold-tortured prisoners, he flipped and flopped throughout the night in an effort to keep warm.

In those rare moments when he did manage to sleep, Austin had horrible dreams. The visions in his sleep were filled with images of violence and war. He dreamt of Camden and holding his dying friend, William Armstrong, in his arms. Even though he had not been present for the battle at Cowpens, he dreamt of the disaster that occurred there. He saw every moment of the battle and watched in dismay as hundreds of men fell from explosions, lead, and steel.

But, his most vivid and perplexing dream invaded his mind in the hour just before the dawn. In that dream, he saw a large army of men dressed in blue coats and black cocked hats descending upon his peaceful home at Jackson's Creek. He watched helplessly as soldiers took his parents and brother captive. The soldiers burned their lovely cottage and barns. Next, he saw his family marching down a dusty roadway. Then, just before he awoke, his vision transported him to Charlestown. He watched helplessly as his family walked up a gangway onto a sailing ship. The Austin family was also on the ship, along with many of their other neighbors. Then, the ship weighed anchor and headed out to the sea. Soon, it disappeared over the horizon. Austin's family was gone. His friends were gone. Then, there was nothing. Everything became black.

Austin awakened with a start. Though he was freezing from the cold, his body was soaked in sweat. It took him a moment to realize that the vivid vision that he had just experienced was only a nightmare. Still, it seemed so very real. It shook him to his core. He relived the disturbing images over and over in his mind. He sat up, threw a few sticks onto the almost-extinguished fire, and then scooted close to the warm flames. As he warmed his hands, he closed his eyes and contemplated the possible meaning of his final dream. Then, the answer came to him. It was obvious. The soldiers were Continentals. All the people on the ship, including his family, were Loyalists being cast out of South Carolina. God, it seemed, had spoken to him. He had been given a glimpse into the future. But, how should he respond to the vision? What was he supposed to do?

Austin was in a state of panic. His politics had been transformed months ago. He no longer considered himself bound by loyalty to the King. He foresaw an American nation, totally free from the kingdom of Great Britain. He knew in his heart that the Whigs were going to win this war. But, what could he do? Surely, he could not simply change sides. He could not even imagine the notion of taking up arms against his friends.

He closed his eyes and prayed. "*God, show me the way. Tell me what to do.*"

Austin prayed fervently. As he prayed, his mind was carried away to another vision. In it he saw his reflection in the glass of a large window. He was standing amongst a large group of men. In his hand was a tall pole, and on the top of that pole waved a flag with thirteen red and white stripes and thirteen white stars in a circle on a canton of blue. He was a soldier in the American army! In the distance were thousands of red-coated British soldiers and he, Austin Newman, was going into battle *against* them.

Austin forced his eyes to open. He tore himself away from the supernatural vision. Immediately, he knew what he had to do. He was going to turn coat. He would join the rebellion. He immediately rose to his feet and then marched toward the tents where the Whig officers dwelt. A guard quickly spotted him and ran to intercept him. He jumped in front of Austin and pointed his French Charleville musket at the center of his chest.

"Where the hell do you think you are going?"

"I need to speak to Colonel Winn."

"Why?" demanded the soldier, his eyes filled with suspicion.

"I intend to swear my oath to the United States and join your regiment."

The man slowly lowered his musket. He gazed searchingly at Austin, looking for any possible hint of subterfuge. Convinced of Austin's sincerity, he waved the musket in the direction of the officer's quarters.

"Come along, then. Let us go and wake the colonel."

Austin sat on a makeshift stool next to Colonel Richard Winn. He sipped steaming tea from a pewter mug. Colonel Winn was pleasantly surprised when he realized Austin's identity. He recalled very well his business dealings and pre-war friendship with William Newman. He sat and listened patiently as Austin described his wartime experience and his evolving change of politics and allegiance, as well as his desire to join the American cause.

"Are you certain this is what you want to do, Mr. Newman?" asked Colonel Winn, genuinely concerned. "I know your father well. He is an avid Tory. He will not be pleased. This may very well cause an irreparable rift in your family."

"Yes, sir. I am sure. Until this morning, I was not. But now my path seems clear. And, in the end, I hope that this decision might actually save my family."

"You must not take this lightly," cautioned the colonel.

"I understand, sir. Trust me. I know that this is a very serious and solemn affair. I have thought long and hard on it. Indeed, it has taken me many months to reach this decision."

Colonel Winn nodded and then stood. "Very well, then. Austin Newman, I welcome you to the cause."

Austin stood. Smiling happily, he offered his hand in friendship to the colonel. They shook.

Colonel Winn explained, "I will call a formation of all the men. We will also make a formation of the prisoners. I must require you to swear your oath on the Holy Bible in front of the entire assembly of men. I trust you have no objections."

Austin inhaled a deep, shaky breath. "No, sir."

"Excellent. Then we shall resolve this issue immediately." He called over his shoulder, "Corporal Davis!"

"Yes, sir." A young soldier appeared by his side.

"See that Private Newman receives some hot food and then see if you can scrounge up a good coat for him. Also, make sure that he gets his weapons and accoutrements back. He is soon to be a soldier in our regiment."

Corporal Davis smiled. "Yes, sir!"

$\sim$

Two Hours Later

THE DEED WAS DONE. Austin Newman swore his oath to the United States of America in full view of all his former mates. He heard angry, hateful curses from several of them. He caught a brief glimpse of Joshua Ginn. The despondent, heartbroken lad was crying like a baby. But John Austin was not crying. Instead, his eyes were filled with rage and hatred.

The wounded prisoner escort had already departed for Camden. With luck, they would reach the British outpost near nightfall. Austin stood in a loose formation alongside his new mates, the other privates in the Fairfield District Militia. They were preparing to make the march to Pee Dee. Austin's first task as an American soldier was not an enviable one. He had to escort his former compatriots to the Whig encampment, where they would all be incarcerated in a military jail.

Soon, the order came to begin the march. As luck would have it, Austin's place in the formation was directly alongside John Austin. His former friend refused to look at him. Austin did not make any attempts at conversation. He thought it best that they not speak, lest he awaken suspicion amongst his new allies. They had been marching for a little over a half hour when, surprisingly, John actually called his name.

"Austin."

"Yes, John?"

"I think I understand why you did this."

"You do?" Austin's heart warmed at the surprising confession from his friend.

"Yes." He paused. "But I am still going to kill you."

Austin's head whipped in John's direction. John was staring at him, his eyes red and swollen with emotion and pain.

John growled, "If it is the last thing I do, Austin Newman, I am going to kill you. Even if I have to use my bare hands ... I *will* kill you."

17

FACING FATHER

Prisoner Convoy – Waxhaws Region, South Carolina
Early Evening - January 28, 1781

"We make our escape tonight," John Austin whispered anxiously to Joshua Ginn. "We will be long gone before they even know we are missing."

Joshua glanced around them to make sure no one could hear their conversation. "What makes you so certain that we can get away tonight?"

John grinned and pointed at the two guards who had just arrived for duty. One was a red-faced, overweight lad. He was sitting on a log stool and slurping from a huge bowl of corn porridge. The other fellow had just emerged from the adjacent woods. His wore neither coat nor weskit and his shirt was untucked from his breeches. He had a most unpleasant look on his face and walked slowly and with his legs spread far apart. He appeared to be in significant pain.

"The fat fellow and that mean bastard are our guards tonight. The big one always falls asleep once his belly is full. The other one has a raging case of the flux. I have heard him complaining about it for the past two days. All we need to do is wait for the big one to go to sleep. Then, when the other one runs to the woods for his scorching hourly constitutional, we make our escape into the night."

Joshua nodded. "We could really use a horse."

"I already thought of that," John reassured him. "We passed by a farm late this afternoon. I saw two horses in the barn. We can reach the farm before dawn, abscond with the mounts and then ... "

"And then we will be half-way home before nightfall tomorrow," Joshua declared, finishing John's sentence for him.

"Right." John grinned gleefully. "There are ample Loyalists betwixt here and home. We should have no trouble finding shelter and food. With a little luck and good weather, we will be sleeping in our own beds in a couple of days."

Joshua sighed happily. "And dining at our own tables."

~

Early Evening - Five Days Later
Home of Will and Lizzy Newman
Jackson's Creek, South Carolina

WILL DOZED CONTENTEDLY in his comfortable wingback chair beside the warm fireplace. His personal copy of *The Life and Opinions of Tristam Shandy* lay in his lap, still open to the last page that he had been reading before he fell asleep. His spectacles dangled precariously on the tip of his nose. A sudden poke to his shoulder roused him from a very satisfying slumber.

"Husband, wake up."

Will awakened with a start and then stared, confused, at his wife. "What is it, love? Is something wrong?"

"No, Will. You have a guest."

"A guest? At this hour of the night?"

"He said that it could not wait. I will fix some tea whilst the two of you visit."

Lizzy stepped to the side, revealing a very gaunt and tired-looking

John Austin. Will's heart leapt with joy at the sight of his son's militia comrade and friend.

"John! How delightful! What on earth are you doing here?" Will stood excitedly. John stepped forward and they shook hands. "But, you look terrible. What has befallen you?"

"I was captured a couple of weeks ago, shortly after the battle at the Cowpens. I was in the hands of the rebels for a little over one week. Joshua Ginn and I made our escape five nights ago, and have only now arrived back at Jackson's Creek. I needed to come and see you before going home to my wife."

Will became overwhelmed with a sudden wave of dread. Trembling, he asked, "John ... where is my son?"

John's weary, unhappy countenance darkened even more. He lowered his chin to his chest. His shoulders began to shake. Tears formed in both of his eyes. Lizzy appeared with a small tea service. She immediately placed the tray on a nearby table and then moved to her husband's side. She took his hand in her own. Already, however, her own eyes were filled with tears. Her heart was also filled with dread. She assumed, like her husband, that John bore the sorrowful news of Austin's death.

"What has happened, John?" inquired Will, his voice cracking. "Has my boy fallen to the guns of enemy?"

John slowly ... almost reluctantly ... lifted his eyes. "No, Mr. Newman. I almost wish that were so. If he were dead in the grave, then, at least, he might retain his honor."

Will's gaze became stern. "You had best explain yourself, John Austin."

"Mr. Newman, I regret to inform you that your son has gone over to the enemy. He has turned coat and joined the rebels."

Will was stunned. He sank numbly into his chair. He turned and gazed at his wife. Lizzy was clearly stunned, as well. She stepped behind Will's chair and then placed both of her hands firmly on his shoulders. She gave him a reassuring squeeze. Will closed his eyes and shook his head in despair and denial.

"There must be some mistake, John. Surely, you have misunderstood his actions. Could he not be on some secret mission for his captain?"

John shook his head slowly and grimly. "No, sir. There was no mistaking what he did. He was captured with me and about twenty other men from the regiment. On the morning after our capture, Colonel Richard Winn called a formation. We were made to stand there and watch as Austin swore his rebel oath." John became choked with emotion. "Then, he was assigned as my guard during the first half of my march to the prison camp at Pee Dee. The last time I saw your son, he appeared quite comfortable and happy amongst the enemy troops."

Will's eyes filled with tears. "I knew that my son was troubled. He seemed confused by his unnatural connection to that rebel boy. He told me that he did not intend to continue in the King's militia once his enlistment was done, but I never imagined anything like this."

"Nor did I ... at least not until a couple of days before he committed his treason. He confessed his changing convictions to me on the night after the battle at Cowpens. He said horrible things about our King. We exchanged some very harsh words that night and had not spoken in the days before our capture."

"Did you speak to him after he turned coat?"

"Only briefly, sir."

"What did he say?" demanded Will, desperate to understand the actions of his son.

"Nothing, really," John lied. "I suppose we have nothing else to say to one another."

Will nodded. It was quite clear that his heart was broken. He stood shakily and then embraced John.

"I am grateful that you were the one who bore this tragic news, John. I would have hated to have heard about it in the form of gossip or loose talk. It is much more preferable to be informed by a friend with first-hand knowledge of the events. Truly, your coming here tonight means much to Lizzy and me."

"It is my honor, sir. I thought that you, of all people, deserved to know the truth."

Will nodded sadly. "How long will you remain here at home?"

"I do not know, sir. Joshua and I are the only ones who escaped. We will stay for a few days to regain our strength and health. Then, we will go to Camden in search of our officers."

Will motioned toward the door. "Go on, then. You have a wife and children who will be quite pleased to see you. Go and tend to them. I wish you luck and good fortune, John."

"Thank you, Mr. Newman."

John quickly exited the house. After he was gone, Will turned and faced his wife. She wept openly. Immediately, she tumbled into his arms.

"Oh, Will, how can we bear this shame? What shall we do about our Austin?"

Will inhaled a deep breath. "We shall love him, my dear. After all, he is still our son."

～

February 11, 1781
Guard Station - American Encampment Near the North Carolina Border

AUSTIN NEWMAN SHIVERED from the evening cold. Truly, serving as a guard at the entrance to the militia camp was the coldest, most tedious, and most mind-numbing duty possible. He longed to be beside his crackling fire and tucked deep into his pine needle and spruce bough bed beneath his two thick wool blankets. But, tonight, that would have to wait.

Austin had settled quite nicely into his new role as a Whig soldier. Duty at the American outpost was typical of most military encampments in the winter season. Thankfully, there were no battles or skirmishes. Any missions outside the camp were usually simple patrols, mostly focused upon procuring food and supplies. When in camp, he endeavored to remain warm, fed, and entertained. He constantly made improvements to his well-constructed lean-to, cut and stacked firewood, and hunted for fresh meat. At night, he and his new friends played card games or rolled dice shaped and carved from lead musket balls.

Austin exhaled hot air into his hands to warm them. He then stood and walked in circles and stomped his feet to keep his circulation going and prevent his toes from freezing. As he walked, he prayed that the next four hours would pass quickly.

"You simply cannot be still, can you?" teased Dread Sutton, his shift-mate.

"My bollocks are going to freeze off, Dread!" Austin whined.

"Well, build us a fire, then. There is no need for us to stand out here in the dead of winter and suffer."

"We can do that?" Austin asked hopefully.

Dread pointed to an open area thirty feet north of their station. "Most men on night guard build a fire right over yonder. There is likely some split wood stacked in that tall grass. If not, one of us can run back and get some."

"I did not know that we could build fires near the road. The light might reveal our position to the enemy."

Dread chuckled. "Hell, Austin ... everyone for fifty miles knows this camp is here. 'Tis no great military secret. You go ahead and build us a fire. I will keep watch on the road. We can rotate short shifts between the barricade and the fire until our work is done."

Austin nodded. "I will be most happy to do so." He peered down the dark roadway toward the west. "Are we expecting anything unusual tonight?"

"We have a group of men who are supposed to be returning from furlough, but we don't know when to expect them. They are several days late getting back. Captain Mitchell is worried they may have encountered trouble back home."

"Well, keep a sharp eye out, anyway. Do you remember the challenge for tonight?"

Dread nodded. "Privy."

"And the countersign?"

Dread laughed. "Thunder."

"That sounds about right, does it not?" quipped Austin. "Though,

I doubt that any of the men returning from furlough will know today's challenge and countersign."

"'Twill be all right, Austin. I know most all of those fellows. If they do come back during our shift, I should be able to recognize them, even in the dark."

"Nevertheless, remain alert," Austin warned. "Signal me if you need me. I will get to work on our fire."

Austin cradled his musket in the crook of his arm and strode quickly to the fire pit. He was thrilled to discover an ample supply of kindling and split wood. He lay his musket aside, whipped out his fire starting kit, and went to work. He had a cheerful blaze going in a matter of minutes. He warmed his feet and hands quickly and then retrieved his musket. It was time to relieve Dread and give him a fireside respite. As he rose to walk back to the barricade, he heard Dread utter a frantic shout.

"Privy!"

The night was silent. There was no response to the challenge word. Austin took off running toward the barricade.

"Did you see something?" Austin demanded. He stepped into position and then held his musket at the ready, aiming it westward down the roadway. Dread aimed his musket in the same direction.

"I heard voices," Dread whispered. He sniffed the air. "And I smell them, Austin! There are men out there on that road!"

"You smell them?" Austin repeated incredulously.

Dread nodded. "I do. I have a nose like a hound, and there is no mistaking the stench of an unwashed man." He cupped one hand against his mouth and shouted again, "Privy! I said, 'privy,' damn you! You had best give me the countersign, or I will shoot you in the arse!"

"We don't know the countersign!" an angry, irritated voice responded from the darkness. "We have been gone from camp for damned near two weeks, you fool."

"Who are you? State your name!" Dread shouted harshly.

There was a moment of awkward silence, and then the voice replied, "Dread Sutton, is that you?"

Dread lowered his musket. He looked at Austin and smiled. "That there is Randolph Carter. Those are our boys, back from home."

Dread shouted, "Come on in Randolph, you stinky jackanape. It smells like none of you have had a good washing since you left camp!"

Moments later, a half-dozen men materialized out of the darkness. One of them, obviously Randolph Carter, approached Dread and greeted him with a warm hug. The other men seemed equally happy to see Austin's fellow guardsman. The men were all filthy and unkempt. It appeared that they had been through quite a traumatic experience. Austin, since he was relatively new to the regiment, remained at a distance and allowed them to enjoy their reunion.

"Where have you fellows been?" Dread inquired. "The captain has all but written you off for dead."

Randolph shook his head. "We almost were! We had a run-in with a big patrol of mounted Tories a few miles north of Camden. They would have skinned our arses iff'n old Dan'l hadn't known about the location of a big cave. We scurried inside, covered up the entrance, and hid there for two days. There was a spring in the back of the cave with good water. We had little to eat and damn near froze our arses off. But, we held on until the Tories went away. Since then, we have been hiding out in the daytime and traveling only at night."

Dread cackled happily. "Sounds like you boys owe Daniel Dansby a drink."

Randolph nodded. "We do, indeed."

Austin's ears perked at the mention of that familiar name. He stepped forward to join the group. He called out, "Daniel Dansby?"

A short, skinny fellow stepped from the shadows. "That is my name," he answered, confused.

The young man's face was covered with dirt and a week's growth of whiskers. Even still, Austin recognized him immediately. It was his old boyhood pal from back home. Separated by politics and circumstance, the two friends had not seen one another in over five years ... not since Daniel's unfortunate captivity at the first siege at Ninety-Six.

Austin's face erupted into a huge grin. "Daniel, surely you have not forgotten your old buddy, Austin Newman."

"Christ, Almighty!" Daniel exclaimed. He stepped happily toward his childhood friend and then grabbed him in a happy embrace.

DANIEL AND AUSTIN sat on the ground near the outpost campfire. Dread offered to stand watch alone for a while so that the two old friends might enjoy some reacquainting.

"Which company are you in?" Daniel inquired.

"Captain James Mitchell's."

Daniel nodded approvingly. "He is a good man. He takes care of his soldiers."

"That is good to know. I figured as much. He has been most polite and attentive to me."

Daniel grabbed a large stick of wood and added it to the fire. "You know ... I already heard that you had turned coat."

Austin was genuinely mystified. "Sincerely? When? How?"

"Word is out back home in the district. The whole backcountry is talking about it. John Austin has been telling everyone who will listen."

"John Austin? I do not understand. How could he tell anyone anything about me? When I last saw him, he was in a column of prisoners headed to the jail at Pee Dee."

"I reckon they diverted the prisoners to the north. They have a big camp for them up in Salisbury, North Carolina. He and Joshua made their escape whilst they were stopped overnight in the Waxhaws. It took them several days to make their way home, but they eventually got there. Both of them are celebrities amongst the Tories around Jackson's Creek. Hell, Drury is, too."

"Drury? What did he do?"

"He was in that big fight at King's Mountain. He survived, but was amongst the hundreds that our boys captured there. A couple of days later, though, he made his escape. Just like John, it took him nigh on a week to get home." Daniel grinned and shook his head. "Those Austin boys are a slippery bunch, are they not?"

"Indeed," Austin agreed. "And rabidly loyal to King George." He sighed thoughtfully. "I served the King because of the politics that I inherited from my father. But, for them, loyalty to Great Britain seems almost like a religion. I only wish that I had made my break long ago."

Daniel leaned closer to Austin. "What did John do when your changed sides?"

Austin chuckled uncomfortably. "He made an oath that he would kill me ... with his bare hands, of course.."

"Of course!" Daniel laughed out loud. "I am not surprised in the least."

"Truly?" Austin seemed perplexed. "I most certainly was. We have been friends for all our lives."

Daniel sighed. "These are strange and difficult times, Austin. One day, if duty demands it, we may be called upon to take the lives of our friends." He shook his head to clear away the deep thoughts. "It is ghastly. I must not dwell upon it."

Austin rolled over onto his knees and then, using his musket for leverage, slowly rose to his feet. Once upright, he extended a hand to Daniel and pulled him up to a standing position.

"Daniel, I have to go and relieve Dread at the barricade, and you need to get some food and sleep. I have light duty tomorrow. Let us spend some more time together. I would like to hear all about your experiences in the Whig army."

"That sounds good."

Daniel gave Austin a quick, friendly hug and then walked briskly down the dirt road toward the camp. Once he was out of sight, Austin turned and then headed back toward the roadway barricade. He still had three frigid hours of guard duty remaining.

∾

February 17, 1781

American Encampment – Near the Border of North Carolina

THE MEN of the Fairfield Regiment were gathered in formation and awaiting Colonel Winn's arrival. Rumor had it that he was about to make an important announcement. The colonel had been gone for several days on a mission into North Carolina and had returned around mid-morning. He was faced with an immediate crisis. His captains hoped that he might provide a solution to their dilemma.

Fever and flux were ravaging the militia encampment. Almost half of the two hundred men in the camp had been afflicted. Already, three men were dead. The only physician serving in the camp was thoroughly confounded by the disease. It bore a striking resemblance to ship's fever, but such a diagnosis did not make any sense. The men at the encampment did not live in cramped quarters. Also, their water came from a spring, so there was no reason to suspect contamination. Still, more and more men were becoming gravely ill. It appeared that many more might die.

Most of the men who were still healthy were eager to leave. They did not wish to become afflicted with the debilitating sickness. As they awaited Colonel Winn's appearance, the group of roughly thirty men chatted nervously. Suddenly, their commander appeared from behind a nearby tent. Austin and his mates immediately stopped talking.

The colonel nodded to his men. "Gentlemen, we have little time to waste. Captain Mitchell has briefed me on the sickness that has invaded this encampment. Right now, it appears largely isolated amongst two of the other regiments." He took a deep, decisive breath. "Cornwallis and his army are currently in North Carolina. Since there will be no campaigns against the British until the spring weather breaks, I am temporarily disbanding this regiment until April 1, when we will re-form at the courthouse in Fairfield District. It seems foolish for us to remain here and carry on our search for Tories." He smiled. "Hell, we can do that back home ... right, Mr. Newman?"

The men all looked at Austin and laughed. Several poked him or patted him on the shoulders and back. Austin's face turned bright red from embarrassment. Deep inside, though, he was so very proud and pleased to have been so readily accepted by the men.

"We have roughly three hours until dark. Pack your belongings. If you have a tent, take it with you. Otherwise, leave your lean-to's as they stand. We will move out as a group one hour before nightfall. Eat something before you leave. I plan for us to walk until well into the night before we make camp. We need to put as much distance as we can between ourselves and this facility. We will remain together throughout the march. There is safety in our numbers. Make sure you have ample rations, lead, and powder before we go. Questions?"

The men looked searchingly at one another. No one responded.

"Good. On your way, then. Get it done. I will see you at the western barricade two hours hence. If you miss our departure, then you are on your own. And, trust me, right now you do not want to be found alone out in the backcountry. You are dismissed."

Daniel turned, grinning, to Austin. "That is damned near six weeks back home! I won't know what to do with myself! I will be fat on my wife's fine cooking and spent from her fine loving."

Austin frowned. "You might be entertaining me, as well. I am not certain that I will receive much of a warm welcome back at my home."

"I sincerely hope not. I love you, Austin, but three will be a crowd at my house. I have plans." He winked. "Simply humble yourself before your father and extend an olive branch. Perhaps you will be surprised."

Austin smiled. "I pray so. But, I still may need a place to sleep until April."

∾

Near Dusk - Four Days Later
Jackson's Creek, South Carolina

AUSTIN WAS HOME. He could scarcely believe it. He had been gone for almost six months. He stood at a distance and stared at his little white house in the fading light of sunset. Everything appeared quiet and serene. The livestock were all inside the barn and protected from the winter's cold. Not a creature stirred anywhere in sight. A thin wisp of smoke escaped the stone chimney and them climbed high into the air. His family had, no doubt, just enjoyed their evening meal. Right now, they were all seated near the fireplace. He could picture his father reading from a book. He imagined his little brother, now sixteen years old, amusing himself with a deck of playing cards. Lizzy, his step-mother, would be sewing or knitting by the firelight.

His heart raced with anticipation. He could not wait to see them all. But, would they share in his joy? Or, instead, might they reject him and send him away? Ultimately, there was only one way to find out.

Austin marched down the hillside and approached the house. He considered announcing his arrival by calling out, but a voice in the night might be even more disconcerting than a simple knock on the door. He decided to just walk up the front steps and knock. He attempted to prepare his heart for every eventuality. Even if his parents rejected him, he knew that he would still love them and honor them ... no matter what.

The sun had just dipped below the horizon when he climbed the steps onto the porch. The top step bowed slightly, emitting a familiar and extremely loud pop. The sound of the shifting lumber alerted the family dog. Inside the house, the hound unleashed a barrage of frantic barking.

"Well ... everyone knows I am here now," Austin mumbled to himself.

Before Austin could even approach the door, it swung open, unleashing a wave of warmth along with tantalizing, familiar smells. His father stood in the open doorway. Will Newman stared for a moment at the dirty, whiskered young man on his porch. It was difficult to see from the warm light of the house into the darkness outside. He did not recognize his son.

Will asked, "May I help you, sir?"

Austin stepped into the light. "Do you have a place where a weary soldier might sleep tonight?"

A look of happy realization washed across Will's face. "Austin? Is it really you?"

"Yes, Papa. I have come home for a visit."

Suddenly, Caesar, now nine months old, sprinted through the open doorway and leapt recklessly into Austin's arms. The excited, wiggling dog assaulted him with a barrage of wet, sloppy kisses. After several seconds, Austin extricated himself from the dog's enthusiastic affections and placed the animated, tail-wagging mutt down on the floor. Caesar continued to jump up and down and paw at Austin's legs.

Austin smiled apprehensively as he patted the dog's head. "It is good to know that at least the dog is glad that I have come home."

Will stepped forward and then wrapped his arms around his son. "Boy, everyone in this house is glad that you are home."

Austin leaned his musket against the wall and then returned his father's embrace. Both men wept with joy.

AUSTIN WAS FINALLY warm and well-fed. Indeed, he could not recall the last time that he had enjoyed such a fine meal. He sat on the stone hearth in front of the roaring fire and sipped hot, honey-sweetened tea from a china cup. Caesar lay sprawled beneath his legs. Will and Lizzy sat in their rocking chairs and gazed happily at their son. They had actually done very little in the way of reacquainting. Austin had been too busy eating to engage in any meaningful conversation. But now, seated in luxury next to a winter night's fire, they would have the opportunity to catch up on one another's lives.

"Can I get you anything, Austin?" Lizzy asked. "Another slice of pie, perhaps?"

Austin shook his head. "No thank you, ma'am. I could not fit another crumb inside me. I already feel as if I am about to explode. But, your supper was so wonderful! I have not dined in such splendor for many months." He paused and grinned. "But, tomorrow morning I am certain that I will be singing a different tune."

"Then I shall prepare you a breakfast feast," she promised, smiling happily.

With a measure of small talk behind them, an awkward silence ensued. At last, Will initiated more conversation.

"How long will you be home, Son?"

"Until the first of April, if you will have me."

Will nodded. "Of course, we will have you. This is your home."

"Even though I am now an enemy of King George and Great Britain?"

Will inhaled deeply and thoughtfully. He glanced at his wife. Lizzy wiped a single tear from her eye. "We shall have to talk about that at another time ... just the two of us."

Austin nodded. "As you wish." He took another sip of tea. "Where is little William, Papa? Is he ordinarily out so late at night?"

Will closed his eyes and inhaled a deep, shaky breath. He sat strangely silent for an uncomfortably long time. Lizzy rose from her chair and disappeared quickly into their bedchamber, closing the door behind her. The sound of weeping emanated from beyond the wall.

"Papa?" Austin inquired, concerned. "What has happened?"

Will opened his tear-soaked eyes. "William is gone, son."

"What?" Austin swallowed hard. "Is my brother dead?"

"No, Austin. He is just gone. He left about a month ago." He paused. "He departed just after John came here to tell us about you turning coat."

"Where did he go?" Austin asked, confused.

"He went east to Pee Dee. He was determined to join a Whig regiment under the command of a fellow named Francis Marion. As far as I know, that is what he did. We have not heard a word from him since he left."

Austin was completely dumbfounded. "I have heard of Colonel Marion. He is a legend amongst the Americans. So, Papa ... are you actually telling me that my little brother has run off and joined the Whig army?"

Will nodded sullenly. His face was filled with shame.

Austin's face expanded into a teasing smile. "I reckon, then, you have raised up a whole litter of rebels here in your little nest of treason."

Will stared at Austin with a horrified gaze. He could not quite believe the words that his son had just uttered in his presence. At first, he appeared furious. Then, as the moments passed, his features softened. Finally, try as he might to maintain a serious look on his face, he could not help but smile. When Austin erupted into laughter, Will could not help but join him. It took a while for their laughter to subside.

"Oh! It is good to laugh together again, isn't it, Papa?"

Will smiled warmly at his son and nodded. "It is, indeed. It has been far too long."

Will looked away from Austin and stared numbly into the fire. After a while, his smile reduced to a guarded frown. He seemed to be struggling with his emotions. Austin allowed him the privacy of his thoughts. After a brief period of silence, Will looked once again into his son's eyes.

"I must confess that I have been angry at you, Austin. I felt hurt by you and betrayed."

"'Tis understandable. I abandoned a set of principles to which you have adhered faithfully throughout your entire life. Some bitterness is to be expected."

Will admitted, "And I have also blamed you for William leaving us."

Austin's left eyebrow raised in a puzzled look. "That is not exactly fair, is it? I doubt that William up and ran off simply because of what I did."

Will shook his head. "No. I reckon he did not. Clearly, it was something that he struggled with for some time. But, I suspect your changing sides in the war did give him a bit of a nudge, though. I know how the boy thinks. He worships the very ground upon which you walk. I have no doubt that your changing sides in the war was the push that he needed to finally make the decision to go."

"I do hope that his mates will watch out for him," declared Austin. "He is so young." He paused. "And I have seen what this war can do to a young man."

"God will watch over our boy. Lizzy and I pray for him every night."

Austin smiled once again. "So, now the two of you are actually praying for the rebel cause?"

"Not for the cause," his father corrected him. "Just for a couple of its soldiers."

Austin patted his father on the knee. "I will take that. I need all the prayers I can get." He turned to his left and placed his teacup on the hearth. "What has it been like for you ... recently, I mean? How have people been treating you? I got word that John Austin has been spreading the news of my change in allegiance."

"He has, indeed. And it has gotten worse ever since William left to join Marion's Brigade. Tongues are wagging, to be sure. There are people here I've known for over twenty years who will no longer speak to me. They actually refuse to acknowledge me in public!"

Austin's eyes widened. "I did not think that your friends would act in such a way."

"Nor did I, Son."

Austin rose from his seat on the hearth and then sat down beside his father in Lizzy's rocking chair.

"You do realize that England is going to lose this war, don't you, Papa? Cornwallis is defeated. He just does not know it yet. He is running short on supplies. The losses at King's Mountain and the Cowpens has them reeling. Men are changing sides left and right. People are beginning to see the changing direction of things, Father. The winds are blowing in favor of the United States. We *will* be a new and independent nation. One would be wise to place himself on the right side of history." He paused. "And quickly so."

Will sighed deeply. "I hear you, Son. I can even see some of the merits of your appeal. But, I cannot simply turn my back on my King. And I cannot abandon my Loyalist friends."

Austin leaned back in the rocking chair and crossed his arms. "Even if those so-called friends turn their backs on you? Because they have ... you have told me so."

Will waved his hand dismissively. "They are just angry. It will pass. You will see."

Austin shrugged. "Perhaps. For your sake, I hope so." He stretched and yawned and then stood. "But, right now I am entirely too tired to solve all of the problems of the New World. I am sleepy. Might I have your permission to retire for the night?"

"Go ahead, Son. Sleep well. Dream of that day when all the members of our family will be together again."

"I will try." Austin leaned down and hugged his father. "Good night, Papa."

Will hugged his son tightly. "Good night, my boy."

Austin turned and shuffled down the short hallway toward his bedchamber.

~

2:00 AM

AUSTIN AWAKENED WITH A START. Something was wrong. His keen awareness of danger had been aroused. Suddenly, he realized what it was. He smelled smoke. Then, he saw an orange, dancing glow through his bedchamber window. He heard the sharp cracking sound of burning wood. He sat up and peered through the window. The barn was fully engulfed in flames.

"Oh, my God!" he wailed.

Austin threw back the thick pile of blankets that covered him and leapt from the bed. He ran in his stocking feet toward the front door.

"Papa!" he screamed. "Wake up! Fire! The barn is on fire!"

Austin heard a loud thud from his parents' room, followed by an angry oath. Almost immediately, his father threw open his bedchamber door. He was rubbing his left shoulder. "Damn it, Austin! What is all the commotion about? You scared Lizzy half to death, and I fell getting out of the bed!"

Austin pointed at the window. "The barn is on fire! Look!"

Will darted to the window, then exclaimed, "God help us!"

Both men ran outside into the winter cold wearing only their shirts and stockings. Will grabbed a bucket and sprinted to a nearby horse trough, but the water inside the container was frozen solid. He slammed the bucket angrily onto the block of ice. The wood shattered into a dozen pieces. He turned and watched, helplessly, as his barn burned in a tremendous conflagration. Austin walked over to stand by his father's side. They were thirty yards away from the blaze, but even at that distance the heat was almost unbearable. Somewhere inside the barn horses whinnied in pain and fear and kicked helplessly against the walls of their stalls.

"All of my animals are in there, Austin," Will moaned. "All of our horses, two milk cows, and a half-dozen sheep. How could something like this happen?"

Something on the ground near the house caught Austin's eye. It was a large, white lump. He walked over to investigate. He soon recognized what it was. One of his father's unshorn sheep lay dead in the dry, brown winter grass. Its throat was cut wide open and a large pool of gel-like blood covered the area around the poor animal's head.

"What in the bloody hell?" Austin hissed.

Lizzy appeared at his side. "What is happening? How did the barn catch fire?" Suddenly, she unleashed a loud, shrill scream directly into Austin's ear.

"What is the matter with you?" Austin demanded.

She pointed over his shoulder in the direction of the house. He turned and immediately gasped at what he saw. There, written in dripping-wet blood across the whitewashed siding boards, were two horrifying words ... "BURN TRAITORS."

April 1, 1781
Mid-Morning
The Richard Winn Estate – Near Winnsborough, South Carolina

WILL Newman eased his wagon to a stop in front of Colonel Richard Winn's house. He set the brake and then he and Austin climbed down from the seat. Colonel Winn came walking down the stairs from the porch of his grand home. He donned his cocked hat as he approached the Newmans. His eyes were wide with surprise. He walked swiftly and confidently up to Will with his hand outstretched.

"Will Newman! How are you, sir? It has been a long time."

"I am well, Richard. And yourself?"

"I have no complaints." He grinned. "Though, I am a bit surprised to see you here, Will, considering your political persuasions. Visiting my place could ruin your Tory reputation."

Will shrugged. "Well, Richard, my boy needed a ride to your muster. And, apparently, my Tory reputation has already been ruined. 'Tis no wonder. I have one son serving with you and one with Colonel Marion." He shook his head angrily. "Then, last month my Loyalist neighbors and friends burned down my livestock barn and murdered all my animals."

Colonel Winn nodded. "I heard about that. 'Twas a horrid, unrighteous act."

Will pointed to the two skinny horses pulling his wagon. "I had to buy these two old nags off of some vagabond Cherokees just so I could have a team to pull my wagon."

Colonel Winn frowned. "I am so very sorry for your unjust treatment, Will. People have no right to abuse you because of the politics of your sons."

"No, they do not. But, in the end, I am glad that they did. They have opened my eyes to a few things."

"Oh?" Colonel Winn seemed genuinely curious. "What manner of things?"

"Matters of allegiance and patriotism, primarily." He tilted his head toward the wagon bed. "Austin and I have a little surprise for you. It should be quite helpful in the upcoming campaign."

"I do not understand," responded Colonel Winn.

"Just wait until you see it," Austin declared proudly. He walked to the side of the wagon and then pulled back the canvas cover.

Will announced, "There are two hundred pounds of ground corn, one hundred pounds of wheat flour, two hogsheads of whiskey, two kegs of gunpowder, and three sacks of dried venison. Plus, there are a few sundry clothing items ... new stockings, neck socks, and such. Lizzy made those herself."

Colonel Winn was overwhelmed. "That will all be mighty helpful, indeed."

"I cannot allow you to take the wagon, of course. It is the only one I have. But all of the cargo is for the good of the regiment. In return, I simply ask that you provide a voucher describing these goods that I have provided to the South Carolina troops."

Colonel Winn grinned. "You shall have it, along with a sincere letter of thanks from me."

"Thank you, Richard. Hopefully, when the fighting is over and we have won this war, I might even get reimbursed by the new government."

"*We?*" Colonel Winn echoed, laughing happily. "Have you finally decided to cast your lot with us ungrateful rebels?"

"No, Richard. I have decided to cast my lot with my sons ... and with liberty."

18

HOPE

The war in the south had taken a dramatic turn. British forces were on the run. General Cornwallis had pursued Patriot General Nathanael Green into North Carolina. He finally engaged Greene at the Battle of Guilford Courthouse on March 15, 1781. It was an enormous and bloody battle. Technically, it was a British victory. However, practically, it was little more than a draw. Cornwallis lost over one-third of his fighting force. He evacuated his exhausted army to Wilmington, North Carolina, to lick his wounds and procure supplies.

Meanwhile, in South Carolina and Georgia, Loyalist support was dwindling. Tories were switching sides in great numbers. With the absence of Cornwallis' main army, Whig forces took control of most of the state. The remaining British and Loyalist troops clustered into small bands and occupied various towns and villages. The American troops, mostly local militia, began to root them out one-by-one. The majority of the British forces became concentrated along the coast, primarily around Charlestown, and in the backcountry village of Ninety-Six.

The American Revolution in South Carolina was drawing toward a climax. It truly seemed that victory for the independence-minded rebels was almost in sight.

May 11, 1781
Mid-Morning
Orangeburgh, South Carolina

AUSTIN NEWMAN, Daniel Dansby, and Thomas Marpole huddled together behind the remains of an ancient stone fence. They chatted happily as the artillerymen reloaded their cannon. When it was time for the big gun to fire, the fellows all pressed their hands tightly against their ears to protect them against the enormous concussion. Then, as soon as the explosion and shock wave subsided, they removed their hands and continued their conversation. They were quite content not to be doing any shooting in this particular fight. Besides, their muskets would be useless against the brick building that housed the besieged British troops.

The three fellows, all friends and neighbors from back home in Fairfield District, had volunteered to go on a patrol commanded by Captain Aramana Liles. But they were beginning to wish that they had remained back in their encampment. Instead of marching out on yet another uneventful long-range patrol, their company, along with a half-dozen others, had been commandeered by Brigadier General Thomas Sumpter. The general had recently received a shiny new six-pounder cannon from General Nathanael Greene and he was itching to use it. The garrison of British troops in the tiny town of Orange-burgh provided the perfect target for his new and deadly toy.

So, Austin and his mates suddenly found themselves as soldiers in General Sumpter's little army. They were part of a force of over three hundred and fifty men surrounding about a hundred Redcoats and Tory militiamen. The enemy soldiers were occupying a large brick building in the center of the town, and General Sumpter was blasting away at them with his six-pounder. The besieged soldiers, though they fired occasional shots from their muskets, were very outmanned and outgunned. The brick walls of their hideout were thick, but they were slowly giving way to the concentrated cannon fire. There were already a couple of small holes in the wall. Soon, the artillerymen would be delivering shots trough those holes into the interior of the house. Then, the battle would be over. They would have no other option but to surrender. It was only a matter of time.

Daniel glanced to his left to observe the artillery team in action. He noticed that they were getting ready to fire once again. "Here comes another one, boys!" he warned his pals.

They lowered their heads and covered their ears. The cannon belched fire once more.

"Damn, that gun is loud! I shall be hearing it in my sleep for a week!" declared Thomas. He nudged Daniel with his knee. "Do you see any progress, a'tall? They have hit that wall at least a dozen times. Surely, it cannot hold for much longer."

Daniel eased up onto his knees and peeked carefully over the top of the wall. He smiled happily. "There are three big holes now. It looks like that wall could go at any minute. I reckon one more shot might do it."

Daniel suddenly leaned to his right. By the look on his face, it appeared that he had seen something unusual.

"What are you gawking at?" Austin demanded.

Daniel turned to his friends and grinned. "They have a big white flag dangling from the second-floor window on the west side. They have surrendered."

∼

Late Evening

It was a lovely, warm, and peaceful spring night. The Fairfield Militia boys had enjoyed a fine supper. In addition to the generous supply of foodstuffs they confiscated from their British captives, Captain Liles had managed to procure a small hog. The Fairfield boys promptly butchered and quartered the animal. They divided the meat and roasted it over their fires throughout the entire afternoon. The delicious, smoky pork was a rare treat for them. Their rations had been sorely lacking in recent weeks. After their supper, Austin and his mates celebrated their victory over the British by brewing and drinking the enemy's confiscated tea and imbibing their ample supply of rum. They were thoroughly satisfied and relaxed. They drank, smoked their pipes, and sang songs. It was a pleasant night, indeed.

Austin reclined against a small stump. His eyes were closed. He was feeling a bit light-headed, having enjoyed a bit too much of the British rum.

"Are you well, Austin?" Daniel asked mockingly. "You look a little green."

Austin scooted his rear-end lower and then lay his head back onto the top of the stump. He chuckled lightly. "I am just trying to make the world stop spinning."

"It will stop spinning by morning," Thomas promised. "You just need to sleep it off. I told you to be careful with the rum. That stuff is potent."

"He is right," Daniel affirmed. "You should just go to sleep. 'Tis a clear night. You can drop your bedroll right there beside the fire."

"I will in a bit. I just need to sit still for a minute."

Suddenly, a swiftly-moving figure darted from the shadows inside the nearby thicket of trees. The swarthy-looking character wielded a huge hunting knife in his hand.

"What the hell?" exclaimed Daniel as he reached for his musket.

But, Daniel was too slow. The man sprinted right past him and then fell upon Austin. He jumped astraddle him, pinning his knee to Austin's groin. He grabbed Austin's neck in a vice-like choke hold with his left hand and pressed the razor-sharp blade of his hunting knife against his throat with his right hand.

"Get off of me!" Austin demanded angrily.

"Who let this son of a bitch into our camp?" growled the knife-wielding attacker.

At last, Daniel retrieved his musket. He swung the weapon around, cocked the firelock, and then aimed it at the man's head.

"Drop that knife! Let my friend go!"

The attacker growled, "Do not aim your gun at me, fool! This man is the enemy! He is a Tory!"

He raised his knee and then viciously slammed it into Austin's abdomen. Austin gasped from pain and instantly vomited the contents of his stomach onto his attacker. The man did not flinch. He remained on top of Austin. He ignored the sickening vomit and continued to stare hatefully into his adversary's face. The tip of his blade dug into Austin's neck, releasing a thin trickle of blood. Austin gasped as he attempted to draw air into his starving lungs.

Thomas Marpole approached the attacker from behind and placed the muzzle of his pistol against the back of the man's skull. "You will release him at once! This man is no enemy, sir. He is Austin Newman of Jackson's Creek. He is our friend, and serves with us in the Fairfield Regiment."

The attacker chuckled sadistically. "Then, it is true! He *is* a spy! I know for a fact that Austin Newman is an avowed Tory!"

Daniel slowly worked his way around so that he could make eye contact with the attacker. "You are mistaken, friend. He *was* a Tory, but he has sworn his oath of allegiance and changed sides. He has served with us since January. I assure you, sir ... Austin Newman is a true Patriot."

"I do not believe you!" the man hissed. "I know who he is!"

Captain Liles suddenly appeared out of the darkness. "What is the meaning of this? You will release that man immediately!"

"And just who the hell are you?" growled the attacker.

"I am Captain Aramana Liles of the Fairfield Regiment. This man is under my command. Now, release him at once!"

"But, sir ... this snake has tricked all of you. He *must* be a spy!"

Captain Liles shook his head. "'Tis true, Private Newman once served the King. But like so many of his former compatriots, he has now cast his lot with the United States. He is a soldier in the South

Carolina militia, and a good one. You can rest assured that he has been proven faithful."

The attacker did not seem to be convinced. The captain stepped closer.

"Look, Son ... this is all simply a misunderstanding. Just put the knife down and then we can talk this out. But, I assure you that you are mistaken about this man."

Slowly and reluctantly, the fellow released his grip on Austin's neck. He gently removed the knife from his throat. After several tense seconds, he stood and then returned his knife to its leather sheath. However, he remained standing over Austin and appeared ready to pounce again at any moment. Austin slowly rolled over onto his side and spit remnants of bile, rum, and partially digested food from his mouth.

"Water!" he begged.

Daniel dropped his musket and fetched a nearby water bucket. He carried it to his friend and helped him rinse his mouth and face. All the while, the attacker stood menacingly over Austin.

Finally, after regaining his composure, Austin rolled over onto his back and looked up at the man. He did not recognize his face, but there was something eerily familiar about his voice.

"Who are you, sir?" Austin demanded. "Pray tell, why did you attack me?"

The fellow's eyes narrowed. He stared at Austin with an icy, incredulous gaze. "Do you not remember me, Mr. Newman? You and I had a nice, long talk in my barn last summer. I am William Wilbanks ... Eliza's brother."

AUSTIN AND WILLIAM departed the camp in order to find a place to enjoy a private conversation. They strolled along the bank of the nearby north fork of the Edisto River, all the while keeping the fires of the army camp in sight. For over an hour, they walked and drank rum and talked at length about their wartime experiences. William inquired about Austin's change of allegiance. Austin explained carefully the series of events that eventually convinced him to turn coat and join the American cause. He even told William about his dreams and his vision of serving in the American army.

"So, you swore your oath shortly after you were captured?" William asked.

Austin nodded. "The morning after. The officer in charge of the patrol that took me captive was an old neighbor from back home. I actually visited his plantation many years ago. Some of the other men in the regiment were my neighbors, as well. It seemed like the perfect opportunity to abandon my father's politics and act upon my own."

"But, did you not say that your father has taken up our cause, as well?"

Austin nodded proudly. "He has, indeed. I did not think it possible, but he, too, is now a Patriot. He claims that he is too old to serve in the military, but he is actively furnishing supplies for the cause."

William shook his head in an expression of disbelief and awe. "Your journey has been an interesting and strange one, indeed. It sounds like divine providence to me ... almost as if God ordained all of it."

Austin smiled at him. "I like to think so."

Soon, they came upon an outcropping of large boulders. It appeared to be a good place to sit. Austin pointed at a particularly large, flat rock near the river's edge. "Shall we rest a while? This rum has gone straight from my empty stomach to my head."

William chuckled and nodded. They both sat down on the rock and faced the river. William took a generous swig from his bottle of rum and then handed it to Austin, who took only a sip. They sat in silence for quite a while.

Finally, Austin inquired, "How is your family? Are Abarilla and the boys well?"

"They are, indeed. The boys grow an inch or two every time I am gone. And Abarilla thinks she is in charge of the whole of Union County. She has the entire valley under her thumb. If a goat farts, she knows all about it."

Austin laughed. "Not much gets past her. The army should hire her out to interrogate their prisoners."

William cocked his head teasingly to one side. "Well, I reckon you got past her easily enough. So, she might not be army material." He paused for a moment. "But, is that who you *really* want to talk about ... Abarilla and my boys? I rather think that we should get down to the matter at hand, don't you?"

Austin nodded. "William, I have never stopped thinking of your sister. Please tell me about Eliza. Have you seen her recently?"

William nodded. "I visited home last month." He paused, picked up a small pebble, and then tossed it into the lazy river. He appeared to be searching for the right words. "She is heartbroken, Austin. The girl has been pining away for you ever since you left. She mopes around the cabin and rarely goes outside. She is consumed with a horrible melancholy."

"Do you truly believe that she still loves me?"

"To be honest, I do not believe that she could ever love another. It seems impractical to me. You only knew one another a couple of weeks at most. But, love sometimes strikes in the most peculiar of circumstances." William paused thoughtfully. "What about you, Austin? Do you still love my sister?"

Austin's eyes began to water. "I *know* that I shall never love another. She owns my heart, and always will. I have loved her from the moment when she walked into that house and my eyes first beheld her."

"Good. It is as I suspected. What, then, are we going to do?"

"That seems entirely up to you. You are her brother. You hold all power over her future."

William nodded. "True. And since I love my sister dearly, I do want her suffering to end."

Austin's heart pounded in his chest. "What are you saying to me?"

"I am saying that your politics and allegiances are no longer an issue. If you desire to court my sister, then you have my permission."

"I do not desire to simply court Eliza. I want to make her my wife."

William grinned. "I reckon I am amenable to that notion, as well."

Austin felt as if his heart might burst with joy. "But, what do I do, William? How can I get word to her?"

William stood. "Can you read and write?"

Austin rose to his feet and faced him. "Yes, of course."

"Good. The men of my regiment are departing early tomorrow. Our outpost is not far from my home. I am reasonably certain that my captain will allow me a short visit. It has been a month since planting, and I need to check on the progress of my corn crop. If you will put quill to paper tonight, I promise that I will deliver your correspondence to Eliza."

"You would do that for me?" Austin seemed genuinely touched by the gesture.

"'Tis the least that I can do for my future brother-in-law." He gave Austin a friendly slap on the shoulder.

Austin grinned. "*If* Eliza will have me."

"Oh, I am quite certain that she will have you. Just write your letter. I will take care of the rest."

"I will find you before breakfast," Austin promised.

"I look forward to it."

They shook hands and then began their hike back to the encampment.

It took a while for Austin to locate a quill and supplies for writing. He finally found a broken desk inside the recently-bombarded brick house that had served as the local British Army headquarters. The desk contained a rather ancient goose feather quill and a small bottle of walnut ink. There was even an ancient stick of sealing wax in one of the desk drawers. After securing a piece of paper and a small board to use for his writing surface, he returned to his campfire and began to compose his letter. He prayed briefly and then dipped quill into the ink, wiped the excess across the mouth of the bottle, and began to write.

Dearest Eliza,

When we last spoke, you made it clear to me that our courtship was a forbidden prospect. Your brother's nighttime ultimatum made the sentiments of your family very clear. My service in the Loyalist militia removed any possibility of a union between us.

It is with great joy that I declare to you that no such barriers of allegiance remain. In January of this year, I departed the ranks of King George's Loyalist Militia and joined the cause of independency. I now serve as a soldier in the Fairfield District Militia, a Whig regiment. I have been campaigning with the American armies for almost four months now. My position as a Whig has been established and proven through faithful service.

Please know that my altering of allegiances was not rooted in artifice or a dishonest attempt to somehow sway your fragile heart. I swore my oath to South Carolina on my own accord. I reached my decision to turn coat after many months of personal searching and struggle. I stand amazed at the fact that my father has also redirected his own personal allegiance and now supports a United States of America.

When I departed you, dearest Eliza, my heart was torn asunder. But, by the providence of God, it has been restored. Recently, your brother, William, discovered my presence in our camp. Following a lengthy and thorough time of counsel, he has become convinced of my change in personal convictions. He has also given his consent for me to pursue a courtship with you. I wish to inform you that I intend to act upon his consent. If I might be so bold as to proclaim it ... the greatest desire of my heart is that you will one day be my bride.

Please accept this humble correspondence as a declaration of my sincerest affections for you. As soon as is practicable, I will make my journey to your district and seek you out so that I may declare my love for you in person. With your brother's consent, I will at that time ask for your hand in marriage.

Please keep watch for me, dearest Eliza. I will come to you. This is my promise.

Until then ... I remain most affectionately yours,
Austin Newman

Once finished, Austin reread the text of his correspondence and them immediately declared it to be perfect. He quickly folded the letter. He heated the sealing wax over a coal from the fire and then daubed the hot wax across the fold. Since he had no seal to stamp it, he simply pressed his thumb into the wax and made an impression of his fingerprint. He then flipped the letter over and wrote two simple words on the front ... Eliza Wilbanks. He placed the finished letter carefully inside his leather pouch.

Satisfied that he had revealed the depths of his heart in the words of the letter, he reclined on his blanket beside the campfire. He was so excited that he doubted he could sleep. However, sleep came surprisingly quickly. Amazingly, the nightmares of battle that so often plagued his dreams were gone. Instead, he dreamt of his sweet Eliza. In his slumbering visions, he saw her standing with him before a preacher as they celebrated a ceremony of marriage.

∽

Sunday - May 13, 1781
Mid-Afternoon
Jackson's Creek, South Carolina

SUNDAYS JUST WERE NOT the same anymore. The growing political divide in the district had all but shut down services at the Jackson's Creek Meeting House. The community, which had once been so united in its support of King George and England, had been torn asunder by the shifting political winds. There were several men like Will Newman who had switched allegiances out of heartfelt conviction. But, there were equally as many others who did so out of political expediency. The Whigs were winning the war, and it seemed that most of the South Carolina backcountry folk wanted to make sure they were on the right side when the last shot was fired.

Lizzy sat quietly at Will's side as he skillfully guided their wagon along a muddy, rutted roadway. They had just endured a very uncharacteristic quarrel. Will was determined to make a visit to the home of Bat and Rachel Austin. Lizzy did not think it was a good idea. The two families had enjoyed little contact in recent months. Will's personal turning of coat had not been well-received by his old friend. The result had been an immediate cessation of their customary family fellowships. Indeed, Bat had severed all personal contact.

Will, on the other hand, could not abide the silence and isolation. He and Bat had been friends for thirty years. Surely, theirs was a bond that was stronger than the unnatural strife caused by politics. It was this simple and, perhaps, naïve conviction that drove Will to extend an olive branch of friendship and seek reconciliation with his old friend.

"They are going to send us on our way. You do realize that," Lizzy declared.

Will shook his head. He appeared very frustrated. "I cannot imagine that Bat would simply cast our friendship aside like this. You will see. Today, we will make everything right again. I am determined."

She placed a comforting hand on her husband's forearm. "I simply do not wish to see your heart broken again."

Will smiled lovingly at his sweet wife. "'Twill be all right. You will see."

Lizzy did not respond. She merely faced forward and silently prayed for the best. Moments later, they rounded a bend in the roadway. The Austin house was on the left, just past the bend. Will guided his team onto the dirt lane that led to the house. His heart beat fast with excitement. It had been almost four months since he had set foot upon Austin land. That was how long it had been since the two families enjoyed their last Sunday evening meal together.

As he scanned the area, Will was quite shocked at the condition of the farm. The fields and barns were unkempt and disorganized. As far as Will could see, there were no crops planted in the fields. There were scarce few animals in the adjacent pastures. Something was greatly amiss. Lizzy immediately confirmed Will's observations.

"Good Lord, Will! This place is a mess! Why is there no corn in the field?"

Will shook his head. "Something must be horribly wrong."

He snapped the reins, urging the team forward. Soon, he pulled the wagon to a stop in front of the house. Will hopped down and then helped his wife from her seat. They slowly climbed the three-step stairway and then approached the front door. Just as Will reached to knock, the door opened. Rachel Austin stood in the opening. She did not look like herself, at all. She was very gaunt and pale. She stepped onto the porch and then quietly closed the door behind her.

"Oh, Rachel!" Lizzy exclaimed. "I have missed you so!"

She immediately swallowed her friend in a loving embrace. It took a moment, but then Rachel slowly returned the gesture. Soon, however, she pulled away from Lizzy. She glared over Lizzy's shoulder at Will.

"Why have *you* come here?" Her question sounded venomous.

Will stepped forward. "Rachel, our families have remained silent to one another for far too long. We have been friends for decades. This barrier between us is abhorrent. It should not be this way. I came today to make things right again."

Tears escaped both of Rachel's eyes. "We have been so alone for a very long time, Will. With all of the other Loyalist men gone, Bat has suffered terribly. He has been outcast by many that he once thought to be friends. There is much work that needs to be done on the farm, but no one will come here and work for us. It is far too much for Bat to bear on his own." She choked back a sob. "He has become so exhausted that he has fallen ill."

"Oh, Rachel!" Will reached out and took her hand. "Is it a fever?"

"No." She wiped her eyes with the hem of her pinner apron. "His illness is not of his body. It is an affliction of his heart. I fear that it may be a sickness of the soul. He is in a very dark place, and I do not know if he will ever return."

"I must go and see him," begged Will. "Will you please allow it?"

Rachel shook her head. "I am not certain that would be wise. I believe that you have been the greatest cause of his suffering."

"Me?" Will asked in disbelief.

"Word of your treason against the King struck a harsh blow to Bat. He could stand the rejection of all the other men in our community. But, he was completely torn asunder when you pledged your allegiance to the rebel cause. He is very bitter and angry at you."

"All the more reason for me to go and speak to him. Might I have your permission? Please, Rachel."

The despondent woman inhaled deeply and then reluctantly nodded her consent.

WILL DID NOT BOTHER to knock. He opened the door and then stepped boldly into Bat's bedchamber. Bat lay on his side atop his plush feather bed with his back toward the door. Mary Austin was seated at her father's bedside. Her eyes brightened when she saw Will. She stood excitedly and gave her father's hand a vigorous squeeze.

"Papa, look! You have a visitor!"

Bat Austin slowly opened his eyes. He rolled over onto his back and looked at Will. He did not smile.

"Leave us, Mary."

"Yes, Papa."

Mary stood and walked around the foot of the bed. As she stepped past Will, she grabbed his hand and gave it a firm squeeze. Will leaned in toward her and kissed her affectionately on the forehead.

"Have you heard anything from my William?" she whispered.

He whispered back, "Not in the past week. And you?"

She smiled giddily. "I received a letter only yesterday."

He leaned close to her ear. "Lizzy is out front with your mother. She would love to hear whatever you might be willing to share. She can tell me all about it later."

Mary nodded. She quickly and quietly exited the room.

"I heard you whispering with my little girl. Does she now keep secrets from me, as well?"

Will exhaled impatiently. "She has no secrets, Bat. She was just asking me about little William. As it turns out, she has heard from him more recently than I."

"I hear that the boy has gone and turned rebel. Now, everyone in your household is an enemy of the King." He turned his face away from Will and stared forlornly out the window. "It seems that the whole backcountry is turning coat."

Will shrugged. "The British are whipped, Bat. Everyone sees it except for you." He paused. "The Redcoats abandoned Camden on Thursday, you know."

"I heard." Bat's voice sounded hollow.

"Most all of their troops have retreated back to Charlestown. The Whigs control all of the backcountry except for a small region around the village of Ninety-Six."

"My sons are at Ninety-Six now," Bat announced proudly. "They are preparing to make their stand."

"It seems a futile gesture to me."

Bat turned and faced him. "'Tis never futile to take a stand for one's convictions, Will."

Will stepped closer to the bed. "Bat, consider the consequences! It is *absolutely* foolish to die for your high and mighty convictions when there is a reasonable alternative."

"On that principle, we will have to agree to disagree."

Will groaned. "Are you truly willing to sacrifice your sons in the name of King George?"

"There is no greater honor than to give one's life for England."

"You have never even been to England!"

"South Carolina *is* England. I am a true Englishman, born and bred."

Will grimaced and shook his head. "You are one hard-headed son of a bitch. That is certain." He paused. "But, you are the dearest friend that I have ever known, and I love you as a brother. Nothing will ever change that."

Bat's face remained emotionless. "I heard someone burned your barn."

Will nodded sullenly. "They killed all my animals, Bat, including my horses. And they wrote a hateful message on my house in sheep's blood. It seems that someone wishes my wife and me to burn in hell."

Bat frowned. "That was an evil thing for anyone to suffer, no matter their politics. There must be civility in this conflict. We are not savages."

"Finally! We have something upon which we can both agree wholeheartedly!"

Will gave his friend a playful nudge. Bat attempted not to smile, but he could not help himself.

"Are we still friends, then?" Will asked hopefully, placing his hand on Bat's left forearm.

Bat slowly reached out his right arm and then placed his hand on top of Will's. "Always."

"Good. Because war or no war, we are destined to be family, you know. William and Mary are going to be wed. I doubt that an entire regiment of Redcoats could stop them."

Bat smiled a huge, happy smile. "Of that, I have no doubt."

"Well, then ... you need to get over yourself and climb your arse out of this bed. You are acting a damn fool and worrying your poor wife to death." Will turned and walked toward the door. As he placed his hand on the doorknob, he declared, "I am all caught up at my place. I will be over right after breakfast in the morning to help you get this farm under control. You had best be up and dressed."

He opened the door, stepped out, and then closed it firmly behind him. Bat smiled and cried as he watched his friend go.

May 20, 1781
One Hour Before Sunset
Near Union, South Carolina

WILLIAM WILBANKS WALKED out of the forest about a hundred yards southwest of his cabin. His son, Marshall, appeared to be the only person outside. The lad was busy tending the garden. The boy was startled by the figure emerging from the shadowy wood. He immediately dropped his hoe and ran for his musket, which was leaning against a nearby fence. The boy grabbed the gun and then pointed it in William's general direction.

William shouted, "Don't shoot, boy! You can't see for shite, but you might up and hit something by accident."

The lad lowered his gun. Smiling, he called out to the cabin, "Mama! Papa's home!"

THE CHAOS of unbridled joy reigned inside the tiny Wilbanks cabin. William had not been home since planting his corn and pumpkin crops in early April. His wife, sister, and children immediately went into celebration mode.

Eliza poured her brother a healthy dose of whiskey and then sat it before him. She also brought him fresh tobacco for his pipe. While William marveled the children with stories of his wartime adventures, Abarilla quickly prepared an extra pie, placed it in her Dutch oven, and then dangled it over the flames of the fireplace. There was already ample goat stew and bread as she had prepared enough for some extra meals over the next couple of days. It took little extra effort to turn her customarily hearty meal into a feast. The family attacked the tasty food with gusto. They talked, ate, laughed, and celebrated life and family. It was truly a wondrous reunion and a memorable night.

Two hours later, the house was silent. The children were all asleep. William was reclined in his rocking chair in front of the fire. Abarilla and Eliza were busy returning the clean dishes to their proper places on the shelves.

"Eliza," William whispered loudly. "Come and sit with me. We need to talk."

The beautiful young woman fluffed her dishtowel and then placed it flat on the table to dry. She approached her brother slowly and curiously.

"Do you need something, Brother?"

"No, Eliza. I just need to speak with you about something."

Eliza sat down in the chair to her brother's right. She cut a concerned glance at Abarilla. The plump, red-faced woman shrugged. Intrigued, she waddled toward the fireplace.

"Is this a private conversation, or might I listen, as well?" Abarilla asked suspiciously.

"Of course, my dear." William patted the seat to his left. "Please come and join us. You also need to hear this."

Abarilla, suddenly *very* curious, quickly joined them.

William turned to Eliza. "I ran across someone after our action at Orangeburgh ... an old friend of yours."

"Oh? Who was it?"

He smiled and cut a quick glance at his wife, then looked back at Eliza. He cleared his throat. "Well ... it was that odd fellow you nursed back to health." He turned to his wife. "What was his name, dear?"

Abarilla replied, "Austin Newman."

He nodded and then refocused his attention on Eliza. "Yes! That is it. Austin Newman."

Eliza sat in stunned silence. Her face flushed crimson. Her breathing increased dramatically.

"I do not understand, William. How did you see Mr. Newman? Was he taken prisoner during the battle?"

"No." William paused dramatically. "Actually, he was a fellow soldier in my camp."

She shook her head vigorously. "That makes no sense."

William uncrossed his left leg and then crossed his right, resting his bony ankle on his knee. "Well, it was the strangest thing. I was walking back to my fire from the thunder hole and a caught a glimpse of him. Naturally, I thought he was a spy in the camp, so I jumped him. I damn near sliced him from ear to ear, but his friends stopped him." He paused. Eliza's eyes were wide and begging for more information. "So, I did some checking and found out that he committed treason against old King George and joined us rebels. Austin has been fighting on our side since January, serving in the Fairfield District Militia. His old pappy has even turned coat."

Eliza was speechless. She sat in stunned silence, her eyes shifting back and forth between William and Abarilla.

"Don't you have something to ask me?" William teased.

Eliza inhaled a trembling breath. "I do not know. Like what, supposing?"

"Something like ... 'Big Brother, do you have a letter for me?'"

Tears began to fill her eyes. "Do you?" she almost whispered.

William reached into the pocket of his weskit and produced a dirty, worn piece of folder paper. It bore a red wax seal. He placed it in Eliza's trembling hand. Eliza giggled as she wiped her eyes with the hem of her apron.

She held it up for Abarilla to see. "Look! He put his thumbprint in the wax."

William grinned. "We were fresh out of fancy stamps out there in the camp."

She broke the brittle wax seal and then carefully unfolded the letter.

William reached teasingly for the paper. "Shall I read it for you?"

Eliza snatched it away from his reach. "No, thank you! I am quite capable of reading it for myself!"

Eliza began to read Austin's letter. She stared for several minutes at the beautifully-scripted words on the paper. As she read, she felt the cold scales that encased her heart disintegrate and fall away. Suddenly, a great hope filled her soul. She began to weep. At long last, she lowered the letter to her lap and then stared disbelievingly at her brother.

She moaned, "Can this all be true?"

William leaned toward her and covered her hand in his. "'Tis true, dear sister."

Her chest heaved slightly. "He says that he wants us to wed."

"Of that I have no doubt," he affirmed. He turned to his wife. "What do you think, Abarilla?"

She grunted. "Huh! Eliza would be a fool, indeed, not to marry that handsome, strapping young man."

Eliza wept openly. "I simply cannot believe it! Oh, William! I love him so! I *want* him!"

William smiled. "Well, then, my dear ... you shall have him."

19

TRUCE

By May, 1781, the British were reeling in South Carolina. The Redcoats and Tories that had once roamed and commanded the backcountry were being rooted out of almost every village and town. There remained only two significant outposts outside of Charlestown still under British control. One was at Georgetown and the other at Ninety-Six. The British presence at Ninety-Six was most important, by far. Cornwallis considered this tiny outpost to be the key to maintaining British control over the backcountry.

Unfortunately for the British, General Cornwallis and his army were three hundred miles away in North Carolina. They remained in the coastal city of Wilmington, still recovering and rebuilding after their costly victory at Guilford Courthouse. Cornwallis' absence from the South Carolina backcountry left the state ripe for attack. Major General Nathanael Greene recognized the opportunity and promptly marched his army southward. He intended to take the outpost at Ninety-Six and drive the British back to the coast.

However, capturing Ninety-Six would not be easy. Lieutenant Colonel John Harris Kruger, Loyalist commander of the garrison there, had heavily fortified the little town and constructed two forts.

One of those was a particularly impressive star-shaped fort, complete with tall earthworks, a defensive ditch, and an abatis. The well-designed and heavily defended forts ensured that driving the enemy from Ninety-Six would prove costly, indeed. To accomplish the task, General Greene needed militia to augment his Continental Regulars. He issued an urgent call to Patriot militias throughout the region. Companies from the various districts began to muster and then make their way toward Ninety-Six to join the campaign.

Greene arrived at Ninety-Six on May 21. The Americans immediately surrounded the town and forts, erected their own defenses, and established a three-gun battery of cannons. The following morning, the artillery opened fire. The Siege of Ninety-Six had begun.

~

June 4, 1781
American Siege Line - Ninety-Six, South Carolina

AUSTIN NEWMAN and Daniel Dansby had just arrived on the line. They were on temporary assignment in a company under the command of Captain Edward Martin of the Fairfield Militia. They joined the over 1,500 American troops that had already dug in around the besieged town and forts. Austin and Daniel stood behind the cover of logs and earthworks and stared in awe at the impressive defenses that surrounded and protected the Loyalist army. A quarter-mile to the east, the Patriot artillery maintained a continuous barrage. General Greene's cannons slowly and methodically took turns firing upon the enemy position. Each impact unleashed a cloud of dust, sand, wood, and debris.

"They are taking quite a pounding," Daniel observed. "'Tis hard to believe anyone can survive such a lengthy and concentrated bombardment. I heard that our boys have been going at them for days."

"I am sure most of them are under the ground right now," Austin responded. He scanned the entire length of the enemy position. "It looks very different than it did back in '75. Those walls at the old fort were pretty ramshackle back then. This, however, is impressive. They have had many months to build these fortifications."

"As well I know it," responded Daniel, smiling. "Don't you remember? I was behind those rickety walls back then."

Austin grinned and nodded. "Indeed, I do. I find it ironic, though, that even though I have changed sides in this war, I still find myself out here and not in there."

"I would much rather be out here than in there," Daniel responded softly.

Austin sighed. "Amen to that."

"What do you think we will actually do whilst we are here? There is no shooting to speak of, other than the cannons. Everyone else seems to be hiding out and taking it easy."

Austin pointed at a feature to their east. There was a narrow depression in the ground that was surrounded by freshly-dug earth. "I imagine most of our work will be at night. Instead of shooting, we will be digging entrenchments."

Daniel stared at the pile of dirt. "Do you think they are trying to get under the walls?"

Austin shrugged. "Either that, or they want to get close enough to set the walls on fire. Either way, I am reasonably certain that we will both find out soon enough. I think we can count on doing plenty of digging."

Almost on cue, Captain Martin appeared by Daniel's side. Daniel nodded politely. "Hello, Captain."

"Good afternoon, Mr. Dansby." He nodded to Austin. "Mr. Newman."

Austin nodded back. "Sir."

The captain peered at the enemy's fort. "So ... do you fellows have everything figured out yet? How shall we win this fight?"

"We have no grand strategy, Captain. But, we figure we are in for some sore backs and hands," Austin answered. "I reckon I should have brought my good pick-axe from back home."

The captain smiled and chuckled. "Well, you are absolutely right about that. You two need to stop gawking at the fort and get some rest. Our company is on digging detail tonight."

Daniel groaned. "Already?"

"These other fellows have been at it for almost a week. In their eyes, we are fresh labor." He pointed toward the rear. "We will muster at that big oak near the battalion headquarters. Bring your musket, cartridge box, and canteens. There are water barrels in the trench, but we need to haul as much extra water as we can carry. It is damn hot out here, even at night." He patted Daniel on the shoulder. "I will see you boys then. Eat a good supper, but do so early. I would not want you to be flashing the hash in my trench later."

"Yes, sir," both men responded, chuckling.

The captain departed immediately. Austin and Daniel continued to stare in silence at the fort. Both men dreaded the hot, back-breaking work that they were sure to suffer once darkness fell.

~

Dusk
Fairfield Militia Regiment Camp Site

AUSTIN WAS WELL-FED AND CONTENT. He reclined lazily on his blanket against a sandy earth berm. He wore his cocked hat sideways and low to cover his face. He and his mates had just enjoyed a hearty meal of rice and stewed beef. Somehow, the captain had also managed to scrounge a sack of corn meal. So, the fellows fried up a mess of corn cakes to accompany the salty, flavorful stew. Each man of the company imbibed a tiny cup of spicy rum for their dessert. They had two hours to rest before going on digging duty. It was just enough time for Austin to squeeze in a short nap.

A crackling, high-pitched voice invaded his post-supper slumber. "Did you save any vittles for me?"

Austin grunted sarcastically. "No, lad. There is no food left in this camp. Go and beg amongst the Regulars."

"You did not even save a tiny morsel for your little brother?"

Austin thought that he must be dreaming. He ripped his hat away from his face and sat up. Standing a mere ten feet away was sixteen-year-old William Newman. The lad was grinning from ear to ear.

Austin exclaimed, "William! Christ, Almighty! What are you doing here?"

He leapt to his feet and grabbed his brother in a warm hug.

"I have been posted here for the past week," William replied. "I just got word that some Fairfield boys had arrived. I hoped that you might be among them. So, I came a-lookin'."

Austin, keeping his hands on William's shoulders, stepped back at arm's length and gave the boy a quick examination. "Good heavens, William! You look older! And taller! Are you fully intact? Missing any fingers or toes?"

William chuckled. "I have been shot at aplenty, but not hit, thank goodness."

"Lizzy will be plenty happy about that. Sit! We have much reacquainting to do."

The two brothers sat down on Austin's blue linsey-woolsey blanket. Austin could not take his eyes off of his little brother.

"Papa told me that you ran off with the rebels." Austin grinned mischievously. "He said you were going east to join up with Colonel Marion."

"You have been home?" William asked, appearing quite surprised.

Austin nodded. "I was home the entire month of March. Lizzy fattened me up and then sent me back to the war."

William shook his head in obvious disbelief. "I almost don't believe you. I can scarcely imagine Papa allowing a rebel under his roof. The man took your turning coat pretty hard. I can only imagine how he must have acted after I ran off into the night to join the rebellion."

"So, then, you have not heard the news?"

"What news?" asked William, suddenly worried. "Is something wrong back home?"

"No, not at all. But, I am pleased to be the one to tell you that our father has crossed over with us. He is now supporting the cause of independency."

"Horse shite!" William exclaimed.

"'Tis true, Brother." Austin's demeanor darkened somewhat. "But, it was a horrific evil perpetrated against him that led him to make his break."

"What happened?" Concern filled the lad's face.

"On the evening that I arrived home, Tories burned down our barn and killed all of the horses and livestock. They wrote a ghastly sentiment on the front of the house in sheep's blood. After that, Papa was done with them. He has been supporting our regiment with food and supplies ever since."

"Holy crivens!" William exclaimed, rubbing his chin. "I never thought it possible."

"Neither did I," swore Austin. "But, we are all together and on the same side now."

"Twill definitely make for more pleasant suppers back home," William declared, chuckling.

"True, indeed." Austin sighed happily. "So, did you make it to Pee Dee and find Colonel Marion?"

William shook his head. "No. I was already tired of walking when I reached Camden. I went to the first militia camp I could find and joined up. It was the Second Spartan Regiment. Lewis Duvall is my captain."

"Second Spartan?" responded Austin excitedly. "Have you met any fellows by the name of Wilbanks?"

"Oh, there's a whole pile of 'em ... three, I think, or maybe four. But, I cannot keep them apart in my mind."

"Is one of them named William?"

His brother smiled. "His is the only name I remember, seeing as how it's the same as mine."

"Well, lovanenty! I don't believe it!"

"What?" asked William, confused. "Do you know him?"

Austin grinned happily. "I am only planning to marry his sister."

William's eyes grew wide with surprise. "You are going to have to tell me that entire story some time."

"'Twill be my pleasure."

Captain Martin suddenly appeared in their midst and gruffly interrupted their conversation. "Newman! Get up off your lazy arse! It is time to go!" He then spun on his heels and marched angrily toward the appointed muster point.

Austin scrambled to his feet. "I have to go, William. I am on trench-digging duty tonight."

William stood, as well. "Keep both eyes open, Brother. It is dangerous duty. Tories hit the diggers almost every night. I lost a close friend in that cursed ditch three nights ago."

"I will." Austin grabbed his brother and hugged him once more. "Come and find me tomorrow." He grabbed his musket, canteen, and cartridge pouch and then sprinted into the deepening darkness.

~

Midnight
Inside the British Star Fort

JOHN AND DRURY AUSTIN huddled with ten other Tory militiamen near the sally port. The port was a tiny opening in the wall, a mere two feet in width, through which the besieged occupants might sneak out and attack the enemy beyond the walls. Both John and Drury were armed with a musket, bayonet, tomahawk, and hunting knife. Like their fellow raiders, they were dressed in dark clothing that would help them blend into the night. Their faces were dirty and black, made so by a thin layer of charcoal and soot.

The brothers were filled with excitement and nervous energy. Soon, they would be sneaking through the sally port and striking at the enemy. Their mission was simple. They were to attack and kill the workers that were digging the invasive trench that was threatening the fort's wall. If possible, they were also to collect the enemy's digging tools and take prisoners. It was a treacherous assignment. It would, in all likelihood, involve hand-to-hand, close-quarters combat.

John whispered to Drury, "They will be expecting us, you know. Our men have hit that trench five nights in a row."

Drury nodded grimly. "I know. They will likely have extra look-outs posted. We must move with the utmost silence. When we attack, we must kill everything that moves. Take no chances."

"What about our orders to take prisoners?"

Drury spat. "To hell with prisoners. It is not worth risking our lives to bring one of those rebel bastards back with us." He stared angrily into the darkness of the silent fort. "No. We will kill them all."

Suddenly, a whispered order worked its way down the line. The man in front of Drury turned around and hissed, "Move out!"

Drury grabbed John by the arm. "After you fire your first shot, drop your musket. 'Twill be worthless after that. Then go to work with your blades."

John nodded. Then, the brothers followed the other soldiers as, one by one, they slithered through the tiny sally port. John was the last man through. They slid silently down the earthworks and landed in the bottom of the dry ditch that surrounded the fort. They crept up out of the ditch and then, crouching low, made their way toward the sound of digging. The raiding party was less than twenty feet from the enemy trench when a frantic shout pierced the night. One of the enemy sentries had spotted them. Then came the sharp, cracking report of a musket. The flash of the rebel gun illuminated the entire area.

"Attack! Kill them all!" Drury shouted.

Instantly, the twelve raiders leapt to their feet and ran toward the trench. More gunfire ensued, but the rebel shooters were firing blind. All twelve men reached the edge of the trench unharmed. Without stopping, they leapt over the side into the darkness below.

AUSTIN AND DANIEL were taking a break. They had earned it. They were reclining, eyes closed, atop a small mound of freshly-dug earth about thirty feet to the rear of the digging party. Their primed and loaded muskets stood at the ready against a nearby wall.

The two friends had been digging non-stop for over three hours. They had only recently surrendered their picks to a couple of hard-working slaves named Kitch and Antony. The slaves had been hauling buckets of earth and rock to the mouth of the trench throughout the night and were eager for a change of task. Likewise, Austin and Daniel looked forward to doing something different. Anything was better than scraping the concrete-like dirt and compacted rock from the face of the trench. Both fellows were actually on the verge of falling asleep when a gunshot awakened them.

"Bloody hell!" Daniel exclaimed, sitting up and fumbling for his musket.

"What was that?" Austin demanded groggily.

"One of the sentries has fired. He must have seen something!"

Suddenly, a chorus of blood-curdling screams echoed in the darkness above the trench. Then, quick as a flash, numerous shadowy figures leapt into the trench from the southern rim. They landed atop the soldiers and slaves who were clustered near the digging face. The handful of dully glowing candles that had been burning on the floor of the trench were immediately extinguished. Numerous shots rang out, illuminating the pitch-black night with brilliant, sizzling white and yellow fire. The men on both sides fought indiscriminately, most of them blinded by the bright flashes of gunfire. Once the initial gunshots were expended, the ringing of steel against steel echoed through the darkness as men fought for their lives with knives, bayonets, tomahawks, picks, shovels, and even buckets.

Daniel and Austin, unnoticed and undiscovered by the attackers, each grabbed their muskets. Daniel was about to take off running toward the fight when Austin grabbed him by the arm.

"Daniel, wait! Bayonets!" he whispered.

Daniel immediately understood. Both men reached for the bayonets that dangled from the leather frogs on their belts. They fixed the blades to the muzzles of their French Charleville muskets.

"Go!" Austin hissed.

Both men ran, side by side, directly at the mass of screaming, clamoring men. As they neared the fighting, they spotted two shadowy figures in front of them. The men were completely clad in black. They were hacking with tomahawks at two screaming, begging Patriots. The wounded victims of their wicked blades cowered before them on the floor of the trench. Immediately, Austin and Daniel dropped to their knees, took aim, instinctively closed their eyes to protect their vision, and then fired. They could not miss their targets. The enemy soldiers were only ten feet away.

Austin and Daniel's musket balls penetrated the backs of the attackers, chewed their way through muscle, bone, and organs, and then exploded outward through the centers of their chests. The two men fell forward and immediately began to bleed out onto the bodies of their mutilated, tomahawk-hacked victims.

Austin and Daniel pressed forward, their bayonets leading the way. Moments later they came upon two more enemy soldiers. Those men were engaged in hand-to-hand combat with two dirt and blood-smeared Americans. Austin attacked the fellow that was on his left, toward the southern side of the trench. The man appeared to have caught a brief glimpse of Austin and was turning to face him when Austin ran him through with the bayonet. The blade penetrated the right side of the man's belly. Austin felt the steel strike the bones in the fellow's spine. He pressed forward, pushing the enemy soldier toward the wall. As he moved, he accidentally stepped on an unseen body that lay sprawled on the floor of the trench and immediately lost his balance. He tumbled to his right and landed hard on his shoulder.

Austin rolled over onto his back and watched in horror as the man that he had just impaled with the bayonet stepped to one side and then pulled the blade from his belly. He tossed Austin's musket onto the body-strewn floor of the trench. The wounded man instantly leapt on top of Austin, his tomahawk high in the air. Just as he was about to slam the razor-sharp blade into Austin's skull, a pistol barked. For a fraction of a second, the flash of the flaming gunpowder illuminated the trench in brilliant light. Austin's heart fluttered. He could have sworn that he recognized the man who sat astraddle him. But, surely, he was mistaken.

Suddenly, something struck the attacker's skull, eliciting a sharp crack. The enemy soldier dropped his tomahawk and then tumbled limply to his left.

A voice pleaded in the darkness, "Austin, are you all right?"

It was Daniel Dansby. He was crouched low and pressing the buttstock of his musket against the head of Austin's attacker. Austin remained disoriented and too stunned to respond.

Daniel demanded once more, "Austin, are you cut? Did he get you?"

Austin did a quick check. "No, I am not wounded."

"That son of a bitch was about to split your skull wide open. But, I was a just a wee bit faster. I popped him with my gunstock."

Austin rolled to his left and then slowly rose onto his knees. "Help me," he begged.

Daniel reached down and helped pull Austin to his feet. Suddenly, dancing light from several bright torches began to fill the trench. Reinforcements were coming from the camp. A handful of surviving Tory raiders near to the digging face slithered over the side of the trench and instantly disappeared into the night. Soon, over a dozen musket and torch-wielding men arrived, flooding the trench with bright orange and yellow light. The sight that greeted them was grisly, indeed. The maimed, bloodied bodies of the dead and wounded, both friend and foe, were strewn everywhere.

"Bring me a torch!" Austin demanded.

"Why?" asked Daniel, confused.

"Just do it!"

Daniel grabbed a torch from one of the newly-arrived soldiers and then handed it to Austin. Immediately, Austin leaned over and grabbed the arm of his attacker. He flipped the man onto his back. He held the torch close to his face.

"Good God!" he exclaimed.

"What?" asked Daniel, confused.

"It is Drury Austin!"

"No! It cannot be!" Daniel knelt beside the man and examined him closely. Then, he looked up at Austin with a gaze of disbelief and shock. "It is Drury!"

"Is he alive?" Austin asked in a frantic tone.

Daniel held his hand close to Drury's face. He nodded. "He is breathing. Yes, he is alive."

"We have another live one over here!" shouted a torch-wielding fellow. "'Tis a Tory, for certain."

The man and one of his mates lifted the unconscious prisoner up off of the ground. Austin turned and held his torch in the direction of the newest captive. He gasped again.

"Daniel, look! It is John Austin!"

Daniel knelt to examine John. "He appears unhurt, other than a blow to the head."

"We must get them both to the hospital." Austin turned to the other Patriots gathered nearby. "Collect the wounded, both ours and theirs. Take them to our surgeons." He turned to Daniel. "Help me. We have to save Drury!"

Austin and Daniel lifted the limp, bloodied body of their wounded friend and then slowly made their way back toward the mouth of the trench.

∾

The Next Morning

"Sir, please! I beg you to reconsider," Austin pleaded.

"You do not understand the gravity of your request. It would not be appropriate," responded Colonel Winn.

"Colonel, you know this man! You know his family! Please allow me to take Drury Austin home to his wife and parents."

"He is an enemy combatant, Son."

"He is *my* friend, sir. We played together as children. I was a participant in his wedding, for Christ sake! He is no more an enemy to me than you."

Colonel Winn sighed and removed his spectacles. He tossed them onto the pile of papers that littered his tiny field desk. "It is my understanding that you are the very one who ran Mr. Austin through with your bayonet. Is that not true?"

"Yes, sir."

He picked up a report containing his notes on the battle and waved it in front of Austin. "Private Dansby reported that Mr. Austin was about to split your skull with his tomahawk right before he struck him with the stock of his musket. Is *that* not true?"

"Yes, sir. But, it was in total darkness and the heat of battle. Colonel, I owe it to him to see that he gets the best care. You and I both know that he will not receive it here in this God-forsaken excuse of a hospital. He will be dead in a matter of days." Austin stepped closer to the colonel's desk. "Sir, I can have him home by supper tomorrow if you will allow me to leave now. All I need is one of the wagons. We have several to spare."

The colonel considered Austin's request for a moment and then shook his head again. "I cannot spare the manpower, though."

"I only need one man to assist me."

The colonel remained insistent. "I simply cannot allow it. We need every man on the line." He frowned. "I lost three soldiers last night."

"It need not be one of our own, sir. Austin's brother, John, is under guard with a handful of the other prisoners. He received a blow to the head last night, but is well enough to travel. If you will grant his parole, John can help me to take his brother home."

Colonel Winn stood and walked to the door of his tent. He gazed toward the prisoner collection area and observed John Austin sitting on the ground in the already-blazing sun. He considered Austin's seemingly absurd idea.

"John is the hot-headed one of the Newman clan, is he not?"

"Yes, sir," Austin acknowledged.

"And likely to cause trouble if he remains here under guard, no doubt."

"No doubt, sir," Austin echoed.

Colonel Winn turned to Austin. "Do you think he will swear an oath of non-aggression in exchange for a parole?"

"I hope so. I will ask him, if you will allow it."

The colonel sighed and shook his head in defeat. "Very well. I will allow it. If John Austin agrees to accompany you on the journey, I will grant his parole and give you three weeks leave. Perhaps, by then, this siege will be over and we will all be home."

"Thank you, sir."

"Go and consult with the prisoner. If he is agreeable, then you may bring him to me."

"Yes, sir!"

Austin darted excitedly out of the commander's tent and sprinted across the field toward the prisoner detainment area. John saw him coming and quickly rose to his feet. The right side of his face, especially around his eye, was greatly swollen and beginning to turn a dull shade of blue. Still, despite his disfigurement, his eyes betrayed his murderous disdain for Austin.

"I have no desire to speak to you, you treasonous bastard," John declared adamantly.

"Then do not speak. Just listen," Austin retorted.

John crossed his arms and turned his back to Austin.

"John, please! Drury is alive. He has a severe wound in the belly and will not survive in our hospital. I have made arrangements to take him home. His wife and your parents can provide much better care."

John spun back around. He stared at Austin, his eyes filled with confusion and disbelief. "How? How can you get him home?"

"I will take him." He paused. "And you can come with me."

"What? How? I ... I do not understand," John stammered.

"Colonel Winn has agreed. If you will swear an oath to lay down your arms, he will grant you parole. Then, you and I can depart immediately and take Drury home by wagon. I will drive whilst you care for him. We can have him in his own bed by tomorrow evening. But, will you do it, John? Will you swear an oath to never again take up arms against the United States?"

John closed his eyes and inhaled deeply. Cleary, he was in turmoil. Austin's request was almost more than he could bear.

"John, please. I beg you. This is Drury's only chance."

John slowly opened his eyes. His countenance softened. He displayed the appearance of a broken, defeated man.

"Take me to Mr. Winn. I will swear his damnable oath."

~

Two Hours After Sunset
Londonderry Highway - Orangeburgh District

JOHN SAT down near the tiny campfire opposite Austin. "He is sleeping. I think he has a fever, though."

"Is he still bleeding?" asked Austin, concerned.

"Just a little. I changed the bandage on the wound."

"He will be all right. You will see," Austin declared optimistically. "We are over half-way home. We shall move even more quickly tomorrow."

"We have been making good time," John acknowledged.

There was a very long period of silence. The tension between the two men was palpable.

"I am very sorry for the rift that remains between us, John."

John shrugged slightly. "As am I. I wish that things could be different." He stared thoughtfully into the flames. "But, I am grateful for this ... for what you have done for my brother. I do not understand why you have done it."

Austin felt his heart swell within him. It seemed that there might be a glimmer of hope for their lifelong friendship.

"I was the one who stuck him during the fight," Austin confessed fearfully.

John glanced at Austin with tired, sad eyes. He sighed. "You had no way of knowing, any more than he knew who he was fighting. It was black as the pit of hell in that trench."

"Drury is like a brother to me." His voice cracked. "You do realize that, I hope."

John nodded. "I do."

"And I love you as a brother, John. Governments and wars and rebellions cannot change that."

A single tear escaped John's uninjured eye and then slowly crept down his cheek. "I know. It has just been so hard. 'Tis an evil thing ... to be fighting against one's friends." He quickly wiped the tear away.

"For me, as well. But, perhaps we can chart a new course now."

John nodded slightly. "I suspect we can ... somehow."

Austin smiled. "So, then ... you no longer wish to kill me with your bare hands?"

John's tortured, damaged face registered an unmistakable smile. "You can rest easy tonight, Austin Newman. I promise not to strangle you in your sleep. I still need someone to drive the wagon, after all."

"Good," Austin declared, grinning. "Then let us get some sleep. We must depart before daybreak."

∽

The Following Afternoon
Bat Austin's Home – Jackson's Creek, South Carolina

A WAGON WAS APPROACHING at an abnormally high speed. Curious, Bat and Rachel stepped onto the porch. They watched as the rig made its way down the long and narrow lane that led to their house. Bat immediately recognized Austin Newman as the driver. Another fellow was riding in the wagon bed. He was bruised and battered about the face. Bat did not recognize him.

Suddenly, his wife squealed, "That is our John in the wagon bed!"

He shook his head. "It cannot be. You are mistaken, my dear."

"But, it *is* him! Look!"

Austin made a wide loop in the driveway and then guided the rig to a stop directly in front of the house. John leapt over the side before the wagon had stopped completely.

"Mother! Father!" he exclaimed. "We have Drury in the wagon! He has a bayonet wound and a raging fever."

Bat's gaze shifted between John and Austin. "I do not understand, Son. Why is he here ... and why is he with you?"

"Father, we will explain later. Did you not hear me? Drury is near death! He needs care!"

Rachel stepped in front of her husband and took immediate charge. "Austin, John ... get him into the house. Take him to your room. Bat, go and fetch clean water and bandages."

Mary Austin, hearing the commotion outside, emerged from the house. "What is wrong, Mother?"

"Drury has been wounded. John and Austin have brought him home."

Everyone stepped aside as the two men carried Drury up the steps and across the porch. Rachel's eyes widened with anxiety when she saw her son's bloody torso and swollen, discolored head. She turned immediately to Mary.

"Mary, I want you to go to Drury's house and fetch Elizabeth. Tell her to come quickly. Then, go to the Newman home and get Will and Lizzy. Tell them what has happened, that Austin is here, and that we are in need of their assistance."

"Yes, Mother."

Mary stripped off her pinner apron and tossed it across the porch rail. She darted down the steps and then took off running across the fields toward Drury's home.

~

Three Weeks Later
June 23, 1781
Jackson's Creek Meeting House Burial Ground

THE PRESIDING ELDER RAISED his hand high in the air and then declared:

O Almighty God, the God of the spirits of all flesh, who by a voice from heaven didst proclaim, Blessed are the dead who die in the Lord: Multiply, we beseech thee, to those who rest in Jesus the manifold blessings of thy love, that the good work which thou didst begin in them may be made perfect unto the day of Jesus Christ. And of thy mercy, O heavenly Father, grant that we, who now serve thee on earth, may at last, together with them, be partakers of the inheritance of the saints in light; for the sake of thy Son, Jesus Christ our Lord.

Into thy hands, O merciful Savior, we commend thy servant Drury Austin. Acknowledge, we humbly beseech thee, a sheep of thine own fold, a lamb of thine own flock, a sinner of thine own redeeming. Receive him into the arms of thy mercy, into the blessed rest of everlasting peace, and into the glorious company of the saints in light. Amen.

The elder motioned to the family, inviting them to come forward. One by one, the grieving members of the Austin clan filed past Drury's grave. Amazingly, there were no tears amongst them. Even Drury's wife and children seemed to possess a supernatural measure of strength and grace. Each member of Drury's family retrieved a small handful of fresh earth and then sprinkled it into the hole. The dirt striking the pine top of the box made a gentle sound, almost like the sound of a soft rain. The solemn rite proceeded quickly. Once the family members had paid their final respects, several friends and neighbors stepped forward to add their handfuls of dirt to the grave. Will and Lizzy Newman were amongst the long procession of grievers.

Then, it was over. The funeral ceremony was complete. Drury Austin, Loyalist soldier and faithful servant of King George III, was dead and buried. All that remained was for the slave laborers to finish the job of filling the grave. Most of the people in attendance dispersed quickly and headed toward their horses and wagons. Everyone seemed eager to get home before dark. It was Saturday, and most had extra chores to perform before the coming of tomorrow's Sabbath.

Austin Newman lingered at the edge of the cemetery. He had been standing in the rear, far away from the other mourners. Young William Newman, fresh back from the failed siege at Ninety-Six, stood by his brother's side. Tears filled Austin's eyes. His spirit was broken, for it was he who had ended his best friend's life. He simply could not believe that he had been the one who sent his lifelong companion into eternity.

Austin wondered all along if it was a good idea for him to attend the funeral. The relationships between the two families had been tense, indeed, since he went over to the rebellion. Surely, after Drury's death, there was now a rift between their family that transcended politics. He had actually ended Drury's life. True, the tragic event occurred in battle. But, he had killed him, nonetheless. How could the Austin family ever forgive that? How could they ever look upon him with anything other than eyes of hatred?

Still, Drury had been Austin's very best friend for over twenty years. Austin needed to attend his friend's graveside service, if only for his own sake. He had to say his farewells. He had to seek some manner of redemption. He needed closure.

William patted his brother gently on the arm. "I am going to go and speak with Mary."

Austin nodded. "I will see you at home. I need to walk around the countryside a bit. Tell Papa that I will be home by supper."

William smiled thinly, nodded, and then walked away. Just as Austin was turning to depart the graveyard, his eyes met those of Drury's father. Bat was fifty yards away, standing in the shadow of the log church house. Austin could see the brokenness in the man's eyes. His heart skipped a beat when he saw Bat whisper something to his wife and then begin walking in his direction. Austin shuffled his feet uncomfortably and awaited the grieving man's arrival.

Bat nodded. He was not smiling. "Austin."

Austin glanced ashamedly at the ground. "Uncle Bat."

Amazingly, Bat smiled at the familiar greeting. Austin felt his heart warming, if only just a little. Perhaps there was some hope for reconciliation, after all.

"We have missed you, Austin. I had hoped that you might have come around more during Drury's last days."

"I did not think it wise." He paused. "And I could not stand to watch him go."

Bat nodded. "It was difficult for all of us to endure. My son died a long, slow, agonizing death. But, it was important for us to be there for him. I am so very glad that he died here at home. And I am grateful to you for allowing that to happen ... for bringing him back to us."

Austin stared sullenly at the ground. "It was the least that I could do."

Bat inhaled deeply and then declared, "I am pleased that you came today, Austin. I feared that you might choose not to attend."

Austin shook his head. "I do not see how or why you could be pleased. Did John not tell you what happened in that trench?"

"He told me. I know exactly what happened."

"But, how could you ever forgive that? How could you ever forgive *me*? I killed your son." Austin was not weeping, but a steady stream of tears flowed from both of his eyes.

Bat placed a reassuring hand on the young man's shoulder. "Austin ... Son, you did not kill Drury. This war killed him. You had no notion of who you were fighting that night. It could just as easily been the other way around." Bat glanced across the meadow at Will Newman. "Your father might have been the one standing over a grave today. So, you rest assured. I harbor no hatred or ill will toward you. You are as family to me. It has always been so, and always will be."

"Then, I am truly forgiven?" Austin asked pleadingly.

Bat reached out and pulled Austin to him. He wept. "Only you can answer that. I have nothing to forgive. Now, you must choose to forgive yourself."

Austin hugged him. He sobbed openly. "Thank you! Thank you, Uncle Bat!"

After a long while, they separated from the embrace. Bat sighed.

"It just has to stop, Austin. All of it. I want no more part of this war. The quicker the British troops are gone from the Carolinas and Georgia, the better off we all shall be."

Austin wiped his face with his sleeve. "Then, are you changing your allegiance?"

Bat shook his head. "No. I am loyal to England to my very core. But, I will no longer be a part of taking up arms against the rebel government. I will not furnish any more supplies for the Loyalist troops. John has sworn an oath of non-aggression and received his parole, and he will honor it. I will make sure of that." He paused. "What about you, Austin? What will you do now?

"I have to finish the job. General Greene is gathering his army and will soon march on Charlestown. He intends to drive the British into the sea. And when that happens, I will be there."

Bat patted him on the shoulder. "Just make sure you come home to us in one piece."

20

FINISHING THE JOB

Though the Patriots failed in their siege of Ninety-Six, the eventual result was still a significant victory. In late July, his men starving and suffering from the intense southern heat, Lord Francis Rowden, now in command of British forces in South Carolina, set fire to the outpost at Ninety-Six and abandoned it. He withdrew his dwindling army to Charlestown. Himself debilitated by personal illness, Lord Rowden returned home to England and left Colonel Alexander Stewart in command of the remaining British forces in South Carolina.

Meanwhile, Major General Nathanael Greene was busy preparing his Patriot army for the final push toward the British stronghold at Charlestown. He moved his army to a remote campsite in the High Heels of Santee. A prolonged stay in the cool, pleasant hills allowed his weary men a much-needed period of rest. It also gave him time to, once again, issue a plea for militia reinforcements. Regiments from as far away as North Carolina responded to his call. He marched his army southward in early September, gathering troops along the way.

On September 7, 1781, Green's force of over 2,200 men, roughly one-third of them militia, was encamped near Burdell's Tavern on the

Congaree Road. Seven miles to the east, Colonel Stewart' British and Tory army of 2,300 men was encamped near Nelson's Ferry on the Congaree, at the Eutaw Springs. The two equally-sized armies would soon meet in the last great battle of the American Revolution in South Carolina.

~

7:00 AM – September 8, 1781
On the Congaree Highway

THE SOLDIERS of the Fairfield District Militia were on the move with General Greene's army. They had been plodding along the dusty, rutted Congaree Highway since before the dawn. They marched with the North and South Carolina militia regiments in the second column of a large four-column formation. The Fairfield men had been assigned to the command of Brigadier General Andrew Pickens. Brigadier General Francis Marion commanded all of the combined militias from the Carolinas. Their destination was the Eutaw Springs, the reported location of an encamped British force. Most of the men were confident that, before the day was done, there would be a battle.

"Reckon how much longer we'll be?" whined the diminutive Willie Addison, age fifteen. It was at least his fourth time asking the same question in the past half-hour. His query elicited yet another annoyed moan from the men marching near him.

After no response to his earlier questions, the talkative Mr. Addison changed tactics a bit. He decided to mention food, which was always a favorite topic of conversation among soldiers.

"Ain't you boys hungry? I ain't had me a decent meal in nigh on three days."

Daniel Dansby sighed impatiently. "Willie, why are you up here marching with us? This is Captain Martin's company. Aren't you assigned to Captain McCool?"

"I like it up here with you fellers better. Them boys back yonder don't care much for conversation. Some of 'em have been downright ugly to me."

Austin cut his eyes at Daniel and grinned. "I cannot imagine anyone mistreating or failing to appreciate such a quiet, reserved, and contented lad as yourself," he teased.

Willie failed to comprehend Austin's insult. Instead, he continued his complaining. "Iff'n we ever get to where we is going, I reckon I won't have any shoes left over for the fight."

"How long have you been serving in the militia now, Willie?" asked Austin.

"Off and on, pretty much every day since last May."

"A fellow with your campaigning and fighting experience should have known to have brought along some extra shoes."

"I ain't got no more shoes!" protested Willie. "Hell, I'm lucky to be a wearin' these. My big brother, Christopher, wore 'em on his last campaign. They 'twas already worned out. 'Twernt much cowhide left on the bottoms when I left home."

"Shoes are optional," countered Daniel. "Look around you. Plenty of the lads are marching this road in their bare feet."

Willie pooched out his lips and shook his head. "Nuh-uh. My dogs is way too tender for that. Besides, all I've done is march for four days straight. It took us two days just to find General Greene's army, and he's been a walkin' us ever since. I wouldn't have no feet left iff'n I 'twernt wearin' no shoes a-tall." He marched only a short distance before declaring forlornly, "Surely, we *gots* to be getting' to our fightin' spot soon. I need to rest a spell."

Gunfire erupted far to the east. There were only a handful of shots at first. Gradually, however, the intensity increased. Somewhere ahead of them the Patriot scouts had engaged the forward elements of the enemy.

Austin glared angrily at young Willie. "You need to be careful what you wish for, boy."

∾

8:00 AM
Gabriel Bourdel's Farm

IT WAS GOING to be a stifling hot day. Already, the humidity was climbing even as the sun was barely peeking above the eastern tree tops. Far to the east, beyond those tall trees, a dull, smoky haze hovered low in the atmosphere. It was the smoke of hundreds of campfires. The Patriots were within striking distance of the British camp.

General Greene halted his ragtag army alongside the highway so that the officers might confer and the men ready themselves for battle. Throughout the four columns, the Patriot soldiers and militiamen checked their ammunition and equipment. Many took the opportunity to sit in the soft grass and rest their weary feet. Some smoked their pipes and conversed quietly. Most were drinking water in great volumes. Thankfully, near their stopping point there were two easily accessible springs. Water was a resource that, on this particular day, they enjoyed in abundance.

The mood among the militiamen was tense. The battle that loomed before them would be vastly different from anything that most of them had ever experienced. Most of the militiamen in Greene's army had been involved in numerous small engagements and skirmishes. They were accustomed to raids or short patrols near home in search of Tories. But, few had actually stood in battalion formations and exchanged volleys with British Regulars. As they sat and pondered the coming fight and their collective destinies, most of the men wondered if they would be brave enough to stand fast and fight ... or if they might turn tail and run.

Austin Newman and his mates in the Fairfield Regiment rested on the front lawn of Gabriel Bourdel, a Frenchman and Patriot. His plantation lay just south of the Santee River. His enormous lawn was shaded by ancient oaks. The shade made the short respite on the Bourdel lawn quite pleasant. Unfortunately, the ample mosquitoes that swarmed the soldiers did not. Throughout the area, the militiamen cursed and slapped at the stinging, blood-sucking critters. The constant battle against the tormenting bugs eventually brought most of the men to their feet. Their canteens filled, they were anxious to get moving and put some distance between themselves and the clouds of annoying mosquitoes.

"Hot damn!" wailed Willie, slapping at his neck. "These skeeters is rough! Iff'n I get hit by a Redcoat's ball, I ain't gonna have no blood left in me to bleed!"

The men around him chuckled. For once, they could not argue with the affable Willie Addison. And they did not fault him for whining about the persistent, painful bugs. They, too, were sick and tired of being feasted upon.

Colonel Winn appeared at the edge of the roadway. He was carrying an eight-foot pole adorned with a flag. The colorful flag had thirteen alternating red and white horizontal stripes. In the upper left-hand corner of the flag, there was a canton of dark blue decorated with thirteen white, five-pointed stars. As he walked toward Austin and Daniel, he motioned for them to approach. Both men strode obediently toward their commander.

"What do you have there, Colonel?" asked Daniel.

"Boys, this here is the official flag of the United States of America. I just received it from General Greene. I was lucky to get us one." He thrust the flag toward Austin. "Mr. Newman, I want you to appoint someone to carry these colors. I must go and confer with the general, so I do not have time to take care of it myself. But, I need you to understand ... this flag will represent our entire South Carolina Militia. The bearer will stand near to General Pickens, who will command our group. You can carry it yourself if you want to, or give the responsibility to someone else. Whichever you prefer. I trust your judgment."

"Yes, sir."

Austin took the flag with trembling hands. The colonel turned and then stomped off in the direction of a nearby gathering of senior officers. Austin stood and stared at the flag for a moment. As he examined the colorful red and white stripes of cloth, he noticed an image far across the lawn. The Bourdel home had a large picture window in the front. In that window, Austin saw his own reflection as he held the colorful American flag waving in the morning breeze. The men of the army milled about all around him. It all looked hauntingly familiar.

Austin felt a shiver run down his spine. Even in the blistering summer heat, massive goosebumps erupted on his arms. He was looking upon an exact image of that powerful dream ... the vision that he saw on the morning after his capture. It was a vision that had compelled him to turn coat and join the cause of independency. That vision from months before had, indeed, been prophetic. Austin was witnessing its fulfillment. His heart swelled with joy and pride.

"Sweet mother of liberty, ain't that a pretty banner!" Willie Addison stepped in front of Austin, instantly cutting him off from his reflection. The lad gently touched the silky, colorful flag. "Lordy, I ain't never seen nuttin' so fine. What is it?"

Austin smiled. "The colonel said that this is the official flag of the United States of America."

"Well, I be deviled!" Willie exclaimed. He whistled in admiration. "Now, ain't that somethin', indeed! It must have come all the way from Philleedelfa. I bet old George Washington paid for it hisself!"

Quite suddenly and unexpectedly, Austin had another revelation. His face erupted into a huge grin. He winked at Daniel, who knew instantly what Austin intended to do.

Austin announced, "Private Addison!"

"What?" asked Willie, somewhat confused. He was not accustomed to being referred to by his military rank.

"Private Addison, Colonel Winn has a special assignment for you." He solemnly placed the flagpole in Willie's hands. "You are hereby ordered to carry the United States colors in honor of the South Carolina Militia. You will remain near General Pickens, our state commander, at all times."

"Gramercy! Are you jokin' on me?"

"No, Willie. I am quite serious."

"But ... but ... reckon what I should do with my musket?"

Austin took his weapon from him and then quickly released the strap. He opened the strap to its last hole so that it would fit over the boy's head. He secured the musket across Willie's back with the barrel facing downward.

"There you go," Austin declared. "If you need it, you can get to it. But remember ... this flag is your mission. Make sure it is always flying high."

"And do not, under any circumstances, allow it to touch the ground," added Daniel.

Willie grinned proudly. "I'll never let this fine silk taste the dirt. I promise!"

"Off with you, then," Austin encouraged. "Report to General Pickens."

Quick as a flash, Willie was gone. He sprinted directly toward the general officers. Austin chuckled as he watched the boy run. Truly, General Pickens did not know what was about to happen to him.

"That was a fine thing you did," Daniel declared, patting Austin proudly on the back.

Austin chuckled. "It is simply perfect, is it not?"

"Absolutely perfect," agreed Daniel. He paused thoughtfully. "Do you reckon Willie will complain to the general about his sore feet?"

❧

9:00 AM
On the American Front Line

DRUMS RATTLED. The shrill voices of officers and sergeants echoed through the various clusters of soldiers. The two armies were forming. They faced one another, separated by four hundred yards of open fields and meadows. The South Carolina Militia was on the front line, positioned near the left flank. Their line included two three-pound "grasshopper" cannons.

Austin and Daniel stood together. They rested the stocks of their Charleville muskets on the ground at their feet as they watched the slow-moving British forces getting into position.

"Is your brother here?" asked Daniel Dansby quietly. "I know there are a few men of the Second Spartan amongst us."

"No, thank God. He is on patrol north of Camden."

The explosions of artillery erupted to their right. The little "grasshopper" cannons had begun to fire. Soon, six-pound cannon balls streaked overhead, fired by the Continentals in the second line. All of the artillery shots landed roughly fifty yards in front of the gathering Redcoats.

"They are getting their ranges. Just two or three more volleys, and they will be dropping balls amongst the middle of them," Daniel observed. His voice betrayed neither regret nor affirmation. He merely stated fact.

Suddenly, large puffs of smoke erupted from behind the British formation. A few seconds later, the sound of the explosions rumbled across the battlefield. Several rounds landed safely in front of the Patriot militiamen.

Austin sighed nervously. "I hope their artillerymen are less skilled than ours."

The two friends stared, transfixed, at the spectacle before them. The scarlet-coated British troops and their Tory allies were spreading out across the open field. Austin and Daniel could see the numerous tents of Stewart's camp in the distance. Just beyond the tents stood a majestic brick home and the smaller outbuildings of a plantation. The smoke of the British cooking fires drifted lazily into the thick, humid air. The Redcoats had been cooking their breakfasts when the American forward patrol appeared on the highway. Clearly, General Greene had caught the enemy by surprise.

"I have never seen anything quite like this," Daniel declared. "It is almost majestic."

"I have witnessed such a gathering of armies only once before," responded Austin. "It was at Camden. But, that time I was counted amongst the enemy. I actually fought *against* the Continentals that day. I think they were from Maryland."

"I was not in that particular fight." Daniel paused thoughtfully. "But, you have to remember ... that was over a year ago, Austin.

Things are different now. You have done a lot of living over the past year."

"And changing," added Austin, turning his head to this friend and smiling.

"Indeed." Daniel reached out and gave Austin a hearty pat on the shoulder. "And how I rejoice that you have." He suddenly pointed to his left. "Look!"

General Pickens was walking around the left end of the formation to take up position in front of his battalion. A sergeant accompanied him, along with an obviously giddy Private William Addison as the color-bearer.

"Here we go," declared Austin, lifting his musket and cradling it in the crook of his left arm.

Daniel sighed nervously. "I cannot believe that General Greene has placed all of the militia in the front line. What do you think that means?"

Austin shrugged. "It either means he has total confidence in us, or none at all."

General Picken's voice echoed across the field. "Shoulder arms!"

Identical commands could be heard up and down the entire line. The militiamen all positioned their muskets across their left shoulders.

"Battalion! Forward!" The color-bearer and the commander took six steps forward. William Addison stopped. The general continued onward two paces in front of the colors, waved his sword, and then shouted, "March!"

Drums pounded their staccato beats as the Patriots, formed in two parallel lines, stepped forward. Across the field, the British Regulars began a similar maneuver. The militia marched roughly two hundred yards. The British and Tories were on the march, as well. As they proceeded, the artillerymen began to find their marks. Deadly cannon balls exploded in the midst of the soldiers, both friend and foe.

Then, General Pickens shouted, "Battalion! Halt!"

The men stopped. General Pickens and the flag bearer fell back to the rear of the formation. The British ranks stood sixty yards to the east.

"First and second rank! Three steps forward! March!"

The ranks moved as ordered.

"Second rank! Close to the front! March!"

The second line stepped to within two feet of the first.

"Front rank! Make ready!"

Austin and Daniel stood side-by-side in the front rank. Austin's heart raced. He could scarcely believe that he was about to engage in head-to-head battle with the British army. Trembling, he pulled the hammer on his musket to the fully cocked position.

"My God!" whispered Daniel. "I can actually hear their officers!"

"Focus," Austin urged him. "Aim at something. Do not fire blind."

The general commanded loudly, "Take aim!"

Austin and his mates brought their muskets to a level firing position. Austin aimed his weapon at the chest of the soldier directly in front of him.

"Fire!"

The sharp explosions of muskets boomed up and down the line. Clouds of white smoke billowed from the pans and muzzles of the weapons, along with cones of bright yellow-orange fire. The militiamen did not even have time to see if their shots had hit home. Already, the general was pressing them forward toward the enemy.

"First rank! Prime your firelocks and load! Second rank! Forward! March!"

The second line of militiamen stepped between the men of the first line and took up position in the front. Immediately, Austin began the fifteen-step process of loading and preparing his weapon. Before he could complete the task, the next series of orders came.

"Make ready! Take aim! Fire!"

The second rank, now in the front, unleashed another volley into the British. However, the Redcoats answered almost simultaneously with a volley of their own. Austin was just returning his ramming rod back into its channel when a spray of warm, sticky blood exploded into his face. He stared in dismay as the man standing immediately in front of him crumpled and then collapsed to the ground. The entire left side of the militiaman's face and head were gone. Austin felt the bile rising into his throat. Immediately, he spewed the contents of his almost-empty stomach onto the ground at his feet. He glanced left and right. He could see at least a dozen men from the front firing line sprawled on the ground. Some of those men remained alive, but most lay prone in death. But, there was no time to reflect upon those who had been lost. Already, General Pickens was pressing on.

"Second rank! Forward! March!"

Austin inhaled deeply and then stepped over the body of the dead man. It would not be the last dead body that he would tread upon on that fateful day.

～

One Hour Later

THE BATTLE RAGED ON. Austin lost count of how many times he had fired. The only thing he knew was that his cartridge box was almost empty. He had been so engaged in fevered combat that he had not even had time to mourn the death of his dear friend. Daniel Dansby, the friendly fellow from Winnsborough township, fell and perished on the fourth volley fired by the British. His body still lay somewhere on the vast battlefield.

The battle had shifted back and forth several times during the first hour of combat. There were moments when the fighting was hand-to-hand as the armies converged upon one another in the center of the field. The Patriots on both flanks, including the South Carolina Militia, held their ground well. However, early in the fight, the center of the line faltered and was almost lost. Then, just at the right moment, General Greene reinforced the center with the men of the North Carolina Continentals. They pressed the British back and, just when it appeared that the British line was collapsing, Colonel Steward committed his reserves, forcing a partial retreat of the American army.

Once again, the direction of the battle had shifted in favor of the British. When it seemed that the ground was all but lost, General Greene committed all of the Maryland, Virginia, and Delaware Continentals, along with Lieutenant Colonel William Washington's cavalry. The concentrated fire of the Continental Army had a devastating effect. The British center broke. Confusion reigned. They fled in retreat.

When the Continentals moved forward to occupy the front line, General Francis Marion finally gave the order for his gallant South and North Carolina militiamen to retire. His soldiers had stood toe-to-toe with British Regulars and two regiments of battle-hardened Tories from New York. During their agonizingly long one hour on the front line, they had fired an unbelievable seventeen shots.

Austin, following the other men in his regiment, turned to make his way toward the rear of the army. His fighting was done. He had survived the battle at the Eutaw Springs. Now, it was up to the Regulars to finish off the enemy.

As Austin marched in formation with the other men of his regiment toward the supply wagons, he passed by a very happy Private William Addison. The lad was standing on a hilltop beside General Pickens, proudly displaying the American colors. He caught sight of Austin and waved excitedly.

"I see you are still amongst the land of the living," Austin shouted as he walked near.

Willie nodded and smiled.

Austin pointed at the wagons. "Come and find me when it is over."

Suddenly, Austin heard a dull whooshing sound, followed by a metallic thud. Willie tumbled backwards, landing flat on his back. He lay absolutely still. The American flag flopped on the ground beside him. Austin darted to the boy's aid. General Pickens glanced down at the fallen lad, but continued to maintain his attention upon the distant battle.

"What hit him?" Austin shouted frantically.

"It must have been a stray ball," the general answered. "Hell, we are over two hundred yards from the fighting right now. 'Twas a fluke. God bless him, though. He was a likeable lad."

Austin knelt over the boy. Willie lay still with his eyes closed. Then, quite unexpectedly, his eyes flew open wide. He squealed in pain and clutched at his chest. Austin quickly pulled back the flap of his coat and then gasped at the sight. A .75 caliber ball from a British Brown Bess was flattened against the brass buckle and leather strap that held Willie's cartridge box. The slow-moving ball, having traveled such a great and improbable distance through the thick, humid air, had not penetrated the leather, nor the boy's skin.

"How bad it be?" Willie wailed. "It's mortal, ain't it? Oh, God help me! It hurts like hell!"

"Calm down, Willie! The lead hit your buckle and strap. You are not bleeding, but you are going to have one mother of a bruise."

Willie raised his head in disbelief. He slowly lifted his right hand and felt of the warm lead lump that was molded to his brass buckle. His face broke into a huge grin.

"I told you the skeeters sucked all my blood this mornin'. Lookee there! A Redcoat ball hit me, and I cain't even bleed."

Three Hours Later

THE HEAT of the South Carolina summer had been merciless. Throughout the battle, each force had tasted both victory and defeat. At one moment the fight had been all but won by the Continentals. They overran and occupied the British camp. But, the starving men stopped to feast upon the food and whiskey left behind by the Redcoats. Despite the frantic orders of their officers, they commenced plundering the camp. Meanwhile, the British regrouped and then drove the Americans back once more.

The back-and-forth continued off and on for four hours. It eventually ended in a draw. Both sides were exhausted. They could fight no longer. In the end, it had been a costly, bloody engagement. The casualties were astronomically high. The Patriots suffered almost six hundred of their men killed, wounded, or missing ... over one-fourth of Greene's army. The British lost almost two hundred wounded or dead, with another five hundred captured. The bodies of the dead and dying littered the South Carolina countryside. In some of the low areas near to the river, the blood flowed ankle deep.

General Greene abandoned the battlefield by mid-afternoon, evacuating his army back to Burdell's Tavern. The British remained in their camp at Eutaw Springs, but would soon retreat back to the safety of Charlestown. Though they did not take the field, the Patriots at Eutaw Springs accomplished far more than they realized. The British were thoroughly spent and defeated. Their hold on South Carolina had been broken. Only a weakened remnant of the British Army endured. The surviving Redcoats lingered in Charlestown, their only remaining refuge in the state. The job of the Patriots of South Carolina was, indeed, done. Within a week, most of the state militias from the backcountry disbanded and the soldiers returned to their homes.

~

Three Weeks Later
Sunday, September 30, 1781
Jackson's Creek, South Carolina

WILL and Austin sat together on the front porch as darkness descended upon the picturesque land. The foliage and fields were still bright green. It would be at least another month before the leaves would begin to turn. But, at least the air was somewhat crisp and dry. Finally, the steamy Carolina summer had broken. It was a pleasant evening, indeed, to enjoy a cup of tea and a smoke on the porch.

"You are certain about this young woman?" asked Will, puffing thoughtfully on his pipe.

"Yes, Father. Eliza is the one for me."

"I only wish that Lizzy and I might have had the opportunity to meet her."

"You will meet her soon enough."

Will took a sip of his sweet, hot tea. "Where will you marry?"

"We shall wed in Union County three weeks hence, on Saturday, October 20. That is the weekend that her preacher comes to her town for services."

"Oh?" Will responded, curious. "A traveling preacher? What denomination?"

"Eliza's family is of the Baptist faith."

Will's eyebrows raised high. He turned and gazed at Austin with a serious look. "I am not certain how I feel about that. I do not actually know what a Baptist is."

Austin grinned and winked at his father. "As soon as I find out, I will let you know."

Will chuckled lightly. Both men sat quietly for a while as they puffed on their clay pipes. Soon, Will's pipe burned out. He placed it on the table and then slowly climbed out of his comfortable woven willow chair. He walked toward the front door of the house.

"Going for some more tobacco?" asked Austin.

"No, Son. I have something that I need to give you."

Will disappeared inside. Several minutes later, he emerged, holding a tiny teakwood box. Reverently, he presented the box to his son.

"I thought that you should have this."

"What is it?" inquired Austin as he lay his pipe aside.

"It is the one thing of your mother's that I kept."

Austin trembled as he removed the top of the box. Inside, there was a wide gold band with a dark green stone. He picked up the ring and held it toward the light of the five-candle stand that sat atop the serving table. The almost-transparent stone twinkled and glistened in the candlelight.

"It is lovely, Father. I am most grateful."

"The stone is an emerald from South America, mined by the Spaniards. It was your mother's wedding ring."

"Was she wearing it when she ... when she died?"

"No, Son. She had not been wearing it for quite some time before she died. As I told you many times before, your mother and I did not get along in those last days. And, as you well know, she was not in her right mind when she took her own life. But, still, she was your mother. I have no doubt that, if she had been right-minded and remained alive today, she would have been very pleased for her one and only son to present such a lovely heirloom to his bride."

Austin was not normally emotional when it came to stories about his mother. After all, he had never known her. But, as he held her ring in his hand, he could not stop the tears from forming in his eyes.

"Thank you, Father. I will remember her in my prayers tonight."

Will nodded. "That pleases me." He returned to his seat. "So, now ... have you decided who will stand with you in your wedding?"

"At first I planned on young William. But, earlier this morning, I decided upon another."

Will cocked his head and stared affectionately at his son. "You are going to ask John Austin, aren't you?"

Austin smiled and nodded. "I am, indeed."

Will nodded in hearty affirmation. "It is a wise choice, and one that will help complete the healing between our two families."

"That is what I thought, as well."

"When will you ask him?"

Austin took a deep, thoughtful breath. "I figured that I might ride over tomorrow morning."

Will smiled proudly. The father and son sat in silence as the South Carolina backcountry surrendered to the purple glow of the dusk.

∼

October 20, 1781
4:00 PM
Lawn of the Wilbanks Cabin – Union County, South Carolina

AUSTIN WAS DRESSED in a smoky blue coat with matching breeches and weskit. His white stockings magnified the rich darkness of his garments. His long, customarily curly queue was braided in the back and decorated with a black ribbon. Eliza wore a matching blue silk gown. Her head was covered in a fine lace bonnet. The lovely bride and groom formed a picture of elegance and grace ... and they were almost married.

Austin slid the gold and emerald ring onto Eliza's finger. As he stared lovingly into her dark brown eyes, he promised, "With this ring I thee wed: with my body I thee worship: and with all my worldly goods, I thee endow. In the name of the Father, and of the Son, and of the Holy Ghost. Amen."

The preacher raised his hand high in the air and then prayed, "Eternal God, Creator and Preserver of all mankind, Giver of all spiritual grace, the Author of everlasting life: send thy blessing upon these thy servants, this man and this woman, whom we bless in thy Name. That as Isaac and Rebecca lived faithfully together, so these persons may surely perform and keep the vow and covenant betwixt them made, whereof this ring, given and received, is a token and pledge. May they ever remain in perfect love and peace together, and live according to thy laws. Through Jesus Christ our Lord. Amen."

The preacher opened his eyes, reached forward, and took Eliza's hand. He placed it in Austin's. He then covered their enjoined hands with his own. He proclaimed to Austin and Eliza, "Those whom God hath joined together, let no man put asunder."

The preacher then lifted his eyes to the wedding congregation.

"For as much as Austin and Eliza have consented together in holy wedlock, and have witnessed the same before God and this company, and thereto have given and pledged their troth either to the other, and have declared the same by the giving and receiving of a ring and by the joining of hands ... I pronounce that they be man and wife together. In the name of the Father, and of the Son, and of the Holy Ghost. Amen."

Again, he raised his hand and then prayed. "May God the Father, God the Son, and God the Holy Ghost, bless, preserve, and keep you.

May the Lord look mercifully with his favor upon you, and so fill you with all spiritual benediction and grace, that you may so live together in this life, and that in the world to come, you may have life everlasting. Amen."

He motioned for them to turn and face the crowd of onlookers. Austin and Eliza obeyed.

"Ladies and gentlemen, I present unto you Mr. and Mrs. Austin Newman!"

The crowd erupted into a great cheer. Austin beamed with pleasure. He waved to his father and stepmother. Bat and Rachel Austin sat proudly beside them. Little William and Mary sat on the row behind their parents. The youthful lovers became so caught up in the romance of the moment that they stole a scandalous kiss. Austin wagged a playful finger of shame at his little brother.

In the midst of the celebration, Austin felt a gentle tap on his shoulder. He turned to face John Austin. The handsome, blonde-haired young man smiled warmly. He extended his hand in congratulations. Austin pulled his friend and former enemy close and wrapped him in a warm embrace.

John whispered, "Drury should have been standing here with you, not me."

Austin replied, "No. God ordained that it to be you standing with me on this day." He paused and then hugged John again. "Besides, I can feel Drury here with us now, can't you?"

John grinned. "Yes, Austin. Yes, I can." He glanced at the crowd. "But, right now I must beg your leave. The work of your best man is just beginning."

John turned and beat a hasty retreat toward the serving tables. Austin raised his hand to calm the onlookers.

"My friends! Eliza and I are grateful for your attendance and support on our special day. For your reward, you will find feasting tables aplenty. Also, my father has generously stocked a table with whiskey, rum, and ale. However, out of a measure of respect, I ask that all men refrain from partaking until after the departure of our dear Baptist reverend."

Austin suddenly felt a very firm tap on his shoulder. He turned to face the rather stern-looking preacher.

The reverend placed his hand on his chest and declared, "Sir, I am not one of *those* Baptists. I will gladly meet with the men at the medicinal table. Perhaps, we might even enjoy some lively Holy Spirit debates amongst the different denominations present."

The men in the crowd laughed out loud and then erupted, once again, in a hearty cheer. Austin's face flushed red with embarrassment.

"All right, then," Austin responded. "Gentlemen, be polite. Do not attempt to out-drink or out-debate the preacher. Now, let the celebrating begin!"

Several men pulled their pistols from their belts and then fired them into the air. Quick as a flash, the people descended upon the buffet tables. Suddenly, a rider rounded the bend and rode his horse directly into the center of the wedding celebration. The people immediately ceased their revelry and surrounded the rider.

"What is the meaning of this intrusion, sir?" challenged the preacher. "This is a private wedding party."

The dusty, sweaty fellow removed and tipped his black cocked hat. "Beggin' your pardon, Vicar." He addressed the crowd. "I am Lieutenant Jeffrey MacLellan of the North Carolina Regulars, and I bear news from the war in Virginia." He inhaled a deep, emotional breath and then announced loudly, "The siege at York has ended. Two days ago, General Cornwallis surrendered his army to General George Washington. The British are defeated. It is over!"

The people all stared silently at one another in utter disbelief. It was almost inconceivable ... the very notion that Lord Cornwallis would surrender to anyone. As the news began to sink in, the people quietly began to hug one another and celebrate. The women wept. The men congratulated one another. Then, the true victory celebration began. Men fired dozens of pistols and muskets into the air.

Suddenly, Lieutenant MacLellan shouted, "Hip! Hip!" The men all answered, "Huzzah!" They repeated the verbal celebration twice more.

Austin turned to his beautiful bride and whispered, "Truly, my darling, this is the very best day of my life."

She smiled mischievously and then pulled his ear closer to her voluptuous lips. She blew gently into his ear and then whispered seductively, "And just think ... this day is not over yet."

EPILOGUE

December 14, 1782
Evacuation Day
Charlestown, South Carolina

I t was finally the day of ultimate victory over the British in the southern theater of the American Revolution. Over 10,000 British and Hessian troops and Loyalist civilians were being forcibly removed from South Carolina. Throngs of mandatory evacuees were being escorted by armed troops to over one hundred and thirty awaiting British ships in the Charlestown harbor.

Most of the Loyalists had already lost their lands and properties. All over the state, regional militia officers had compiled lists of men who had taken up arms against the United States. If those men had not sworn their oaths to South Carolina and to the Congress in a timely manner, they were automatically placed on the removal list.

Will Newman was safe from prosecution. He held letters of recommendation from Colonel Richard Winn. Likewise, Austin was exempted from the consequences of his previous crimes because of his later service in the Patriot militia.

Tragically, however, Bartholomew, John, and Drury Austin were all on the evacuation list. Of course, Drury was already dead. But, that did not keep the government from declaring his lands forfeit. His widow, Elizabeth, lost everything. Despite the pleadings of Will Newman, Colonel Winn refused to grant clemency to Bat and John. Indeed, Colonel Winn was the officer who identified them from removal from the state.

So, on December 14, 1782, the members of the Austin family stood near the Charlestown docks and awaited their spot on board an evacuation ship. Mary Austin Newman, freshly married to young William, clung to her mother and wept. Bat and John stoically stood watch over their baggage. Elizabeth Austin, Drury's widow, sat nearby on a small wooden barrel and held her two fatherless children close to her breast. Will, Lizzy, William, Austin, and Eliza Newman unashamedly stood near to them all. They were determined to support their friends right up until the bitter end.

"Surely, Bat, there must be some manner of recourse," Will blurted, exasperated. "This is simply wrong! You only took up arms once, and that was back in '75."

Bat shook his head. Clearly, he was defeated. "No, my old friend. I have exhausted every possible appeal, right up to the acting governor. I am afraid that this is our last day in America."

"But, you have never been anywhere else!" Will protested. "America is your home!"

Bat patted his friend on the shoulder. "Worry not about us, Will. We will be just fine. We are better off than most of the folk getting on these ships today."

"But, where will you go?" moaned Lizzy.

Bat held his head high. "Our particular ship is bound for Newfoundland. We shall make a life there."

"That is in Canada," Austin declared. There was a glimmer of hope in his voice. "You can get back here from Canada. After things calm down in a few years, you *must* make your way southward again."

Bat shrugged. "Perhaps. We shall see." He smiled thinly. "I would think that John might be much more likely to undertake such a journey." He turned to his son. "Eh, John?"

John smiled. "I imagine that I will be back home in a year or two."

A Continental Army Major approached with a paper in hand. He announced, "Austin! Bartholomew Austin!"

Bat raised his hand. "I am he."

"Mr. Austin, I see that we have eight souls in your family under orders of evacuation."

"No, sir. There are only seven."

"Please explain," demanded the major impatiently.

"My daughter, Mary, has wed to William Newman. He was a soldier in the rebel ... I mean ... the American militia. She is now bound to him and not to me."

"I see," the Major remarked skeptically. "Is she here?"

Bat gently pulled Mary away from her mother and placed her hand in William's. "Show him the document, William."

The young man reached into the interior pocket of his linen coat and produced a parchment stamped by the county clerk in Camden. It was his and Mary's marriage license, attested by the regional commissioner.

"Very well then," the major declared, handing the paper back to William. "Mrs. Austin will, of course, remain here with her husband. But, the rest of you must follow me now. I have special quarters for you on the boat."

"I do not understand," Bat protested. "Special quarters?"

The major glanced at his paper. "I have orders describing a request by one Colonel Richard Winn that we treat your family with the utmost courtesy and endeavor to meet all your needs and comforts. I assume that you know Colonel Winn?"

Bat nodded. "Yes, Major. I do."

"Very well then. Let us get on with it. If you will accompany me, please." He motioned his hand toward an awaiting boat.

Will and Bat shook hands, as did Austin and John. Mary once again clung to her mother and wept even more loudly than before.

Austin whispered to John. "I will be waiting for you, old friend. Come back as soon as you can, and I will help you find new land. There is ground aplenty up in Union County."

John smiled. "Set an extra place for me. One day, I will be back."

The major shouted, "Mr. Austin! Please! I have much work to do!"

Bat and John immediately picked up the family's bags and then proceeded toward the gangplank that led up onto the awaiting ship. Rachel walked behind her husband. The widow, Elizabeth, carried her children's tiny bags. The little ones followed their grandparents and walked ahead of their mother. They slowly marched up the dancing, bowing plank and then disappeared past the railing onto the deck of the ship.

The Newmans waited for almost an hour for the ship to set sail. They scanned the decks constantly, hoping to catch a glimpse of their friends, but the Austin family never came back up on deck. Then, the dock hands released the ropes and the ship and slowly began to pull away. It sailed across the harbor at a frustratingly slow pace. Eventually, it rounded the tip of James Island and then disappeared completely from view.

"Will we ever see them again?" Lizzy mused.

"I certainly hope so," declared Will. "But, for now, we must see to our own care. Let us return to the tavern and have supper. We must retire early tonight. We have a very long journey upriver tomorrow."

The members of the Newman family, Patriots of Fairfield District in South Carolina, turned and walked sadly toward Charlestown's business district.

They never saw their friends again.

THE REAL NEWMAN AND AUSTIN FAMILIES

Austin Newman is one of my thirty-two fourth great-grandfathers. I stumbled across him several years ago while doing personal genealogical research. I was always intrigued by his given name. "Austin" was not a very common name in the 18th Century. I became determined to find its origin in my family line.

After digging into some land and military records, I discovered the connection between William Newman, Austin's father, and a fellow named Bartholomew Austin. They truly did serve together in the same company in the Cherokee Wars, and they were actually neighbors at Jackson's Creek. There are several land records that connect them. There remains no doubt in my mind that Austin Newman's given name arose out of the connection with the family headed by Bartholomew Austin. So, of course, I had to include that familial connection in my story. As the plot and chapters poured from my computer keyboard "pen," the intimate familial relationship almost took on the role of an actual character in the narrative.

Of course, my greatest area of interest is the American Revolutionary War. It is the context of all my novels. Being in the *Sons of the American Revolution*, I am always on the lookout for Patriots / soldiers in my family tree. And, during my research, I discovered a rejected pension record in the name of Austin Newman. In 1839, his widow (Austin died in 1818) applied for a pension for his Revolutionary War service. However, that pension was rejected because the service could not be corroborated. Indeed, there was no record of the officers she named as being in her husband's chain of command.

Well, that *really* intrigued me. So, I did a *lot* of digging. Amazingly, I discovered a rather obscure record that listed a payroll for the soldiers of the Jackson's Creek Regiment of Loyalist Militia. That one-page payroll contained the name of Austin Newman. He was reimbursed by the British government for roughly six months militia of service that ended in December of 1780. Amazingly, the name of his captain was James Millar (Miller), which was the very name that Elizabeth Newman listed in her pension application. As a soldier in the Jackson's Creek Regiment, he did, indeed, fight for the British at Camden. The regiment is listed in the record among the British combatants.

So ... Elizabeth Newman (I called her Eliza in my story because there were so many "Elizabeths" amongst Austin's friends and family) actually filed for a Revolutionary War pension with the United States government for her husband's service in the Loyalist militia! I must confess that this awkward enigma was one of the most interesting discoveries that I have ever made in my personal genealogical studies.

But, my quest for information did not end there. Interestingly, the application process continued for many years, and the cause was even taken up by a daughter named Edith (Edy) Newman Hall. In some of her later depositions, Edy Hall named several other officers served by Austin Newman. The officers named served in the Fairfield District Militia (American). So, I had actual documentary records indicating that my ancestor first served the British cause and then "turned coat" and joined the rebellion against England.

Elizabeth's file for a pension on Austin's service contains one very interesting and amazing letter. It is an affidavit from his brother, William Newman (i.e. "Young William" in story). He swore the document at the courthouse in Rutherford County, North Carolina, on

October 9, 1839. It also includes his "mark" with an "X," indicating his illiteracy.

We must, of course, address the big issue of "turning coat." Changing sides was a relatively common occurrence in South Carolina in the year 1781. Many Tories would eventually make the decision to cast their lot with the independence crowd. It is, however, an aspect of the war in the Southern Theater that many modern readers do not understand. That is precisely why I wrote this particular novel. I wanted to show how there were some Americans who were once *Tories*, but them became *Turncoats* and joined in the battle for independence. I wanted to attempt to demonstrate the circumstances and thinking that might lead to such a dramatic shift in personal politics.

The Jackson's Creek Presbyterian Church was real. It was the center of culture and community in the small, primarily Tory community. It began as a log structure in 1774. By 1780, it had been replaced with a stone building. The church was later renamed Lebanon Presbyterian Church. The remains of that stone church remain, along with its cemetery. It is now known as the Old Lebanon Church, since the modern church has relocated to another site. I have never been to the original church site before, but my wife and I will be visiting it later this year when we attend the annual Revolutionary War Field Days in Camden, South Carolina. Perhaps I can include a photo in future printings.

For those of you who have read my other novels, you know that this is the portion of the text in which I customarily confess who was real or was not, what did or did not happen, etc ... So, allow me to enter into a brief period of authorial confession.

I regretfully admit that the early details of the life of William Newman were all fictional and utter figments of my imagination. I wanted to create an imaginary environment in which the loyal friendship of William Newman and Bartholomew "Bat" Austin might be given birth, nurtured, and then blossom and grow. I hope that I achieved that goal.

The name of William Newman's first wife is fictional. Her real name has been lost to time. I created her character in its entirety ... name, personality, and circumstance. Needless to say, her suicide was fictional, as well. William did, however, marry some time shortly after his arrival at Jackson's Creek. So, his second wife, Elizabeth (I called her Lizzy, again, to reduce the number of Elizabeths in the book), was quite real. I do believe, because of the timeline, that Austin and his younger brother, William, had different mothers. That is why I created the mechanism of a failed, tragic marriage in the elder William's life followed by a loving, successful one. In the end, I was quite pleased with the dynamic.

Bartholomew Austin was a real, historical person and has many descendants in America today. There is some debate, however, as to when he died. Many Ancestry.com trees show him dying in 1771, and that the Bartholomew of Jackson's Creek was actually his son. That timeline did not fit my plot line, at all, so I adapted it to allow for more creativity and deepening of the relationship between the families. Bartholomew had a quiver full of sons and daughters. However, I limited the sons to only two for simplicity's sake. I actually combined a couple of the brothers into the single character of John.

Drury Austin did, indeed, die from wounds suffered in the British service. After the hostilities ended, his name and the names of all of his brothers appeared on a widely-circulated list of men who took up arms against the United States. Col. Richard Winn was truly the author of the list. Interestingly, Austin Newman's name was not included. His absence from the roll of "traitors" provides a confirmation of silence that he had, indeed, changed sides and cast his lot with the revolutionaries.

The evacuation scene at the end of the book really happened ... or at least something very similar to it. After the formal surrender of Cornwallis, all British troops and Loyalists who refused to repent of their Tory ways and give oaths of allegiance to the United States were forced to leave the country. In South Carolina, all of their lands and property were confiscated by the state. December 14, 1782, was and is still celebrated today as "Evacuation Day" ... the day upon which the Redcoats and their followers were all loaded upon ships and promptly sent away. The civilians who departed went in many different directions. Some went to Canada, the West Indies, and Bermuda. Many others returned to England, Ireland, and Scotland. There are numerous fascinating records recording how they made monetary claims for their personal losses to the British government after the end of the war. It was quite a tragic ending, indeed, for the South Carolina Loyalists.

Which brings me to yet another big confession. Since I have already told you that Bartholomew Austin has numerous descendants in America, you can probably guess that his family did not evacuate (as far as I know). However, I thought that the image of the stark separation of the families would provide a heartbreaking, powerful ending to the intimate relationship between the two families, as well as a bitter "twist" at the end of the book. I hope that the scene tugged at your heart ... at least a little bit. That was my goal.

I do know with documentary certainty that Drury Austin's lands were all taken by the state after his death. But, I am not sure about all of his siblings. Context would seem to indicate that they must have sworn their oaths and remained in America. It appears from the various family trees that I examined that they scattered throughout North Carolina and Virginia.

When I first envisioned this novel, I fully intended for Austin, the primary turncoat, to be the "star" of the story. But, as the account developed inside my mind, it became a bigger, multi-generational, multi-family "thing." Still, in the end, I did manage to refocus the story back onto Austin. At least, I hope it did.

Austin Newman married Elizabeth Wilbanks (sometimes spelled Woolbanks) on March 18, 1786, in Union County, South Carolina (obviously, a few years after the date in my story). I am not sure when or how they met. Most likely, they met after the war, since courtships tended to be a lot shorter during those days. But, as with many other things, I tweaked the timeline just a bit and brought her character into my story, as well. I always like to introduce the love interests and future spouses of my key characters.

Austin and Elizabeth lived in Union County at least through the year 1790, when he appeared on the first United States Census in that community. In 1800, I located him on the census living in Rutherford County, North Carolina (also the home of brother William). At some point after that, Austin and his family moved into east Tennessee, just a short over-the-mountains jaunt to the west. We know from his wife's pension applications that he died in Dandridge, Jefferson County, Tennessee, on September 22, 1818.

Austin and Elizabeth Newman, like most married folk in their day, raised a large family. As best I can calculate, they had six daughters and four sons who survived past childhood. I descend from them through their third daughter, Edy, who married a man named Moses Hall. Her oldest son, and my 2nd great-grandfather, was named Austin Hall. So, the name that seemed so very odd in the 18th Century was passed on into the 19th Century.

Austin Hall fought for the Confederate States in the Civil War, which was unusual for a fellow from East Tennessee. That was generally considered to be Union country. I actually have a copy of his pardon issued immediately after the war. Austin Hall married a woman named Elizabeth Miller (another Elizabeth!). One of their daughters was Sarah Caldonia Hall. She married Thomas Jefferson Baggett in 1872 in Giles County, Tennessee. They were my great-grandparents. One of their sons was Claude Thomas Baggett, who was my paternal grandfather. I, of course, am the son of George Farrow Baggett, the son of Claude Thomas Baggett and Fannie Jo Hollingshead. Thus explains my connection all the way back to Austin Newman.

As for those older generations, I have precious little information on this particular line in my ancestry. I do not know Austin's burial place, nor the burial place of his father, William. I wish that there were graves that I could visit. But, like so many of my ancestors of old, their final resting places lay somewhere beneath fields, parking lots, and buildings. This story will, I hope, serve as my own personal *homage* to these amazing people who helped give birth to this country that I love so very much. By putting pen to paper, I can, in at least a small way, keep at least a tiny portion of their memory alive.

And I have one last "sidebar" to add. William Addison, found only in the final chapter, was a real person. He actually lived out his last years about fifty miles from where I live today. In fact, he lived to a ripe old age and died in 1853 in Todd County, Kentucky. His burial spot is known and has a Veterans Administration headstone. William Addison is the Patriot ancestors of one of my fellow SAR members. I was honored to lead the ceremony to dedicate his grave in 2014.

As I was approaching the final chapter and the Battle of Eutaw Springs, I had a sudden flash of memory that took me back to William Addison's pension record. I remembered that he had been wounded at Eutaw Springs by a "spent ball" and was standing only a "few paces from General Pickens." Amazingly, when I pulled the record, I discovered that he, too, was in the Fairfield District Militia ... the same regiment as Austin Newman! So, obviously, I could not resist writing him into my last chapter.

And, that's about it. No more confessions. I do hope that you enjoyed my story. I have already begun preliminary on the next book in my series. My working title for Book Seven is *Virginians and Continentals*. As it turns out, I have a 4th great-grandfather who was a sergeant in the infamous 1st Virginia Regiment of the Continental Line. He is actually in the family line of Elizabeth Miller, the wife of Austin Hall (grandson of Austin Newman). This ancestor served for three years in the Continental Army and took part in many key battles in the northeast. It is going to be quite a demanding and in depth research project. Therefore, I must bid my farewell and get to work. Huzzah!

Cheers,
Geoff Baggett
September 10, 2020

ABOUT THE AUTHOR

Geoff Baggett is a Tennessee native and a retired pastor. Prior to his career in Christian ministry, he served in the U.S. Army Reserve, and also worked in clinical laboratory medicine. He holds degrees in the fields of chemistry, biology, counseling, and Christian theology. His hobbies include metal detecting, genealogy, Revolutionary War history, and writing.

Geoff is an active member of the Sons of the American Revolution. He has discovered over twenty Patriot ancestors within his own family tree from the states of Virginia, North and South Carolina, and Georgia. He is also an avid living historian, appearing regularly in period uniform in classrooms, reenactments, and other Revolutionary War commemorative events. He and his lovely wife, Kim, enjoy dressing in their period attire and operating their *"Cocked Hat Book Shoppe"* tent at various Rev War and 18th Century events throughout the eastern United States.

Geoff and Kim live on a small, quiet piece of land in rural Trigg County, Kentucky, with their daughter, Katie, and grandson, Jackson.

THANK YOU FOR READING MY STORY!
PLEASE HELP ME MEET NEW READERS!

I hope that you enjoyed my work of fiction. It was a pleasure preparing and writing it for you. I am just a simple, "part-time" author, therefore I am sincerely grateful for every individual who chooses to read one of my books.

I would humbly ask that you help me spread the word about my growing library of Revolutionary War novels. It is very difficult for an independent writer to "break through" and find success in the overly-saturated American book market. But, you can help me in a number of ways!

1. **Tell your friends!** Word of mouth is always the best. Please recommend my books to the people in your circle of influence. Or, better yet, buy them a copy!
2. **Mention me and my books on Facebook.** This is just a "high tech" form of word of mouth. Be sure to "Like" my author page and tag me in any posts that you write. Simply search for my name, or "Cocked Hat Publishing," on Facebook.
3. **Write a review for me on Amazon.com and/or Goodreads.** Reviews are critical in today's marketing

environment. I am grateful for every review that I receive and review my titles daily in search of any new ones.

4. **Consider using my student books in your school curriculum.** Obviously, this is a plea to all you educators out there! I have been honored to have four schools choose my books for inclusion in their reading curricula. The potential for "crossover" between history and reading makes my short novels for kids an attractive addition to your educational arsenal. I have available a teaching supplement for my first book for kids, *Little Hornet*. Similar products are under development for my other children's titles (this is an ongoing project that my wife is pursuing). The completed resources are available as free PDF downloads on my web site. If you would be interested in a "class set" of a particular title for your school, please contact me directly. I make copies available for classrooms at production cost plus shipping.

5. **Book me for a presentation!** I have several fun, interactive, unique, engaging, and interesting Revolutionary War presentations available for groups or classes. I am a professional speaker and living historian. I will travel moderate distances if I can have the opportunity to connect to readers and sell some books! It is particularly helpful if I can arrange multiple audiences at one location over a period of a few days. Simply contact me through my web site, geoffbaggett.com, or through my Facebook author page to arrange an event.

6. **Finally ... Please follow me on Twitter and Instagram!**

Twitter - @GeoffBaggett
Instagram - geoffbaggett

Thanks again for reading this product of my personal history and imagination! Please be on the lookout for my next novel. *Book 7* in the

Patriots of the American Revolution Series, Virginians and Continentals, should be in print before the end of 2021!

Huzzah!

Geoff Baggett